THE BRIDESMAIDS

CARA KENT

The Bridesmaids
Copyright © 2023 by Cara Kent

All rights reserved. Without limiting the rights under copyright reserved above, no part of this publication may be reproduced, stored in or introduced into retrieval system, or transmitted, in any form, or by any means (electronic, mechanical, photocopying, recording, or otherwise) without the prior written permission of both the copyright owner and the above publisher of this book.

This is a work of fiction. Names, characters, places, brands, media, and incidents are either the products of the author's imagination or are used fictitiously. The author acknowledges the trademarked status and trademark owners of various products referenced in this work of fiction, which have been used without permission. The publication/use of these trademarks is not authorized, associated with, or sponsored by the trademark owners.

CHAPTER ONE

THE BRIDE

HER BOOTS DOUSED IN MUD AND SOCKS SOAKED, TAYLOR Sherman squelched toward Sherwood's quietest corner, a glass of chardonnay in one hand and a crumbling flower clenched in the other. A trail of orange florets mapped her journey from door to bar to booth, and her best friends—Mariah King and Cheyenne Welch—followed it like Hansel and Gretel, stopping to collect each petal and glaring at anyone who dared to look in their direction.

"Beautiful flowers," Mariah said as she sat opposite Taylor, her gesticulating fist full to the brim with their debris.

Taylor looked down at the firework-shaped chrysanthemum and unfurled her grasp, revealing the pulverized and oozing stem. Still defrosting from their lakeside requiem, Taylor nodded numbly and wiped her frost-chafed hand on a napkin before arranging the flower as a flaccid centerpiece.

"Where'd you get them?" Mariah pressed, unable to bear the lengthy silence any longer.

Taylor looked up, eyes darting from Mariah to Cheyenne on the other, her lashes wet from thawing and the thickly applied mascara starting to run. Cheyenne had already resorted to tapping away on her phone with her long, glittery nails, but Mariah's attention was focused, intent, and unbearably earnest. Running a hand through her frizzy, ombre locks, Taylor offered her friend a small smile as if it answered the already-forgotten question.

"Taylor," Mariah said more insistently. "Did you hear what I said?"

"What?" Taylor stuttered.

"Where did you get the flowers?" Cheyenne articulated, enunciating each syllable of the question, her eyes briefly parting from her always fascinating screen.

"Oh," Taylor replied, her voice hoarse as if that, too, had frozen over. "I got them at Blooming Maidens over in Hallington."

"Oh, I'll have to check them out. It's so nice over there, I need every excuse I can get to visit," Mariah said dreamily.

"Yeah, it is. Plus, it was the only place I could find that does spider and pompom chrysanthemums. Jenny's favorites."

"Well, there's no accounting for taste," Cheyenne remarked dryly.

"Cheyenne!" Mariah protested.

"What?" Cheyenne laughed. "We all loved Jenny, but she was hardly *Vogue* material. Not that she wasn't pretty, but the poor thing couldn't put together an outfit unless she saw it on a mannequin first. And don't get me started on her bedroom. Green and pink? Glow-in-the-dark stars? Butterfly fairy lights? I mean, come on. All she was missing was a tutu and a Barbie Dreamhouse."

"Seriously, Cheyenne," Mariah repeated gravely.

Here we go, Taylor thought. *More fighting.*

"Oh, come on! Lighten up. It's not like I sugarcoated anything when she was alive. I told her to her face when her outfits were lame and her hair was flat. Why should I behave any differently just because she's dead?"

Mariah pursed her lips. "Well, it's not 'to her face' now, is it?"

"I doubt she minds."

"Jesus," Mariah hissed, tucking her purple hair behind her ear and glancing at Taylor with concern.

"Well, am I wrong?" Cheyenne questioned.

"I guess not, but you could tone it down a little, considering what day it is."

No longer able to reduce her friends' bickering to white noise, Taylor intervened. "It's okay, Mariah. Thank you for defending Jenny, but Cheyenne's right. As soon as we stop talking about her, then she's really gone."

Cheyenne smirked, triumphant. "Exactly."

"Plus," Taylor continued with an expression to match, "Jenny always thought you were a spiteful bitch in life, and when you give me a reason to agree, I feel close to her."

"The bitch part is accurate," Cheyenne admitted, flicking her long, silken hair over her shoulder. "But spiteful implies that I have, at some point, been jealous of either of you, and we all know that's not true."

"If you say so," Mariah murmured.

Cheyenne's glossy mouth coiled at the left corner, causing an almost-imperceptible twitch in her corresponding eye. "Well, maybe I've been jealous of Taylor's nail beds once or twice," she joked. "But now she chews them, so... shots anyone? On me."

Mariah shrugged. "Sure, why not? I don't do anything on Saturdays."

Taylor hesitated. She actually did have stuff to do tomorrow—visiting her parents before they went away on vacation for one—but after laying the bouquet on where they'd found Jenny's body, all she wanted to do was numb the pain. Come midnight, her little sister would have been dead five years to the day, but even after half a decade of healing retreats, therapy, medication, exercise, and staying busy, the wound in Taylor's heart still oozed when poked.

"Hello?" Cheyenne asked, placing her precious phone face down on the sticky table and clicking her fingers loudly in Taylor's face. "Shots?"

The sound of acrylic clacking was enough to break Taylor of her cogitating haze, and she bobbed her head with fake enthusiasm. "Yeah. Tequila."

Cheyenne scoffed. "As if I'd get anything else. Now, move your fat ass, Mariah."

Mariah glared at Cheyenne. "I'm not going anywhere if you're going to speak to me like that."

"Ugh, why are you so moody today? Are you on the rag?"

"No, Cheyenne, I'm not 'on the rag,'" Mariah repeated with a disgusted expression. "I just don't feel like being called fat."

"Oh my god, I'm just joking... You're seriously not going to move?"

Mariah shook her head indignantly, her arms folded. Taylor could tell she wanted to laugh at her own childishness and Cheyenne's outrage but needed to stand her ground. Cheyenne drummed on the table, an eyebrow cocked in disbelief. She waited for a few seconds, but when Mariah didn't still didn't budge, she stood, revealing her silver, cowl-necked slinky jumpsuit that left little to the imagination.

"Prepare yourself for a face full of pancake," Cheyenne warned, shimmying past and pausing to wriggle her size 0 rear in Mariah's face.

"Jesus, how do you even find underwear that fits?" Mariah asked, her voice betraying her amusement.

"I don't," Cheyenne replied with a wink before galloping to the bar in her high-heeled boots.

Mariah and Taylor looked at each other, their mouths twisting this way and that before they couldn't suppress their howls anymore. They laughed until tears streamed down their faces, and they couldn't even remember what was so funny. All Taylor knew was that it hurt, but she didn't want it to stop. It was beginning to ebb when Cheyenne returned with a tray of limes, salt, and golden shots, but then they made the mistake of eye contact, and round two erupted from their mouths.

Cheyenne's face lit up, illuminated by sheer joy and lights above bouncing off her reflective outfit.

"Thank God. There's still life in the old girls yet." She handed out shots to the still-hysterical Mariah and Taylor and hollered, "Cheers, bitches!"

Taylor gulped hers down and shoved a lime in her mouth, momentarily tamping the hysteria until Cheyenne shimmied past again. Soon all three of them were laughing hysterically, and the booze warmed the coldest recesses of their insides. Not wanting the feeling to end, they reached for another. The second shot burned even better, and Taylor looked at her friends fondly.

"Cocktails?" she asked. "My treat."

"Yes! No more wine!" Cheyenne enthused. "Margarita time!"

Amber Horton—fiancée of the titular Bobby Sherwood—groaned comedically from the nearby bar, and Taylor looked at her apologetically.

"Sorry!" she exclaimed.

"Hey, you don't have to be sorry," Cheyenne corrected. "You have a dead sister to mourn."

It was a jab, and it worked. Amber's pretend pout went slack, and she pressed her hands hard against the bar's edge, straightening from her slump.

"I'm so sorry, y'all. I had no idea. I thought this was some sort of woo-girl work do. Taylor, my condolences. Really."

Amber was good at remembering names. Taylor liked that about her. They hadn't spoken often, and never for long, so they couldn't be considered anything more than minor acquaintances. Yet Amber pronounced her name as if each letter was important to her personally. It was sweet. Too sweet to be on the receiving end of Cheyenne's lashings, so Taylor intervened, shushing Cheyenne with her eyes and flashing a smile at Amber.

"Don't worry about it," Taylor said. "It happened before you moved here. Five years ago tomorrow. September 9th, 2018. We do this every year. First, we lay flowers on where she was found, and then..."—she picked up her third and final shot—"we drink heavily to celebrate the night we last spent with her."

"She was murdered," Mariah clarified, noticing the question on Amber's face. "By her asshole boyfriend, Mason Fowler."

"Well, the case was a bit holey," Cheyenne added, always the devil's advocate, despite having been convinced of Mason's guilt over time. It was a windup and a chance to take potshots at the local police force. It happened whenever she drank, without fail, and honestly, it was getting old. As were her ridiculous conspiracy theories about the police murdering Mason and making it look like suicide to avoid a court case they'd inevitably lose.

"Come on. Not tonight," Mariah groaned, rubbing her forehead with vigor. "They found the murder weapon in his car, and his suicide letter was all about hurting women. What more do you need?"

"A seance," Cheyenne deadpanned.

More groans from Mariah. "Seriously?"

"Yeah, I'm with Mariah," Taylor said. "We're twenty-eight years old. We're not going to do a seance at the Fowler shack. Plus, that place is horrible."

"The Fowler shack?" Amber asked, all her chores and customers passed along to a disgruntled Bobby at the other end of the bar.

"Yeah," Cheyenne said, putting on her best ghost-story voice and wriggling her fingers. "Mason Fowler lived in a little tin shack out in the middle of the woods, living on roadkill with his abusive and possibly inbred—"

"Cheyenne!" Mariah opposed loudly. "You can't just say stuff like that."

Taylor agreed but resented the hypocrisy. After all, it had been Mariah who started the inbreeding and incest rumors about the Fowler family lineage back in high school. Sure, there were already whispers, but she amplified them, even if only to get a rise out of Mason and destabilize his relationship with their precious Jenny. It was weird because, at the time, they'd had a somewhat ambivalent friendship with Mason—even before he and Jenny got together. Yet they spent so much of their time winding him up and, frankly, ridiculing him. It turned out to be well deserved in the end, though she still felt a little guilty.

"Anyway," Cheyenne said, ignoring Mariah. "Mason and his definitely not inbred dad, Roy, lived on the edge of town in this little deathtrap they called a house. They spent their days flirting with their cousins, drinking moonshine, and making hats out of raccoon pelts. Then, when Mason murdered little Jenny Brooks, he went home, wrote his disgusting little note, and ate a bullet. Roy then spent the next six months drinking himself to death. Died in his sleep of cirrhosis of the liver. Took weeks for them to find his body, and by that time, the wolves had had their fun with him."

"There weren't any wolves," Taylor hastily clarified to a terrified-looking Amber. "Well, not that I've seen, and I was born here."

"Still, that's awful." Amber looked distant until Savannah began to wail through the tinny baby monitor, and she blinked rapidly. "Sorry again for your loss. I'll be right back, and then I'll grab you girls those drinks. On the house."

"Thanks, Amber," Taylor said kindly.

"Yeah, thanks," Mariah said with a grin.

"Thanks," Cheyenne said with a sarcastic, saccharine smile.

If Amber noticed Cheyenne's lack of manners, she didn't let it show as she waved the group's gratitude away and opened the skinny door, revealing a dark, narrow staircase that led upstairs. The wailing intensified, and Cheyenne shuddered.

"Ugh, babies. Who'd have them?" she asked, picking her phone back up.

"I would," Mariah said.

"*Would* being the operative word."

"What's that supposed to mean?" Mariah retorted.

"It means that you need to find someone who's father material first, and considering your taste in men..."

"Sid was nice!" Mariah insisted. "Right?"

"Babe," Cheyenne said sadly. "Sid got shot breaking into some old lady's house."

"He turned himself around after that."

"Yeah, in prison. Where he'll be for the next ten years."

Mariah huffed, but Taylor could see a smirk forming. "Okay, maybe Sid wasn't so nice."

"No, he wasn't," Taylor said, putting an end to the discussion and downing the shot she'd been holding. "So on the night Jenny died...," she began.

Cheyenne sucked her teeth and held up her hand. "Come on, Tay. You know we're happy to come here with you every year and have a nice time, but I don't think we have to rehash the plot points."

"Why not?" Taylor asked, her head starting to spin.

"Because it never leads to anything good. Sure, it'll start out fun like, 'Oh, remember the nightclub,' 'Oh, remember the limo,' 'Oh, remember Mariah falling over on the dance floor.' But then it'll turn into how we left her at the diner, and then you'll fall into a guilt spiral and get snippy with us. I'm happy to reminisce about Jenny—cute stuff like her orange foundation phase or how much she loved country ballads—but once the blame game starts up, I'm out."

"I just want to talk about my baby sister. That was the last time I was..." she trailed off, her throat constricting.

Cheyenne sighed. "Babe, the more you dwell, the more you get stuck. And if you get stuck, then you never stand a chance of being that happy again."

"I can talk about what I want," Taylor insisted, the alcohol seeping into her tongue, making it heavy and lazy.

"You can," Cheyenne agreed. "But that doesn't mean I have to listen."

"Then go."

Cheyenne checked her phone. "Fine, I've got places to be anyway."

"Seriously?" Mariah asked. "You're just going to leave? What happened to cocktails?"

"Listen, I've known you ladies long enough to know when the night is over. Enjoy your overpriced drinks."

Cheyenne squeezed past Mariah once again, but there was no humor in it. Only frustration and grunting. Once she made it through the crevice, she bent to pick up her shot with her teeth and threw her head back, swallowing with ease. She lowered it back onto the tray with a dainty hand, popped a lime in her mouth, and spit it into the glass from afar. Basket made, she blew a kiss to her friends and walked away.

Mariah watched her go in disbelief. "I've got to hand it to her. She knows how to make an exit."

"I really do want to talk about that night," Taylor pushed as Amber reemerged and got to work on their cocktails.

Mariah frowned. "Taylor, honey, you've talked about it to death. In therapy, to us, to Hunter, to your parents. We all know what happened. We all feel terrible, but I really don't think there's anything more to talk about."

"What about Hazel?" Taylor asked. "That's weird, right?"

Mariah's face tightened, and she nervously re-tucked her hair behind her ears, revealing her old eyebrow stud and piercing-covered ears. Mariah opened her mouth to speak and fiddled with one of her studs, pulling it back and forth in its hole. Just as she opened her mouth to speak, Amber placed two margaritas in front of them before being whisked away once again by her crying daughter.

"Why do you want to talk about this crap, Taylor?" Mariah asked, her expression pleading.

Taylor pulled her margarita close. "You really don't want to talk about the fact Hazel went missing last year?"

"No, I don't want to talk about it," Mariah hissed, lowering her voice. "I spend enough time thinking about the fact that two out of the five of us are dead, and we're not even thirty. It feels like we're cursed, like *Final Destination* or some shit. So, no, I don't want to talk about it. I want to get drunk with my friend, whom I never see, and have a good time."

Taylor threw her hands up. "All right. You're right. Good times. Let's go."

"Are you sure?"

"I'm sure," Taylor assured her.

"Great," Mariah said, lighting up and lifting her drink. "To good times."

"To good times," Taylor said, a little less enthusiastically.

As the drinks kept coming, the conversation grew lighter, and Taylor managed to clamber out of the dark hole that she'd started to dig. Once they had both reached the point of slurring and dancing to nostalgic jukebox tunes, the "good time" status had been achieved. Then Taylor's phone buzzed, stopping her mid-spin and sending her hurtling toward the booth with a giggle. Her face dropped when she flipped it over and saw several unread texts from her husband, Hunter, asking the same question in three different ways.

Hunter: *Where the hell are you?*

A flash of irritation rose up in her, but she tamped it down and tapped out a response to the best of her ability, double-checking for spelling errors.

Taylor: *Where do you think? It's the anniversary of Jenny's death.*

He didn't reply for a few minutes, clearly unsure of how to keep the argument going considering that response. Still, despite the odds, he managed it.

Hunter: *Well, come home soon. I don't have any clean clothes for work. Not to mention there's a pile of dishes and nothing to eat.*

Taylor: *And where have you been?*

Hunter: *At work. Doing my job.*

Taylor: *On a Friday night?*

Hunter: *Not all of us get to work 9 to 5s.*

"Give me a break," Taylor murmured to Mariah before turning the screen off and putting her phone away in her purse.

"Hunter being an asshole?"

"Yup. And the argument is only going to get worse if I don't leave now."

'Wait, you're leaving?" Mariah whimpered, giving puppy eyes. "But we were just starting to get going. Screw Hunter!"

"Screw Hunter," Taylor agreed. "But also, he is my husband, and I do have to live with him. So, I'm afraid I'm calling it a night."

Something flickered in Mariah's eye, and she held out a hand to squeeze Taylor's. "I have…" she started before drifting off into silence.

"What?" Taylor asked, squeezing back in concern.

Mariah loosened her grasp and offered an unconvincing laugh. "Already forgotten. Damn goldfish brain."

"Okay," Taylor replied, unconvinced. "You want to share a taxi?"

Mariah looked past Taylor's shoulder and waggled her eyeliner eyebrows. "No. You go on ahead. Text you tomorrow."

"Text me *tonight*," Taylor insisted. "Let me know when you get home safe."

Clearly not listening, Mariah made an ambiguous noise, and Taylor followed her friend's gaze to a good-looking group of young men at the big circle table. They still had their high-vis jackets on from work and had dirt on their hands and under their nails. Most of them were covered in tattoos. Exactly Mariah's type. It was hunting time.

Taylor sighed, her expression amused. "Seriously, Mariah. Text me."

"Yeah, yeah, Mom. I'll text you. Now get out of here, your wedding ring makes us seem old."

"All right, give me a hug," Taylor requested, and Mariah offered a half-assed embrace before picking up her drink and sauntering over to the tanned, muscular strangers.

Taylor turned to leave but felt momentarily uneasy about leaving Mariah. Then she caught Bobby Sherwood's eye, and he offered her a wave. He was the kind of guy that made sure people got home safely. She herself had been in the back of his truck more times than she could count, especially when she was twenty-one, and never felt even remotely in danger. And now, with Amber helping run the joint, it was safer than ever before.

She watched her friend ingratiate herself with a chuckle but shot Amber a meaningful look before doing the same to Bobby. In return, he offered a small salute, and she stepped out into the bitterly cold night, where a taxi waited eagerly for their clientele to come stumbling out into the dark.

CHAPTER TWO

THE DETECTIVE

Though the sky above bordered on bleak, Heather Bishop's smile provided enough sunshine to warm up the entirety of Glenville. Possessed by the spirit of joy itself, she induced suspicion and awe in the passersby who knew her. This only tickled her more, and she waved to the glum, frost-bitten townsfolk, intending to spread this newfound merriment.

After parking outside the station, she swiveled in the driver's seat and planted her feet firmly on the sidewalk. Soles to the earth, she inhaled deeply and closed her eyes. Though the numerous yoga sessions had primarily educated her about her terrible inflexibility, they had also taught her how to savor the moment. This moment was delicious—the crisp country air laced with pine needles and rime crystals—she wanted to stay there and keep supping. Yet, much like her three-week vacation with her parents, all good things must end.

She opened her eyes and stared at the police station ahead. As soon as she passed that threshold, that was it, back to work. Yet her smile remained, her heart thrummed enthusiastically, and when she got to her feet, she felt light and limber. She cracked her neck and transitioned from play to work, clipping her detective badge to her belt and scraping her long hair back into her signature ponytail. A blue-and-purple thread-wrapped braid hung loosely at her temple, marking her trip to a sunnier land. She knew the addition bordered on unprofessional, but she hoped that Tina would neither care nor notice.

Tina, Heather thought, zealously bouncing to the trunk to collect the goods.

The heavy bag—which she was eager to dump on the nearest desk—was filled with a dozen goodie bags for her coworkers, each one containing a branded bottle opener, a tin of fudge, and a bar of chocolate-shaped wax melts that smelled as tasty as they looked. The items had been obtained from her three favorite trip destinations, but she knew her hardworking boss needed—no, *deserved*—something special. So after a lot of tasting, Heather finally selected the perfect bottle of wine from the Southern Californian vineyard and B&B she'd stayed at for the entirety of her vacation.

Minding the ice on the concrete, she shuffled forward and threw the station door open, feeling akin to Saint Nick himself. She stopped herself from saying something cheesy—*ho, ho, ho* being top of her list—and bid everyone good morning with gusto. Crickets answered her, and she froze. Peeling her eyes from the muddy welcome mat, she looked ahead and was met with an almost-tangible wall of gloom. Her smile, which she'd worn since she'd rolled out of bed, melted away as gray faces tried and failed to match her jolly energy. No one smiled, no one laughed, and no one even looked surprised by her newfound happiness. Even Gabriel faltered and fell apart, looking back at his empty desktop screen.

"Is there something on my face?" Heather joked, looking around, begging for engagement.

She spotted Lisa Simmons—their resident crime scene officer—zipping up a large black bag to her left. Before it sealed completely, Heather caught a glimpse of yellow evidence markers.

"Hey, Lisa. What are you doing here?"

"I think you better talk to Tina," she replied softly.

Heather knew it was coming. Those fateful words. She'd heard endless iterations of them over the years, and they always meant the same thing. Somebody was dead.

"Will do," Heather replied, setting her stuff down by the door and moving quickly toward the sheriff's office.

Gabriel made eye contact and partly swiveled as she passed. "Welcome back," he said dryly.

"Thanks." Heather sighed and looked over her shoulder at the front door. "Squad car or mine?"

"Don't pretend I have a choice," he half-heartedly quipped. "I'll meet you outside by the Granada."

She'd hoped he'd be confused by the question, but there was clearly a crime scene to go to, and Heather chewed her lip as she moved toward the freshly painted white office door. She knocked twice, pushed it open, and Sheriff Tina Peters looked up, forcing a tired smile.

"Wow," she said, looking Heather up and down. "California has certainly treated you well. You must miss it already."

"I do, but don't worry. I won't be back for a while. Too expensive."

"Your hair looks cute too," Tina added.

Heather touched the braid sheepishly. "Mom forced it on me. She wanted one but didn't want to go to the booth alone. Honestly, I'm kind of into it."

Tina's smile flickered before dropping. Chitchat was over, and Heather sat in the red leather armchair before leaning forward and resting her forearms on the black, bean-shaped desk. Tina rocked back and forth in the inner curve of it, her brand-new ergonomic desk chair swishing seamlessly. Heather waited for the awful punchline, but they both took the time to stare around at the white walls and neatly organized, black-framed family photos before landing on the red roses in the corner. Tina's husband replaced them every couple of days, and though this batch was starting to wilt, the smell and color were still incredibly vivid. Heather hoped their pleasantness would soften the incoming blow but doubted it.

"We have a suspected homicide on our hands," Tina said, delivering the punch with a limp wrist.

"I figured. Lisa is packing up by reception. Has she marked the scene already?"

"Yes. I remember what happened last time," Tina said bitterly. "She'll come back and gather up the evidence later after we take a look."

The venom wasn't aimed at Heather but was instead pointed squarely at the past. She was referring to the tragic murder of young Jenny Brooks back in 2018.

The twenty-one-year-old woman had last been seen at Dottie's Diner enjoying a cheeseburger after abandoning her old sister's bachelorette party for greasy food and a reduced hangover. She was found the next day by the edge of Whitetail Lake, having been bludgeoned, dumped, and left for dead. She'd crawled out of the lake and died of either blood loss or exposure. Heather didn't know. Dr. Melvin Melrose—who did not deserve his honorable prefix—had never sent the full report over. Or if he had, Heather had never seen it.

However, she did know who killed poor Jenny Brooks. As was often the case, the crime had been committed by her boyfriend, Mason Fowler, who killed himself shortly after via gunshot. The debacle had occurred just three months after Heather's arrival in Glenville and had been her very first case in the town and the messiest of her career.

Despite becoming a wonderful gardening mentor after his shameful "retirement," Gene had been an incompetent sheriff, to say the least. This had led to the scene being destroyed by ignorant cops long before Heather had even been informed of the case. Footprints and mud marred evidence, and the lack of labels or CSI made it a minefield to navigate. To call it a disaster would've been generous, and had they not discovered the apologetic suicide note—in which he apologized for hurting women—and the poorly concealed murder weapon in the bed of his truck, the case would likely have gone unsolved.

"Well, thank God for that," Heather said. "Hopefully, this time will be easier. If it wasn't for Mason's posthumous confession…" she trailed off. "Wow, that was about five years ago now. Time flies."

Heather watched as Tina's dark-brown skin adopted a faintly grayish hue. Lowering her gaze to the floor and looking as if she might vomit, Tina stayed quiet.

"Wait," Heather said, looking at the kitten-themed calendar on the wall. "Today's the eleventh. When did you find the body?"

"This morning, but she was floating. So, Lisa reckons she died on the ninth. Shortly before, she was reported missing by her best friend, Taylor Sherman."

"Taylor. September 9th," Heather muttered. It all sounded so familiar. "That was the day that Jenny…"

Tina nodded. "Yeah, that's when we found her too."

Heather shuddered. "That's spooky."

"I think it might be more than that," Tina replied, her voice as distant as her gaze.

"What do you mean?" Heather asked to no reply. "Tina? Whom did you find?"

Tina finally met Heather's gaze. "She hasn't been formally identified yet, but we believe the victim is Mariah King. One of the girls in Jenny Brooks's friendship group. She was at the bachelorette party and diner that night."

Heather put a hand to her lips and pawed at her mouth. "You don't think the same…"

"No, I don't. Like you, I still believe it was Mason Fowler, despite Gene's ridiculous obsession with Thimbles. And Mason is dead. And not Dennis Burke dead either. Definitely dead. But it seems like an almost-impossible coincidence."

Heather nodded, unpleasantly reminded of Thimbles, a local pest and criminal transient who wore thimbles on his fingertips to prevent cuts when digging through people's garbage. He'd been Gene's number one suspect in the murder of Jenny Brooks, and though he'd ultimately been innocent, the mere mention of him still made Heather's skin crawl.

Heather spoke through the cracks in her kneading fingers that formed a Bane-like mask over her face. "Oh, it's weird, all right. And a crime of passion isn't exactly copycat behavior."

"I agree. I don't want us to get bogged down with this until we know more, but I think it's important to bear in mind."

"Agreed."

There was a lot of agreement going on, which was unusual but a good start. Despite the tragedy, Heather could see silver linings appearing already and felt more motivated and clear-headed than ever.

"Are you coming to the scene?" she asked.

"I am. We'll bring Gabriel too. You two seem to work well together."

"Great," Heather said enthusiastically and received a justified raised eyebrow in response. She cleared her throat and reduced her eagerness by sixty percent. "You'll have to fight him for shotgun, but—"

"I'll take my car," Tina hastened, not a fan of Heather's driving style and always keen to show off her pimped-out Sheriffmobile.

For once, Heather let the unspoken jab go and pulled her faithful, battered notebook from the inner pocket of her new wool coat. "Sure. What's the address?"

Tina paled again, and Heather watched her throat move as she swallowed. "Edge of the lake," she answered quietly. "Just like last time. I'll drop you a pin."

Heather put her notebook away and drummed on the desk before standing. It was another unpleasant, unsettling coincidence, hurtling her back to that cold September of 2018 when she'd trudged through the silt to reach Jenny Brooks's pale, soaked body. She'd met Jenny the night before at Dottie's Diner and spoke to her in some depth after her sister and friends had left.

Taylor, Heather thought. Jenny's sister's name. Except she hadn't been Taylor Sherman at the time. Poor girl, having to endure such an ordeal not once but twice. However bad Heather felt, Taylor must have been feeling it ten times over, and Heather felt terrible.

She and Jenny had talked and laughed that night, and Heather had given her money for a taxi, thinking she was in safe hands with the trustworthy owner, Missy Jenkins. Unfortunately, she'd been terribly wrong, and to see her like that—soaked through and face down, after being so full of life less than twelve hours before—had been one of the darker moments of Heather's career. Now to have another woman—"punk rock chick" Mariah with her wild hair and tattoos—in the same position made Heather's insides roil.

Looking down at Tina, the pair of them sick to their stomachs, Heather gulped and croaked a feeble farewell before leaving the odiferous room and charging through the station toward the already-waiting Gabriel.

CHAPTER THREE

THE DETECTIVE

Whatever warmth Heather had radiated had long since been snuffed out by the time Mariah King's body came into view. Though her coals—stoked hot by her time in the sun—had burned molten hot, a good dousing of cold water always won out. Now all that remained of what she'd so lovingly cultivated was a bunch of soggy stones that rattled inside her skull, knocking against nerves and lobes. She ground her teeth from the flickers of pain and the beginning of a migraine, her serotonin depletion feeling awfully like withdrawal.

"I keep telling you, you're going to end up with no teeth," Gabriel chided, staring straight ahead at the body. Slowly he turned to Heather, who had only increased her noisy mastication. "Joke," he added flatly.

She stopped momentarily and opened her mouth, popping her jaw with a crack that made them both cringe. "Maybe you're right," she said, thinking of her recent dental work and the fragility of her repaired molar. "Maybe I'll swap to gum."

Gabriel shuddered. "Maybe I'm wrong. Maybe you should keep grinding."

Heather shot him a quizzical look. "Can't stand the sound of chewing, huh?"

He shook his head, his mouth downturned.

"Well, it's either chewing, no teeth, or lung cancer. Take your pick."

Gabriel weighed it up and groaned. "I guess gum it is."

Heather leaned across Gabriel, opened the glove box, grabbed an ancient pack of gum, and popped three pieces in her mouth. She chewed loudly, smacking her lips and sucking saliva, and she could see that Gabriel was close to breaking into either laughter or screaming. Then they both remembered where they were, composed themselves, and opened their doors in perfect synchronicity.

The cold chill made her bones ache, and everything, except for the small squares of yellow, was washed out and dingy. Even the crepuscular rays that had shone so brightly earlier had been crushed by the merging of the clouds. Now the sky was consumed by an ashen, soupy haze, which not only drained the color from their surroundings but also lowered the ambient temperature by at least ten degrees.

It was a good thing, she reminded herself as she rubbed her hands together. A frozen body was a preserved body, and that refrigerated state would lead to a much more fruitful autopsy than someone who'd been lying in the hot, insect-beguiling sun. This would have also benefitted the investigation of Jenny Brooks's murder, had Gene not insisted her autopsy be performed by incompetent Dr. Melrose. Thinking about it, even the preliminary findings regarding Jenny's death had been passed along by word of mouth—Gene's mouth, to be specific—which, considering his memory, was about as trustworthy as Dr. Melrose's medical license was legitimate.

Heather could feel herself prickling at the memory and took a big, grounding breath as she pulled on her latex gloves and shoe covers.

This isn't about Jenny, she told herself. *This is about Mariah. And this time, we're going to do it right.*

Looking around, her pep talk didn't feel delusional. Lisa and her helpers had constructed an organized scene that surpassed even Heather's high Seattle standards. The barrier was taut and neat, the evidence had been labeled, and best of all, the cops that had retrieved Mariah from the lake kept their distance and were dressed in appropriate protective gear.

This was a stark difference from the cops who'd watched over Jenny Brooks. Fortunately, that pair of buffoons realized that police work wasn't for them shortly after and left the force entirely, allowing more competent people to join the force. So now they had Lee Pearson, a gray-haired man with a dimpled chin and acne pockmarks, and Gretchen Keller, the most androgynous, muscular woman Heather had ever met. Heather didn't know either well, but she knew they were professionals and knew when to stay out of her way.

They were chatting to Tina as Heather and Gabriel approached, and as soon as they joined the sheriff at the barrier, all chitchat ceased. No small talk, no jokes, no overfamiliarity. Just silence and a lifted barrier for the three superior officers to duck beneath. It was exactly as it should be, and Heather nodded appreciatively at the pair of them once she was on the other side.

"So, you two pulled her out of the lake?" Heather asked.

"Yes, ma'am," Gretchen said, her posture military perfect. "We received a call from one of the waterside residents at 8:13 a.m., informing us that there was a body floating in the water about thirty feet from shore. So, Officer Pearson and I investigated and found that there was indeed a dead body—a female, approximately thirty years old—floating on the surface of Whitetail Lake. We then requested a boat and went out to retrieve her. While looking around the area, Officer Pearson noticed blood in this clearing, leading us to believe this was the original crime scene. Thus this is where we decided to lay the young woman for further inspection. I would like to add that we handled her with gloves and were incredibly careful not to damage the body. However, the rope that was around her wrists did come loose during transportation and is now placed adjacent to the body. Additionally, we have noted that there was no sign of a boat here prior to ours. No marks by the water."

Heather nodded. "Great work, Officer Keller, Officer Pearson. I trust only you, Lisa Simmons, and her team have been at the site so far?"

"Yes, ma'am," the pair said in sync.

Heather nodded again, genuinely impressed. "Thank you. Feel free to go warm up in the back of my car."

Despite their stances, the two of them smiled appreciatively and ducked under the barrier, quickly flocking toward the promise of warmth. Heather watched as they nestled into the back seat and held their hands in front of the fan.

Heather turned to face the young woman who lay on her back atop the frozen ground, her arms by her sides and her open eyes reflecting the dull sky. She was in surprisingly good condition, having been submerged in a lake for at least forty-eight hours. They had the cold water temperatures, the stillness of the lake, and the shallow depths to thank for that. Had it been warmer, rougher, or deeper, she would be far more decayed, significantly damaged, and might not have surfaced at all if she had sunk too far down.

Still, she didn't look like Jenny had. She didn't look like she was sleeping. She looked dead. Even from a distance, Heather could see the blue tinge, the purple extremities, the swollen lips, the sloughing of the waterlogged flesh, and the bloating that had allowed her to float. She also knew that now she was out of the water, putrefaction would take hold much quicker than someone who had not been in the water. So they had to act fast and get her to Julius before the day was done. If they couldn't manage it, they would have to hope a tent would do the trick, but Heather knew, even in these thirty-degree conditions, that it wouldn't.

There were only five markers at the scene, but Heather trusted that Lisa had thoroughly swept the location and that nothing of note had gone unnoticed. So they started at the first one, which had been placed not in order of importance as TV shows might depict, but in order of observation.

It was a partial footprint. A very partial footprint, in fact, with only the outer curve of the toe visible on account of the compacted ground and abundance of grass. It was better than being a muddy, sludgy mess covered in a thousand footprints, but Heather doubted that neither she nor the forensics would be able to do much with it. Still, she appreciated Lisa's eagle eye, as that sliver of an imprint would've been imperceptible to Heather without the yellow triangle by its side.

Putting his arm around her neck, Gabriel hovered his foot over the print, the shadow of his toe and its toe lining up.

"I'm a size 11," he said. "What do you think?"

Heather tilted her head from side to side, scrutinizing the print. It looked about right, but too much was missing to be sure.

"If opinions were evidence, I'd guess it's a men's shoe between a 9 and a 12, but unfortunately…"

"They're not," Gabriel finished, putting his foot back down, far away from the print, and unhooking his arm.

"Nope," Heather confirmed.

"And the tread?"

"Probably a hiking boot. But considering we're in rural Washington during a particularly cold fall season…"

"Everyone's wearing hiking boots," Gabriel finished.

"Not to mention. A lot of hiking boot brands are unisex. My pair are indistinguishable from men's shoes."

"Okay, so the print's a bust," Tina said impatiently, bouncing from foot to foot. "Let's keep it moving."

"Sure thing, boss," Heather said, leading the pack toward marker number 2. The blood spatter. "Has Lisa taken a sample of this to send to the lab?"

"Yeah, but only with a cotton swab," Tina said, squatting to get a better look. "She said she'll scoop some of it up when she comes back later to bag and tag everything. Send it all up to Julius with the body."

Heather hadn't even asked about using Dr. Julius Tocci's team of forensic experts to help with the case. She was going to mention it soon, knowing she would need to contact him in advance, but seemingly she could go right ahead. As she sent him a vague text with a cold hand about clearing his schedule, she was glad that she and Tina were on the same wavelength without the need for exhaustive, futile communication.

"All right, Gabriel," Heather said. "What can you tell me about this?"

Gabriel, who'd been hanging back, widened his eyes and took a shaky step forward. "Right now?" he asked.

"Why not? You've been doing your course prep, right?" Heather inquired, knowing he was balking not because of the blood but because of the presence of their boss. If he was going to do this—the job and his bachelor's degree—he needed to function under all circumstances, not just the ones that made him feel safe or comfortable.

"I have," Gabriel said, his voice small as he made accidental eye contact with an expectant Tina. He'd asked to go part-time just last week, as his Bachelor of Criminology degree, with a minor in forensic science, would inevitably take up great swatches of his time for the next several months. Now was his opportunity to prove it wasn't just an inconvenience.

"Well, considering the size, shape, quantity, and castoff," he started before dropping to the ground. "I'd say it was caused by a heavy impact, a bat or a pipe…" He gestured the lines of cast-off speckles surrounding the larger splats and splotches. "And it was slow. Low velocity and impact. Blunt-force trauma. And I'd say that she was standing about there when she was hit."

Heather agreed with all of it, give or take a few inches regarding the victim's position. "Very good," she said. "That would also be my assessment. Now, on to marker 3."

Evidence number 3 had been in their eyeline for some time—the huge pool of dark, congealed blood—but no one had wanted to look for long. Not until they had to.

"And this is where she fell," Gabriel said. "After being struck."

"Yeah," Heather replied. "It is. And from the look of it, I'll hazard a guess and say she didn't get back up again."

"Agreed," Tina murmured, her hands in her pockets.

Heather craned her neck. "And it looks like our fourth piece of evidence is the rope that came loose from her wrists."

They padded over to it, where it lay close to shore. Heather cocked her head. There were no knots, but there was denting and fraying where it had clearly been tied at both ends. "So, I guess whoever did this was trying to make sure she didn't come back up."

"Well then, whoever did this is no Boy Scout," Gabriel added. "Anyone with any kind of knowledge of the outdoors knows there's a big difference between a wet and dry knot," Gabriel said. "Clearly just did a double knot or something."

Heather made a note in her head, her hands too cold to scribble in her book. "So, probably not an outdoorsman."

"Maybe it's someone who likes to think of themselves as an outdoorsman," Gabriel suggested. "They must've been pretty confident that it would work."

"Cocky," Heather stated, agreeing with the beginnings of his profile.

They stood there quietly for a moment before Heather clicked her tense jaw once again and turned to face Mariah. The others joined her, and as they made their way toward the deceased—a young woman in a nice dress soaked through to the bone—a terrible sense of déjà vu took hold.

They all gathered around and looked down. The deceased was undoubtedly Mariah King. That much was obvious. She hadn't changed much since Heather had last seen her, except her bob of hair was now a dark purple and her tattoos had tripled. She was wearing a black, long-sleeved dress with a heart cutout in the front and thick, black tights, the soles of which were covered in mud. This implied she had, at some point, ditched her shoes and ran through the woods without them. This meant she had known she was in danger. That she was frightened. That her last moments had been ones of horror.

Though Heather had seen most of the damage from afar, what she hadn't noticed, due to the angling of the head, was the crater in the left side of her skull at Mariah's temple. It was blunt-force trauma, as indicated by the blood spatter, just like Jenny Brooks. However, unlike the injury at the back of Jenny's head, Heather was confident that this powerful blow had killed Mariah almost instantly rather than knocked her unconscious.

Despite that minor quibble, it was another similarity that was hard to ignore.

"Heather," Tina said, her intonation summing up all of Heather's thoughts into one word.

"I know. It's similar."

"It's too similar," Tina corrected.

Heather exhaled, a cold cloud bursting forth. "Mason's dead. So, someone must be screwing with us. Or this is... I don't know."

"The coincidence of all coincidences?"

"Yeah. Or that."

CHAPTER FOUR

THE DETECTIVE

By three o'clock, Mariah King had been transported from the increasingly frigid clearing to an almost equally chilly basement in the Ellsworth Family Funeral Home. Heather had been waiting by her side ever since for the formal identification to occur. It felt like the right thing to do, even though she was more uncomfortable being alone with the dead in the windowless, clinical space than she cared to admit.

Not much longer, she told herself, checking her watch and realizing that an hour had passed. Soon enough, Mariah would be on her way to Dr. Tocci in Seattle, where she'd be put on ice, awaiting her autopsy. Though, knowing Julius, he'd probably get to work right away. He knew better than anyone that time was of the essence.

Heather bobbed her knee, watching the second hand tick, tick, tick. She was trying hard not to be impatient, especially considering the unexpected complexities of finding someone to make the identification. As it turned out, Mariah had no next of kin to call. She was childless, single, and an only child. Her parents, too, were only children, so there were no cousins, aunts, or uncles to speak of. They also had tragically died in a snowy car accident in 2020, and any remaining grandparents lived out of state.

So Heather had turned to the first person she could think of. Taylor Sherman, née Brooks—one of Mariah's best friends and Jenny Brooks's older sister. While she could've contacted the other remaining members of the fateful 2018 bachelorette party—Cheyenne Welch and Hazel Brock—she'd soon ruled them out based on temperament and location. She and Cheyenne had butted heads in 2018, and the last Heather had heard, Hazel was away studying at Washington State. So it had to be Taylor, even if it felt unkind to inflict something so awful on her for the second time.

At least I have Foster, she thought, her eyes still glued to the ticking clock. He'd made a career out of calming the grief-stricken, and Heather was confident he could bail her out should she start to drown in the inevitable tears. Then he could whisk Taylor away to the crackling fire in the parlor and ply her with tea until she was steady enough to drive home.

Heather hadn't been present when Taylor and her parents, Jeff and Diane, identified Jenny. Instead, Gene had taken that upon himself. Heather had been grateful for this at the time. However, in retrospect, it had only removed her further from the chain of command, and Gene had used this to his benefit. Jenny was in Dr. Melrose's hands by the following day, despite the parents' protests and Heather's failed attempts to redirect her to someone more competent.

She knew she was lingering. She knew it wasn't helpful, but five years on, she still couldn't believe how badly they'd botched that case. Dr. Melrose—a notorious pill popper who'd only just returned from his suspension—had been far from the correct choice, and she was sure that the full report, wherever it was, would be sloppy at best.

Everyone else had seemed to be aware of this too. Everyone except Gene. Jeff and Diane, in particular—who worked as defense lawyers—had been highly opposed to using Dr. Melrose. They'd seen in the flesh how his testimony failed to hold up in court. Though Mason's suicide was unpleasant, Heather was glad that Jenny's case had never reached the courts, because if it had, Mason would have likely walked free after a couple of years. That was if he ever saw the inside of a cell in the first place.

Heather's phone rang, and she answered without looking.

"Detective Bishop. How may I help you?" she asked flatly.

"Hello, Detective Bishop," Julius replied coyly.

"Julius," Heather breathed. "Hi."

"Hi. How are you?"

"Crappy. To say the least."

"I figured as such," he replied. "How's everything going? Is Mariah King on her way?"

"Not yet. Still waiting on identification."

"Of course," he said, soft and understanding.

"Sorry," Heather croaked anyway.

"Don't be. She's being kept cold, yes?"

"Yes."

"And you found her in the lake?" he asked.

"Yes."

"Well then, she'll be fine for a while longer. I promise."

Heather hummed in response, unable to speak.

"I promise," Julius repeated. "You have no idea of the things we're able to do at the lab now. I promise I have examined worse and still provided thorough reports that stand up in court. Perhaps you should accompany her, and I can show you."

"I can't," Heather replied. "I've got way, way too much to do here."

"Well, as I said, I'm happy to come to you."

"You know that the funeral home isn't equipped for this."

"I could make it work. I did for Roland Ellis," he reminded her.

"Roland worked because you had cyanide test strips in your kit. Mariah needs x-rays and full blood workups."

Julius sighed. "I know. I know. Worth a shot."

"I'll visit when the case is done. *I* promise."

"I'd like that. But more than that, I think it would benefit you to watch me work. To know your cases are in the right hands."

"I know they are," Heather assured him.

Julius paused. "At this rate, maybe I should set up a shop in Glenville. I'd certainly manage to stay in business."

The door at the top of the stairs creaked, and Heather fell silent.

"Sorry, bad joke," Julius added hastily. "Though that town of yours is certainly afflicted by bad luck of late."

"Bad luck or bad people?" Heather asked. "Anyway, don't be sorry, but Taylor Sherman is here to make the identification, so I've got to go."

"Okay. Talk soon. I'll let you know when Mariah arrives."

"Thank you. Bye."

She liked that Julius used their names. As hardened as he had become about death and as crude as he could be about it at times, a level of respect was always maintained. She could relate. Sometimes it was hard to sound sympathetic when you'd seen so much horror, but it was crucial to maintain your humanity in the face of atrocities. At least that was what Gabriel's therapist had told him when he'd opened up about using humor as a coping device.

"She's down there, my dear," Foster croaked from the distant doorway.

"Thanks," a woman's voice replied, and soon dainty feet descended the steep steps into the overlit room.

Taylor squinted at the base. "Should've brought my sunglasses."

"I'm thinking the same thing. I swear, it gets worse every time I come down here."

"No kidding," Taylor replied, glancing around before her eyes landed on the slab. "Is that her?"

"Yeah," Heather said. "Do you want to...?"

"Give me a second," Taylor requested, her fists clenched. "Just need to get my bearings."

"Of course. Take your time."

Taylor smiled weakly at Heather, tearing her gaze away from the sheet. "It's weird," she said. "I know it's her under that sheet. Everyone knew Mariah, and if you all say it's her, I know it is. But I just keep hoping that you'll pull back the sheet and it'll be some stranger staring back at me. Some out-of-towner that I have no connection to. It would still be awful, but it wouldn't be her."

"I get that."

"I know it's not," Taylor clarified. "But right now, I still have some hope."

"Do you want to be alone?"

Taylor half laughed, half shuddered. "God, no. Not down here."

"Glass of water? Tissue?" Heather asked, even though Taylor didn't look remotely close to crying.

"No. I'm fine," Taylor said kindly. "I'm not the type to fall apart, so if you want to ask me some questions, go right ahead. Saves you having to come to my house."

"It does. Thank you. And feel free to ask me anything in return. I don't want this to be a one-way transaction."

"Like it was with Jenny?" Taylor asked before closing her eyes. "I'm sorry. That was unfair."

"It's not unfair. And don't be sorry."

Taylor nodded and took a seat on the counter next to Heather. "Where did you find her?"

"In the lake. She was floating. Two of our officers retrieved her."

"So, she was there for a while?" Taylor asked.

Heather looked at her profile, and Taylor turned to make eye contact.

"It probably sounds weird, but despite everything, I'm obsessed with crime shows."

"It's not weird," Heather said softly, turning back to Mariah's sheet ghost silhouette. "I think we all become obsessed with the things that affect us most, and we all have our ways of coping."

"Yeah, I think being informed about all of it makes me feel… safe." Taylor exhaled. "So, she was in there for a while?"

Heather nodded. "From my estimation, which you should take with a pinch of salt, I'd say she died Friday night or early Saturday morning."

"Jesus. That's ironic."

"How so?"

"Mariah couldn't swim," Taylor answered, a nervous giggle-burp escaping her lips. "Sorry. But, um, it would've been early Saturday. That she died, I mean. I was with her until 1:00 a.m. that night."

"Yeah, at Sherwood's, right? I read your missing persons report. I'm sorry I wasn't here to follow up on that. I was away."

"You're allowed time off. Besides, it wouldn't have made a difference if she was at the bottom of the lake."

"I guess not," Heather admitted.

"I filed the report after I couldn't get ahold of her in the morning. It hadn't been twenty-four hours yet, and there was no evidence of foul play, so it was just a waiting game." Taylor paused. "It's awful, but I'm actually glad she died before I filed the report. It would be so much worse if she'd died afterward and we just didn't get to her in time. I feel guilty enough as it is."

"Guilty?"

"Yeah," Taylor said softly, looking at her friend, cold and still on the slab. "I abandoned my sister at the diner and Mariah at Sherwood's, and both of them were murdered because they were alone. Hard to not feel like a shitty friend at the very least."

"Well, there were plenty of other people around. Trustworthy people. It wasn't like you abandoned them in the middle of the woods to fend for themselves."

"I bet you have to tell yourself the same thing about Jenny. Probably why it sounds so rehearsed," Taylor said bluntly but without malice.

Heather felt her heart palpitate and opened her mouth, but Taylor shook her head.

"Don't worry. I don't blame you. As you said. There were plenty of people around. You even gave her taxi money, right?"

"I did."

"Well, there you go. It's not your fault Mason showed up."

"So, I'm taking it you left before Mariah?"

"Yeah. We were at Sherwood's. She wanted to stay and party, but my husband—you remember Hunter—wanted me to come home."

Heather did remember Hunter Sherwood, and not especially fondly, but she kept such opinions to herself. "Do you remember who else was at Sherwood's when you left?"

"No, sorry. You'll have to ask Bobby. I'd had at least three too many. That's Cheyenne's fault. She always buys shots."

"Was Cheyenne still there when you left?"

"No, she left at around eleven-thirty, I think. We fell out as usual."

"What about?"

"Does it matter?" Taylor asked, not angry but genuinely curious.

"When it comes to homicide, I find that everything matters."

Taylor bobbed her head. "Okay. Well, we argued about Jenny. Or rather, we argued about Cheyenne not wanting to talk about Jenny and the past. It was the anniversary of her death—well, technically the day before—and I always get a little…" Taylor screwed up her face, her relaxed hands turning back into fists.

"Wait," she said, turning to Heather again. "That means they both died—"

"I know," Heather said softly, acknowledging the long list of parallels and coincidences.

"You still sure it was Mason?" Taylor asked, clearly half joking. "Don't answer that. I know the blood on the tire iron was a match."

"Yeah, it was."

"Weird."

"Well, before we take the next step, I'll ask you what I did back then. Do you have any idea who could've done this? A boyfriend I don't know about? A stalker?" Heather probed.

"Well, unless you want to look into Thimbles again—which, no offense, I still think is a ridiculous theory—then I've got nothing. Sorry."

"Don't be."

Taylor exhaled and slid from the bench top. "Okay. Let's do this."

"Now, I should warn you, her injuries are severe, and the water—"

"I understand," Taylor said. "What happens after this?"

"We'll send her to Seattle, where my friend Dr. Tocci will perform an autopsy."

"Well, thank God she's not going to Dr. Melrose. You know he lost his license two years back?"

Heather wanted to scream and throw things but kept her composure. "That figures," was all she could say as she also slid from her seat. "Are you ready?"

"I have no idea. Let's just get it over with."

"All right," Heather said, approaching the head of the body as Taylor sidled up beside her.

Slowly she began to peel the sheet away, the fabric sticking to the wound and the wet, and unveiled Mariah's ghastly visage bit by bit.

Despite her claims, Taylor fell apart instantly. Tears welled, her knees weakened, and her lips paled, contrasting with her caramel-colored fake tan. Knowing the symptoms of fainting well by now, Heather moved to her side and wrapped an arm around her shoulder. Taylor leaned into her, sputtering and gasping.

"Breathe with me," Heather said, and together they breathed in and out, in and out until Taylor regained her balance.

Snaking an arm around Heather's waist, Taylor kneaded at her shirt, her fingertips digging into the skin beneath. "It's Mariah," she said at last. "It's Mariah King."

"Okay," Heather said softly, quickly moving to cover the swollen face.

Taylor reached out a hand and stopped her. "No. Please. Let me look."

She stared down at her friend for a solid minute, unblinking, mascara running down her cheeks in black rivers before she released Heather and turned away.

Heather covered the body and turned to the shivering woman. "Are you okay?" she asked.

"God, that was…" Taylor muttered, rubbing a thumb fiercely over her prominent collarbone.

"I know. I'm sorry."

Taylor turned, wiping her face with the back of her hand. "Are those tissues still on offer?"

Heather retrieved the pack from her pocket and handed them over. Taylor carefully pulled one out and dabbed at her face, but all the blotting did was hollow the streaks, and black outlines remained where the tears had been.

"Thank you, Detective," Taylor said.

"Heather's fine."

"Heather. I hope you catch the bastard who did this."

"I will do my best."

"Well, I suppose that's all anyone can do," Taylor sniffed.

Heather, feeling her own eyes prickle, led them to the stairwell and gestured up the flight. "Cup of tea?"

"I'll take a coffee with bourbon."

"That can be arranged."

CHAPTER FIVE

THE BRIDE

TAYLOR STIRRED AWAKE IN THE DRIVEWAY, HER HANDS on the wheel of the still-rumbling car. She wondered how long she'd been sitting there, staring at nothing, and though she couldn't remember, the stares from her nosy suburban neighbors gave her some indication. It was weird. Not only could she not remember pulling up, but she also couldn't remember driving. She knew the car hadn't driven itself, but the journey was dark and impervious to her attempts at recollection. All her prodding soon inspired a headache, and she decided to leave the black spot alone. On any other day, this lack of recollection would've frightened her, but she was too tired to care and focused on her next journey instead—the one from the car to the house.

Prying her hands from the wheel, she put the car in park, grabbed her bag from the passenger seat, and exited the vehicle. Under the watchful gaze of dozens of eyes, she checked her car for damage—or worse, blood—as discreetly as possible. Fortunately, there wasn't a single mark on her precious hand-me-down 2001 Audi TT, and she relaxed a little as she moved to lock it. However, a new problem presented itself as she stared down at the well-worn key fob, unable to remember what buttons did what. She'd pressed them daily for the past six years, yet it seemed her muscle memory was temporarily atrophied. After some further dithering, she guessed correctly; the lights flashed, and the locks clunked. Yet she still wasn't satisfied and lunged forward to pull hard on the handle.

The oversensitive alarm system roared to life, its blaring calls deafening the entire neighborhood. She struggled again with the keys, becoming further disorientated by the cacophony. She felt the stares burning on the back of her neck and spun on her heel to confront the onlookers with a potent glare. They hastily pretended as if they weren't looking and resumed their hedge-trimming and weed-whacking. Living in the cult-like confines of an HOA irritated her at the best of times, but on days when she wanted to scream and day-drink on her front lawn, it felt downright oppressive.

After a lot of button-pressing, the sound stopped, and she shuffled to the front door. As she fiddled with a second lot of keys, she resisted the urge to flip Mrs. Mackensize off. The old biddy was still watching from her living room window while her vicious, ankle-biting chihuahuas thrashed against the glass.

If she even thinks about bringing me a casserole, Taylor seethed, slamming the door shut behind her.

Eyes pricking with tears, she leaned back and slid down the length of the door until her buttocks hit the floor. She didn't know what to do or what to think, so instead, she stared down the hallway to the kitchen doorway, hoping Hunter would come running. She wanted to be scooped up, coddled, and loved. She wanted him to make decisions for her. However, despite all the calamity, he didn't come to her rescue.

She mewled like a lost lamb for him, hoping he would materialize. Then she realized his car hadn't been in the driveway, blocking hers like it always was. He was somewhere else even though she'd begged him to be home when she returned from the funeral home. He knew she had to go identify Mariah. He knew, and he wasn't there. He rarely was anymore, and when he was, it was awkward and quiet until he wanted something—usually dinner or sex—and then he'd turn on the charm. Still, she craved his touch because his hands were the only ones she could turn to.

Fueled by frustration, she managed to drag herself from the floor and into the living room, where she collapsed onto the couch instead. The laundry had piled up over the weekend while she'd been worrying about Mariah's whereabouts, and through the slight gap between the double barn-style doors, she could see that the dirty dishes were in a similar state. She hated mess, but she knew her hands were a liability and would only result in broken glass and shattered plates.

Hunter also hated mess, and the mounting pile had become a state of passive-aggressive contention over the weekend. Sure, he could do them, but it wasn't his job. Seemingly, nothing was aside from his work at the mill. That place was his main excuse. He was always too tired when he got home, and it didn't seem to matter that Taylor was doing double shifts at the care home twice a week. Seemingly, even her best friend going missing on the anniversary of her sister's death could not spur him into action. Though, in his defense, he had complained less about eating the bland leftover meatloaf than he usually would.

Taylor curled up into herself and fell sideways, looking around the sparsely decorated room, her eyes landing on one of the photos that sat on the mantlepiece. It was the bridesmaid photo from her wedding day. She stood in the middle of the image with Cheyenne on her left and Hazel and Mariah to her right. It was supposed to be symmetrical, but of course, the maid of honor was missing. However, she wasn't entirely absent. The four women held their arms out in front of them, their palms facing the sky, Jenny's plum-colored dress draped across their steady limbs.

THE BRIDESMAIDS

Most people—including Hunter and her parents—thought the image morbid and certainly a poor choice of decoration. Yet it was Taylor's favorite wedding photo, and the bride always won when it came to these sorts of things. She liked that it was honest. The day itself had been bittersweet, filled with more sad tears than happy ones, so why hang a falsehood on the wall? After all, her sister had only been dead two weeks by the time the big day rolled around, and her funeral had only been five days earlier. She'd wanted to move the date, but Hunter countered her, insisting she needed something positive to look forward to. Secretly, she thought it was because he was worried she'd run away if given more time, a grief-induced case of cold feet nipping at her heels.

If she was honest with herself, it had been more than the grief that had given her second thoughts. Hunter had been best friends with Mason Fowler, the man who'd butchered her little sister. How could she trust that her husband didn't know? That he, too, wasn't a monster? Over time her suspicions had fortunately faltered, and she'd been convinced of his innocence. It wasn't his fault. He was a safe person. A trustworthy person. A man, not a monster. Of this, at least, she was certain.

She began to sob when the realization hit her. Only two of the women in the photo remained. There were only two of them left. Jenny was dead, Mariah was dead, and Hazel had been missing for over a year now. Her once-happy friendship group had been completely decimated by tragedy.

And then there were two, she thought bitterly, hoping the day that two turned to one—or worse, none—wouldn't come to pass anytime soon.

Despite the bachelorette party being the last night they were all together, those photos were not on the walls. They were hidden away in a box in the attic. It was too painful seeing her sister laughing and dancing, with no idea of what was in store for her only a few hours later.

So instead, there was a photo of the five of them about to go to prom sans boyfriends. It was sad to acknowledge, but high school was when they'd all been their happiest. Adulthood had only wrought disappointment—Mariah and Cheyenne's failed career attempts, bad relationships, lack of fulfillment—and tragedy on the group.

One memory stuck out in particular. It was on the last Friday before their junior year summer break. She wasn't sure what it was exactly about that day, that lunch break, that was so memorable. Yet she thought about it often, and every time she did, it was as if she could feel the sun shining on her face.

They'd decided to venture out during lunch break and head to the local park. They'd sat on a picnic blanket on a grassy bank, drank wine that Cheyenne had stolen from her mother, and smoked a skinny joint that Mariah had pieced together from her hippie dad's stash. Supposedly, he smoked it to ease his cancer pains, but they knew the truth. He was a stoner, and they loved him for it.

As they got tipsy and a little too high, they told rude jokes, talked about boys, and laughed until their stomachs hurt. They ended up getting so stoned that they had to ditch their final class of the day and miraculously didn't get into any trouble. This was probably because they were generally good girls with perfect attendance and were in the good graces of their young surprisingly cool, young female principal. Plus, the final week was mostly spent watching movies on the ancient TVs they wheeled into classrooms.

Taylor closed her eyes, and there she was, on that grassy bank, her bare hands and feet pressed into the lush green as she giggled absentmindedly.

"You know, in a year from now," Hazel said, "we'll be a week away from graduation… except for Jenny."

Everyone cooed and awwed at "Little Jenny," and Cheyenne pinched the slightly younger girl's blushing cheek.

"Aw, poor little cutie. We'll have to come back for your graduation and show everyone how successful we've all become."

"Wait, you're leaving?" Jenny asked, wide-eyed and horrified by the possible disintegration of her only friendship group.

She didn't even hang out with them all that often, not until they were in their senior year. She only tagged along at first because she was Taylor's younger sister. Yet over time, the girls grew to love her far beyond mere toleration. Then she'd become one of the wolf pack.

"Of course I'm leaving," Cheyenne said dramatically, as if she was offended by the question. "I'm going to go stay with my cousin in New York. She's the receptionist for a major modeling agency. She's going to help me become a supermodel."

"Wow," Jenny said, her awe evident and completely genuine.

Taylor had to agree that it did seem very glamorous, but she swallowed her jealousy, knowing that envy was an ugly look on anyone, and she was already the less attractive friend.

"What about you, Mariah?" Jenny had asked.

"Oh, I'll probably just get a job in town. Maybe take some classes at the community college in the next town over. It would be cool to be a vet, but I don't have the grades."

"You could be a veterinary nurse," Taylor suggested, and Mariah lit up.

"Yeah," Jenny agreed. "Our cousin is a vet nurse in Seattle, and she didn't even finish high school. Ended up getting her GED afterward."

"Wow, a veterinary nurse," Mariah said dreamily, fiddling with the nose stud that Cheyenne had pierced for her.

"Hazel?" Jenny asked with a smile, always making sure she didn't leave out their more quiet friend.

"I'm going to Washington State to study English," Hazel said shyly, not wanting to brag.

Jealousy burned hot again, but it was soon crushed by pride. Sure, all Taylor was going to be doing in a year was dating Hunter Sherman and working at the grocery store, but her parents had promised to help her find a place once she was eighteen, and small-town life didn't sound so bad if she was with the man she loved in a home of her own.

The front door handle jiggled, and Taylor snapped out of her dreamland, finding herself in a cold, rapidly darkening living room instead of out in nature, surrounded by the sun. She launched onto her feet and turned to face the door as Hunter let himself in. He turned to face her, his expression already gloomy as he stared around at the unlit interior.

"Sweetie?" he asked slowly, his tone filled with concern.

"Hi," Taylor said quietly.

"What's going on? Why are you in the dark?"

"Mariah's dead."

Hunter sighed and strode toward his wife, wrapping his arms around her tightly. She found she didn't want his touch and stiffened in his embrace. He'd come home too late, and the ghosts of her past had comforted her plenty in the meantime.

More than that, with the vividity of her memories still burned into the back of her eyelids, she also felt resentful. It wasn't his fault, but all she could think was, if they hadn't gotten married in Glenville and they'd moved further afield like she'd wanted, the bachelorette would've happened elsewhere, placing Jenny far away from Mason. Maybe they could've convinced her to break up with him over text and stay with them in the city, and her wildest wishes would've come true. Similarly, had he not insisted she come home early from the bar, Mariah too would be safe and warm, maybe recovering from a hangover in the guest room and not on a slab in a funeral home basement. The thoughts compiled, forming fury, and she pulled away, looking up at him, unsure of everything.

If he noticed her coldness, he didn't mention it. Instead, he smiled and tucked her hair behind her ear. "Go take a bath. I'll crack open a bottle of wine and order Chinese," he whispered kindly.

Decisions, she thought, nearly falling to her knees in thanks. Her mood spun 180 degrees and pointed toward gratitude as she dipped back toward him and wrapped her hands around his waist. He kissed the top of her head. They stayed there for a moment before she let him go and headed up the stairs. As she went, she felt nerve endings connecting and memory returning, and her sister's laughter echoed in her ears.

CHAPTER SIX

THE DETECTIVE

"**P**ENNY FOR YOUR THOUGHTS?" GABRIEL ASKED, opening the glove box and handing over the pack of gum.

As Heather opened her mouth to thank him, another sickening crack rang out. Had Heather not felt the source of the sound of it burning hot in her jaw socket, she would have thought a rock had hit the windscreen. She grimaced and massaged her tender mandible while Gabriel looked on in disgust. She hadn't even realized she'd been grinding again, but clearly, the same could not be said for her partner. If he'd rather hear her smack and chew on a wad of spearmint, then the terrible, crunching milling must have reached unprecedented levels of audio unpleasantries.

"You should go to the dentist," Gabriel said.

"I was just at the dentist," Heather groaned.

"I know, but at this rate, you're going to end up with a mouth full of bone meal."

That made Heather smirk. Her ex-husband, Daniel, used to say similar things about using her jaw as a mortar and pestle. That was the last time the grinding had gotten out of control, and understandably, Daniel's joviality hadn't lasted long. It got so bad that he couldn't be in the same room as her when she was working, and she ended up moving into the guest room so that he could sleep in silence. Retrospectively, these were probably also indicators of a marriage in decline, but at the time, it was easier to blame the grinding.

"You're doing it again!" Gabriel exclaimed

"Crap. Sorry," Heather said, popping four pieces of stale gum into her mouth and chewing fervently.

"What's going on with you?"

"It's just the case. I did it when I was investigating the Paper Doll Case too," she said.

"Why didn't you do it with the Warrens, or the Ellises, or the Flemings?"

Heather stopped chewing for a second and thought about this. What if this habit was caused by something else, something subconscious, something she was trying to ignore? Then it struck her. It was Daniel—not the killers—triggering the desire to pulverize enamel. Back then, it had been the dissolution of their marriage, the falling out of love, the worry of him leaving her, and now it was an entirely different can of worms. One that was somehow even more painful—the murder of Katy Graham by her fiancé, Daniel Palmer. Not that he'd been convicted yet—at least as far as Heather knew—nor did she believe him to be guilty. Instead, it was the possibility that bothered her. The mere suggestion that she could've been married to a murderer for five years without realizing it was enough to upturn everything she believed in and send her running back into the arms of the bottle.

"Heather," Gabriel said softly.

"Penny for my thoughts?" she asked, snapping out of it and remembering what Gabriel had said earlier.

"Yeah, I mean, there's clearly something on your mind."

Heather turned the rearview mirror toward her, pulled her hair down, and got to work on readjusting her ponytail. "I don't know. This case is just weird. I've seen my fair share of copycats, but Jenny Brooks's murder—a domestic homicide and possible crime of passion—is not what copycats look for. It's too personal and not nearly famous enough."

"It's famous around here," Gabriel noted.

"I guess. Still, it's unusual. But if it's not a copycat and a separate, unlinked murder, then why all the coincidences?"

"Is there any possibility they were committed by the same person? No copycat. No coincidences. Just one guy five years apart."

"Mason Fowler is dead, so no. Not unless you believe in zombies."

"I don't." Gabriel paused and looked away. "You're going to hate me for asking, but what if it wasn't Mason?"

Heather thought about it, finally securing her unusually unruly hair and dropping her hands into her lap. "Did I ever tell you about when I met Mason?"

"I don't think so."

"I'd been watching him celebrate at the football game for hours, a big old smile plastered on his face. We'd just found Jenny's body, and there he was, drinking beer and eating hot dogs. Then I followed him out to the parking lot and confronted him. I'm telling you, when he looked at me, all the hair stood up on the back of my neck. Honestly, he scared the shit out of me. The things he said, the way he moved, his eyes... No, he was evil all right, exactly the same brand of monster as all the other scumbags I've locked up."

"Okay. I trust your judgment. It was Mason. So, what about a different kind of copycat?" Gabriel asked.

"Go on," Heather replied.

"Well, I know there are the ones who want to be famous, who idolize the killers, but what if this is personal? Maybe they want to hurt Taylor for some reason, or maybe they want to screw with you. You got any psycho enemies in town that I don't know about?"

"Not as far as I'm aware. But I like the theory, even though that level of meticulousness sort of falls apart when you factor in the crappy knot-tying."

Gabriel shrugged. "Unless they wanted you to find her."

Goosebumps erupted across Heather's arms, and she rubbed at the downy part at the back of her neck. "Then why would they put her in the water at all? Why not just leave her in the clearing? I don't know. It's probably not even half as weird as it seems."

"Is that what you actually think or want to think?" Gabriel asked skeptically.

"Both," Heather admitted sheepishly. "But let's hold off on the theories until we get the autopsy report and witness statements."

"Yeah, of course. Sorry."

"Don't be. I like your thinking and enthusiasm. Honestly, you remind me of me at twenty-six." She paused and lowered her brows before turning to look at Gabriel. "Wait, you're twenty-seven next month, right? Were you and Jenny in the same year at school?"

"We were actually in the same class," Gabriel admitted.

"Why didn't you tell me?"

Gabriel frowned. "To be honest, I had a major crush on her, and her death really freaked me out. I mean, it wasn't like she knew I existed, but still. Mason definitely did though. Knew I existed, I mean. Even back then, that guy was a freak."

"Typical high school bully, huh?"

"And then some. Roadkill-in-your-bag kind of bully. Swirlies-in-an-unclean-toilet kind of bully. Gross-out stuff. Weird stuff. Never did much to me, thanks to all my older brothers."

"That's one thing I still don't get. What the hell did Jenny see in him?" Heather questioned. "I mean, it makes sense that she wanted to leave him, but how'd they end up together in the first place?"

"She must've seen some good in him, I guess. Or maybe she wasn't as nice as we all think."

"She seemed nice to me," Heather said sadly.

"Me too. I guess it's just another mystery."

"I guess," Heather replied, suddenly sullen.

"Come on, let's start unraveling some of this crap," Gabriel said, strangely assertive, tilting his head toward Sherwood's with a half-cocked, coaxing smile.

"Sounds like a plan, boss," Heather teased, slipping on her sunglasses and adjusting her belt.

She pushed open the door with the bottom of her hiking boots and smirked as she heard him repeat the word *boss* under his breath as he unbuckled his seatbelt.

CHAPTER SEVEN

THE DETECTIVE

As the door swung shut behind them, Heather paused. There was something different about Sherwood's, but she couldn't put her finger on what until she inhaled deeply. She did it again, awestruck. Somehow the perpetual stench of deep-rooted cigarette smoke had been eradicated and replaced by the smell of citrus and bleach. It seemed there were no bounds to the miracles Amber could perform given the correct dose of cash flow injection.

"What the hell have you done?" Heather asked Amber, grinning ear to ear, looking around at the glistening interior.

"Good afternoon to you too," Amber laughed, pausing her counter wiping to beckon them further into the warmth.

"Sorry, it just smells really good in here."

"We power-washed the walls. Did you know that that one was originally white?" Amber asked, gesturing at the section of eggshell by the back door.

Heather furrowed her brows. The rest of the walls still were and always had been black, but gun to her head, she couldn't remember what that specific wall had been before. It certainly hadn't been white. In fact, if she had to guess, she'd have said it was a bisque brown with a hint of mustard.

"I did not," she said slowly. "Was it covered in nicotine?"

"Among other stuff," Amber said.

"I wish I could've seen that."

"Oh, I'll send you the video. It's practically pornographic."

Heather continued to inspect the room. Though the booths themselves looked the same—maroon, faux-leather upholstery, and wooden tables; there was something new about them.

"Did you reupholster the seats?" she asked.

"Some of them," Amber said. "Thanks for noticing. Bobby insisted we keep them the same color. Don't want to freak the locals out too much, but it's nice not having to sweep up all that spongy crud at the end of the night."

With increasing horror, Heather wondered whether that "spongy crud" that had so often comforted her aching body had been, in fact, asbestos. A little leftover from the bygone era of Bobby's grandfather. She didn't mention this; the possible damage was already done. All she could do was hope they wore masks during the renovation.

"So, how can I help y'all?" Amber asked. "Tying one on after a tough day?"

"Unfortunately," Heather replied, taking a seat at the bar. "Our work is not quite done. And I'm afraid we need witness statements from both you and Bobby. Is he around?"

"Yeah, he's upstairs." Amber dropped the cloth and turned to the open doorway that led to the second floor. "Bobby, get your ass down here!" she hollered at a drum-rupturing volume.

Thundering feet followed, and Bobby emerged in a panic. "What is it?" he began before catching sight of Heather and

Gabriel. "Oh, thank God. Don't do that, baby. I thought you'd fallen off that damn stool again." He took a second to catch his breath. "Hi, Heather. Gabriel. Guessing you're here about Mariah King?"

"We are," Heather replied. "We need your witness statements. As far as we know, you were some of the last people to see her."

Gabriel laid two blank statement sheets on the table and clicked a ballpoint pen. "Don't worry, I'll write, you sign."

Bobby poured himself a scotch with a sigh. "So it's official? The body in the lake was hers?"

"Yep. Taylor identified her less than an hour ago."

Amber shook her head. "Poor girl. Poor Taylor too. Especially considering her sister… Wait, that's—"

"Weird? I know," Heather said, the word *weird* beginning to sound like gibberish. "So, who served them that night?"

"I did," Amber answered. "Tequila shots and margaritas."

"Great, we'll start with you. Any idea of a timeline?" Heather began as Gabriel hovered his pen over the page.

"I've got some idea. We were slammed on Friday, as usual, but I think they came in after dinner, and Cheyenne left sometime before midnight when I checked on the baby. Then Mariah and Taylor continued to drink and got pretty loose before Taylor took off. I'm not exactly sure when that was."

"It was 1:00 a.m.," Bobby supplied. "Or near enough. I remember her making eye contact with me."

It was all lining up with what Taylor had said, which was a good start, and Heather nodded, not prompting them with what she already knew. "What about Mariah?"

"I was with the baby again, sorry," Amber said.

"I remember," Bobby said, and Gabriel jumped to the other sheet. "Last call is at 2, and she, the five guys at the big table, and a couple of regulars stayed behind for the lock-in. So, there weren't too many heads to count, and she was the first one of them to leave. I know for sure it was 3:31 a.m. when she went outside to wait for her taxi. I remember because I'd microwaved a snack and saw the time on the little digital clock as she stormed past. Then the guys she was with left a little after 5, and we both went to bed."

"Okay, the guys. You're sure none of them left with her?"

"I'm sure. There were five of them at the start, and there were five of them when I kicked them out. I know those boys well, and I keep close to sober on busy nights."

Heather nodded. "Right. And did anyone see her get into the taxi?"

They both shook their heads.

"No," Bobby said.

"And I went out for a cigarette probably ten minutes later," Amber added. "She wasn't there anymore, so I assumed she got in."

"Did you hear it pull up?" Gabriel asked, doing an excellent job of alternating between statements.

"Music was all the way up," Bobby said. "And these walls are thick. And with the windows being painted over, you can't hear much of anything when it's busy."

"Do you know which taxi company she used?" Heather asked.

"You'll have to ask the guys," Bobby replied. "They ordered it for her."

"Do you have their contact details?"

"Sure. They've all got tabs here. And I always take a number in case a tourist tries to disappear without paying up. I'll send you a list if your number is still the same."

"It is," Heather confirmed.

"Joey Marsh is the one you should talk to," Amber added. "She was trying to hook up with him. I could tell he was into her too, but she was too drunk. He's a nice guy. *Really*," she emphasized.

"Okay. So, to recap," Heather said, glancing at Gabriel's statements. "They arrived after dinner."

"Probably eight, thinking about it now," Amber stated. "They mentioned going down to the lake to lay flowers for Jenny beforehand."

"Okay, so they arrive at eight. Cheyenne leaves at what, 11:30, 11:45 p.m.?" Heather asked, remembering what Taylor had said.

"Yeah, that sounds right. She and Taylor seemed pretty heated," Bobby interjected. "Taylor also seemed pretty drunk."

"Okay, and then Taylor left at 1, but Mariah didn't join her and set her sights on Joey Marsh and joined him and his friends?"

"Yeah, Joey and the other boys from the mill," Bobby confirmed.

"Then Mariah leaves at 3:30 a.m., and they stay another hour and a half until 5."

"That's about it," Bobby cemented.

"All right. Anything else? Maybe somebody else went out the front when she did and saw her get in the taxi?"

Bobby shook his head. "Nobody followed her out. Most folks go out the back to smoke, and as you might know, that's all fenced off now. Can't enter or leave except through the front."

"Okay, was there anything or anybody that stood out to you? Regardless of the timeline."

Bobby hesitated. "Thimbles. He came in close to last call. He'd already been on the hooch, and when he started getting weird, I made him leave. Probably about two hours before Mariah left," he clarified. "And I'm sure you remember what I told you last time."

Heather did remember. Back in 2018, Bobby had told her that Thimbles wasn't and couldn't be Jenny's murderer. He was just a strange old man at best and a nomad, an alcoholic, a petty criminal, and a pest at worst.

He'd also told her that Thimble's real name was Michael Ford and that he'd lost his daughter to her husband's domestic abuse and his wife to cancer shortly after. Supposedly, that was the reason he stalked young women to their homes: to protect them. Heather wasn't sure if she bought that any more than she bought his boogieman status. Still, the mention of him, regardless of Bobby's feelings, made Heather's blood run cold. Here he was again, skulking around the scene of the abduction as he had at Dottie's Diner on that fateful night. Another troublesome parallel.

"Do you have cameras?" Gabriel asked.

"'Fraid not," Bobby replied. "Maybe I should look into it."

"Guessing it's too late to talk to Joey Marsh tonight?" Heather asked.

"More like too early," Bobby answered. "Those guys work late on Mondays."

"All right," Heather sighed. "I'll reach out tomorrow. Or later. But for now, I could really do with a beer."

"Coming right up," Amber said.

Gabriel cleared his throat, spun the witnesses' statements around, and laid the pen on the counter. He tapped where to sign, and the two did so gladly before resuming their bar duties. In sync, Heather and Gabriel stretched, stood, and moved to their favorite booth, awaiting a frosty pitcher to soften the edges of their harrowing day.

CHAPTER EIGHT

THE DETECTIVE

Heather hadn't stopped by Dottie's Diner in over a month and was pleased to see that, unlike Sherwood's, it hadn't changed a single inch. Not that there was anything wrong with Sherwood's facelift; the bar had been in desperate need of its makeover, whereas the diner was already perfection itself. Well, maybe not perfection, but it certainly had charm in abundance, and Heather liked it just as it was, from the garish mustard-and-ketchup color scheme right down to the novelty salt and pepper shakers. In fact, she coveted the latter and had often considered trying to liberate the ones that looked like a pair of fat, pink pigs even though she knew their true home was right here, the ceramic glaze being worn away from excess use.

It had taken Heather a long time to go back to Dottie's after what happened to Jenny Brooks, but once she'd mustered up the courage to go back during the day, she'd become a frequent visitor—so long as the sun was out.

It was mostly the nostalgia that kept her coming back. Bought and furnished in '92, it reminded her of the endless diners her dad had dragged her to during her childhood in Seattle. Despite being English, Adrien Bishop was obsessed with authentic American cuisine and had embarked on a three-year mission to find the best cheeseburger in the city. He eventually found it in a hole-in-the-wall place that looked almost exactly like Dottie's. It was called The Greasy Grill, and it became their secret Sunday spot while Heather's Hindu mother, Sima, went to lunch with her friends. It felt wrong, but the covert nature undeniably improved the burger.

Heather planned to take her dad to Dottie's when he and her mother eventually visited. They promised that they were coming soon, and for once, after such a lovely trip, that didn't feel like a threat. She just hoped they loved her house and the town as much as she did. However, at the very least, there was Dottie's, which would inevitably be a hit with her dad, even if it didn't quite stack up against The Greasy Grill.

Dottie's Diner was owned by a woman named Missy Jenkins, who'd christened the joint after her late mother, Dottie Jenkins, who was apparently a fried chicken genius. Like Amber, Missy talked a big game about completely renovating the joint, but as of yet, she had not walked the walk. It was evident from her vague rambling that she had no concrete refurbishment plans and that her beloved diner would remain unaltered until her retirement day.

Selfishly, Heather hoped that was an event set far in the future. With all the city yuppies sniffing around the growing town, the plot of prime real estate would inevitably get snatched up and butchered once back on the market. Likely turned into some overpriced, hipster taco joint run by white Americans with neon signs that say things like "Tacos Are Bae."

Heather shuddered at the thought, and Missy looked sympathetic.

"It's a cold one, all right," she cooed. "Feels like every September is colder than the last, but that could just be my mind going."

"No, I think you're right," Heather replied, pulling the door closed behind her.

She glanced around and spotted a young man with a black ponytail, who raised his hand in hello. She did the same, and a toothy grin appeared at the center of his goatee. His facial hair was out of place on his narrow, delicate face, giving him the distinct appearance of a small boy dressing up as a pirate for Halloween. As he'd said on the phone, he'd brought his friend along—a thickset, ruddy-faced blond who offered a straight-line, close-mouth smile before returning to his menu.

Heather approached, Gabriel shadowing her every move, and hovered by the side of the booth.

"Joey Marsh?"

"That's me. And this here's my buddy, Ollie Simmons."

"Simmons?" Heather questioned.

"Lisa's my mom," Ollie explained.

"Huh," Heather replied, realizing how little she knew about her coworkers. "She told you anything about the case I'm working on?"

Ollie chuckled. "Not a single thing. She's so secretive you'd think she works for the damn FBI."

"Well, she's certainly good enough to," Heather said.

"I'll tell her you said that."

"Please don't," Heather laughed. "If we lose her, we're screwed."

"Seriously," Gabriel added.

Ollie chuckled again, and Joey gestured to the opposite bench. "Please sit," he requested, half standing out of politeness. "Can I get you guys anything? Coffee?"

"I'll have a coffee and a doughnut," Gabriel said.

"Got it," Joey said, straightening to match Heather's height. "Detective?"

"Heather's fine. And just coffee for me. Black. No sugar. Two sugars for him and some creamer."

"Coming right up, Heather," Joey said, sprinkling powdered sugar on her name, making it sound like something delicious.

There was the charm that Mariah was so taken in by. Admittedly, it did nothing for Heather—Joey was too young, too ponytailed, too greasy—but she could see the appeal somewhere. She also mentally noted that while he was an evident flirt, he didn't come across as sleazy. He moved like he was God's gift to women, but his gaze was appropriate and his manners intact.

Ollie drummed on the laminated menu, pretending to be absorbed in it while his friend ordered. Heather left him to it and pretended to be equally fascinated by the world outside until Joe returned.

"So," Joey said, sitting back down with two packets of sugar and a sachet of creamer in hand. "How can we help you, Heather? Officer?"

Heather had been vague on the phone, worried they wouldn't agree to meet with her if they worried they were in trouble. After all, they were a group of young men who'd not only assisted in getting the victim drunk, but there had also been sexual attraction on the table. Had Bobby not provided somewhat of an alibi, Heather would be highly suspicious of all of them, Joey in particular.

"Can you tell me where you were on Friday night?"

"We were at Sherwood's with three of our buddies," Joey answered, his cheerful expression faltering. "Wait, are we in trouble? Nobody broke anything, did they? 'Cause I'll pay for it if they did. I've got plenty of cash on account of being promoted."

Heather was surprised by how clueless they were and shook her head. "No. You're not in trouble. I'm just trying to fill in some blanks about that night. Is it okay if we take your statements?"

Joey and Ollie looked at each other. "Sure," Joey said. "Ask us anything, we're open books, but can you tell us what this is about?"

"I'm sure you heard about the body we found in the lake."

"Yeah," Joey murmured, his skin blanching. "We heard. Who was she?"

"Mariah King. You met her that night at Sherwood's. In fact, she came and drank at your table for a while."

Ollie stopped drumming, and Joey looked as if he might vomit. He began to pull at his goatee and cleared his throat shakily. "Yeah. She did. Jesus Christ, that's… I liked her. Never met her before. Not directly. But she was a nice girl."

"Real nice," Ollie added earnestly. "Fun too. Wanted to dance a lot even though nobody would join her."

"To be honest, I thought we'd end up going home together," Joey admitted. "But I swear nothing happened. She got really drunk, and I called her a taxi."

"That's kind of you," Heather noted.

"Just basic human decency, ma'am," Joey croaked. "Didn't want anything…" he trailed off, pressing his palms hard into his eyes before releasing the pressure. His expression was wet, like a newborn calf, and he spoke again. "I didn't want anything bad to happen to her."

Ollie unfurled a clenched fist to pat his friend on the shoulder. He spoke, his voice low and thick. "I'm afraid we don't know what happened to her after that."

"That's okay. I just need to substantiate the timeline we have. So, what time did you arrive at Sherwood's?" Heather asked.

"Around seven," Joey said.

"It was seven-fifteen when Joey and I got there," Ollie corrected confidently. "I know because the others were giving us crap about being late as usual."

"Yeah, seven-fifteen. That's right," Joey confirmed. "We had some burgers and bought a couple of pitchers. We meant to leave around midnight, but being single guys, all of us living with roommates or parents…"

"You didn't want to go home," Gabriel said, finishing the sentence and writing everything down in his perfect handwriting. "I know the feeling."

"Hey, man," Joey said, clicking his fingers, "I've seen you at Sludge. Hanging out with Beau. Your band is all right, man."

"Thanks, man," Gabriel replied shyly.

Heather resisted a smirk and kept the ball rolling. "So, what time did the group of women come in?" Heather asked, verifying Bobby and Taylor's versions of things. "Taylor Sherman, Cheyenne Welch, and Mariah King."

"They all arrived at eight or just a little after," Joey answered. "I noticed Taylor because she's married to our foreman and comes around sometimes. I noticed Mariah because she's my type. I like weird, edgy girls. And obviously, I notice Cheyenne because, hell, no one can miss Cheyenne."

"Because she's pretty?" Heather inquired.

"Kind of," Ollie said. "But mostly because she's loud."

Joey concurred. "Yeah. I don't want to sound like an asshole, but that girl loves attention."

"Okay. So when she came to your table, did you guys buy Mariah drinks?"

"I bought her two beers," Joey said. "But she hardly touched the second one and bought herself a couple of shots and another margarita. We tried to stop her, but it was hopeless. When I couldn't understand what she was saying anymore, I texted the taxi company. That was probably around ten past three, and he said he'd get there close to half past."

Missy arrived with the coffees and Gabriel's donut and quickly scurried off, detecting official business was occurring. Gabriel's portion went unconsumed as he began to write, but Heather gulped her coffee, needing something to do with her hands.

Feeling the pleasant warmth through the porcelain, Heather cupped the mug with both hands and spoke between sips. "Did any of you see her get in the taxi?"

"No," Joey said. "The guy texted me at…" he checked his phone, "3:30 a.m., saying he'd be there in five, and she stormed off. I think she was pissed off that I didn't want to hook up. Or maybe she just didn't want to go home either. Seemed like she'd had kind of a rough night."

"Can you give me the driver's number?"

"Sure," Joey agreed and noted the number to Gabriel, who jotted it down. "And in case you're wondering, we left just after 5:00 a.m. Same taxi service, different driver."

"Great," Gabriel said, noting it all down.

"Anything else we can help you with?" Ollie questioned.

Heather nodded. "Yeah. Last question, I promise. Did you notice anything weird?"

The two conferred thoughtfully, silently before Joey spoke. "Only Thimbles. Came in around a little before lock-in and got kicked out pretty quickly. Long before Mariah left though, and it was cold, so I doubt he lingered."

All the statements lined up, so despite the minimal amount of new information, they at least had a solid, corroborated timeline of the events at Sherwood's, and hopefully, the driver could fill in the rest of the blanks. In fact, as far as she was concerned, he was their newest suspect.

"Thanks for your time, guys," Heather said, reaching out to shake hands. "And thanks for the coffee. If you can just sign those statements, we'll be out of your hair."

"No problem, Detective," Joey exhaled, all his flirtation drained away. "Think it's time for us to tie one on over at Sherwood's."

"Put two on my tab," she said, standing and stretching. "Drink responsibly."

The men chuckled weakly and thanked her profusely. Heather directed them to the dotted line, Gabriel handed over his pen, and Heather moved to the counter to speak with Missy. Her stomach had been painfully shriveled all day, but now, in the absence of breakfast, she was starving and craving some of that famous fried chicken.

"Hey, Missy. Chicken sandwich to go. No tomato. Extra pickles."

Missy declared the order through the kitchen window in that famous, unintelligible diner code and cocked her head. "So I guess you were asking those boys about the body by the lake? Is it true that it was Mariah King?"

Heather gave her a tired look that answered both questions and collapsed onto a stool.

Missy hung her head. "Now, that's a sorry thing. First Jenny, then Hazel, and now Mariah. Those girls are dropping like flies."

Heather perked up, her eyes wide. "Hazel? Hazel Brock?"

"Yeah, that's the one," Missy lamented. "Went missing from campus at Washington State about a year ago."

"Please don't tell me it was a year ago exactly," Heather begged.

"No, it happened in October, after a Halloween party on campus. I'm friends with her mother, so I know all about it. Well, as much as there is to know. Which isn't much." She paused and rested her chin on her hand. "It just doesn't seem right. Three out of the five being gone. If I was the kooky-spooky type, I'd say those girls had been messing around with one of those Ouija boards."

It wasn't a horror movie, and Heather knew there weren't any ghosts involved, but Missy was correct in her assessment. It wasn't right. It wasn't right at all.

"I know this is a long shot, but there wasn't anything else—I don't know—weird, about the night Jenny disappeared? Something you forgot to mention at the time?"

"Like what?"

Heather laughed bitterly. "I honestly don't know."

"Jeez, I wish I could help you, honey," Missy said. "But I don't remember much of anything from 2015 to 2019. In fact, I don't remember that night at all other than the girls coming in hooting and hollering and little Jenny turning up dead the next day."

Heather's face must've asked a question because Missy lowered herself further onto the counter and whispered, "Pill popping. All day every day. Started stealing them from my mom when she was dying in my spare bedroom."

Heather swallowed. An unreliable witness. Another thread of Jenny's murder investigation pulled loose. She composed herself and forced her expression into a kind, congratulatory mold. "Well, I'm glad you're sober now."

"Me and you both."

There was a crashing sound in the kitchen followed by an echoing smash, and Missy cursed under her breath before straightening. "Let me go check on that and grab you that sandwich."

Gabriel approached, and they watched Missy through the window as she scolded one of the fry cooks for breaking a plate into the sink. Heather recognized him, even from the back. Victor, one of the two fry cooks she'd spoken to when Jenny went missing. He had been determined that Jenny got into

Mason's truck, whereas Grady—the untrustworthy tweaker—was sure she hadn't.

Seeing him again, remembering his conviction as well as her own, gave her a little jolt of confidence. It was Mason. It had been Mason. It was someone different this time.

"Oh, that's Victor Wu," Gabriel said, "I forgot he worked here."

"You know him?"

"Yeah, we were buddies back at school."

"He was one of my key witnesses back in 2018," Heather informed her partner. "And probably the only trustworthy one, as it turns out."

"Well, at least we have at least four this time around. Not to mention a competent sheriff, pathologist, and partner." He nudged her with his elbow.

Heather smirked, staring at the ceramic pigs beside the napkin dispenser, their expressions merry in their ignorance. "Yeah, you're right. I'll leave the past alone for now."

"So, staying in the present, what's next?"

"Time to talk to the taxi driver."

CHAPTER NINE

THE BRIDE

It was after lunchtime when Hunter came home from God knows where. Taylor wasn't even sure when he'd left. After a piping-hot bubble bath and three glasses of rosé, she'd been out for the count and had woken around nine, disorientated, dehydrated, and surprisingly tucked up in bed. She'd almost definitely fallen asleep on the couch and had turned to thank Hunter for bringing her to bed and beg him for a glass of water, only to find him gone. Suddenly dying of thirst, she'd padded downstairs in her flannel pajamas and found that Hunter was not home.

She'd returned to bed after that, but it didn't last long. Soon she'd become restless, and not knowing what else to do and finding it chipping away at her sanity, she'd forced herself to clean the house from top to bottom.

Despite having been home for twenty minutes, Hunter did not seem to notice her efforts. If he had, he didn't say anything a word. No "thank you," no "good job," no appreciative kiss. Just a blank expression and total neglect. He could be an asshole, but this was out of character. He loved carpet lines, sparkling floors, and she'd even gone so far as to light his favorite candle—leather and vetiver—and still, nothing. Not even a glance.

She watched him tap away on his laptop, entirely ignorant of her seething. She opened her mouth, wanting to yell, but thought better of it and sealed her lips shut. When he finally looked up, she was gripping her mug so tightly that she thought the ceramic might splinter. In fact, she willed it to embed its shards in her palms so that Hunter would have to get off his ass and help her. She imagined him sitting her down, picking out the pieces with tweezers, and wrapping her hands in bandages. Despite the blood, it made her feel warm inside. That, in turn, made her feel sick.

He didn't seem to notice her hands as he winked and rolled his shoulders. "Going for a shower. Care to join me?"

Taylor looked at him in disbelief. "Where have you been?"

"Work. Where else?"

"Seriously?"

Hunter slowly closed his laptop lid. "Honey, you know the guys work late on Mondays. So, I kept my phone on in case of a disaster, and lo and behold, at around eleven, there was one."

"So you're telling me you've been at the mill for over twelve hours and haven't slept at all."

"That's what I'm telling you," Hunter replied solemnly.

"You're so full of it," she laughed. "Look at your face! You're fucking glowing!"

Hunter pouted, faux wounded. "Babe, what's gotten into you? You hate that word."

Taylor laughed again, an awful hysteria-tinged yelp, and Hunter flinched at the sound. "*You* hate that word. And what's gotten into *me*? Are you serious?"

"Babe, calm down."

"Don't tell me to calm down, and don't tell me to calm down," she retorted, sibilating like a feral cat backed into a corner. "If you can't figure out why I'm upset, you don't get to pretend to love me."

"Wow, Tay," Hunter said, throwing up his hands. "Pretend to love you? Really? Also, I'm sorry about Mariah, really I am, but I don't know how I can help you. Grief is personal, you know?"

"You could be here for me. Hire someone else to work nights."

Hunter stiffened. He'd wanted her soft and pliable like she always was, but today he was up against a brick wall. He stood and approached, his hands by his sides.

"Stay over there," Taylor instructed. "I don't want to smell you."

Hunter did as he was asked and perched at the end of the dining table, returning the height advantage to Taylor. "You don't want to smell me?" he asked, jovial, his head cocked. "What the hell does that mean?"

Taylor didn't answer.

Hunter straightened his head, his expression darkening. "You like this house, don't you? You like the things I buy you, right?"

"Yes."

"Okay, and could you afford it on your own?"

"No," she answered, her voice breaking.

"No?" he imitated her, bringing a fist to his eye to imitate the oncoming tears. "Well then, how about you keep your paranoid delusions and negative opinions to yourself, and I'll keep this roof over your head? Deal?"

"Yes. Deal," Taylor whispered.

"That's more like it. So, how about joining me in the shower instead or whipping up some lunch like you used to do?"

"I don't think I've joined you in the shower since before we got married."

"Yeah, and that's exactly the goddamn problem," Hunter growled, getting to his feet. "You've let your sister's death ruin your life and our marriage."

"You think it's ruined?" Taylor asked, her eyes wide, and she looked up at Hunter.

He sighed. "It will be if you let Mariah's death make things worse. You don't want to do anything, Tay. You used to have ambition, and now all you do is come home, work, and sit on the couch eating ice cream. It's pathetic."

He may as well have slapped her in the face. She almost wished he had, instead of wounding her so deeply. "I'm ambitious. I just got promoted to head nurse."

"Oh yeah, and that's so fulfilling. Wiping old people's asses and tending to bedsores. If it really 'fulfilled' you, you'd be there today instead of using up all of your paid vacation days to mope around at home."

"I—" she began to protest but was soon interrupted.

"You know what would actually fulfill you? A baby. A couple of rugrats running around. A dog. Some hobbies. Learning how to cook."

"Hunter," Taylor protested weakly.

"Don't look at me like that. I'm not the one who's changed. That's what we both wanted when we met, it's what we wanted when we got engaged. You know, if I'd been able to see into the future, maybe I wouldn't have…" he silenced himself, seemingly with difficulty, realizing he was about to encroach on new territory.

"Finish your thought. What wouldn't you have done?"

He sighed. "Maybe I wouldn't have married you if I'd known we'd end up wanting such different things. Kids are not the kind of thing you can agree to disagree on. There's no compromise. You can't just have half a baby."

"I do still want those things… but I can't."

"Don't say you can't when you can. Plenty of women *can't*. You just won't. And I know why. I get it. You're scared the kids will die, or the dog will get hit by a car, and you think you'll be overbearing and anxious. But, Tay, you can't let death stop you from living." He didn't sound cruel. It wasn't his intention. Instead, he was verbally on his knees, begging and pleading for his wife to come back to him. What he didn't know, and Taylor did, was that woman no longer existed.

"You don't understand," she said, ever so quiet, her lip beginning to tremble. "You didn't lose your sister. You don't even have a sister."

"Tay, come on. My best friend turned out to be a killer and shot himself. Of course I understand."

"That's different. He wasn't the prey, he was the predator. You have no idea what it's like to be a woman, to fear for children and other women like we do. To wear your heart outside of your body, terrified that a man might rip it apart."

Hunter rolled his eyes. "Give me a break with the stereotyping. Sure, some guys are freaks, and what happened to Jenny and Mariah is messed up. But nothing is going to happen to you or our kids."

"How come?"

"Oh, come on, babe. Everyone knows you shouldn't hang around alone in dark places at night, especially while drunk."

Taylor's mouth fell open again, her jaw muscles turning slack. She looked away and blinked away hot, angry tears. "I don't like what you're implying. Besides, considering Jenny was murdered by her own boyfriend, it doesn't really fit your slut-shaming narrative. That's something that could happen to our daughter. That's something that could happen to anyone."

"Okay, Mariah then. She got wasted at Sherwood's with a group of guys like she does three nights a week. I mean, yeah, whoever did it is a monster, and when they catch him, I hope they ship him off to some hick state to face the firing squad, but it's not exactly shocking."

"Are you serious?" Taylor laughed in shock and anger, willing for the words falling from her husband's lips to be nothing more than a cruel joke.

"Yeah. Again, whoever did this should be castrated or whatever, but I don't know, it's like, what did everyone expect? That's how I know your cockamamie theory about her death being tied to Jenny is a bunch of crap. Jenny was a tragedy, and Mariah was living on borrowed time." His voice was level as if he was delivering a TED talk. As if he was an expert on femicide and this was his clinical conclusion.

Taylor shook her head and moved to leave, but Hunter held her fast with one strong hand on her wrist.

"Let go," she warned.

"Come on, you know the type of guys she was into. Drug addicts, ex-cons, all kinds of freaks. Plus, you told me she used all those skeezy dating apps that are just for one-night stands. I liked Mariah well enough, and I'm sorry she's dead, and I'm sorry you're hurting, but you have to admit, she was trashy."

She could barely control her shaking. "Do—do you think the same about Jenny? I mean, she dated Mason, who was all of the above. Was she trashy too?"

"No. I think she was too young to know better and incredibly naive."

"So, still asking for it?" Taylor spat, actual spittle flying toward Hunter's face.

He grimaced and released his grasp. "Don't put words in my mouth. All I'm saying is, you don't have to worry about our hypothetical kids because this kind of stuff won't happen to them. We'll raise them right. Give them Tasers and curfews. Tap their phones. Scare off boys with shotgun threats. Whatever it takes."

"And if we have boys?"

"Well, if he's gay, the same applies, and if he's not, we'll raise a gentleman. Make sure he has better friends than Mason. Send him to military school like my parents did to me. And listen, we have our issues, but I'm not a sleazebag, and you know it. I've only ever been with you, I have treated you like a princess, and you know I'd never hurt a woman." He rubbed her upper arm, the one her contraceptive had been implanted into two years ago. "Come on, our kids would be perfect. And our parents only have us to make them grandparents."

Taylor was queasy. She'd been with Hunter since sophomore year, and here he was, standing before her, suddenly a complete stranger in their home. A stranger trying to impregnate her.

Or, maybe it's worse than that, she thought. *Maybe this was him all along.*

"Go take that shower," she commanded, unable to bear his face or sickly cologne any longer. "I'll make us some lunch."

"That's my girl," Hunter said, swooping in for a forehead kiss that Taylor failed to dodge.

She had no intention of making sandwiches and waited for his footsteps to recede and the water to start running before calling Cheyenne.

"'Sup?" Cheyenne chirped after a single ring, her phone never far from her grasp.

"Want to go grab a drink?"

"Sure, babe—ouch! Bitch! You're supposed to count down! Are you trying to kill me? What time?"

"What are you doing?" Taylor asked, furrowing her brow at the outburst.

"Getting waxed. Full Brazilian, which is not usually my style, but ya girl *miiiight* have booked a bikini shoot up in Seattle. The new girl is a bit rough, but it's a pretty good place. You should come with me some time and get a pedicure while you're at it. Might help with your intimacy rut."

"We're not in a rut," Taylor protested.

"Oh, come on, babe. I can smell it all around you, the frigid, stale air. You smell like a goddamn farmhouse pantry." Cheyenne paused. "That's why you're calling, isn't it? You've had another argument."

"Yeah."

"Well, you get your skinny ass in the car and head to Sherwood's. Put whatever you want on my tab, and I'll be there in an hour after I get my nails infilled."

"He insulted Mariah and Jenny," Taylor said numbly.

Cheyenne sucked her teeth, and Taylor didn't know if it was from what she'd said or her hair being ripped viciously from her pores.

"Ooh, that little shit. You better tell me everything, so I have an excuse to slap him next time I see him. I've been dying to do so for a while now."

Taylor smirked a little. "Please don't slap him, but I will tell you everything. I think if I keep it to myself, I'll go crazy."

"Well, please don't go crazy. Can't lose you too. Ow, crap, Jesus! I'm getting mauled over here, so I've got to go, babe. See you soon. Kisses!"

Cheyenne hung up, and though Taylor knew not making lunch would lead to more strife down the road, she grabbed her keys, left the house, and turned her phone off for good measure.

CHAPTER TEN

THE DETECTIVE

Heather sat in the parking lot of the Greenman Grocery Store with a bag full of cheese, crackers, sourdough, prosciutto, pickled cucumbers, chili-stuffed olives, and figs. Looking at it now, it was a little much, but she was heading to Gene and Karen's for a much-overdue lunch and wanted to impress. She'd had no idea what to bring, so naturally, she'd asked Julius's advice on what one brought to an autumnal luncheon if looking to seek forgiveness for being incredibly busy.

Julius retorted with a list of things he expected Heather to bring to his home when she eventually visited. She had rolled her eyes and laughed but ended up buying all of it and even sought his advice when faced with the overwhelming cheese section. One soft and one hard was his general advice, but even that wasn't specific enough for her, and she ended up with what he referred to as "beginner cheeses"—camembert and aged gouda.

He noted, however, that he expected her to have upped her game by the time she swung around. He wanted things he'd never even tried, unpronounceable names, boutique delis. He wanted to be wowed. Of course, she knew he was kidding. However, when their nonwork meetup finally occurred, she intended to try her best in the tidbit department, and if that failed, she planned to bring the ingredients for a mean martini and a bottle of Merlot to accompany whatever delicious feast he'd inevitably prepare.

Her stomach rumbled from the yeasty, sour scent of the warm sourdough, and as she typed in the taxi driver's number, she hoped he wouldn't be able to hear the growls through the receiver.

"Hello. Whitetail Taxis. This is Carl," he answered with a thick Chicago accent.

Heather wondered briefly if he'd also relocated from the city for a quieter life, and she was curious if, unlike her, he'd found it. Surely he had. Navigating Glenville must be much easier than making one's way around America's third most populous city.

"Hi, Carl. This is Detective Heather Bishop," she said.

"Detective... That's a new one, all right. How can I help you, Detective? Guessing you don't need a ride, considering the fancy introduction and all."

"I don't. Do you have a minute to answer some questions?"

"Sure, I'm just sitting outside Luigi's, waiting for the bottomless mimosa session to let out."

"Great. So this might be a long shot, but do you remember picking anyone up from Sherwood's on Friday night?"

"Sure do. A couple of people. Who are we talking about specifically?"

"Mariah King. Around three thirty. Joey Marsh ordered the ride."

"Oh yeah," Carl rasped. "I remember. That was a weird one."

"Weird, how?" Heather prompted.

"Well, I texted Joey and told him I'd be five minutes. He says she's waiting outside in a long, purple fur-lined leather coat with hair to match. Can't miss her. Except, I pull up out the front, and there's nobody there. That skinny patch of dirt is completely empty except for some trash cans. Still, I waited for a few minutes, honking the horn, thinking she might be in the can. When she still didn't show up, I called Joey, but he didn't answer. Phone was on silent, I guess. So, I left. I've got other gigs to get to, you know. Busy night. Didn't think too much of it. Figured she went back inside or got picked up by someone else in the meantime. Our competitors, Glenville Taxis, often linger around there at night."

"So you left without her?"

"That's right."

"What time did you arrive?"

"I'm going to say, three thirty-seven. My internal clock is pretty good at this point, but I'll send you the dashcam footage to be sure. Got one of those fancy gadgets that uploads to the cloud, so no skin off my back. Send me your e-mail, and I'll get that to you once I get off work." He paused. "She missing or something?"

"Or something."

"Shit," Carl exhaled. "Poor kid. I knew something felt wrong, but I was busy, you know? Just hoped my gut was wrong. Turns out it never is. Hey, I'm not a suspect, am I?"

"Not if your dashcam proves you didn't pick her up."

"It does. There's even an interior cam in case somebody tries to rob me. I'll send that over too."

"Thank you, Carl. Well, I won't keep you, but I'll send over my e-mail address. I definitely need to take a look at that footage. Enjoy the mimosa rush."

"Will do. Have a nice day, Detective. Oh, and if you ever need a taxi, choose Whitetail."

He hung up, and Heather was left to ponder something very strange. If Mariah left at 3:31 a.m., as confirmed by Bobby and Joey, but had disappeared by the time Carl pulled up, that only left a six-minute window for her abduction. Had someone offered her a ride? Had someone been waiting in the bushes to snag her? Had someone followed her outside, unseen? Had someone been waiting for her? Had she gone willingly? Did they hit her for the first time there? Did they use chloroform? If any of the above, had they targeted her specifically, or had they been an opportunist, overjoyed to stumble across a lone, drunk woman?

Heather wasn't sure, but having an ending to her timeline was undoubtedly helpful, even if the eradication of a possible suspect was not. Additionally, Julian's preliminary findings had confirmed that Mariah had died between 3:00 and 5:00 that morning. With the additional information provided by her witnesses, Heather had further narrowed that down to the hour between four and five. This also helped to further rule out Joey Marsh, Ollie Simmons, and their friends, considering they had all left after five. It was a tighter timeline than she usually had, with many more witnesses, and though she had no further leads beyond the incoming footage, it all was compiling into something she could really sink her teeth into.

She arrived at the cozy, well-kept home of the two retirees, paper bag in hand and best slacks on. The door opened before she got the chance to knock, and Karen wrapped herself around Heather with a bone-crushing bear hug while the two teeny dogs nipped at her ankles. Karen, surprisingly, had covered her usually dirty feet in sheepskin boots. She'd painted flowers on them that matched the colors of her clearly homemade knit hat. It came to a flaccid, gnomelike point, and her vivid henna-dyed hair stuck out the bottom, wet from a shower and stinking of patchouli shampoo.

"Heather!" Karen exhaled, having winded herself from their forceful embrace. "Don't you look healthy!"

"Thanks. I just got back from vacation."

"I love the braid. Very becoming. I used to wear them all the time. You should consider adding a feather."

"I'll do that," Heather promised, holding out the bag of goodies.

Karen's eyes widened. "Well, what do we have here?" She snatched it away from Heather, propped it up on a raised knee, and began to forage with the tenacity of the hungriest raccoon.

Eventually, after a lot of enthusiastic, approving nodding, she plucked the camembert from the rest and held it to her collarbone.

"My favorite cheese. How did you know?"

Heather thanked Julius internally and shrugged. "Just a good guess."

"Oh, you must've used those detective skills on me! And here I was, thinking I could get away with murder!"

Heather chuckled. "Maybe you could."

Karen tutted and smacked herself on the back of her ring-laden hand, her expression unusually grim. "Oh, I shouldn't be joking about that sort of thing at a time like this. Isn't it awful?"

"It is."

"Well, come in, come in. And don't be afraid to talk shop with Gene. I know he's dying to do so. Been muttering about poor Jenny Bishop nonstop." Karen reached around Heather and pulled the door shut. "I'll lay all of this out on a platter. He's out the back by the fire pit, grilling some hot dogs. I'll call you in when ready." Karen whirled and pointed a warning finger. "Don't you tell me about any of this murder stuff though, or else I won't be able to sleep."

"Deal. We'll get it out of our system outside."

"Good girl. Now get, before these dogs have a damn asthma attack."

Heather grinned and scuttled away as a dishcloth snapped in her direction. She hadn't been to the Wellses in far too long and was glad to see that the place seemed tidier, airier, and there was a distinct lack of whiskey bottles in view, empty or otherwise.

She approached the back door, admiring the little stained-glass window of a willow tree, and pushed it open to reveal a colorful garden and a circular bench surrounding a large fire pit.

That hadn't been there on her last visit, and like the fantastic, otherworldly garden, she envied it fiercely. Not that she knew how to grill, but there was another thing she was sure Julius—or Gene at a push—could teach her.

There was a grate over the flickering flames and abundance of coals, and Gene turned the hot dogs atop the heat like a pro. A tray, mustard, caramelized onions, and buns at the ready, Heather felt her stomach rumble again. The chicken sandwich had satiated her for a couple of hours, but her anxious energy had tripled her metabolism, and she was a growing teenager once more.

Gene acknowledged her presence with a nod, and she sat a few feet away, warming her hands over the heat.

"This is nice," she said.

"Yeah. I can't stay cooped up inside all the time, so I needed something to make the colder months bearable."

"I'm jealous. Build it yourself?" Heather asked.

"Of course. Not letting any of those young idiots stomp around my backyard, overcharging me and blasting all that crap music."

"Understandable. My hot water tank barely works, but if I call someone, then there's going to be some guy in my house for hours, ass crack hanging out."

"I can fix that for you," Gene offered.

"Well, consider this advance payment," Heather replied, rummaging around in her shoulder bag and plucking out a couple of carrots, potatoes, and onions. "From the seeds you gave me."

Gene nodded in thanks, but his expression didn't lift as much as she'd expected. "So, how's the case?" he asked.

Heather leaned forward, warming her face as well as her hands. "I have a lot of witnesses and a tight, corroborated timeline. I just don't have any real suspects aside from the ghost of Mason Fowler. Or goddamn Thimbles."

"It's that similar to Brooks, huh?"

"Similar enough that it's freaking people out. Taylor Sherman especially. I get why. Bludgeoned. Lake. Same friendship group. Same day. I'd be lying if I said it didn't freak me out too."

Gene paused his grilling to scratch at his stubble, his jowls moving with his fingertips. "How often do you see coincidences like that?" he asked, turning to look at her for the first time with sleepless, bloodshot eyes.

"Not often. But come on. Mason Fowler is dead."

"He is," Gene replied gravely.

"Wait. You don't think it was Mason."

"I didn't say that," Gene grumbled, resuming his turning, stoking, and prodding.

"You might as well have."

Gene didn't reply, his eyes reflecting the dancing embers, his pupils focused past the food.

"You did at the time, right?" Heather questioned, sounding a little too desperate for her liking. "Right?"

"I was convinced by our findings at the time, yes."

Like Karen after their greeting, Heather too felt the air being sucked from her lungs as she continued to prod.

"And now?"

"And now I realize we used a scumbag doctor for the autopsy, my men screwed up the crime scene, and if Mason was alive—guilty or not—his case would've been thrown out. I messed up, we didn't investigate enough avenues, and now I just don't know."

"So, if it wasn't Mason, who do you think it is?" She paused and analyzed his stoic, unblinking expression. "You still think it's Thimbles, don't you?"

"Once again, I don't know. Never bothered testing the blood at his campsite because we were all so convinced that we already had our man."

"The tire iron matched Jenny's DNA, right?"

"It did."

"Any paperwork for that?"

"I doubt it."

"Well, could we have it rechecked to be sure?"

Gene began to place the hot dogs on a paper towel atop the metal tray. He was sloppy and aggressive, his piles collapsing instantly. "We could if we hadn't lost it. Tried looking for it a few years back. Just gone."

"You think someone who worked at the station took it?"

Gene shook his head, his turkey neck waggling. "No. Nothing like that. Just plain old incompetence. Lack of capable staff and a drunk sheriff. Probably ended up in the trash, just like all the other stuff that was taking up space. If it wasn't a cold case…"

"You threw it out. Got it."

"'Fraid so."

Heather leaned back and looked up at the plain white sky. With Missy turning out to be an unreliable witness, Thimble's duplicated presence, the blood by the tent having gone untested, the murder weapon missing, and a second, bizarrely similar murder having occurred, not only were a few threads being pulled loose from the original investigation, but the entire sheet of fabric was coming undone and unspooling onto the ground. Though her gut still held its earlier convictions, her mind no longer did.

"Heather! Gene!" Karen called, piercing the unpleasant atmosphere.

Without a word, the two gathered up the food, trudged toward the house, and wiped their boots on the bristly mat before entering the abode, hungry smiles plastered on their tired faces.

CHAPTER ELEVEN

THE BRIDE

"**W**HAT A DICK!" CHEYENNE EXCLAIMED AS SHE slammed a pair of Long Island iced teas down on the table.

Taylor followed her back to their seat, her throat hoarse from ranting, and looked at the drinks warily. She hadn't even registered Cheyenne ordering them, nor Amber making them.

"Seriously?" she asked. "I haven't had one of these since I was twenty-one. Remember that night at Mariah's house?"

"That," Cheyenne said with a coy smile, "is exactly the point. You need to loosen up. Go crazy. Stay out all night. Make Hunter wonder where you are for once."

"I don't know. I wanted to go to the gym in the morning."

"Ugh!" Cheyenne grunted, slamming her hands palm down on the table. "The gym? Really, Tay? Just find a personal trainer to screw instead. Seriously, that gym is infested with venereal diseases."

"Ew, Cheyenne!" Taylor giggled. "You're awful."

"I am. And you used to be too. So, drink up."

"Chey…"

"Do it for Mariah."

"Jesus, pull my arm," Taylor muttered.

"Come on, you know she'd want us to live it up in her absence," Cheyenne coaxed. "That girl loved a drink. Hey, who knows? Maybe she's lifting a glass to us up in heaven. Getting tipsy before her date with God's own personal trainer."

Taylor laughed. "You think God's jacked?"

"I mean, look at his son. Abs for days."

Taylor shook her head, a grin plastered on her face, and slid the glass toward her. It left a wet trail from the condensation across the wooden tabletop like snail slime, but it looked a lot tastier than the escargot she had tried on her one and only foreign vacation. She raised the brown cocktail high to the sky and called out, "To Mariah."

Cheyenne beamed and raised her own glass, clinking it hard against Taylor's and sloshing liquid over both of their hands. She retracted and slurped it off, unladylike and noisy, and Taylor continued to giggle as she tried to capture her straw that seemed to have a mind of her own.

Cheyenne snorted. "You look like a fish trying to catch some bait." She opened and shut her mouth, gulping dramatically and tossing her head around.

Despite the admittedly accurate mocking and the resulting cackles, Taylor succeeded and took a long sip. The sweetness, warmth, and citrus spread across her tongue in a fizzy wave. It was delicious, and her sounds of pleasure reflected this to the point of turning heads.

"Jeez, babe, do we need to get you two a room?" Cheyenne teased.

"Thank God for Amber," Taylor moaned. "I remember when you could only get beer, wine, and mixers at this place."

"That's because men only care about what other men like."

"Aw, Bobby's not like that," Taylor protested.

"Don't get me wrong. I love Bobby, but, babe, they're all like that. They're all dicks in some way or another. Seriously, they don't have a thought of their own. They like the cars the magazines tell them to. They marry the women their friends think are hot and dump the ones that don't get the bro seal of approval. Even their pickup lines are unoriginal. Some guy with a podcast tells them what to think, and no doubt he's just copying his dad, who copied his dad, and so on. That's why they're the weaker sex."

Taylor shrugged. "I mean, I'm sure they say the same about us. Magazines. Beauty trends. Mariah dumped that guy because you said he was too short."

"That's because Mariah was weak-willed."

"Cheyenne!" Taylor hissed, suddenly realizing how "fine" her friend seemed. Her makeup was perfect, her outfit was glamorous, and though Taylor was holding it together in public, she was shaky at best, dressed in track pants and a sweatshirt, her eyes puffy and devoid of her usual mascara.

"Oh, please. Don't give me that speaking-ill-of-the-dead crap."

"I'm not, but you don't need to be cruel. She was our best friend."

"She was, and she is, but facts aren't cruel. They're facts," Cheyenne retorted.

Taylor tilted her head to and fro, still frowning. "I guess she was a little… easily swayed." She hated herself as soon as it came out of her mouth. There she was, disparaging Mariah's resolve when she was just as eager to agree with whatever came out of Cheyenne's mouth.

"She was, and if I was the dead one, she'd be right here calling me a loud bitch. Because I am. No shame in it. At least I don't try to be something I'm not," Cheyenne stated, head held high before adopting a gentler stance. "You know I'm right. Now, we can talk about Mariah till the cows come home, and we will, but first, I want you to tell me why we're really here."

"I already told you, Hunter—"

"Is a dick. And a misogynist. Yeah, but there's something else on your mind." Cheyenne paused and scrutinized her friend. "Are you thinking about leaving him?"

"No! I mean, no. I don't think so."

Cheyenne took a long drink, eyebrow raised. "Uh-huh."

"What?"

Cheyenne shrugged. "I don't believe you."

"No, seriously. I love him, and I want to make it work. I'm just not sure he feels the same."

"You love him?" Cheyenne asked skeptically. "Didn't sound much like love. Sounded more like you were scared of him."

"I love him," Taylor insisted.

"All right. Whatever you say. You love him. So, what's the problem?"

Taylor chewed at the end of the straw and spoke with a lisp, the tip held by the vice of her teeth. "I don't think he feels the same."

"Really?" Cheyenne gasped, leaning forward. "But he was always the one who was desperate to get married. Is it because you're frigid?" Cheyenne demanded, waggling a punitive finger. "We can practice kissing again if you need to up your skills."

"Cheyenne, oh my god," Taylor replied, burying her head in her hands, not wanting to revisit that particular fourteen-year-old memory.

"I'll admit, you were never very good, so I don't know, maybe you need a booster course."

"Cheyenne, stop flirting with me!" Taylor insisted as another bout of giggles erupted.

"As if, babe. I'm merely offering you a service. Plus, you're not my type," Cheyenne stated, flipping her hair over her shoulder with a smirk.

"Oh yeah, what's your type?"

"Women who look like me and very rich men."

"You're so vain," Taylor scolded.

"Hey, there's nothing wrong with a woman knowing what she wants." She paused to lean forward again, her silky hair careening back over her bony shoulders. "So, what's the problem with you and Hunter?"

"Kids," Taylor admitted. "He wants them. I don't."

Cheyenne rolled her eyes. "Well then, just pop one out. Give him what he wants."

"Cheyenne. I can't just have a kid. As he said, it's an uncompromisable issue."

"Well then, babe, I'm sorry to say, but he'll find someone that will pop one out, and gladly."

Taylor sighed. "That's the problem."

"Wait," Cheyenne said, drumming on the side of her glass before pointing again. "You think he's having an affair."

Taylor drained her drink, and Cheyenne watched with widening eyes as the liquid level lowered to nothing.

"I'll take that as a yes," she said.

Taylor crumpled, her eyes welling up for the millionth time that day. "He's gone all the time, and I can tell he's lying about where he's been."

Cheyenne reached across, grabbed her friend's hand, and adopted an unusually compassionate tone. "Hey, maybe it's something else. Maybe he really is working overtime."

Taylor shook her head. "No, I know it's not work. They're busy, but not…"

"That busy. Gotcha. Gambling problem? I know that crappy Irish bar does some backroom poker."

"No. It's not that."

"What about drugs? I know he liked a little sniff back in the day."

"No," Taylor said mournfully. "It's not that either. I've seen him high often enough to tell."

"So, you really think it's an affair?" Cheyenne enquired sadly, offering a little squeeze.

"Yeah. I do. And I thought I was crazy, but then on Friday, it seemed like Mariah really wanted to tell me something. Something important, but she ended up pretending it was nothing." Taylor looked down into her empty glass. "You don't know anything, do you?"

"God, no. Honestly, I couldn't tell you three facts about Hunter besides his name, the school he went to, and his being married to you." She removed her grasp and drew a heart in the condensation before putting a big wet cross through the center. "Cross my heart and hope to die."

Taylor looked up and nodded glumly. "I believe you."

Cheyenne nodded and leaned back, retracting her hand. "Well, shit, babe. Do you think he's going to leave you?"

"No," Taylor said firmly. "Which is another problem. He won't pull the trigger, and I don't want to. So we're in the world's longest Mexican standoff."

"Why won't he? Too chicken shit?"

"The prenup. My parents helped me and made me make one. I get fifty percent of everything, which is standard. However, if there's evidence of an affair, I get a hell of a lot more than that. Including the house."

Cheyenne's expression soured. "Seriously? A prenup? Babe, I thought you were a romantic."

"I mean, with today's divorce rates, it seemed like the safest bet," Taylor reasoned. "And again, my parents."

"I know, I know. But an affair clause? I mean, no wonder he feels trapped. And as I'm sure you know, men don't like being caged. Makes them flighty."

Taylor flicked her straw from edge to edge, her lips puckered. "Why do I feel like you're on his side now?"

"I just think it's cruel. Imagine if the situation was reversed. You fall in love with someone else, someone that can give you what you want, but you're stuck being married to someone you don't love because you don't want to lose everything you've built."

"The difference is, I wouldn't have an affair."

"You don't know that."

"Yes, I do," Taylor scoffed.

"Whatever," Cheyenne said flippantly. "I just think it's low."

"Seriously?"

"Seriously. But I also want to drink. So, let's drop it and move on. We're friends, not identical twins. We're not supposed to agree about everything."

From Cheyenne's tight tone and excess movement, Taylor knew that "dropping it" meant passive-aggressively conversing for the rest of the evening. However, like Cheyenne, she also wanted to drink and definitely didn't want to go home, so she was willing to endure it, especially if the drinks were free.

Cheyenne blew a kiss as she stood—her royal-blue bandage dress emphasizing her amazing elongated figure—and rolled her tongue around the edges of her open mouth until Taylor's protests finally stopped her.

"You know you love it," Cheyenne said, leaning in for a kiss on the cheek and leaving a circular gloss residue behind.

While she waited for their fourth round of drinks, Taylor propped herself and looked around the bar. Faces that had once been friendly, familiar to her, now looked like strangers. Wolves in sheep's clothes. She couldn't help but wonder, as they sat in their usual spots as they had on Friday night, slunk low, blending into their furniture, had any of them had their eyes on Mariah? Did any of them follow her out into the cold, trying to pick up the scraps that Joey Marsh had dropped from his toothy maw?

Did she reject them? Did she laugh? Did they intend to kill from the start? Did they hate women? Were they obsessed with them?

Would they do the same to her?

CHAPTER TWELVE

THE DETECTIVE

Despite her initial reservations about the name and clientele, Sludge—Glenville's newest and only music venue—had quickly become one of Heather's favorite haunts. It filled a certain void that Sherwood's innumerable renovations had left behind. Once again, there wasn't anything wrong with the newest iteration of her favorite bar; it looked great, it smelled great, the food was amazing, and Heather was over the moon for their abundant success. Yet sometimes she found herself nostalgic for the dark, dirty dive it had once been.

In particular, she missed the inoffensive white noise that the old jukebox had provided. That too had received an update. Or more accurately, it had been replaced entirely by a new digital machine that hosted a vast collection of modern, poppy chart toppers. That in and of itself wasn't the end of the world. Sure, Heather liked listening to the blues with a bourbon to match, but she could also get down with some Taylor Swift.

No, the problem was the karaoke attachment and the resultant caterwauling. It was off-putting, distracting, and demanded your attention. Worse still was that not a single participant was even a halfway decent singer.

Sludge was loud too. Very loud. However, it wasn't piercing; it was a constant thrumming that quickly became just as much background noise as the rattling mullet rock had once been. As a bonus, the deafening music, live or otherwise, provided a veil of conversational privacy, allowing her to discuss the case without eavesdroppers.

Beau and Gabriel attended regularly, and when she got the invite text from either of them, she was there within half an hour. Often, she'd only have a single drink followed by a soda before leaving, but it was good for her head to socialize.

Tonight both young men were present, dressed in their death metal T-shirts and black jeans, while she donned a more gothic version of her usual shirt-and-slacks combo. The whole place made her feel old at times and more than a little uncool, but Beau had informed her that it was *caring* that was uncool, so she was trying her best not to.

She tried not to look at Beau too fondly either as it made him uncomfortable, but sometimes it was hard not to "mom all over him" as he chugged his nonalcoholic drinks and enthused about his friends from AA. His go-to drink had become a can of zero beer called Straight Edges, apparently a Seattle brand started up by sober punks. She'd tried some, and though she wasn't an IPA kind of gal, it was incredibly tasty.

The guys were enthusing about some online video game that seemed to involve a lot of ghost hunting when Heather returned to the circular standing table with a pitcher of beer. She hated to interrupt, but there were important matters to discuss, so she cleared her throat and watched as they swiveled, ever attentive.

"Excuse me, gentlemen," Heather said, already raising her voice so her audience could hear her. "But I have some official business to talk about."

Beau groaned. "Don't you ever take the day off?"

"Not during a murder investigation," Heather replied, filling her glass to the brim. "So, the taxi driver sent the footage over."

"And?" Gabriel asked, wide-eyed.

"And nothing. I mean, he was right about arriving at 3:37 a.m., and he was right about Mariah not being there. He waited for another five minutes, but she was nowhere to be seen. The interior cameras further proved that she never got inside."

"So he's innocent?" Gabriel questioned, sliding the pitcher his way.

"Seems like it. Joey, Ollie, and their group too."

"So, we don't have any suspects?"

Heather sipped, foam coating her upper lip. "Well," she replied thoughtfully. "I guess we sort of do." The two stared expectantly, and she elaborated, shattering the suspense, "Thimbles. Or rather, Michael Ford."

"No shit," Beau said, grinning. "I didn't know he had a real name. Why's he on the list? Other than for being a total freak."

"Well, he was loitering around Dottie's when Jenny Brooks went missing, and he was at Sherwood's a little before Mariah vanished. Plus, I spoke to Gene, and as it turns out, he never tested the blood we found by Thimbles's tent. Not to mention, with all the other issues with the Brooks case, it's becoming increasingly possible that Mason Fowler was innocent."

Gabriel sipped thoughtfully. "Meaning we can't rule Thimbles out for killing Jenny, and considering the cases are so similar…"

"He's our new number one suspect," Heather confirmed with a heavy heart.

"Didn't Mason admit to it in his suicide note?" Beau asked.

"Sort of," Heather admitted. "He talked about hurting women, and we assumed he meant Jenny."

"Maybe he was abusing her, but somebody else killed her, and his guilt finally caught up to him when the grief set in," Beau theorized.

Heather nodded. "Yeah. Maybe. I don't know what to think. But it might help me to know more about Thimbles. So what do you two know? I know I've been here for a few years, but I'm not a local. So, hit me."

Beau bounced up and down, eager to talk, so Gabriel held out a hand and let him take the floor.

"Okay. So he's a bit of an enigma. A local cryptid or boogieman."

"Like Dennis Burke and the Whitetail Forest Monster?" Heather asked.

Beau shook his head. "No. Way more well-known than that. A real boogieman. Not just Gabe's mom's wacky theory."

Gabriel punched him gently in the upper arm. "Hey! My mom's theories aren't wacky." He paused. "Well, maybe a bit, but she was kind of right about Dennis."

Beau rubbed his arm. "Yeah, I know, man. All I'm saying is that I'd never heard about the 'Whitetail Forest Monster' until that case hit the podcasts. Thimbles, on the other hand, loomed over our childhoods. My dad used to say if I was bad, he'd put me out with the trash because that's what Thimbles loves most. Supposedly, he'd gobble me up the same as all the leftover scraps."

Gabriel nodded in agreement. "Yeah, my dad used to say he'd drop me at the edge of town, and Thimbles would get me and take me down the lake."

"What happened at the lake?" Heather questioned.

"I guess he'd eat me," Gabriel said, smirking slightly. "God, that's terrible, isn't it?"

"Yeah, a little bit," Heather said, half laughing. "My parents just used to tell me they'd take me back to the little girl store and swap me for someone nice. No cannibalism involved."

"Yeah. I don't know what they were thinking," Beau replied, cracking up. "I guess every town has its thing. It's weird, though. Like, we knew Thimbles wasn't actually eating kids, but…" Beau trailed off and looked at Gabriel, who returned his gaze. "I don't know, maybe it was just me."

Gabriel shook his head. "No, I was scared of him too. Sometimes I'd be walking home and could hear him limping and wheezing in the distance, and I'd just start running."

"Remember his metal fingers on the trash can lids?" Beau shuddered. "That noise haunted me, man. Still does. Honestly, I probably had occasional nightmares about him until I was fourteen."

"So all that stuff is true?"

"Oh yeah," they replied.

"Do you think he's actually, you know, dangerous?" Heather asked.

Beau and Gabriel looked at each other again and then back at Heather. "I don't think so," Gabriel said, and Beau nodded. "But at the same time, if you found a body down there by his tent, I also wouldn't exactly be shocked."

"Yeah," Beau concurred. "Like, I don't *think* he's a serial killing monster, but I wouldn't need much evidence to be convinced otherwise."

"Really? He freaks you out that much?" Heather inquired, almost awestruck by their visceral reactions.

Beau nodded and burped out the side of his mouth. "Oh yeah. He's not like some misunderstood drifter and we were just dumb kids making up stories. Well, maybe there's a bit of that, but he's scary. For real."

"I hate to be judgmental," Gabriel said. "But I agree with Beau. My brother got dared to go down to Thimbles's tent once, and from how he tells it, yeah. The guy is an asshole at minimum."

"And a killer at the maximum. Got it," Heather acknowledged. "You know, Bobby figures he is misunderstood. Said Thimbles lost his daughter to domestic abuse and his wife to cancer and that he follows women home because he wants to protect them."

"What a crock," Beau snorted. "Bobby just wants to see the best in people. It's why he never got around to banning me until it was too late. Sure, that story might be true—and let me emphasize *might*—and if it is, that's really sad. But Thimbles has lived here for thirty years, and the stuff he moans to women isn't exactly protective, in my opinion."

"What kind of stuff?"

Beau frowned, his nose scrunched up as if a terrible smell had wafted past. "My sister said he followed her home once and kept talking about her legs in between barking at her like a rabid dog. I don't know about you, but that sounds pretty pervy."

His visceral disgust spread to Heather's face as she sipped her beer. "Yeah, it does. So what happened to your brother, Gabriel? When he went down to the tent?"

Beau rubbed his hands together. "Oh, I love this story."

Gabriel hesitated. "Honestly, Matías is probably full of it… Well, actually, I know he is because he also said he hooked up with Traci Hendricks that night and—"

Beau barked a laugh. "No way in hell did he pull Traci Hendricks, the babe of all babes. Maybe now that he's hit the gym and that pizza face of his has cleared up."

"Yeah. I trust my brother, but he was like seventeen when he told me this story, and he's never repeated it. So take this with a pinch of salt," Gabriel warned before starting his tale.

"It was July 2009. Matías was on summer break between his junior and senior year, and considering most of them would be off to college in 2010, it felt like the end of an era. The last real summer of their lives. So they decided to do something they'd always been too scared to do: go camping in the depths of Whitetail Lake, way off the beaten path. They'd been camping out there before, as had everyone in town, but the campsites were always packed during summer, and they didn't want to be bothered by tourists or other kids from school, nor did they want to get busted for underage beer drinking, and they knew the cops patrolled all the well-known campsites on weekends.

"Matías didn't want to go. He was a horror movie fan with a paranoid spiritual mother who had rubbed off on him more than he liked to admit. He wanted to be scared from the safety of his bedroom, not out in the unknown, unmarked wilderness where the bears reigned supreme and the snakes were eager to bite. Not wanting to be a 'pussy,' he didn't voice these fears to his friends, claiming he was grounded for smoking."

"Your mom lets *you* smoke," Heather interrupted.

Gabriel shrugged and smirked. "Perks of being the baby. Anyway, when the girl of his dreams—the one and only Traci Hendricks—said she'd go if he did, he immediately caved."

"Huh, maybe they really did hook up," Beau said.

Gabriel laughed. "I have a feeling that's yet another embellishment, but who knows. Anyway, so the group of five teenagers—two girls and three guys—headed off to the woods. They'd each told their parents they were going camping on Tunwood Trail, and Scott, their leader, was permitted to borrow his mom's minivan. Scott, of course, took them miles out of town, claiming to have found the perfect place to set up camp. Considering he had the car, the tents, the food, and the bears, no one felt like arguing, despite an air of unease building in the car. Matías supposedly almost spoke up when they passed the rusty 'Welcome to Glenville' sign but thought better of such an uncool move.

"To Scott's credit, the clearing they'd trudged to, after parking in a covert spot by the side of the road, was ideal for camping. It was elevated compared to the lake, so it lacked the bogginess of other such rural areas, and there were plenty of dry sticks and wood to get a decent fire going. Soon enough, they had warmth and music, and Matías began to settle in with the help of Traci by his side. They'd roasted marshmallows and hot dogs, drank crappy lite beer, and laughed like it was a sin not to. However, when the vodka emerged from Traci's backpack and the shots began, Scott finally revealed his hidden agenda. He hadn't just chosen the spot because it was nice. He'd also chosen it because it was a mere half a mile from Thimble's current bivouac."

"What's a bivouac?" Beau asked. "I don't go camping."

"You live in a trailer in the woods," Gabriel laughed. "You're always camping."

"You know what I mean."

"It means temporary campsite," Heather clarified, and the story started up again.

"*'In fact,'* Scott said, *'if you take that path through the trees, it leads to his tent.'* Supposedly, Thimbles had worn the trail himself with his heavy clomping boots. Which meant if he decided to head into town that night, soon enough, they'd all be face-to-face. With this declaration, their campsite turned from cozy to cold, and everyone began to look over their shoulder and jump at every sound.

"A little drunk and not wanting Traci to insist on leaving, Matías foolishly suggested that it was time to play a game. Everyone was excited until he unveiled a pack of cards. No one wants to learn card games while drunk, it's simply a fact of life. What they wanted to play was an old classic. Spin the bottle. Never have I ever. Truth or dare. In the end, the vote went to the latter, and Matías's cards returned to his pocket.

"When it was Matías's turn to make his big decision, he'd forgotten all about Thimbles and instead admired Traci's beauty in the firelight. Hopeful that his buddies would have his back and dare him to kiss her, he chose dare. Unfortunately, his friends didn't have his well-being in mind.

"The dare, of course, came from Scott. '*Go down to Thimbles's tent and bring back something to prove it.*' It was cruel, and everyone knew it, but a morbid fascination had taken hold, and no one protested the request except Matías. Insults rained down, and the more disinterested Traci looked, the more motivated he became. Resolve weakened, he took a shot of vodka and traipsed off along the path, eventually coming to a tent by the lake."

"Do you think your brother could still find the spot?" Heather wondered.

"I have no idea, but I can ask. Why? Do you want to go look for bodies?"

"Maybe," Heather admitted. "So what happened next?"

"What happened next was Matías reached the campsite, being as careful as possible not to make any sound. He turned off his flashlight too, using his adjusted eyes to guide him toward the tent, and spotted a fish pinned by a spear into the ground. He thought that would be the ideal evidence and moved forward to wrench the head from the recently deceased creature. There was no way his friends would ever think him capable of catching a fish.

"Just as he had it twisted in his hands, he heard movement ahead and spotted a figure on the shoreline. Thimbles—solid-built and wild-haired—was standing about ten feet away, just watching Matías. Then he drummed his fingers, and they clanked against something. Matías held his breath, and in the moonlight, he saw the glint of a Bowie knife and began to back away, fish head tearing off in his seizure-stiff grip.

"*'Drop the fish, or I'll gut you and eat you instead,'* Thimbles said. He said later it was like an almost-unintelligible growl. Matías did as he was told, dropped the head, and ran back to camp. The only evidence was the smell on his hands and the fear on his face, but his friends believed him. So they packed up, killed the fire, and moved to another spot, far away from the lake. The fun never quite reached the same heights after that, and all attempts at telling ghost stories from Scott were swiftly shot down."

"Jesus," Heather exhaled, blowing her cheeks out. "I mean, it was probably an empty threat, but yeah, that's pretty scary."

"Yeah, no kidding," Beau said, shuddering once again. "And that's not the only story. There are hundreds of them. Talk to anyone our age around here, and they have their own Thimbles tale."

"Most of them are crap," Gabriel noted. "But my brother was really shaken up after that. Didn't go camping again until he moved out of state."

Heather leaned forward onto the table. "Do you guys seriously think he could've killed Mariah?"

"I think he's capable," Gabriel said. "I think anyone is technically *capable*. So, it's not so much the killing but the location."

"What do you mean?"

"How did he get her all the way out to the lake? I mean, he's strong, but I'm stronger, and I couldn't carry an unconscious woman all the way out there."

"Yeah," Beau agreed. "If you want my two cents, it was someone she knew. Someone with a car. Maybe someone she wanted to hook up with."

"I agree with both of you," Heather said. "It just doesn't seem feasible. It's why I wrote him off the first time around."

"Yeah, if this is a 'hit' against that group of girls, what's his motive? And how would he get to Hazel at Washington State?" Beau challenged. "Honestly, when it comes to Thimbles, I think it's all just a ghost story. Creepy but probably not what you're looking for. Still, as I said before, if you make it make sense, I'll believe it."

"I don't want to make it make sense. I just want it to make sense," Heather groaned, topping up her drink.

"It will soon, I'm sure," Gabriel said reassuringly. Heather noted, however, that he didn't sound entirely convinced. "What's next on the agenda?"

"Interview Cheyenne," Heather replied flatly.

The other two laughed, stopped, looked at each other, and laughed again.

"Good luck," they said simultaneously and roared as Heather laid her head down on the table.

CHAPTER THIRTEEN

THE DETECTIVE

By 10:00 p.m., Heather had swapped to soda water, and shortly after, she'd begrudgingly called it a night. Her new sleeping pills were to be taken a good hour before one's desired sleep time, which for Heather was midnight, allowing her to reach all five stages, including REM, by the time her alarm went off at 7:30.

Understanding the magnitude of the case at hand, her friends hadn't tried to guilt her into staying out late and watching their friend's band play. Instead, they offered hugs and parting advice on how to deal with Cheyenne Welch.

"Meet her at Sherwood's," Gabriel began. "She's real talkative after a drink."

"And she loves cocktails," Beau added. "Pretend you love them too."

"And compliment her hair."

"Wear yours back though. So she doesn't get jealous."

"And whatever you do," they said in sync, "don't look her in the eyes."

They'd fallen about laughing at their banter, and though Heather chuckled along as she said her goodbyes, her nerves grew into a nerve-gnawing monster once she was in the taxi. The last time she'd interviewed Cheyenne, it hadn't exactly gone well. The younger woman had a sharp tongue and a steely disposition, and their brief interaction had only culminated in frustration.

Fortunately, at home, the meds had proved effective despite her nerves, and she achieved yet another night of fulfilling deep sleep. Six weeks ago, this had been something she thought impossible to achieve, resigning herself to a life of insomnia. However, upon opening up to Julius about her restless nights, he'd referred her to his general practitioner friend, and the day after their first appointment, Heather had her first perfect night's sleep in six years.

Heather had called Cheyenne first thing in the morning, reminding her about their plans to meet and wondering if she wanted to meet at Sherwood's around 4:00 p.m. Unfortunately, Cheyenne was one busy woman and was booked out all day except for a half an hour slot starting at 11:15 a.m. Sherwood's wasn't even open that early, so it looked like it was back to Dottie's.

Fortunately, after five minutes of small talk, it was apparent that coffee made Cheyenne almost as loose-lipped at tequila shots. As a bonus, Heather didn't feel half as scummy as she would have getting a witness drunk in exchange for information.

It was strange. It was almost as if Cheyenne had forgotten their past and talked as if she and Heather were friends that went way back, relaying gossip and telling her all about her gradual return to modeling. It was all undeniably fascinating—Cheyenne was a natural storyteller, and her imagery was beyond vivid—but Heather kept an eye on the clock on the wall, knowing their time was short.

She cleared her throat. "I'm sorry to interrupt—good luck at the casting call—but, Mariah."

Cheyenne nodded vigorously. "Oh, of course. Mariah. Look at me gabbing away. Sorry, it's just the only people I really talk to are Taylor and Mariah, and both of them are currently mute."

"Not a problem. So, the timeline has already been corroborated for that night, but can you tell me exactly when you left?"

"Eleven thirty-five is when I went outside. My friend picked me up three minutes later."

"Friend?"

"Guy friend. Not quite a boyfriend. He was visiting from out of town and staying at the Black Bear Motel."

"Gotcha. So, you went to the motel?"

"No, we went to my place, which is a lot nicer, I assure you."

"And you were there all night?"

Cheyenne smirked. "Am I a suspect, Detective?"

"No, not really," Heather admitted.

Cheyenne hummed. "I suppose everyone has to stay on the list until you've solved it. That's smart, not ruling out the friends. While I'd rather not involve my man, should you ever find me at the top of your list, I'll happily provide a solid alibi, video and all." Cheyenne winked.

"Hopefully, that won't be necessary," Heather replied, picking up what Cheyenne was putting down and not wanting to be subjected to the video in question.

"I'm sure that's not everything," Cheyenne said, maintaining an unsettling amount of earnest eye contact.

"No, I..." Heather faltered. "Honestly, I don't know what to ask you. I've already spoken to Taylor, Bobby, Amber, the guys Mariah was with, and the taxi driver that was supposed to pick her up."

"And you've got nothing."

"Not exactly."

"But you're still hoping I'll wave a magic wand and it'll all come together." Cheyenne let out a tinkling laugh and flipped her slinky, waist-length hair over her shoulder. "I'm just busting your nonexistent balls. Of course, you're not going to find the guy who did it—not yet anyway—because no one except Mariah knows who he is."

"What do you mean?"

Cheyenne leaned forward conspiratorially. "Heather—can I call you Heather?" She didn't pause long enough to get an answer. "Mariah liked her men fast, crazy, and criminal. Met them all on these awful anonymous hookup apps and even *Craigslist*." She shuddered. "Seriously, look no further than her phone to find her man."

"We couldn't find her phone."

"Huh, well. There you go. There's something on there that someone doesn't want you to see." Cheyenne paused, a gleeful expression taking hold on her magazine-ready face. "Maybe I am waving that magic wand after all."

"It's certainly very helpful information. Did you ever meet any of them?" Heather asked, laying her notebook on the table.

"God, no. I found the concept repugnant. Not that she wanted me to meet them either. I always 'ruin' men for her apparently."

"How so?"

Cheyenne held up her long fingers and pressed them down into her palm one by one. "Too bald, too short, too poor, too rude, too old, too meth-riddled. The list goes on. I just wanted her to have higher standards, like me and Taylor, so she didn't end up barefoot and pregnant, living in a trailer park with some ex-con wife beater. Maybe I should've just kept my mouth shut, I don't know. I guess all my chiding did, in the end, was make her secretive."

"You don't need to feel bad for wanting to keep her safe," Heather assured, though she didn't think Cheyenne was entirely wrong in her self-assessment.

"You're right," Cheyenne agreed, immediately perking back up. "But no matter our interventions, it was always going to be a lost cause. She had no self-esteem, poor thing. It's a shame too, because she was pretty underneath all that black lipstick and resting bitch face. She could've married well, like Taylor, if she didn't love the bad boys so much. I suppose she and poor Jenny had that in common. Such a pity when women don't know their worth. I know they would've been content with someone nice eventually, but they didn't want to try." She paused to sip her low-fat soy latte. "And now they're both dead," she said matter-of-factly, any grief she might have possessed buried deep.

"Do you blame them?" Heather queried, keeping her tone neutral but inquisitive. She wanted to sound like she could be swayed by Cheyenne's opinions, knowing it would generate many more assertions if she made the woman feel she was in good company.

"No. God no," Cheyenne insisted. "They were just naive. Couldn't see the monsters inside 'ordinary' men. The type of girls to accept a ride from Bundy, you know?"

It still sounded like victim-blaming, but Heather let it go, allowing Cheyenne to express her sorrow in the form of frustration. "So, what did Mariah do for work?"

"Well, she wanted to be a vet tech, but that didn't end up working out, so she washed dishes at Luigi's. No judgment. It got us great discounts, plus I can't exactly talk. It's not like modeling really pays the bills. Not anymore at least."

"But it used to?"

"Oh, yeah. But I sort of partied a bit too hard and got dropped by my agency. Then my mother died and left me her house in Glenville, so I figured I'd go home for a year and sort my life out. Took a job at that ugly boutique by all the waterfront properties, and now, five years later…" she faded out with a smile and a shrug. "It is what it is. But I'm slowly getting back out there."

"I get it. I've been here for five years myself."

Cheyenne clicked her fingers. "I thought you were new back when Jenny went missing. You seemed hardened but also super nervous. I think that's why I gave you such a hard time. I can smell weakness. Sorry."

"It's fine," Heather replied, her eyes dry from staring. She looked down at her own coffee and blinked. There was something magnetic about Cheyenne; the combination of being both wholly fake and utterly honest was disorienting and fascinating all at once.

"It's not. Really. You don't have to coddle me. I know I can be a bitch."

The corner of Heather's mouth curled up at the corner as they resumed eye contact. "You're not being a bitch now."

"No, but that's because I like you now. Well, at least I think I do. I definitely like that you don't stink of booze anymore."

"Well, I like that part too. And I like that you're not telling me to get lost."

"But you don't like me?" Cheyenne teased.

"Not just yet," Heather admitted.

"Honesty. That's refreshing. We could do with more of that around here. It would save us a heap of trouble. I'm sure it would make your job a hell of a lot easier."

"You have no idea."

"I'm sorry too for making it harder back then. I did you and Jenny a disservice. But it was our first tragedy, and I thought Mason was innocent."

"You don't now?" Heather asked.

"Well, I'll admit, your evidence isn't very compelling, but also, I figure, why wouldn't it be him? Abusive boyfriends and beautiful innocent girls. It's a tale as old as time."

"What about Hazel?"

Cheyenne sipped her coffee thoughtfully. "No, Hazel was a good girl. And I'd hazard a guess that if they ever do find her body, she won't fit your pattern."

"So you think there's a pattern?"

"Don't you?" Cheyenne asked, leaning further forward. "I mean, they're near identical. Girls going missing from venues late at night and being found by the lake bludgeoned to death. Taylor told me all about the body. Awful stuff."

"But you think Mason killed Jenny?"

"Yes. I suppose my theory is that there's a hive mind among these limp-dicked perverts. Can't bear to lose something out of their league. Perhaps Mariah's killer was inspired, perhaps bludgeoning is the way to go if someone rejects your advances. I really wouldn't know, Heather. I've never killed anyone."

"Fair enough. So you think Hazel is dead?"

"Oh yeah." Cheyenne laughed before stopping herself with a hand pressed hard against her mouth. "Sorry. I don't mean to be callous. It's just that the theories are outrageous. That girl was never bold enough to run away or fake her own death. No, she's dead, all right, probably for rejecting the frat boy variety of male monsters." She pointed a long nail at Heather's face. "See, that's why you have to be tough, like us. You have to have bite. Or else you'll only ever be a piece of meat that someone wants to screw or, worse, eat."

Cheyenne's two cents were poignant, pragmatic, and cold in Heather's palm, and Heather pocketed them thankfully. Cheyenne, for all her apathy, was a better informant than most. Her opinions on women were not aligned with Heather's, and her opinions on men were much more extreme, but she didn't mince her words and laid entire slabs of insight down because of it.

"What about Thimbles?" Heather asked.

Cheyenne shrugged but looked amused. "I think it's silly. Everyone sees a scary-looking man and assumes he must be a serial killer. It's—what do they call it?—the halo effect."

"Yeah," Heather replied. "People see someone with a good job and conventional looks and assume they're a good person."

"And the reverse."

"You contradict yourself, Cheyenne," Heather said, tapping the nib of her pen to the page and leaving inky dots in the corner. "Considering your frequent mentions of ex-cons and meth users."

Cheyenne grinned. "Well, you've got me, Heather. I suppose you can consider me a victim of the halo effect too. To be honest, though, I think all men are scum. Only good for one thing, really, and even then not all that good at it. But thinking about it and questioning my apparent biases, there was an exception to Mariah's taste. A banker over in Hallington. Alain Durand. Maybe you should speak to him. Or his wife."

Heather raised her eyebrows. "Mariah was having an affair with a married man?"

"Sure was. Honestly, I don't know how I forgot. Maybe it's because she didn't tell me herself. I know," she said, seeing Heather's quirked brow. "Weirdly enough, I received a text three days before she died telling me all about it. I don't know if it was blackmail or what, but it was weird. Had a picture attached too."

"Can I see it?"

"Sorry. Deleted. I'd have kept it if I knew she was going to die, but I don't mess with blackmailers and figured the less evidence of her… indiscretion, the better."

Heather nodded but wasn't convinced by the claim of deletion. She wondered if there was more to the text, something Cheyenne didn't want her to see. Maybe she too was the victim of a blackmailer. Even her expression was different, less self-assured, her persistent gaze dropping. It smelled like self-preservation.

"Though," Cheyenne added, looking back up, "I did a little research on this particular bacterial specimen and found his address. Spin your book around, and I'll jot it down." Sensing Heather's hesitation, she continued, "I won't read your little notes. Your handwriting is illegible anyway."

Heather relented, spun the notebook, and handed over the pen. "Thanks. This is a big help. An affair is—"

"Yeah, I know. Sometimes it's the wife, but sometimes it's the mistress. In this case—"

"It was Mariah," Heather finished.

"Go get him, Heather," Cheyenne said, turning the notebook back around to reveal a neatly written address complete with hearts over the *i*'s. "Well, it's been great talking to you, but I have appointment after errand after appointment today. So, unless you have anything else to ask?"

"No, that's it for now. Thank you for your cooperation, and here's my card if you think of anything else."

"You must be handing these out like candy on Halloween," Cheyenne said, pocketing the card. She stood and looked down at Heather. "Be quick. We don't want this one to eat a bullet too. I have an outfit planned for his court date."

Heather held out a hand to shake, but instead, Cheyenne reached out and stroked the top of her slicked-back hair.

"Beautiful, but it needs some coconut oil."

"Noted."

"See you around, Heather."

Cheyenne stalked out, her model-esque walk catching the attention of everyone in the room, including Heather's. Heather blinked again and laughed to herself, the interaction bizarre and overwhelmingly useful. As she stuffed her notebook into a too-small jacket pocket, she looked around the room and caught sight of a struggle.

The fry cook, Victor Wu, was fighting with his backpack at the counter. The zipper had come undone on either side of the toggle, and its innards were spilling out onto the plastic. Fortunately, Heather knew just how to fix it and approached with an outstretched hand.

"May I?" she asked.

"Please," Victor exhaled.

Heather tried not to look at his belongings, but she couldn't help but notice the abundance of hardback books.

"Jesus, no wonder you broke your zip," she joked. "Lugging around a bunch of bricks."

Victor smiled. "I know. I picked them up from the thrift store about a week ago and keep forgetting to put them on my bookshelf. It's nice reading them on my breaks though while everyone else is smoking."

Heather craned her neck to look at one of the dated front cover illustrations. "*A Beginner's Guide to Entomology*? That's insects, right?"

"Yeah. They're not all bugs though. Some history too."

"That's cool," Heather said.

"Most people *do not* think so," Victor laughed. "I'm obsessed with beetles. Everyone just thinks it's creepy."

"Listen, I've seen creepy, and beetles don't make the list. Do you own any? Like as pets?"

"Yeah. Some."

"Well, I'm more of a dog person myself, but whatever floats your boat. Hey, maybe you should become an entomologist. Study beetles around the world. It's got to beat burning your hands on fried chicken," she said, noting the blisters.

Victor hid his hands but smiled meekly. "A guy can dream. Maybe if I get around to getting my GED. So I saw you were talking to Cheyenne. Was that about Mariah?"

"Sure was. You don't know anything, do you?"

"No. I don't go out to bars—very strict parents—but if you're looking at Thimbles again, I still think you're wrong."

"Why?"

"I don't know," he admitted. "Call it intuition. I'm sure you've got that in spades to do what you do."

Heather nodded. "Any better ideas?"

He shifted uncomfortably and stared at his beat-up sneakers. "Okay, maybe I overheard your conversation. About the affair."

"Uh-huh," Heather encouraged.

"And maybe I do know something."

"Go on."

"I saw her having breakfast here with a guy about a week ago. Real clean-cut. I'm guessing that's the same guy."

"Well, he's a banker, so probably."

"Well, from what I overheard on my way out the door, it sounded like she was giving him an ultimatum. *'Me or her,'* she said. He didn't seem to like that," Victor added, his black eyes implying a much worse conversation.

Heather zipped his bag closed and looked past him thoughtfully. "Huh. Well, I think Alain just jumped to the top of my list. Thanks for the intel, and enjoy your books."

Victor looked at his fixed bag in awe before beaming at Heather. "Will do, Detective. Good luck with everything."

Deeply affected by Cheyenne, Heather nearly winked but thought better of it at the last moment and rubbed at her twitching eye as if something was in it. She offered a little wave before turning to face the door. As she went, she felt an air of relief, not only at the solid new lead but also the reminder that Cheyenne was wrong. Not all men were monsters.

CHAPTER FOURTEEN

THE BRIDE

The Sherman household felt oddly empty as Taylor wrestled with loneliness and the resulting déjà vu while nestled beneath a tartan blanket on the couch. It was as if the walls were distant land, the fire the promise of civilization, and her leather two-seater a small boat lost at sea. All of what she wanted was out of reach, and she was without paddle nor supplies out in the vast, inky black.

Perhaps the living room had always been like this—the walls too far away, the couch too small—and she just hadn't noticed before. Or maybe she was shrinking, and everyone had been too polite to point it out. That was the thing about grieving; everyone who didn't disappear entirely became unsettlingly mild-mannered, like some sort of robot impostor. They became soft smiles and gentle reassurances and gaslit you into believing everything was okay.

"I'm shrinking," you could say, disappearing right before their eyes.

They'd look sympathetic before offering pats, tea, and advice. Things like, "Have you tried stretching? It's very good for the brain. Might make you big again." Or something like, "Go get some sunshine. How about a run? Might do you good to get some vitamin D. The sun makes plants grow after all."

"I can't, I'm lost at sea, and the sun isn't out," you'd insist to glum faces.

"Well then, you'll have to swim," they'd retort as if it were the easiest thing in the world.

Maybe it was, but you had to work up to it to be sure. They'd be patient at first, eager for you to make the plunge. Then, as days passed, they'd tell you what you already knew: that you'd starve, freeze, or die of exposure if you didn't get a move on. That you were missing out on everything. That everyone was already back onshore waiting for you. But you were so very tiny, and the way was so very long. So you didn't jump in, and they gave up on waiting for you to do so.

Taylor checked her hands to ensure some type of *Alice in Wonderland* situation wasn't taking hold and sighed with relief upon spotting her wedding ring. It was still too small, sunken into the skin, unremovable without a saw blade. She knew she hadn't actually been shrinking, but drinking in the early afternoon always rendered her loopy in the same way staying up late at a childhood sleepover once had. Strange things happened when exhaustion, hyperactivity, and sugar were combined, and she wasn't sure she enjoyed the effect as much as she used to.

I guess it is the room, she thought, looking around at the shadow-covered walls. She'd always considered her home roomy, but now she was concerned it was simply empty. In her discomfort, she jumped to blaming Hunter, but rationally, she knew they were both to blame.

The main things Taylor and Hunter agreed upon were style and taste, and once they moved in together, she got to work on executing his wildest interior design fantasies. She'd been unemployed at the time, and grieving her sister, so Hunter gave her a budget, provided some Pinterest boards and magazines, and gave her complete control over what was to be their family home. It felt good to have a job of sorts, and she worked hard every day. Whether she was at the hardware store, looking for antiques, building, painting, or decorating, she was doing something. Then her paid leave ended, and it was back to the care home, leaving the majority of the ceiling trim unpainted and the guest room and would-be nursery still half done.

Still, she thought it looked beautiful and only ever thought about the trim or the rooms when Hunter brought them up. Though even he agreed that the rest of it was close to perfect. They both loved the shabby, chic, upscale-farmhouse, rustic all-American look—an aesthetic Cheyenne referred to as "Mormon realness"—and Taylor nailed it from the whitewashed floorboards to the genuine oil lamp chandelier. The furniture was a mixture of vintage and upcycled. There was a tasteful amount of antiques, including a set of French copper cookware, a butter churner turned umbrella stand, and several leather trunks for storage. There were also a lot of animal hides instead of rugs and blankets and a plentiful amount of taper candles and accompanying bronze prickets to really sell the pioneer-era fantasy.

It was around then, in January 2019, that Taylor had given herself a makeover, changing her look from mall rat to pioneer woman with her wardrobe full of conservative floral dresses. It was only in the past year that she'd even owned a pair of jeans, and that was only to go on walks to find kindling without tearing her nicer clothes.

However, beyond the beauty, the most essential thing was that the house needed to be minimal and clean. This was partly to make the most of the square footage but also to save Hunter from his hereditary hoarding disease. Honestly, Taylor didn't think his parents were that bad, but perhaps his dad's model plane collection and his mother's buildup of romance novels had gotten a little out of control.

Because of this, Hunter was highly organized and loathed any form of clutter, decorative or otherwise. So other than some tasteful, practical pieces such as the butter-churning bucket, the living room was essentially just a fireplace, a leather couch, two matching armchairs, a coffee table, and four small framed photographs on the mantle that flanked a sheathed knife that had belonged to Hunter's grandfather.

Usually, this lack of junk, personal belongings, and material goods didn't bother Taylor. In fact, she loved it. She loved the slight echo the house had, she loved how easy it was to clean, she loved how ecofriendly it was, and she loved how it gave her somewhat modest home the illusion of mansionlike proportions. Plus, it wasn't like they were actually living the lifestyle of nineteenth-century homesteaders. She had her bookshelf, arts and crafts projects, and beautiful clothes. Not to mention the TV above the fireplace, claw-foot bathtub, high-pressure shower, underfloor heating, and a well-stocked pantry. What more could a person ask for?

If she was to answer that question literally, she would answer with, "A lot." Yet nothing she craved could be sated by a trip to the store. She wanted love, romance, friendship, and excitement, but with her marriage on the rocks and most of her friends dead, she felt the unfulfilled pit in her stomach growing all the time. She tried to feed it the best she could, but right now, all she had in her hands was dread, anxiety, and guilt. She gulped it down regardless, but it was always rejected and regurgitated. Still, she'd try again soon. Try to make it stick. Try to make the most of her life.

While these feelings did not fill her, neither, as it turned out, had the granola she'd eaten eight hours ago. Her stomach jolted with real hunger pains, and she decided to call Hunter begging for takeout and wine even though she'd promised to cook tonight.

He didn't answer, which wasn't unexpected, so she texted him instead, making sure to provide plenty of emojis promising his favorite variety of rewards for this favor. She wasn't in the mood, but it never lasted long anyway, and she was desperate for comfort food.

The text went unread. As did the next two sent over the next ten minutes. This was slightly more unusual but not inexplicable, so she moved on to her only other option, Cheyenne.

She pressed the dial button, waited, waited some more, and eventually reached Cheyenne's voicemail. Taylor hung up and pressed again with an angry jabbing finger. Unfortunately, this more aggressive attempt also garnered no results. Neither did the next two or the stream of texts. This, unlike her husband's neglect, was unusual. Cheyenne was what one might call phone savvy, as in she was completely, utterly addicted to that accursed rectangle. It was an extension of herself to the point that not seeing it in her hand was perturbing, as if looking at a friend post-amputation.

Trying not to jump to worrisome conclusions, Taylor told herself that Cheyenne was probably with someone. Taylor was vaguely aware she had a big-city suitor she'd occasionally see, though Taylor had never met the man. She wondered if it was because the relationship was too casual or if Cheyenne could dish it out but not take it. She'd undoubtedly given Mariah a hard time about the few men she'd met and had often been critical of Taylor and Hunter as a pair. This, however, Taylor suspected, was based more on jealousy than contempt. It was a well-known fact that she'd liked Hunter first, back in sophomore year, and when he'd unexpectedly asked Taylor to Homecoming, the claws had been unsheathed, and Cheyenne had swiped at Taylor for months to come.

She'd gotten over it by the start of junior year—having become extremely popular with boys of all ages due to the kindness of her puberty—and she and Taylor were best friends once again. Still, she never forgave Hunter, and the two had remained icy cold to one another ever since.

Begrudgingly, Taylor ordered a pizza from the ridiculously named Saucy Dish Pizzeria, even though it meant a long wait for delivery, human interaction, and a handsome tip. The pizza wasn't particularly pleasant nor cheap enough to compensate for the lack of quality. It certainly couldn't hold a candle to Luigi's wood-fired, thin-crust offerings, but sadly, they did not deliver. Even if they did, she was sure they would be far too professional to pick her up a bottle of chardonnay, unlike Ricky—Saucy's only delivery "boy"—who always eagerly obliged the outlandish request.

Gooey pepperoni pie on its way, Taylor realized how silent her home was aside from the ticking of the kitchen clock and the crackling of the fire. The new medical procedural she'd been binging had been paused for over an hour, the screen dimming from lack of interaction. Though she'd somewhat forgotten the plot, she forced herself to press Play, if only to have some humans in her home, albeit interactive, two-dimensional ones.

She tried to pay attention, but when an affair was unveiled, she tuned it out altogether, her attention drifting back to her husband and, in turn, her bridesmaid photo. But instead of awaking memories from that day, it—combined with the crackling fire and the cold, dark night—unleashed something much more ancient: their last camping trip before Hazel had left for college. It was something she hadn't revisited in a long time, and though it projected against the walls of her mind like an intact film reel, she couldn't remember the end before it arrived.

At first, she enjoyed the blast from the past. It was comforting, warm, and full of laughter, but soon something dark took hold as Cheyenne began to read from a book of ghost stories. The others had been into it, but Taylor had protested, which quickly turned into her receiving a forfeit for being a killjoy. Like so many before her, she was to go down to Thimbles's tent and take something to prove it.

She'd managed to avoid that particular dare for her entire life up until that point, and despite her anxiety, the jeers from her peers eventually persuaded her. Once her back was to the group, she'd been near tears as she made her way through the woods to the lake. She had some mace that her dad had given her, but it was of little comfort as she flinched at every owl hoot and cracking branch. She also had a flashlight but kept it pointed toward the ground, terrified of what she might see lurking behind the thick trunks.

She knew she was close when she reached the embankment and nearly turned back, but something in her—liquor or otherwise—was tired of being a coward. So she'd continued, and fallen down the slope, coating her back with wet mud as she slid and making plenty of noise in the process. Scrabbling forward, she'd reached for her light and shone it in all directions. Her blood turned cold when she realized she'd seen something and moved past it in panic. Braving a second look, she pointed her light ahead toward the lake edge, and there he was, facing her.

She'd screamed and choked on her spit as she turned back around, coating her other side in the same viscous brown as she tried and failed to scramble up the steep, sludgy ledge. Just as the footsteps behind increased in speed, she made it to the top, rose to her feet, and ran back through the woods.

She'd gotten lost for nearly twenty minutes and cut her head on a broken branch, but eventually, the blaring radio guided her back to camp, and she rejoined her friends in complete hysterics. Everyone had been sympathetic—except for Mason and Cheyenne, who'd thought it hilarious—but they didn't move camp. The boys were too macho, and Mason had, for whatever reason, brought one of his dad's guns along. Though she was fairly staunchly anti-gun, his weapon had reassured her, just as the one in the closet under the stairs did now.

She considered grabbing it from the safe but knew, in her paranoid state, it was probably an accident waiting to happen. She tried to assure herself that she was safe to stop the hyperventilation, but all she could think about was Thimbles. She could hear his footsteps clear as day. The sound was awful, that arrhythmic lollop initiating a chase.

Ring. Ring. Ring.

Covering her mouth, she successfully muffled her scream as someone rang the doorbell. Her doorbell camera app informed her that someone was at the door, the ominous notification popping up on her upturned phone. She hesitantly checked the video feed to see greasy Ricky and his tomcat smile waiting at the door. Self-soothing, she rubbed at her aching chest as she moved to the door with her wallet. She opened it, mustered some friendliness, and handed over the money along with a generous tip.

"You all right?" Ricky asked, his hair slicked back and oily.

"Yeah. I'm fine," she answered, convincing neither of them.

"You sure? I know you must be pretty shaken up by Mariah. I can hang out front with my piece to keep the freaks at bay till your man gets home."

"That won't be necessary. Good alarm system."

"All right. But if you ever need anything, I'm available and cheap."

Taylor began to shut the door. "Thanks for grabbing the wine. Have a nice night, Ricky."

"You too, Taylor."

The door clicked shut, and she locked the rim cylinder just for peace of mind. She knew Hunter couldn't get in without her opening the door, and she also knew she would soon be asleep, but she thought, *Screw him and his other woman,* as she turned back toward the house.

The fire was nearly out, and no longer feeling safe in that space, she ventured upstairs and teetered between the bedroom and guest room. The idea of getting into her marital bed made her feel queasy, so she opted for the latter, turned both side table lamps on, got under the covers, and tucked in. She drank from the bottle, ate from the box, and continued her show on the little TV in the corner.

It was the best she'd felt in days, but once she was done and had washed up in the en suite, she locked the door to the room and slept with the lights on for the first time in a long time.

CHAPTER FIFTEEN

THE DETECTIVE

Heather collapsed on the couch beside Gabriel and scooched into the saggy depression left by repeated corkboard analysis. She gestured at the collection of photos, evidence, statements, and sticky-note theories with limp arms.

"So, that's what I've got," she exhaled, a little out of breath from her endless journeys between printer to board.

"Well, there's a lot going on, I'll say that much," Gabriel replied.

Heather shot him a nasty look, and he chuckled.

"Okay, it's a masterpiece. Whatever. Where do we start?"

"Where do you think we start?"

"The scene," Gabriel said confidently.

Heather nodded. "All right. The scene. So, we have the body of Mariah King, twenty-eight years old, 170 pounds, and five-foot-four. Local residents discovered her floating thirty feet from shore after the weight keeping her asunder came loose from its bounds. We still have not found said object. She was then removed from the lake, placed in a boat, and laid on her back in the clearing, arms by her side. She was on the grass, and this is when her blood began to settle in her back. Her wrists were red and raw, having also been bound by a rope that came loose as she was moved. As you noted, the rope must've been poorly tied by someone without knowledge of wet knots."

"Someone confident that they knew what they were doing."

Heather stopped him. "That's a theory, not a fact. Hold on to it."

"Will do. Keep going."

"We also found blood spatter that indicated blunt-force trauma. This matched the wound on her left temple and also indicated that this was where she had been killed before being dumped. First responders also noted that no evidence of a prior boat had been discovered, which means whoever dumped her must've swum her out there with the weight. Meaning..." Heather began, asking an unspoken question.

"Meaning they're either very strong or the weight was not very heavy. Either way, a great swimmer."

"Correct. We also found a partial footprint that is inconclusive of style, sex, or size."

"Have we gotten a preliminary back from Julius?" Gabriel questioned.

Heather nodded and pointed at the printout in the bottom-right corner. "She had not been sexually assaulted, and there was no trace of semen, fresh or old. The cause of death was the impact to her brain and skull combined with intracranial hematoma."

"Internal head bleeding?"

"Very good," Heather replied, trying not to sound condescending. "Her skull was crushed and cracked in several spots, though the skin had not always broken in this area. There was a particularly nasty dent at the back of the head where I believe—again, theory, not fact—she was initially struck before falling. Then, I believe, she was turned onto her back, where the fatal blow was delivered. Something strange that I didn't notice because of her black dress was that she had also been stabbed multiple times in the upper body and arms, but after she was dead. There was blood, but not as much as one would expect if her heart were still pumping."

"Sounds personal. The intimacy of straddling, hitting her in the head, and then stabbing. A lot of anger."

"Maybe," she said, and Gabriel gave her a curious look. "I've seen this in serial killers too. The ones that really hate women. But in truth, I agree with you. Though what's more of note is how methodical the stabbing was. The wounds were entirely symmetrical, one in the base of the throat, one just below the sternum, one in each shoulder below the collarbone, and one in each bicep."

Gabriel cringed and whistled low. "Jesus. That's… something."

"I know," Heather murmured, her blood running cold.

"Maybe he's a Satan worshipper."

"Why do you say that?"

"I don't know, I'm imagining her pinned on her back, dead, arms outstretched, and this person bringing a dagger down on her throat. It seems almost ritualistic."

Heather raised her eyebrows. "Huh. I hadn't considered that."

"You're welcome."

"Thanks. I still think you listen to too many paranoid true crime podcasts, but it's not impossible. It could point to someone with mental health problems."

"Like Thimbles?"

Heather chewed her lip. "Maybe."

"Was Jenny stabbed?" Gabriel asked, brow furrowed.

Heather groaned. "And there's another issue. I never flipped her body all the way over to check. Didn't want to disturb the scene any further and figured she'd be going to Julius, not goddamn Melvin Melrose."

"Wait, is that really his first name?"

"Yep, and though I never heard anything about stabbing, I also never got to look at the report. In fact, he never sent it over, just relayed the details to Gene, who relayed them to me. Like a really messed-up game of telephone."

"Can you get it now?"

Heather tasted copper and stopped chewing, instead turning her attention to giving her neck a friction burn.

"Shredded, apparently, according to his old receptionist. During the investigation into his questionable ethics and practices."

"Seriously?" Gabriel exclaimed.

"Seriously," she confirmed, her voice low and raspy.

"Man, that is one hell of an 'I told you so.'"

"Yeah. Gene knows it too. I feel sorry for him, but…"

"You also don't."

"I—" Heather started and stopped, slumping a little onto the arm of the couch.

"Hey, he screwed up a lot of stuff. A lot of people got hurt because of it. Don't get me wrong, I like the old man too, but he was one hell of a crappy boss."

Heather sighed. "Yeah."

"So," Gabriel said, keeping the momentum going. "At the moment, the main differentiation between Jenny and Mariah is the stabbing. At least as far as we know. But that's pretty much the only difference, so if that was the same…"

"Then we're looking at the same killer. Especially if no one knew, except for Melrose, that Jenny got stabbed. And before you say anything, he didn't kill Mariah either. He's on house arrest."

"Oh goody," Gabriel said dryly. "Very trustworthy."

"Yeah," Heather muttered, starting to flag.

"Hey, take your own advice," Gabriel insisted. "Let's focus on Mariah and see if that sheds any light on the past. It's not like an innocent man is rotting away in jail, and we can't resurrect Mason. So, let's just stay in the present."

Heather nodded and reached for her chow mein. "You're right. Let's circle back to Jenny. Suspects?"

"Suspects," Gabriel confirmed, squinting at the board. "So, we've got an 'unknown stranger/drifter,' Thimbles, Alain

Durand, and the ghost of Mason Fowler." Gabriel gave Heather a withering look. "Really?"

"Hey, it doesn't have to be a literal ghost. Just someone carrying out more killings in his honor. Or someone trying to screw with me. A copycat. A duplicate. A pale imitation. A..." she trailed off and pointed to Gabriel.

"Ghost. Okay. I get it. I still think it's stupid."

"Yeah, me too. But you know I don't like to rule anything out, including the undead."

"I respect it, and I think you're nuts. But you have a pretty good track record, so I'll hear you out," Gabriel teased.

Heather rolled her eyes. "Okay, so obviously, Thimbles has to be suspect number one. We found a bloody axe and a pool of the stuff by his tent back in the day, which was never tested, so we can't rule him out for back then either. He also has a terrible reputation, a criminal record, and some unsettling fixation with women. And if your brother is to be believed, he's also threatened minors with bodily harm. Of course, none of this means he's guilty, but our lineup is pretty weak, and he's the obvious choice. Though at this stage, the obvious doesn't mean much. Plus, there are some significant improbabilities regarding his ability to transfer a woman who weighs as much as he does down to the lake."

"All right. I'm getting that you're still not totally convinced. So, tell me about Alain Durand. Considering he has a name and actually exists, I'm guessing he's your second favorite."

"Correct. I haven't met him yet, but I'm driving over to Hallington to speak with him. He's a rich banker, and from what Cheyenne said, he's married, and Mariah was the other woman. Victor Wu also saw them together at the diner and heard Mariah give—who he believes was—Alain an ultimatum."

"So, maybe he chose the wife, she threatened to expose the affair, and he killed her to cover his tracks."

"Yeah, or something along those lines," Heather agreed. "It's a tale as old as time."

"Well, it makes sense to me," Gabriel concurred. "More so than seventy-something-year-old Thimbles with his bad leg. Plus, it would mean you're still right about Mason and that this really is just the coincidence of all coincidences. Did Mariah tell Cheyenne all of this?"

"No, that's the weird part. Cheyenne got a text from an unknown number saying that Mariah was sleeping with Alain three days before she died. Which seems… weird, to say the least."

"No kidding. Maybe the wife found out and sent it out as revenge. Trying to brand Mariah with a scarlet A."

"Maybe. Cheyenne also said she'd deleted the text before Mariah died to protect her friend, but that seems weird too."

"Maybe she found out another way? Like, maybe Mariah was boasting about sleeping with a wealthy guy, and she didn't want to, I don't know, posthumously embarrass her?"

Heather shook her head and spoke between noodle slurps. "No, Cheyenne wouldn't shy away from something like that."

Gabriel chuckled. "Yeah, true. I forgot who we were talking about. Well, maybe there was some sort of separate blackmail scheme, but then she died, so they retreated."

"Maybe. Or maybe someone wants the suspicion cast on Alain and knew I'd speak to Mariah's friends."

"That sounds complicated."

"It always is," Heather sighed, her mouth half-cocked.

"So, Mason's ghost. That's mainly someone screwing with Taylor or you, right? A personal copycat."

"Yeah. That's pretty much it, but I don't have any real suspects."

"All right, and I hate to ask, but what about the ambiguous stranger/drifter theory?"

Heather groaned. "It's as weak as it sounds, and it's really a theory, not a suspect. Basically, a drunk woman goes outside alone at night, some guy offers her a ride, maybe even a guy she knows, and you put the rest together. Cheyenne said she was involved with a lot of shady guys from a lot of shady websites, but all the sites are anonymous and encrypted. Going to take a while to pull any suspects from them if we ever break through."

Gabriel leaned back, beer sloshing. "Well, I hope it's not that one. It might be impossible to find the guy." He drank deeply and burped loudly. "So, to recap, we've got a methodical stabber, who bludgeons and ties knots poorly and who may or may not have killed two women, and we only have two real, living suspects. That about sum it up?"

"Yep," Heather said glumly before lighting up. "Oh, the dashcam footage. As I said, it doesn't show much of anything, but I don't know. Could be worth another look."

She stood and grabbed her laptop, but just as she was about to put it on the coffee table, Gabriel placed a hand beneath it, stood, and carried it toward the TV.

"We won't be able to see anything on this old thing," he said. "Let's plug it into the TV."

"Plug it in?" Heather asked, feeling less tech-savvy than she ever had.

"Yeah, with the HDMI cord in your DVD player." Gabriel rested the laptop on the floor, unplugged a cord, shoved it into the side of the laptop, and sure enough, the screen duplicated onto the TV like a second monitor. "And this is the video?"

"Yep."

"All right," Gabriel said, turning off both lamps and squatting beside the device. "Showtime."

He pressed Play and scurried back toward the couch, landing hard, his eyes focused on the screen. For whatever reason, the image being so enlarged unsettled Heather. It was like watching a horror movie, waiting for the inevitable jump scare, and she crumbled her takeaway box in her hand until sauce began to ooze out the bottom. Though it dripped, she stayed put, watching with bated breath.

"Okay, so he's pulling in," Gabriel said. "It's 3:37 a.m. And she's not there."

The car honked loudly through the TV speaker, and they both jumped.

"Why is this so scary?" Gabriel asked, laughing a little.

Heather glanced at his face just in time to watch it fall. His Adam's apple bobbed the full length of his throat.

"Wait, what the hell is that?"

"What is what?" Heather asked, not wanting to look back at the screen.

"Behind the trash cans," Gabriel whispered.

"Are you screwing with me?" she demanded, equally as quiet.

Without answering, Gabriel stood and rushed toward the laptop. He skipped back forty seconds, pressed Play, and watched the laptop intently. His eyes widened, and he paused before standing in front of the screen.

"What the hell is that?" he asked again, and Heather forced herself to look.

"Oh my god," she said, her heart in her throat and sauce all over her lap. "It's…"

"Thimbles," Gabriel confirmed, his finger right next to the old man's haggard face as he peered out from behind the trash cans. "Hiding out right in the time span that Mariah disappeared. I'll bet you anything that she's back there with him."

All other theories melting away, Heather also got to her feet. "I have to call Tina. We need patrol cars out. We need him in custody. I am not letting this fall apart again. Not in court, not in Glenville. I'm going to catch this fucker."

CHAPTER SIXTEEN

THE DETECTIVE

While Tina sought approval for the somewhat unorthodox search warrant required to search Thimbles's tent, Heather was determined to keep busy with other avenues. This was not especially popular among some of her coworkers. They had decided Thimbles was a killer on the loose and wanted him locked up immediately. Heather understood that, despite not holding the same convictions. What she didn't understand, however, was that to them, Thimbles's place of residence being a tent made it unworthy of law adherence. Heather had fought this trigger-happy would-be malfeasance by listing the laws regarding search warrants. In turn, they'd countered by reminding her that Thimbles's tent currently resided on private property—Paul Warren's, specifically—without permission.

Technically, this meant they could do whatever they wanted with the tent—bulldoze it, burn it, rip it to shreds—with little governmental flack. However, Heather liked to think they all were better than a bunch of uncouth animals. A home was a home, no matter how flimsy and small, and respect was essential if they wanted to look good in court, present an airtight case, and retain their humanity. It would also help them avoid unflattering headlines like "POLICE BULLIES BRUTALIZE ELDERLY HOMELESS POPULATION."

In truth, Heather hoped that Thimbles had graduated from tent to house, allowing them to simply acquire Paul's permission to search the area and put Thimbles behind bars for squatting. Not only would it allow him to clean up, eat a good meal, and sleep in a warm room, thus priming him for an interrogation, but it would also put Heather's mind at ease to have a possible serial killer off the streets.

While Tina happily handled all the paperwork, the alternate avenue that topped Heather's list was heading to Hallington anyway to talk to Alain Durand. While the footage of Thimbles had graduated the old man from suspect number one to Glenville's most wanted, there was no point in ignoring other possibilities until they had evidence. Mason Fowler and his shifty behavior had given her tunnel vision back in 2018, leading to potential oversights and a precarious conclusion. A rookie mistake to be sure, and one she was learning too much from to repeat.

She and Gabriel arrived in Hallington after a scenic thirty-five-minute drive and found themselves in an even more scenic town than their own. Heather didn't know something occupied by humans could be so beautiful, but there it was. Driving through the smooth streets, they passed people dressed in designer clothes, redbrick buildings, and black-and-white half-timber cottages. This helped her figure out the algorithm. Take Glenville, inject it with money and European expats, and you get Hallington.

"Wow," Gabriel said, removing his sunglasses and looking around at the clucking backyard chickens, topiaries, free-roaming tomcats, collie dogs, rose gardens, and thatched roofs. "Look at this place. This is… Oh my god, is that a peacock?"

"It is," Heather said slowly, her expression lifting with amazement as she stared at the albino Indian peacock. It spread its fabulous snowflake tail feathers and shimmied them, seemingly trying to impress the less beautiful turkeys with whom it shared a bowling-green perfect garden. "You've never been?"

"Nope," he replied. "Too expensive. No point. That's what my parents say anyway. They come out here for their anniversary though. Apparently, there's a really great winery and European-style tapas place."

"Wow," was all Heather could say. She too had never been, but with a paid-off house, very few bills, and a substantial paycheck, she could see herself indulging in its offerings from time to time.

"Not to justify extramarital affairs, but if Mariah really was coming out here to sleep with Alain, I see the appeal. Maybe I need to get myself an Alain. An unmarried female one," he hastily clarified. "I'd retire tomorrow and become a house husband if I could live here."

Heather laughed. "Maybe we can grab a coffee after we talk to Alain and see if the man-in-uniform gimmick works around these parts."

"Or woman-in-uniform," Gabriel nudged.

Heather rolled her eyes. "I'm good, thanks."

"Oh, come on. I'd hate to see you become an old maid."

Heather punched him in the arm. "I'm not going to become an old maid, you turd. I just think Hallington is a little fancy for the likes of me."

"You could be someone's *Pretty Woman*. We could go to brunch and play croquet, talk about stocks and our bratty kids, or whatever rich married people do."

"I could go for a little caviar and champagne before horse-riding," Heather admitted. "But my ex-husband already tried to make me into a lady, and it didn't turn out so great, as you can probably tell."

Thinking about Daniel Palmer and when she was once Heather Palmer made her stomach twist, and her happy expression faltered. She'd been avoiding her ex-husband, dropping the Lilly Arnold case shortly after discovering his potential involvement in the murder of his new fiancée, Katy Graham. She'd stayed far away from the news and placed all reminders of him in the furthest depths of her house. Her parents tactfully avoided the subject, Julius mainly kept mum, and Gabriel knew nothing about anything, including her ex-husband's name. Despite this, Daniel managed to sneak inside her mind every now and again and pull on her nerves till she wanted to scream.

"What's wrong?" Gabriel asked, noticing her pained expression.

She shook it off and smiled weakly. "Nothing. Bad headache."

"I have some aspirin."

"Already taken some, thanks."

"If you're sure," he replied warily, still staring.

"We're here," she said enthusiastically, desperate to distract and gesturing to a beautiful brick cottage on their left. Its front path was flanked by perfectly sculpted hedge rows, and its cherry timber door was decorated with an autumnal wreath that appeared to be real rather than plastic.

"As I said, I need to find myself an Alain Durand," Gabriel said, slack-jawed.

"Aside from the married-man part and his being a possible murderer," Heather reminded him, smirking.

Gabriel shrugged. "Honestly, I could probably make the first two caveats work if it landed me in this place. Maybe once he gets divorced…"

Heather shook her head in disbelief and barked a laugh. "You tart."

Gabriel threw up his hands. "Hey, I've never pretended to be anything but easy."

Containing her amusement, Heather altered her face into something more serious as she turned off the engine and opened the door. A wall of sound rushed forward, filling the car, and they both cringed. A baby—possibly colicky or teething, considering the intensity of the guttural sounds—was screaming its throat raw inside the house, shattering the paradisical peace.

Heather grimaced. "I hope he's the one on baby duty and not his wife. She's going to have questions if she's home."

"Hey, he made his bed. Their marriage isn't our problem."

"Yeah," Heather said, drumming her fingers on the wheel before stepping out of the car.

Single file, they made their way up the stepping stone path and used the door knocker in the absence of a doorbell. It took a minute or two for the door to be answered. Fortunately, by that time, the baby's yells were distant, clearly having been confined to some faraway nursery.

A woman answered. She was about Heather's age, if not younger. It was hard to tell on account of her messy mouse-blond hair and the gray bags beneath her eyes, but her skin was taut, and the hand that fiddled with her wedding ring was smooth and devoid of raised veins.

"Good morning, ma'am," Heather said, using her most professional voice. "Is Alain Durand in?"

"Alain?" the woman repeated, sounding distant. She blinked, some life returning to her glassy eyes. "No, no. He's not. Can I help you instead?"

"Are you Alain's wife?"

"Yes. I'm Leah Reed... I mean, Durand."

That was a bad sign, Heather thought, and she cleared her throat before asking, "Do you know where your husband is?"

"What's this all about?" Leah asked, glancing back into the house.

"It's probably best we speak with your husband first, ma'am."

"Right," Leah said, her voice clipped and mouth disapproving. "If you must know, he's at the Renaissance Hotel and Courtyard."

"Is that in town?" Heather asked.

"It is. Let's just say it's somewhat of a luxurious doghouse that I send Alain to when he's been, well, a dog."

"You kicked him out?" Heather asked.

"Yep. Seven days ago now. Apparently, he was having an affair with someone in Glenville. At least according to the anonymous text I received. Our son is two months old, and while I've been here, pumping and feeding, he's been out there doing a different kind of pumping."

Heather tried to forget the unpleasant phrase and visual and said, "I'm sorry to hear that, ma'am."

"Me too. You know, I always thought we had a fairy-tale marriage. Turns out it was, but just one of those awful Brothers Grimm or Hans Christian Andersen ones where the little mermaid turns to sea-foam and Rapunzel gets nonconsensually impregnated with twins."

Heather swallowed and hoped Alain was not, in fact, their man. If he was, the end of their marriage would challenge the conclusions of even the darkest fairy tales. Unfortunately, Heather could relate to Leah's plight and was troubled by breaking the news to this poor woman.

Leah narrowed her eyes, scanning Heather's badge. "Glenville Police Department, huh?" She paused thoughtfully, then stopped fiddling, her eyes turning circular, the bloodshot whites haloing the chocolate brown. "Wait, is this to do with the affair?"

"To a degree, yes," Heather confirmed.

Leah turned red with rage. "Oh god, what the hell has he done now? Public indecency? Screwing in the park? Blowjob in the car?" She stopped for breath, trying to read Heather's unwavering expression and moving to Gabriel's more expressive face. "Something worse? Battery?"

Heather gave in, her shoulders slumping slightly. "I'm afraid to tell you that the woman your husband was having an affair with, Mariah King, was found dead on Saturday morning."

If Leah had been holding anything, she would've dropped it as her body went limp, and she fell against the doorway. Heather moved forward, but the woman held up a hand.

"I'm fine, I'm fine," she insisted. "Just shocked."

Using the wooden frame, Leah righted herself and stared directly into Heather's eyes. For whatever reason, this extended, unblinking eye contact made Heather's gut burn and contract as if she'd downed a shot of gasoline. Her instincts were on fire. Something wasn't right. Everything Leah was doing suddenly felt like acting.

"I hate to ask," Heather said. "But can you tell us where he was on Friday night?"

"At the hotel, I guess. We weren't speaking at the time."

"And yourself?"

Leah scowled. "Why do you need to know?"

"It helps me get a full picture."

"I was here. With the baby. Not like I could murder someone with him in tow."

"No one is accusing you of anything, ma'am," Heather assured her.

"Yeah. Sure. I took a video of Theo, my son, that night. Do you need to see the time stamp?" Leah asked, condescending and increasingly hostile.

"That won't be necessary," Heather replied. "But if you could show us the text you received regarding the affair, that would be extremely helpful."

"Yeah, sure," Leah grumbled, rummaging in her dressing gown pocket, turning on her phone, scrolling, and tapping before turning the screen around.

Beneath the unknown number at the top of the screen—202-555-0179—was a brief text that read: "Mariah King of Glenville is having an affair with Alain Durand." That was it. Nothing more. Underneath the single sentence was a blurry portrait photo of two people kissing in the street, clearly taken with a phone camera, but not a good one. A burner, most likely, which meant the number was of little use. Still, the woman was undeniably Mariah, standing on tiptoes, wrapped around a taller, blurry man with graying hair.

"Can you screenshot that and send it to me? Here's my card."

"I guess," Leah muttered.

"Thank you, ma'am. Much appreciated. Please contact me if you think of anything that could assist the case."

"Sure," Leah replied flatly, taking the card and shoving it into her pocket along with her phone. "Now, I have to get back to Theo. He's teething."

"Of course. Have a nice day," Heather said.

"I'll try," Leah said sarcastically and slammed the heavy door in Heather's face.

"Guess we're going to the—what was it—Renaissance Hotel and Gardens?" Gabriel asked over his shoulder, already walking back toward the car.

"And Courtyard," Heather corrected. "And yes, we are."

"Sounds fancy," Gabriel said, opening the passenger door.

Heather didn't reply, walking in silence, but her brain caused a racket. She wandered to the driver's side, got in, and sat down. She didn't start the car or remove the keys from her pocket but gripped the wheel and stared straight ahead.

"There's something wrong," Gabriel said.

"Yeah," Heather said quietly.

"What is it?"

"I don't know," Heather admitted. "But there was something weird about her."

"I got that too. I don't have your freaky instincts, but it seemed like she knows something."

"Yeah."

"Or like she killed Mariah," Gabriel said, his tone unusually serious.

Heather looked at him. "I mean, the wife finds out, goes into a jealous rage, and kills the girlfriend. It's not out of the realm of possibility."

Gabriel nodded. "And at least we know Cheyenne's text is legit."

"Yeah, unless she was the one who sent it to Leah. Or Leah sent it to herself and Cheyenne."

"Why would either of them do that?"

"Well, maybe Cheyenne wanted to teach Mariah a lesson about ruining a marriage by letting the wife know, but she doesn't want to admit it because she thinks doing so got Mariah killed. However, she still wants us to catch whoever did it without implicating herself in the process. Or maybe Leah sent it because she already knew about the affair, planned to take revenge, but wanted to cast aspersions on her husband as revenge for his indiscretion."

"This is making my head hurt," Gabriel groaned.

"Mine too," Heather replied, rubbing her temples, her faux headache having manifested into a migraine. "Let's go see what Alain has to say for himself."

CHAPTER SEVENTEEN

THE DETECTIVE

THE HOTEL WAS, AS EXPECTED, ELEGANT AND EXPENsive, built from red brick, its modest four stories caressed by ivy and vines. It was clearly older than most of Hallington, perhaps nearly a century, but it was made to appear more ancient like the historical hotels of London. Thus the lobby looked like something stripped from an English castle, complete with dark wooden paneling, intricately carved glossy furniture, tapestries, imported oil paintings, and suits of armor on either side of the counter. It was beautiful like the rest of the town, but the feigned history felt a little forced as they trudged across the faux-worn rug. Heather tried to guess how much a week in this place would set someone back, and the resulting sum made her queasy.

"Hello, welcome to The Renaissance," the young woman—who was dressed in a black pantsuit—called out with a red-lip-sticked mouth.

Heather was no history buff, but the Renaissance era was not what the hotel reminded her of. It lacked the opulence, the cherubs, the golden gilding. It was more like something from the Tudor era—dark, drab, and musty, yet still costly. A visiting place of Henry VIII, a hunting ground for his next well-to-do wife. She felt as if she should be wearing a square-necked velvet gown complete with a corset and rubies. In fact, she could practically smell the nonexistent suckling pig and mead in some adjacent dining hall.

"Hello. Detective Heather Bishop. That's Officer Silva. We're looking for Alain Durand," she informed the clerk.

"Badges, please," the woman requested in a thick Italian accent, and Heather wondered whether they hired Europeans to sell the fantasy.

They handed their badges over, and as the young woman approvingly handed them back, she sent a wink flying in Gabriel's direction. The uniformed hypothesis proven correct, Heather smirked as her partner blushed.

"He's in room 202," the woman said with a brilliant smile.

"Thank you," Heather replied.

"And should you need any further assistance, this is my personal number," the woman informed them, scribbling some digits onto a paper napkin.

Heather moved to grab it, but the woman politely dodged her and handed it to Gabriel. He took it gratefully but was tongue-tied at the moment, spluttering embarrassingly as he tried to speak.

Heather, about to burst out laughing, moved quickly toward the stairwell, and Gabriel raced after her. Heather heard the woman giggle affectionately in the distance and finally joined in her amusement.

"Nice one, slick," Heather choked up through her tears.

"She took me off guard, is all," Gabriel protested, his ears turning ruddy.

"Sure."

"Seriously. I have game," he insisted.

Heather waved an invisible white flag. "Okay. I believe you."

"I'll call her, and you'll see. I'll take her to Luigi's, and she'll be putty in my hands."

Heather's mocking echoed down the dark hall of the second floor. "Gabe, she's actually Italian. Luigi's to her would be like taking your parents to Taco Bell or my mum to…" she faltered, unable to think of an Indian equivalent.

"Huh," Gabriel said. "Guess there's not really any Indian chain restaurants. Untapped market. Something to look into for your upcoming middle-aged crisis career change."

"Well, for one, I'm not middle-aged, and secondly, I can't cook."

"That's why I said 'upcoming.' You've got at least seven years to learn, and I know Julius would love to teach you how to make a fiery vindaloo." Gabriel waggled his eyebrows, and Heather responded with a disgusted, silent gag as she raised a fist to knock on the door of room 202.

Gabriel controlled his bubbling amusement as a tall, narrow man opened the door and looked at the uniformed pair in confusion. He had a large nose, crinkly crow's feet, and salt-and-pepper hair cut short at the side but long on top like a cockatoo. Heather pegged him for being in his late forties, if not fifty, roughly two decades older than Leah.

Despite their age gap, Heather could see the appeal. He was handsome in that rugged Vincent Cassel sort of way, and his asymmetrical expression communicated an unspoken charisma. His grays and subtle lines reminded her of Julius, though she preferred the latter's beard and curls.

"Alain Durand?" Heather asked.

"Indeed," Alain replied, his French accent almost as thick as the Italian clerk's downstairs. He shifted, his expression curious as he loomed above them.

Heather quickly looked him up and down, hoping he wouldn't notice but knowing he most certainly would. He was barefoot and dressed in suit slacks and a white undershirt. He was also notably freshly showered, shaved, and smelled of rich, musky cologne. Alain smiled, lines appearing on his cheeks as he surveyed the pair.

"And you appear to be Heather Bishop, detective extraordinaire."

Heather frowned. "How did you—"

"I watch a lot of news, and I listen to a lot of podcasts. True crime, mostly. Exciting stuff compared to banking. Your name crops up frequently, not to mention I was living in Seattle when you caught the Paper Doll Killer."

"Go figure," Heather said flatly, her celebrity status a constant source of irking.

"Indeed. Normally I'd ask for your signature, but considering you've come to me, I fear that may be inappropriate."

"It would. We're here to ask you a few questions."

"Of course," Alain said, resigned. "Well, come in. Apologies for the mess."

Alain turned and ventured back into the large hotel suite, and the two followed him in. The supposed disarray was nonexistent. His suitcase was open but empty, his belongings packed away into the wardrobe and chest of drawers. Heather supposed after a week of banishment, he'd figured he was here to stay. The only actual "mess" to be seen was an empty coffee cup, a crumb-covered plate, and a slightly unmade bed upon which Alain sat down before gesturing to a velvet teal couch beneath a still-life oil painting of a fruit bowl.

The pair of investigators took their seats, and before Heather could speak, Alain asked, "I presume this about the text my wife received? The repugnant blackmailer?"

"It is, and it isn't. While we will look into who sent the text, it's the content of said text that we're here for."

"Oh?" Alain asked, cocking his head. "Now, why would an upstanding officer of law such as yourself be interested in a tawdry affair? Unless… Oh no. Is Leah okay?" he queried, his eyes lighting up with panic.

"Leah's fine. We just spoke to her."

Alain rubbed at his chest and leaned forward. "Thank God. So what's the matter?"

"Mariah King, the woman you were having an affair with, was found dead on Saturday," Heather answered, deciding not to beat around the bush.

Alain crumpled, his lanky body folding in half. He waved a hand apologetically. "I'm sorry. *Pardon.* But Mariah is dead?"

"When was the last time you spoke with Mariah?"

Alain laughed bitterly. "You won't believe me, I'm sure, but I last spoke to Mariah two years ago. She accidentally hit me with her car over in Glenville while I was on my bike. I was fine, but she treated me to a drink at some bar as an apology."

"What were you doing in Glenville?" Gabriel asked.

"Better trails, Officer," Alain said. "It's near metropolitan around here, and I like to be in nature."

"Okay. And that was the last time you spoke?"

"In person, it was. She added me on Facebook, and we liked each other's posts, but that was it. I promise. The affair is a complete fabrication. Some *connard* trying to hurt me, Mariah, or Leah. God knows what their intention was, but none of it is true. I swear."

His earnest, pained expression seemed truthful, but Heather wasn't ready to let him off scot-free just yet. "What about the photo?"

"Pfft. The photo? Come on, Detective. You know better than that. It's a blurry photo of a man who looks vaguely like me and Mariah kissing. You can't see his face, not to mention it looks like he has a bicep tattoo, whereas I"—he gestured to his bare arms—"do not. Terrified of needles, in fact."

Heather opened her phone and saw that Leah had, in fact, texted the screenshot to her. She examined the photo and admitted that there was a shape that could be a tattoo on the man's right bicep.

"Could be a shadow," Heather argued.

"Yes, that's what my wife thinks too, but I'm telling you, that's not me. Surely, by now, you're aware that Mariah had a lot of lovers."

"I am."

"Well, surely one of them shares my physicality? Is that so out of the realm of possibility? Perhaps he's innocent too, but he's not me." Alain straightened a little and pleaded with raised palms, the backs set against his knees. "I love my wife and only my wife. To be respectful, Mariah is not my type. Tattoos and goth clothes have never been my thing."

Once again, it sounded like the truth, but Heather pushed forward. "I appreciate the information, but your word is not evidence, so I'm going to continue to ask you the question I came here to ask you."

"Go ahead," Alain said, relaxing somewhat. "Ask me anything."

"Where were you on Friday night and early Saturday morning?"

"That's when she died, I suppose? Well, I was here, in the hotel. The CCTV should prove as such, and I think you'd agree that I'd have trouble escaping through the windows. I would have certainly wrecked the ivy had I attempted and been caught in the process."

"Okay, I'll ask at the desk for the CCTV."

"Please do. I'd love to get this cleared up so I can stop pissing away money and return home to my wife and son. And here, take my card in case I might be of more assistance." They swapped cards, and Alain continued, "You're barking up the wrong tree, however. I believe whoever orchestrated this fiction is who you should be looking into. Think about it. All you have on me is a tenuous affiliation, an anonymous text, and a vague resemblance. I know it's always the boyfriend or the husband, and if there's an affair involved, the guilt multiplies, but Detective, I believe you are smart and good at your job, so I'm telling you to save your time and look elsewhere."

His pleading expression made Heather uncomfortable, and she stood, thanked him for his time, and headed toward the door with Gabriel hot on her heels. They didn't speak during their descent, nor did they say a word to each other as Heather requested the CCTV footage from the night of the murder. It was only when they had their hands on the car door handles that Gabriel spoke.

"That was weird," he said.

"You're telling me," Heather replied.

"He didn't seem like he was acting."

"No, he didn't." She looked up at the hotel and inspected the intact vines. "You still want that coffee?"

"No, let's get out of here. This place is giving me the heebs," Gabriel shuddered.

"Agreed," Heather concurred and pulled the door open, surprisingly eager to get the hell out of such a beautiful dodge.

CHAPTER EIGHTEEN

THE BRIDE

"**A**RE WE SERIOUSLY DOING THIS, TAYLOR? AGAIN? Aren't you tired?" Hunter asked, taking off his work boots and placing them on the rack.

Next to go were his hat, scarf, and coat, and once all the autumnal layers had been shed, he stormed past his wife—who stood in the living doorway with hands on her hips—and headed toward the kitchen.

Taylor moved through the large, square opening, rounded into the hallway, and stalked after her husband in her sheepskin slippers. "Yes, Hunter!" she despaired. "I am tired! Very tired!"

Hunter stopped, turned, and put a hand on her shoulder. He lowered his voice, cocked his head sympathetically, and squeezed just a little too hard for her liking. "Yeah, you look tired. Why don't you lie down while I finish off some paperwork?"

Taylor winced, imagining her collarbone bending like a willow branch beneath his thumb. She ducked to escape his grasp and shuffled backward. "More work? Seriously? You were gone all night."

There was that déjà vu again, nearly potent enough to knock her to the floor. Was this all that her life was going to be? The same day recycled but a little worse with each reiteration?

"Yes, more work," Hunter huffed. "There's always more work when you run a business. What don't you understand about that?"

"You know my parents are high-end criminal defense lawyers, right? And that I work in a care home full-time. I know about work."

Hunter ran a hand through his hair, which was graying around his temples and behind his ears. It was freshly cut, she noticed, the shorter hairs still stuck to his neck.

"Babe, your parents make so much money getting mobsters off the hook that they only need to work four cases a year. And you don't have to take your work home with you. It's not the same thing." He said it slowly, as if explaining cellular biology to a five-year-old.

"I want you to show me," she said, her hands returning to her hips.

He frowned, his discomfort directed at her diamond-shaped stance. "Show you what?"

"I want you to show me what work you have to do."

Hunter groaned and went slack as he transformed from a condescending father to an insolent child. Suddenly a six-foot-tall boy in a shirt and tie stood before her, refusing to show his mother his phoned-in homework assignment. Taylor nearly dropped her hands to her sides but fought the urge to accommodate his discomposure. She held out her hand, demanding, fulfilling her role as the nagging matron she'd never wanted to become. All he could see was his mother, her mother, and whatever love he had left drained from his expression. This too made her want to stop, but the dance was nearly at the end, and she planned to see it through.

"Jesus, fine," Hunter grumbled, turning back toward the kitchen and slamming his bag down on the wooden island. He unclipped the buckles, pulled out a black folder organized via colored tabs, and flipped it open to the red section to reveal some blank paperwork.

"See this?" he asked. "See those boxes? See how they're all blank? Well, I need to fill them in."

Heather hovered over the paperwork and looked up at Hunter, unimpressed. "So you've got to fill in a few numbers, tick some boxes, and sign your name on the dotted line? Wow. I get it now. That definitely couldn't be done during work hours."

"Clearly, it couldn't."

"You're such an asshole." She laughed, her tone reaching painfully high tones that strained her vocal cords. "Seriously," she emphasized, her eyes filling over with tears. "There's something wrong with you."

Hunter stared at her unblinking, and she wondered if this was how Victorian women felt before they got shipped off to some grisly asylum with a diagnosed case of hysteria.

He closed the book, his frustration mutating into concern. "There's something wrong with *me*? Babe, look at yourself. You're losing it over nothing. When I took over the company, I told you that it would be a headache, but it'll get easier, you just need to be patient." He sighed. "But hey, if it's gotten this bad, I'll take the week off. Joey could take over for that long. Maybe we can go to the shelter and pick out a puppy. Get you a little companion, huh?"

Taylor swallowed a scream. "A week off? And you're going to act like that's your idea? Seriously?"

"Babe, I don't know what you're talking about."

Taylor pointed a finger at his face as if brandishing a knife. "I have been begging you to take time off and be here for me. My best friend was just murdered by some lunatic on the anniversary of my sister's death. I'm traumatized, terrified, and exhausted, and you're not here for me. You're supposed to be my husband, and you're not here. Where are you, Hunter?"

"I am here," he insisted.

"No, you're not. You know, I've heard of guys being married to the job, but you seem to actually be screwing it."

"I'm trying to provide for us," he sniped. "So that you can quit your job and pursue your passions."

Heather let out a disbelieving rasp of amusement. "I don't want to quit my job. I love my job. You know this."

"Taylor, come on," Hunter replied, lowering himself onto a stool. "You seriously want to wipe old people's asses and clean bedsores for the rest of your life?"

"Yes, I do. Because I actually care about other people."

Hunter barked a laugh. "That's rich."

"It's the truth."

"Come on, babe. Be reasonable. You were a bitch in school, and frankly, you're still a bitch. I love that about you. You're a bitch, I'm an asshole, and that's why we're successful. We have what it takes. Frankly, with your cutthroat sensibilities, I'm surprised—and honestly disappointed—you didn't end up CEO of Microsoft or something. But there's still time. You're only twenty-eight."

"I wasn't that bad," Taylor murmured, ignoring the latter half of his sentiment.

"Oh yeah?" Hunter scoffed. "I wonder if Penelope or any of the other girls you terrorized would agree."

"That was a long time ago."

"I'm sure it feels like yesterday for your victims."

Victims. The word made her feel sick, and she wanted to throw it back at him, but a knot formed in her throat, and she couldn't move her mouth to speak. The problem was that he wasn't wrong. If he was, it would be water on a duck's back, but there it stayed. That word. *Victims.*

She hadn't always been like that. In elementary school, she was sweet as pie and a total teacher's pet. She'd remained the same way at the start of high school, but forming a clique late freshman year—and a popular one at that— had brought out the worst in her. *Cruel, callous,* and other *c*-words were how she'd describe herself, but no matter her parents' involvement, she only got worse. Her friends were her new parents and boys her new gods. The more attention and respect she garnered from either party, the more she showed off, desperate to remain one of the elite. She stomped on hands, climbed on shoulders, and reached the top of the food chain by the time her sophomore year rolled around.

The group enabled each other too, working together like clock cogs, passing painful seconds, minutes, hours, and days for their unfortunate peers. If Mariah had a problem with some girl in science class, Cheyenne would invent a rumor to spread. If Hazel needed to reject an ugly boy, Taylor would help her write the insult-ridden note to stuff into his locker. If Cheyenne didn't make head cheerleader, the other three would wreck and infiltrate the team to get what they wanted.

They became good at them—the insults, the mocking, the humiliation. Their insults weren't surface-level, childish rhymes and nonsense; they cut deep. They'd point out things that only that person had ever noticed about themselves, and soon enough, everyone else noticed Debbie's penile-shaped birthmark, Chrissy's hairy forearms, or Derek's bladder issues. So much buried information—disguised with scarves, long sleeves, and adult diapers—was all dug up eventually by the group of bloodthirsty truffle pigs.

There was one girl in particular, Penelope, who was their favorite to pick on. Taylor honestly couldn't even remember how it had started. Perhaps she'd borrowed Cheyenne's pencil and forgot to give it back, eaten a smelly lunch near their spot in the library, looked in their direction the wrong way, or simply had an irritating face. They were undiscriminating in their hatred, so it could have been anything, and Taylor felt even worse for being unable to remember. That was how little she thought of all these children and the damage she'd done to them.

Maybe, she thought, *that's the real reason I don't want to have kids. Just in case they end up coming across someone like me—or worse, becoming someone like me.*

Come the end of sophomore year, they were all wholly mutated by their accumulated power. Even sweet Jenny—for all her attempts to soften their blows early on—became infected with time and formed her own disease-ridden posse in their absence.

Poor Penelope must've been even more excited than they were to graduate. The poor thing couldn't do anything right. Painfully shy but incredibly pretty was a bad combination when it came to jealousy-ridden teenagers. The boys hated her because she rejected them, causing them to turn on her. After all, they were "lowering their standards" for her anyway, and who was she to say no?

Similarly, the girls hated her because of the boys' wanton obsession with hooking such a slippery catch. They pouted their lips, desperate to be reeled in, but it was all about small-fry Penelope, who seemed above all of it. Which made them feel about as desirable as long strands of fish shit.

Of course, it was all projection and invention, but they, the sharks, frenzied once blood was in the water. It took awhile to come, but those salty tears allowed that group of predators to swim and snap worse than ever before.

In reality, Penelope just wanted to be left alone and tried her best to make herself small and unappealing with her baggy black clothes and curtain of hair. Taylor could still picture her now, perched on the brick wall surrounding the old pine tree, her legs crossed and an Edgar Allan Poe collection in her lap. Despite her age and distance from the person she had once been, Taylor still felt a burning hatred for the perfect, porcelain girl and her glum expression. A loathing that made her want to yank hair, slap, spit, and punch. It made her feel disgusting, though it had felt justified at the time.

They never laid a hand on her, wanting to maintain good grades, but the emotional abuse was probably more soul-crushing than the occasional bruise. Cheyenne was undeniably the worst at doling out cruelty, but Taylor and Mariah often rose to and surpassed her level. Hazel even had some choice words, but she was more of an enabler.

She'd approach their corner cafeteria table by the window and whisper, "Did you see what Penelope is wearing today? I think she's making an effort. I could smell the cheap body spray three rows back in home ec."

"Ewww," Mariah would say, and Taylor would concur before Cheyenne got them really fired up with a combination of slut-shaming and good old-fashioned appearance-based insults. Then it would be Taylor's turn to come up with something really clever, and everyone would giggle and cheer while patiently waiting for Penelope to come close enough to yell it at her.

She'd cry sometimes, and often she'd scowl, but most of the time, she just quickened her gait and sped off to wherever her newest hiding spot was. None of her safe spaces ever lasted long. They found them all eventually and snapped at her diver's cage, the threat enough to make her swim to shore. Which, in this case, was her parents' home, lowering her attendance to expulsion-worthy figures.

She never turned them in for whatever reason. Never said a word in fact. They were lucky she didn't, but her lack of revenge only culminated in disappointment. In fact, it made them seethe. They wanted an outburst, an attack, something to justify the hatred that kept them awake at night.

A memory came to Taylor—one of Penelope and Hunter standing close together in a busy hallway. He'd asked her out the year before he'd decided Taylor was the one for him. They'd been freshmen, so popularity hadn't mattered as much as it would later on, and Penelope was beautiful and brilliant. Smart girls were Hunter's type, and though Penelope had rejected him, Taylor and her burgeoning crush had never gotten over it.

"Why did you ask me out?" Taylor asked of her husband, back in the present. "There were so many other girls. Cheyenne included."

Hunter shrugged. "You were pretty, smart, and popular. You impressed me in math class, and I knew you'd impress my parents too. Which you did."

"Do you still think that about me? Do they?"

"I think we'd all be a lot more impressed if you got a better job or became a mother."

"What kind of job does she have?" Taylor asked wryly.

"You know what my mom does. She was an accountant, then a stay-at-home mom, and now she's the manager at the local bank."

"No, not your mom. The woman you're sleeping with."

Hunter scraped his chair back and stood suddenly, towering above Taylor. "Are you actually accusing me of having an affair, Taylor?"

"I…" she stuttered.

"Let me warn you now, if the answer is yes, we're going to have a problem. So, I'll give you one chance to admit you're being a paranoid idiot."

"And I'll give you one chance to answer the question," Taylor replied, standing firm despite her rapid heartbeat.

"No. I'm not having a goddamn affair, Taylor," Hunter growled, shaking his head at her and turning toward the liquor cabinet.

"Where were you the night Mariah died?" Taylor asked.

Hunter wheeled around. "Excuse me?"

"Well, you asked me to come home, but when I got here, you were nowhere to be found."

"I was in the guest bedroom. You fell asleep on the couch. I left for work before you woke up." His voice was leveled, but she could see his jaw muscles twitching.

"I would've heard you. I'm a light sleeper."

"You were drunk and snoring," he explained, his voice still calm though the effort to keep it so was evident.

"I'll ask you again. Where were you the night Mariah died? How do I know you didn't just want to lure me away and—"

Hunter closed the gap and struck Taylor hard across the face with an open palm. He was stronger than ever since becoming the big boss at a physical job, and the blow knocked her into the counter with ease. Hitting her side, she fell back down and hit the ground hard. She scampered back with her feet, one hand placed on her side and the other pressed to her cheek.

Hunter stepped forward, his mouth hanging open and his eyes wide. He lowered himself to her level and moved closer again. Taylor moved her hands, creating a barrier before her face.

"Stay right there! Don't come any closer!" she whimpered.

"Taylor, I'm so sorry. Baby, I didn't mean to," Hunter whispered.

"Leave me the hell alone!" she screamed, loud enough for the neighbors to hear, and Hunter backed off.

"Okay, okay, I'll leave you alone. I'm sorry I overreacted. I think Mariah's death has affected me more than I thought, and for you to accuse me of something so…" he trailed off, his voice froggy with emotion.

She'd never seen him cry, not really, and the following sniffles softened her into putty. "I'm sorry too," she said softly. "I'm really sorry, Hunter. I know you'd never do that. I'm just tired and scared."

"Uh-huh," he said, his head in his hands and his ass on the ground.

Slowly, cautiously, Taylor crawled toward him and rubbed herself against him like a hungry cat, prying him open. Once he relaxed, she laid her head in his lap, and he toyed with her hair, both of them ignoring her pink and swollen cheek.

CHAPTER NINETEEN

THE DETECTIVE

As Heather parked her Ford Granada in its usual spot outside the front of the police station, her usually fortified skull was creaking against the strain of her throbbing, swelling brain. It was as if all the new information received—about Thimbles, Leah, Alain—was physically stretching the lobes, cerebra, and cortices to their limit, like a stomach after Thanksgiving dinner. It was gravid with knowledge and growing increasingly uncomfortable within its bony constraints. She'd given in to Gabriel's Advil offer and donned sunglasses, but all she wanted to do was nap. However, upon turning her head and seeing Tina in full uniform and hiking boots, it was apparent that resting was not on today's cards.

Heather opened the door and faced her boss. "You've got the warrant," she said.

"Yep," Tina said. "Approved for the house and tent. No arrest."

"You tried for arrest?" Heather asked, surprised.

"Figured we might as well bring him in and ask him some questions. Hopefully, he's squatting and we won't need to ask," Tina replied, mimicking Heather's earlier thoughts.

"Fingers crossed," Heather muttered, not bothering to move from her seat and turning the engine back on.

"How was Alain?" Tina questioned, her feet constantly moving and ready to go.

"According to him, innocent of the affair and the murder."

"And what do you think?"

Heather sighed and massaged the back of her skull, her tight ponytail not helping the situation. "My instincts say he's innocent, but it's not like that will hold up in court. His wife certainly isn't his biggest fan right now, and the photographic evidence of him kissing Mariah could go either way. Honestly, it could be anyone. Just waiting on the CCTV to solidify his alibi."

Tina nodded. "Good work, Detective. For what it's worth, I believe your gut. Mainly because I have a feeling we're about to wrap all of this up once and for all."

"You're that convinced by Thimbles?"

Tina looked up at the sky, squinting, her braided bob falling backward. "I never thought it was him. I really didn't. But now it just makes sense, doesn't it? I guess Gene will be relieved."

Heather swallowed, the pain nearly blinding. "For all of our sakes, I hope he's our guy."

"You going to be okay?" Tina asked, looking back at Heather. "Considering your history with the Warrens."

"I'll be fine."

"You sure?"

"I'm fine," Heather snapped. She held up a hand. "Sorry, headache."

"Have Gabriel drive," Tina instructed. "I'll see you guys over there."

"Yep," Heather grimaced, stepping out of the car as Tina strode away.

"You sure?" Gabriel asked, looking at the wheel.

"Just drive," Heather said, rounding the front of the vehicle, her eyes closed and fingertips guiding her.

As it turned out, Heather wasn't fine. She hadn't seen the Warren house in over a year, and even with her eyes closed and brain pulsating, she could hardly remember what it looked like as they made their way through the eternity of trees. Then Gabriel swerved, and she forced her lids open and let the blinding gray light in. Soon after came the house and all the associated memories along with it.

The enormous midcentury modern cuboid sat on the horizon, overhanging the lake on spider-leg stilts. It was cold, dark, hungry, and somehow alive, looking as if it might pluck its anchors from the dirt and drag itself toward them before eating the car in a singular bite with them trapped inside like some sort of metallic, bony turducken.

It was silly, but it frightened her, and she avoided the oversized windows, fearing the appearance of Alice Warren's ghost within the expensive frames. She noticed Gabriel, too, had stiffened, his knuckles white and shoulders raised toward his jaw. They'd let her down, and now she was never going to leave them, especially not in a place like this.

It was strange how places changed with context. Heather remembered seeing it for the first time and being grateful they'd retained and refurbished the past without destroying it. A wonderful time capsule to what had come before. Now she wished they'd bulldoze it, erasing all the filth and misery that was imbued in its glossy, tinted walls. What was once beautiful was now hollowed out, the rose bushes wilting, and everything that remained, from furniture to jacuzzi, had turned into oddly shaped sheet ghosts.

Tina was waiting for them alongside Officer Tim Reeves—a paunchy, disagreeable, but capable officer who was quickly becoming Tina's right-hand man. He laughed at something Tina said, her hand over her mouth and her face tilted toward him. Whatever was said was clearly insulting, but Heather didn't have the capacity to dwell on it. Any reserved space in her head was for the case and the case only. So she smiled, her headache fading, as Gabriel parked and they exited the car.

Peters and Reeves came to them, looking like a pair of detectives from a canceled cop show with their serious expressions.

"You two checked the house yet?" Heather asked.

"Nope," Tina called over the lashing wind. "We'll split up. Silva and Reeves, you check the house. Detective Bishop and I will investigate the tent," she said, gesturing to the yellow tent by the water's edge that was near tatters and browned with filth. Once again, despite the heinous possibilities, she felt sorry for Thimbles and swore to herself she'd gift him with the best tent on the market should he prove to be innocent.

"Okay," she replied, even though splitting up felt like a bad idea.

She knew it was silly to think; she was armed and trained, as were the rest. But she supposed Beau and Gabriel had worn off on her with their slasher movie talk.

She reassured herself by reminding herself that Thimbles was well on his way to eighty, if he hadn't reached it already, and Heather had handled worse, far more dangerous men who wielded much more dangerous weapons than axes or tire irons.

Tire irons, she thought, wondering whether Thimbles could have planted the murder weapon in Mason's truck. Mason hadn't lived far from the lake after all, and his door was permanently unlocked. That was how they'd gotten in after all and seen him with his brains blasted against the plaster. Could Thimbles have subdued such a tough young man, who'd been a promising linebacker and a wrestling king? It seemed unlikely, but if Thimbles was their man, he'd also carried full-grown women for miles, so perhaps Gabriel was right about the superhero—or supervillain—strength.

She supposed that Dennis Burke had been much the same. Just a man living in the woods who was capable of feats of strength that were both unbelievable and apparently entirely possible. Heather didn't believe in the devil, but there was something about human monsters and the things they did that would always be inexplicable, unknowable, and impossible for everyone but themselves.

Adrenaline soothing her pain, Heather and Tina skittered down the slippery embankment, leaving the other two to permissibly break into Paul Warren's home. The poor man had never managed to sell it with all the beating hearts beneath its floorboards, and as far as Heather knew, he still lived with his parents to recoup his losses. Another failing on her part. Had she managed to save Alice, Holly would have a mother, Paul would have a wife, and the beautiful home by the lake would've likely found new owners in new times. A rescue story was good luck, especially with the would-be murderous beast rotting in the ground with a bullet in his forehead. However, death—multiple deaths—rendered it beyond undesirable. So there it would stay until he decided to bulldoze the unsavory piece of history that had once been a promising family home to two innocent women.

At first, as they landed in the marshy grass, Heather thought it was her own foul memories that stank. That they'd so permeated and made residence inside her that she could smell them without them actually exiting. Then she spotted the fish guts and the buzzing flies that feasted upon the grayish, rotting innards. All the stories about Thimbles had involved fish, but they had never been rotting. They'd needed to be edible. Thus, they were freshly caught, so why had these been left to go bad? Heather's head pulsed again, and her guts twisted as she covered her face with the T-shirt beneath her uniform. She noticed Tina do the same and was at least relieved that the smell was real, even if it was of little comfort.

Even through the fabric, Heather tasted copper on her tongue, and the thick miasma of foulness seemed to seep into her pores, making her feel greasier than ever before. Then she saw the basket, more fish rotting away in piles, beside them a fish knife, and a little further away—atop what looked like a square of leather—was an axe. It was completely covered in gore from top to tip.

Tina glanced at Heather and drew her gun but kept it by her side. Heather decided to do the same and hoped their mere presence would spook the old man into submission without any sort of violent exchange. The last thing she needed was an axe being hurled her way.

Deciding it was better not to scare him, the two agreed via eye contact, and Tina called out, "Mr. Ford?"

Using the man's real name was tactful, and Heather cautiously joined her, asking, "Michael? Can you please exit the tent? We don't want to hurt you, we just have some questions."

They continued this line of communication, keeping their voices clear over the ambient wildlife, making sure that they wouldn't surprise him. Though, as expected, Thimbles had no interest in making this easy.

"Michael Ford," Tina said sternly as they made it to camp. "Please exit the tent now. We have a search warrant, and I do not want to have to physically remove you from your home."

Still nothing. Tina sighed and pressed the button on the walkie. "Reeves, you got anything? Over."

"Nothing, boss. Doesn't even look like he's been inside," Reeves replied. "No footprints, no breakages, and no unsheathed furniture. Plus, the fridge is empty, and the water has been turned off."

"Crap," Tina hissed, her eyes on the tent. "Okay. Call Lisa. Tell her I'm going to need her to mark up this campsite."

"Why, what have you found?" Reeves responded

"A whole lot of blood and a couple of possible weapons too. We're going to have to take him in and get forensics to take a look at some of this stuff."

Heather expected Thimbles to come running, axe in hand, at any second, yet despite the loudness of the conversation, not a single rustle sounded from inside the tent. On the one hand, she figured, he could be asleep or going deaf—or both. Then there was the other hand, and that might be that he was simply that stubborn after thirty years of open-air freedom. Alternatively, maybe he wasn't there at all. Heather had no idea, but she'd had enough of waiting around, and despite Tina's hisses and whistles, she carefully rounded the scene to the lake-facing tent flaps.

Her memories of 2018 were overpowering. The smell, the blood, the tent. Being in this exact situation before with Gene. Him being so convinced it was Thimbles, just like Tina was now. Maybe they were both right, and Heather was the idiot, but something felt wrong. It didn't feel like a penny dropping or a puzzle piece falling into place; it felt like a copper-colored herring letting go of the hook.

Carefully, gun pointing forward in case there was an opposing firearm, she placed one hand on the flap and pulled the entrance aside. She jolted and realized she was right about the sleeping part. There he was, a mass of white head and facial hair like Santa's terrifying evil twin, wrapped up beneath animal hides and decaying blankets. It smelled like fish and rot, and Heather honestly pitied this man, forced to sleep in soggy, stinking filth.

"Mr. Ford, wake up," Heather said loudly as Tina joined her.

"Christ," Tina muttered, covering her own face with her shirt. "Mr. Ford, please get up," she added, nudging his foot with the toe of her boot.

Thimbles did not stir. Not one bit. He didn't snore. He didn't groan. He didn't breathe.

"Shit," they said in sync.

"He's dead," Heather said, carefully touching his protruding posterior tibial area to check for a pulse and finding none.

"Yeah, and look what he's holding," Tina stated, gesturing toward Thimbles's outstretched hand.

It was the blade of a hunting knife pressing against the fabric of the tent. A knife just like the one from Mariah's autopsy report. From eyeballing it, they could tell it was also the same width and length, and just like the axe, it was covered in dried blood.

"Looks like we've got another killer who won't see his day in court," Tina groaned, backing away from the stench.

"Yeah," Heather replied, unable to move, her voice distant.

"And I'd say, if he killed Mariah, then he also killed Jenny."

"Yeah," Heather said again, her voice now miles away.

"Don't feel bad, Heather. We all make mistakes. And it's not like you killed Mason. That kid was going to kill himself regardless. Your only sin is ruining his posthumous reputation, which, frankly, was never going to be glowing anyway." She darted forward, offering a single pat to Heather's shoulder, before moving further to the lake, being careful to avoid the fish guts. "Seriously, don't sweat it," she shouted. "You got the right one in the end. It's my fault too. I should've locked this creep up the moment I became sheriff."

Heather nodded, staring at the knife. There it was. There he was. It made sense. Here was a man who was mentally ill, wild, scrappy, a known criminal, strong for his age, and a hater of women holding one of the murder weapons in his hand. Yet there still were pieces missing.

What about the affair? The texts? Hazel? Still, nothing else made half as much sense. Maybe Cheyenne was right about Hazel's disappearance being an unrelated and unfortunate coincidence. Maybe Mason's letter had merely been made of guilt for being an abusive boyfriend, not a murderer. Maybe Alain really hadn't been having an affair and Leah's energy was conjured by stress. After all, Thimbles had been present at both crime scenes around the time both girls disappeared. It made sense; it did.

So Heather let everything melt away as she stood on the sidelines and watched Lisa and her crew mark the scene. Then she let herself be the center of attention as champagne flowed back at the police station and allowed grabbing hands to congratulate her.

The case was closed. It was. It had to be.

CHAPTER TWENTY

THE BRIDE

"**W**HAT DO YOU FEEL LIKE, BABE?" Hunter asked, one arm slung around Taylor's neck, the other swinging synchronously with the empty shopping basket.

She watched it oscillate like a Newton's cradle to the beat of the tinny pop music on the loudspeakers without blinking, and the rumbling bass of Hunter's voice only served to remind her they were due for a storm at the end of the week. Just what her sodden lawn needed, more rain.

"Taylor?" Hunter prompted, pressing his fingertips into her denim-clad upper arm.

Taylor looked up for the first time and scanned the interior of Greenman Grocery with narrowed eyes. The lights were too bright in contrast to the gloomy outside world, and the unexpected reorganization of the aisles rendered her completely lost in what had once been a familiar place.

Hunter didn't know this, but it had been months since she'd physically been inside the minimarket. Ever since they'd started offering online orders and delivery, she'd been shopping from the comfort of her home, her feet up and the TV on. She'd always hated grocery shopping, and the ability to luxuriate over the options, press a few buttons, and have a chipper, dreadlocked vegan show up at the door the next day had been one of the most significant improvements to her life thus far. Her parents dismissed it as a fad, born from the younger generations' sheer laziness. She pitied their inability to relish in the perks of modernization, thanks to their workaholic mindsets; but she knew Hunter, despite his age, would agree wholeheartedly. So the indulgence remained a secret between her, the well-tipped employees, and her nosiest neighbors.

"Tay," Hunter said, firmly this time, his grip bordering on painful.

Taylor snapped out of her fugue and mumbled, "Let's do pasta."

"Pasta, pasta, pasta," Hunter reiterated, looking up at the signs hanging from the dropped ceiling. "This way," he said confidently, moving his hand to hers and pulling her along.

If her memory was correct, Hunter hadn't been grocery shopping since they moved in together. Still, regardless of his experience, she was happy to assign him as the leader of this particular mission.

Faced with a plethora of sauces, Hunter lowered his arm and the basket, scratched his face, and reached forward, grabbing two jars in his catcher-mitt hands. One was alfredo; the other was puttanesca, and he looked back and forth between them as if watching a tennis match.

"White or red?" he asked, turning to present them.

"White," she confirmed.

"With shrimp?"

"You read my mind," she replied, his good mood wearing off on her despite the unpleasantness of the night before.

Hunter ducked down and kissed Taylor chastely on the cheek. She flinched. The pain was still there, and though the mark wasn't anything her foundation couldn't handle, the sharp reminder of its existence was unpleasant. Hunter retracted hastily—looking as unsure and anxious as a schoolboy attempting his first kiss—until she smiled and reached for his hand. He was trying harder than he had in years, even going so far as to take five days off. It wasn't the week he had promised, but he was on a roll, and she had no desire to lay herself down on his bullet train's tracks. Preventing progress would only mean grinding to a halt, and she did not want to end up stuck in an eternal yesterday.

Hunter lifted their hands and spun Taylor one-eighty degrees until she faced the other side of the aisle. Confronted by a wall of dry pasta, she tilted, feet planted, trusting him to keep her from falling, and grabbed a box of fettuccine. He yanked her backward, she plopped it into the basket next to Alfredo, and then they were off again, barreling toward the fish counter, picking up speed and out of breath upon arrival.

Reliving her high school romance, Taylor couldn't stop the happy giggles and looked away from the counter, embarrassed. As a result, she didn't notice Hunter ordering an excess of shrimp until it was too late, but it didn't matter. They had board game plans in the sunroom tomorrow, and a shrimp and avocado salad would go perfectly with such a breezy, relaxing day.

The giggles spread to the young attendant as they continued their manic shopping trip, Hunter once again leading the way with gusto as they hurtled into the wine department. It was a dark room embedded in the side of the building, and in the partial privacy of the alcove, Hunter discarded the basket, wrapped his arms around Taylor, and kissed her deeply on the mouth. She almost recoiled, her instincts telling her to retreat, but instead, she parted her lips, returning the affection before shoving him away playfully.

He chuckled as he turned to a display and plucked an expensive Chardonnay and downright overpriced Shiraz from the offerings. He offered them to Taylor, holding the bases like a waiter at an upscale restaurant.

"Same question again, madam. Red or white?"

"White again. Chardonnay and alfredo go together like…" she trailed off, thinking.

"Like us," Hunter finished, his expression smug.

Taylor grimaced. "You cheeseball."

"Well, luckily, you love cheese."

"I do."

"Anything else?" he asked.

"Well, it wouldn't be a cheat meal without more carbs."

"Garlic bread?"

"Garlic bread," she confirmed, the hibernating butterflies in her belly remembering how to flap their wings.

They'd agreed to remain unplugged from the outside world until after dinner: no phones, no tablets, no laptops, no smartwatches, and no carrier pigeons were permitted. To Taylor's surprise, Hunter stuck to his promise, and they replaced the usual beeping, buzzing, and clattering of keys with conversation and their favorite crooner records. After such an extended period of muted interaction, they were so interested in each other's lives that it took them until after seven to start cooking. Then the aprons were donned, and they got down to business.

Taylor, of course, was the head chef, while Hunter took on the role of her sous-chef. For the dozenth time that day, Hunter surprised her, taking to his duties as if he'd spent a decade under the wings of a Michelin star chef. There might not have been much to chopping garlic and peeling shrimp, but she was enamored by his fervor and impressed by his handiwork.

Sadly, his role was a brief one, but he didn't leave once his work was done. Instead, he stayed to watch the show, swaying in his seat and singing along to Sinatra. Occasionally, she'd look over her shoulder and smile, all her worries and anxieties melting away. There he was, the man she'd fallen in love with all those years ago: her husband, protector, and friend.

She knew what her friends and mother would say if they knew what had happened and how easily she'd forgiven him, and it wasn't anything good. She understood, of course. It was part of human nature to judge others—especially couples. God forbid a friend should complain about her boyfriend's gambling habits or unusual relationship with his mother should she want the man in question to be able to show his face at a dinner party without receiving the cold shoulder. Which was why—looking at Hunter now—she so regretted having aired her dirty laundry to Cheyenne. Once your friend hated your partner, nothing could undo the vitriol.

"I feel bad," Hunter said abruptly.

Taylor turned sharply, spoon in hand, a little sauce on her lips. "Why?"

He was slumped in his seat, looking up at Taylor as if she were a holy figure. "This whole time, I thought there was something wrong with us, with you, with me. But all you needed was for me to be here." He held up a finger. "One day, just one day, of quality time and a little TLC, and we're right back where we used to be."

Taylor shrugged. "Well, I told you that's what I needed. You know I'm not high-maintenance. I'm not Cheyenne. I'm not my mom. I just want you to look at me. Talk to me."

"I know, I know," he groaned, burying his face in his hands.

His distress felt genuine, and she softened her tone. "Hey, you're making an effort now, and that's what counts."

"Is it?"

"It is," she reassured him, convincing herself in the process. "Now get that bread out of the oven and crack open the Chardonnay. It's shrimp alfredo time."

"Yes, ma'am," Hunter said, getting to his feet like an attentive soldier and saluting.

Taylor laughed and returned to the food, spooning it into locally made ceramic bowls and topping it with fresh basil leaves. It smelled amazing, and she turned, mouth watering, to steaming bread and a full glass of wine awaiting her. Hunter sat attentively, illuminated by candlelight, his eyes focused on her every movement. He looked even hungrier for her than the food, despite the fact that she'd donned pajamas and removed her makeup shortly after they'd gotten home.

For once, his desire made her feel confident instead of withdrawn. Likely because, for the first time in three years, his attraction was fully reciprocated. She laughed quietly, the concept of him being unfaithful suddenly seeming ridiculous as she blushed under his gaze.

"What is it?" he asked, grabbing his bowl from her hand.

"Nothing. I'm just happy, I guess."

"I'm so glad, baby," he said, using their most rarely used and tender pet name.

They ate quietly, making frequent, flirtatious eye contact, and when they were done, Hunter poured another glass of wine. Mouths no longer full of Italian food, they sipped their drinks between enriching conversations and ensured that trauma and work were kept at arm's length. Then, after the third glass, despite feeling sleepy from their decadent dinner, Hunter proposed a shower, and Taylor joined him under the water for the first time in five years.

Afterward, they took to the living room and lounged on the couch. The conversation had run dry, and with the fire crackling and the TV on, they finally agreed it was okay to check their phones. If only to see how his employees and her parents—who were away in Seattle on a case—were getting on.

As Taylor's phone turned on, the screen underlighting her face, it buzzed three times. A text from her mom, a missed spam call, and an email from *mariahhh1995*—Mariah's email address. In her panic, Taylor nearly dropped her glass of wine, attracting Hunter's focus. She growled, tempted to smash both her receptacle and phone against the wall as Face ID failed to recognize her in the dim light.

"Baby, what's wrong?" Hunter asked. "Are your parents okay?"

"They're fine," she said, calming herself and placing her glass on the table.

Hunter did the same, waiting for the inevitable blow. "So, what's wrong?"

THE BRIDESMAIDS

Taylor hiccupped, almost laughing, as she stared at her inbox. "Mariah just sent me an email."

Hunter's concern changed shape, his expression morphing from worry to wariness. "You know that's not possible."

Taylor turned her phone around defiantly. There, at the top of the screen, was an email from Mariah with a subject line that read, "Surprise." Whatever Hunter said next was like static to Taylor as she tapped the screen and began to read.

It began:

Hi Tay bae

So I'm sure you remember it's our friendaversary tomorrow, so I went ahead and booked us dinner at Luigi's. Yes, even I, pot washer extraordinaire, have to book two weeks in advance nowadays.

Taylor's heart shattered, despite knowing that Mariah was dead. "She scheduled it. It's from two weeks ago," Taylor whimpered.

Hunter looked relieved. "For a second there, I thought ghosts were real."

"Yeah," Taylor sniffled, reading on.

That place is poppin, but you know ya girl has that sweet 25% discount, so we're going to get our drink on. Expect a taxi at 7 pm and dress sexy. Love you forever,

M.

Taylor blinked away tears. "I miss her so much."

"Aw, baby," Hunter cooed, rubbing Taylor's arm. "I know you do."

"Her killer is still out there," Taylor said, beginning a spiraling descent into panic. "What if I'm next?"

"Baby, I'll never let that happen," Hunter promised. "What kind of husband would I be if I left you alone at night?"

Taylor didn't reply but began to breathe heavily. Hunter increased the speed of his rubbing until her pajama sleeve began to burn.

"Look, you're still alive. Nothing bad is going to happen to you. So don't think like that. It won't make you feel any better." He paused, his flat palm turning into walking fingers. "Maybe we can go to bed, and I'll cheer you up. Take your mind off things."

"No, I..."

Running out of words, Taylor shook her head and coiled into herself.

Hunter retracted his hand. "Come on, babe. It's okay. I bet they already know who did this. One of my buddies was hunting by Whitetail Lake and saw Detective Bishop and the sheriff looking at Thimbles's tent. Blood everywhere, he said. They're probably arresting him as we speak."

"Uh-huh," she choked, hyperventilation and hiccups limiting speech.

"Hang on, I know what will help."

Hunter got to his feet, padded across to the sliding doors, and disappeared into the dark kitchen for a minute or two before emerging with a fresh glass of white.

"Last of the bottle," he said. "Drink up. You'll feel better in no time."

She grabbed the large glass greedily with both hands and drank deeply and quickly. When he returned his touch to her back, she leaned into it and turned to him with a sleepy, grateful smile. He was right; it did make her feel better.

"You're right," she slurred, all the alcohol consumed hitting her like an eighteen-wheeler. "It's all over now."

"That's right, babe. It's all over."

She smiled toothily, her eyes growing heavy. When her hand began to tip and the drink began to spill, Hunter grabbed the glass and placed it on the coffee table.

"Want me to carry you to bed?" he asked.

"No, no," she protested drowsily. "I'll have some more in a minute. And I want to finish…" She gestured at the TV, forgetting what they were watching. "Whatever that is."

"Okay," Hunter chuckled, grabbing a blanket as she fell sideways onto the couch arm. He placed a cushion under her head and the knitted throw over her body and kissed her cheek. "I'll go clean up in the kitchen. You take a nap. I'll wake you up in a little while."

"Uh-huh," she said weakly, her eyes fully closed.

Sleep came quickly once those shutters were pulled shut, and it held her down like a two-hundred-pound weighted blanket. For once, she didn't wake every five minutes, and if she tossed and turned, she didn't notice it. This was strange, but not half as bizarre as the dreams themselves, which were oddly dark, empty, and unbearably noisy. Water ran, pots clanged, and footsteps walked past, yet she saw no source until Thimbles appeared on the black horizon.

The old man held Hunter's heirloom knife and pointed it in her direction, his thimble-covered fingertips drumming on the curved blade. He'd come to seek his revenge for her visiting his tent all those years ago, but even from a distance, it was clear that he was dead—his body swollen, rotten, and stinking. This dark world was a place beyond the veil and thus his domain; she had no power or protection here.

She tried to run, but it only seemed to bring them closer together, and when he was close enough to strike, she tried to look away but was forced by unseen hands to look him in his bloodshot eyes. He smiled, and his wrinkles softened, revealing a much younger man that looked less like the infamous shadow lurking in Glenville's edges and much more like her husband.

Bang.

The sound of a door slamming woke her with a start. The room was dark, the fire reduced to smoldering coals, but the reassurance that it had all been a dream calmed her rapidly beating heart. She yawned, and craving her husband's reassurance, she tried to call out, but her exhausted body wouldn't let her. Despite her fear of returning to that terrible place, her eyes shut once more, confident that her protector was home and ignoring the phantom draft wafting from the front door.

CHAPTER TWENTY-ONE

THE DETECTIVE

"**Y**ou're shitting me," Heather cursed. "Please tell me you're shitting me."

"I, unfortunately, am not shitting you," Julius replied apologetically.

Heather didn't reply and instead pressed her forehead against her steering wheel, forcing her horn to do the screaming for her. She held her stance for at least five seconds before sitting, and the world was momentarily silent until her dog's dissonant howls reached the driveway.

"Do you feel better?" Julius inquired with dry amusement.

"Not even a little bit." She sighed. "I can't believe I'm going to ask you this, but can you please repeat yourself? I need to know if this is really happening."

"It is."

"Come on, just hit me again."

Julius wavered. "The blood samples retrieved from Mr. Ford's campsite neither match Mariah's nor were they human."

"Oof. Yeah. That hurt."

"Do you want me to keep going?"

Heather laughed bitterly. "No… but I need you to. What animal did the blood belong to?"

"Deer mostly. Some raccoon. A little fish."

"And Thimbles?"

"Heart attack. Not surprising, considering his alcohol consumption."

"When did he die?" Heather asked, crossing her fingers that the answer wouldn't be "An hour before Mariah did."

"I'd say about two days ago, considering the level of decay."

"That's something, I guess. It means he could have killed her. Shame that most of our evidence is circumstantial, and the rest is 'hearsay' or 'character.'"

"Surely, three is better than zero."

"Barely. Maybe if those three were forensic, physical, and direct."

Julius sighed. "I know. I'd say at least you don't have to take him to court, but I'm sure that's of little consolation."

"It is and it isn't. On the one hand, I don't have to tangle with lawyers, write a deposition, or risk him ending up back on the streets. On the other, he could be innocent and the real killer is still out there. Honestly, I'd spar with the defense any day if it meant knowing for sure."

"Well, for everyone's sake, I hope he was guilty," Julius said. "Mine included. This has been a nasty case."

"Yeah," Heather murmured, zoning out and watching the birds—having recovered from the devastation her horn had wrought on their delicate dispositions—return to the worms. She morbidly mused about whether such a noise could kill such a tiny creature and whether scaring something to death accidentally would make one a killer. She supposed it technically did—murder by lack of common sense.

"Heather, are you there?" Julius asked.

Heather blinked rapidly and sipped black coffee from her travel cup. "Yup. Just trying to figure out how to break the news to the department. Everyone was so happy that we'd caught the killer."

"Well, maybe you still have. There could be another knife out there in the woods, along with whatever rounded object he used to bludgeon them."

"So the axe wasn't a match in shape or blood?"

"No. It wasn't. Which either means he didn't do it…"

"Or he kept his murder crap somewhere else." Heather rubbed her chin. "It's possible. I think Gene's brother-in-law's bloodhound is still kicking. He might be partially blind and mostly deaf, but his nose still works."

"Well, I'm sure your keen senses will compensate for what he lacks."

"Let's hope that's true. I can't screw this up again."

"You won't," Julius assured, always kind, if a little irritatingly optimistic regarding her investigation skills.

"We'll see," Heather grumbled, unconvinced, and pulled out of her driveway just as the predicted flakes of frost began to fall.

"Now, I know this is disappointing, but it doesn't necessarily mean that we've got the wrong man," Heather said, addressing a dozen forlorn faces while trying to harness some of the confidence Julius had attempted to install.

"Yes, it does," Tina interrupted loudly, her face thunderous as she stepped through her open office door.

Heather frowned, stepping down from her imaginary podium but ready to protest. Tina had spent the entirety of her somewhat rousing speech on the phone in her office. Her hearing might have been batlike, but she must've missed great swathes of information to come to that conclusion.

Heather coughed. "As I was saying, the timeline adds up, he was present at both secondary crime scenes, and he was known to stalk women at night. Some have even said he was violent, so as far as I'm concerned, he's still on the table."

Tina waited for Heather to finish, her arms crossed. "A couple of kids just found another body. A fresh one."

All hell broke loose, and as everyone whipped themselves into a frenzy of cross-talking panic, Heather and Tina stared silently into each other's eyes. She didn't need to ask if the body was female; she didn't need to ask if she was found by the lake; and she didn't need to ask if she'd been bludgeoned. Tina's mournful and furious gaze told her everything she needed to know. It wasn't and had never been Thimbles. Their killer was still out there, and a third woman had been butchered by this person right under their noses.

Three, Heather thought miserably. An interesting number, to be sure. There were three sides to a triangle, the world's strongest shape; three stages of existence, birth, life, and death; and three requirements to becoming a serial killer. Murder, murder, and another murder. Excluding Hazel Brock—whose disappearance was, as of yet, nothing more than a coincidence—it seemed their killer had finally graduated.

"All right, everyone, back to work!" Tina thundered. "I let you take it easy yesterday, considering most of you were hungover, but there's plenty of paperwork filled out and vandalism to investigate. Reeves, you're in charge while Detective Bishop, Officer Silva, and I head down to the crime scene. I expect to see some progress when I get back."

Reeves—who most of their coworkers called Uncle Pat— looked a little disappointed not to have made the invite list but dutifully herded the protesting and panicked officers back to their desks anyway.

Secretly, Heather was glad he wasn't coming along. It felt like one more job well done by him, and she'd no longer be the only detective in town. The concept troubled her. What would it be like to try to work a case as Tina's second favorite investigator?

However, as Tina nodded toward the door, it seemed that was a worry for another day, and Heather ventured outside feeling a mix of mild confidence and profound nausea. The chilly, wet wind lashed at her face, and despite being fed up with an unseasonably cold fall, she was temporarily grateful as the shock-induced fire in her face fizzled out.

"So, we're heading to the lake," Heather confirmed, glancing conspiratorially over her shoulders as Tina and Gabriel joined her on the frosty sidewalk.

Tina nodded. "It's close to where we found Mariah. Maybe half a mile away. Close to the boutiques."

"Who is it?" Heather asked, not sure if she was ready for the answer.

"The EMTs were unable to make an accurate identification," Tina said, looking away and swallowing her disgust with a look of distaste. "The victim's face has been… disfigured beyond recognition."

"Disfigured?" Gabriel asked as if he didn't understand the word.

"Caved in," Tina elaborated, even though the phrasing wasn't the problem.

Gabriel blanched, and the phrase hung in the air for a minute before Tina clapped her mittened hands together.

"Right. Follow my car. I'll lead the way."

Despite saying this, it took Tina another thirty seconds to move, her boots glued to the sidewalk but by dread rather than ice. Heather understood. Whatever they were about to see could not be unseen, and for all of them—Heather included—it was going to be a very harrowing day indeed. However, there was no point in making it a long one, so Heather unlocked her car with a loud clunk, snapping Tina from her stupor.

"See you there, Sheriff."

"Yes, right. See you there."

CHAPTER TWENTY-TWO

THE DETECTIVE

Heather watched, brows raised, as Tina abruptly pulled over on Main Street without indicating. They'd only been driving for three minutes and were miles from their destination. Still, after waving apologetically at several honking locals, Heather followed her boss to the curb.

After nearly breaking her neck slipping on a shockingly icy puddle, Tina explained through Heather's partly rolled-down window that she was getting coffee for the CSI crew and the EMTs. She wanted to boost morale and give Lisa a chance to comb the scene before getting in her way. Despite feeling twitchy and impatient, Heather agreed but was dismayed when

Tina beckoned her to exit the car, apparently unable to carry all the coffees on her own.

Tina's choice of café—a narrow newcomer called Pestle & Mortar—was unbearably busy, made worse by the fact that its meager square footage was occupied by every young person in town, several haphazard tables, and enough plants to rival Hallington's botanical gardens. In typical trendy café fashion, everyone else's orders were a mile long, and the two baristas spent more time wooing than they did working. Finally, after nearly twenty minutes, Tina and Heather managed to walk away with their eight black coffees.

By the time they arrived at the scene—another fifteen minutes later—the yellow markers indicated that CSI had already worked their magic. Lisa, blonde with broad shoulders and mile-long legs, had her back to them as they ducked beneath the barrier. Her two protégés flanked her, and together the three of them obscured the body from sight.

It was snowy in the clearing, the layer of white at least an inch thick already. Usually, Heather liked the snow. She appreciated how it made the rest of nature seem exceptionally vivid, but today, as her eyes flicked from crimson splatter to sangria pools, she resented the contrast. There was so much blood. So much that would have gone unobserved in other scenes. In some ways, it made their jobs easier, but mostly, it just made her feel queasy.

Heather chewed her wad of gum into liquid as she made her way forward, awaiting the dreaded reveal with dry open eyes. She wasn't going to balk—not from this, not when it was their fault that the killer had struck again. Gabriel was similarly focused, keeping pace, but Heather could hear Tina panting and snuffling about ten feet behind them. The combination of perpetual colds and a deviated septum had turned her boss into a mouth breather, and Heather was reaching her limit.

Maybe I'll make her a GoFundMe to pay for the surgery, she thought, tossing a scathing look in Gabriel's direction.

He didn't return it. His eyes remained forward, his mouth hanging open. Heather looked forward. Lisa had tilted, turning toward them, her coworkers peeling from her sides. The curtain was being drawn in slow motion, and slowly but surely, the body was unveiled. Heather stopped dead in her tracks, the impact of what lay ahead as halting and painful as running into a brick wall.

The woman was flat on her back, her arms outstretched and her ankles pressed together. A kind of semi-snow angel in a sequin minidress, the powder turned to slush around her from body heat. She wore a strappy high-heeled shoe on her left foot, but her right was bare. Both were reddened from frostbite, though neither was as red as her face, which was as unrecognizable as Heather had feared. Yet she still knew who the woman was. She'd known since she'd first seen the halo of black hair and the quilted Chanel bag tossed to the wayside. The EMTs might have mistaken her for a wealthy waterside resident, some Seattle tech bro's trophy wife, but Heather knew better.

"Oh my god, it's Cheyenne Welch," Tina panted, her brown complexion leaden.

Heather nodded. "So it is the bachelorette party. Somebody is targeting that group of girls in particular."

"Could it be a coincidence?" Tina asked, her flat tone indicating no hope of an affirmative answer.

"I don't think I believe in those anymore," Heather replied.

"I don't think I do either," Tina admitted, the tray of coffees trembling slightly.

Lisa strode forward, meeting them in the middle, and grabbed a coffee, easing Tina's load. She took a long sip and moaned with pleasure. "Oh yeah, that hits the spot. Pestle & Mortar?"

"Yeah," Tina replied quietly. "They're pretty good."

"Mm," Lisa added in agreement before an awful silence—punctuated by sipping—took hold.

"So," Heather eventually said. "Did you find much?"

"A little." Lisa checked her watch. "Ollie volunteered to take the little one to school, and my doctor's appointment isn't until midday. Want me to guide you around?"

"That would be great," Heather replied appreciatively, glancing over her shoulder and noticing that Tina had begun to move toward the EMTs at the edge of the perimeter.

Heather suspected it was less a relinquishing of power and more a tactical retreat from the gore, but Heather was happy to thin the herd regardless. Too many cooks in the kitchen would only lead to more mess. Plus, there were people to call, barriers to guard, EMTs to console—things that Tina excelled at and Heather despised.

"There's not as much this time," Lisa said, guiding them toward marker number 1. "No footprints—"

"No footprints?" Heather questioned, looking around at the snow. "How is that possible?"

"Don't worry, we're not dealing with a killer ghost. Whoever it was just covered their tracks." She gestured to a trampled-down pathway that revealed grass underneath. "Wherever they walked, they wiped," she explained, demonstrating with her own foot and a wiper motion.

"Right," Heather said sourly.

"So, what we do have is blood, her personal effects—aka that handbag—and this." Lisa pointed toward a small hole in the ground with another marker beside it.

Heather tilted her head. It was the kind of cavity a cicada might make. Yet upon sticking her gloved pinky finger inside and feeling the narrow point at the end of the two-inch indent, it evidently did not belong to the underground invertebrate.

"What is this?" Heather asked, looking up at Lisa and Gabriel.

"Beats me," Lisa said. "It looks familiar, but I can't place it."

"Maybe it's from a camping peg?" Gabriel suggested.

"No, it's not big enough," Heather said, standing and wiping the dirt on her slacks.

The three stared down at the little hole, knowing it meant something but having no idea what. They continued to look, hoping it would click, but when it didn't, Heather rolled her head back and turned her attention to the blood. The majority of it was where Cheyenne currently lay, but there was another significant pool about eight feet away. Joining these two patches of cruor was a trail about as thick as Heather's forearm was long.

"She moved," Heather stated. "She fell there and crawled over here."

"Yeah," Lisa said. "And whoever did this watched her do so."

"Why do you say that?" Gabriel asked.

"Her position," Heather said, noting Cheyenne's unnatural arrangement. "They waited for her to die before positioning her like that."

"Jesus, that's so sadistic."

Heather agreed. The identical stab wounds to Mariah—which had not been made public knowledge, ruling out a copycat—and the severity of the facial injuries were far from lost on her. She had a lot of experience with dead bodies and had seen them in all shapes and forms, but she'd never quite seen a face so irreparable—a real close-casket case, as one of her Seattle coworkers used to say.

She feared they were right, that even with almost a century of expertise under his belt, even Foster Ellsworth would be able to do very little with what was left. Even her beautiful hair had been crudely cut into a choppy mess of lengths and scattered around her. It reminded Heather of her mutilated childhood Barbie dolls, and though it was silly, she felt as if she owed the plastic women an apology.

All of it spoke of burgeoning violence, and more than the awfulness before her, that scared Heather. The town wasn't safe. A serial killer was on the loose, and it was time to take action. Curfews, patrol, you name it, and she'd enact it. This was not happening again, not on her watch.

"I hope this doesn't sound callous," Gabriel began and looked at Heather expectantly, who gestured for him to continue. "Cheyenne was famously vain. Not in a bad way, just that she put a lot of effort into her appearance. Especially her hair and face. To destroy both, I don't know… it almost seems like whoever did this wanted to take her down a peg."

Heather's stomach lurched; the black coffee and minty gum were a bad idea on an empty stomach. "Yeah, it seems that way. It also seems like they're gaining confidence. To mutilate in this way…"

"You keep saying *they*," Lisa noted. "Surely you don't think a woman did this?"

"At this point, I'm not ruling anyone out," Heather said, looking up at her. "Most of the killers I've put away have been men, yes, but I've certainly met my fair share of killer women. In fact, a woman nearly killed both of us just a few weeks ago."

Lisa's frost rash deepened into a brilliant pink, and she looked away. "Yes, of course. Sorry, that was silly."

Heather was almost too focused, too exhausted, to feel guilty, but not quite. However, just as she opened her mouth, an apology brewing in her brain, Gabriel interrupted, speaking just as the wind picked up coming in fast off the water's surface.

"What?" Heather asked blankly, his words inaudible.

"She's not wet!" he yelled over the swell.

"What?" Heather asked again, though she'd heard him loud and clear.

He pointed to the sequins. "She's not wet like the other two were."

He was right. Aside from the blood pooling in her sunken parts, the top of her legs and dress were bone-dry to the touch.

"They wanted us to find her," Heather yelled back. "They didn't try to hide her. They left her here for us to find." Heather looked around. "And the trees are sparse. You can see this clearing from the road if you look hard enough."

"What else did you find?" Heather asked Lisa—who, ever the professional, seemed to have shaken her humiliation off.

"Her purse," Lisa answered, pointing at the quilted Chanel bag in the middle distance.

Heather meandered toward the bag before dropping low to the ground by its side. With gloved hands, she rummaged through the crap—tampons, tissues, lip gloss—and laid it out on a plastic sheet that Lisa quickly provided. None of it was of much interest until she found something strange—a hidden pocket, clearly custom, embedded in the side. Heather unfolded the Velcro flap, unzipped the compartment, and retrieved Cheyenne's violet smartphone. Heather inspected it momentarily, not quite understanding, until Gabriel leaned over her and flipped it open. The screen looked seamless, and though Heather had never seen anything like it, she tried not to be distracted by technological advancements and pressed the On button. The screen lit up, the battery still half full.

Hoping the others and Cheyenne—wherever she might be—would forgive her, Heather moved quickly back toward Cheyenne.

"Sorry," she said, lifting Cheyenne's stiff hand, uncoiling her index, and pressing her blue finger against the Home button. As it unlocked, Heather was grateful that Cheyenne had been a Samsung woman, not an Apple addict. A passcode—or worse, Face ID—would've taken a lot longer to figure out.

The phone unlocked with a click, and Heather ventured to the most logical place—the chock-full Photos app. There she was immediately bombarded with nudes of all varieties. Many of the images and videos were extremely graphic, and not all of which were of Cheyenne. From a quick glance, it seemed about half either featured men or starred them.

"Look no further than her phone," Heather murmured, repeating what Cheyenne had told her about Mariah at the diner.

"Jesus," Gabriel whispered, looking over her shoulder as Heather swiped and scrolled.

Heather picked up speed, similarly repulsed by the bombardment of genitalia, but then Gabriel stopped her.

"Wait, go back."

She did—one, two, three times, until she landed on a selfie of two fully clothed people. They were smiling, tucked away in a Sherwood's booth with drinks in hand. They were clearly drunk, and their body language transcended romance and crossed the threshold into unbridled lust. She knew their faces well—Cheyenne Welch and Hunter Sherman, his hair much grayer than the last time Heather had seen him.

"Holy crap," Lisa exclaimed. "That's my son's boss. You don't think..."

"I do think," Heather confirmed.

Lisa gasped, causing Heather to flinch. "That hole! I *knew* I recognized it. My son and his dipshit friends were pretending to be javelin throwers with this tool from the mill. I've got holes like it all over my yard. What's it called?" she asked herself, rubbing fiercely at her forehead and leaving it red.

"A peavey," Gabriel said. "My dad works there too."

"What's a peavey?" Heather asked.

"It's a heavy metal pole with a sharp point that they use to separate wood," Gabriel explained.

"A peavey," Heather repeated, looking between Cheyenne and the hole and remembering what Julius had said about rounded objects. "I think we have our murder weapon."

CHAPTER TWENTY-THREE

THE DETECTIVE

With Thimbles permanently struck from her list, the once–crystal clear case had become impenetrably murky. Thimbles, much like Mason, had made sense. They were both violent men. They killed animals, got into frequent bar fights, were aggressive drunks, and had complicated relationships with women. They also had the means, knowledge, and ability to efficiently subdue and kill both in weaponry and hunting experience. These were the types of men that murdered.

According to William of Ockham—a fourteenth-century English philosopher—the more straightforward answer was often the right one. In Heather's opinion, Ol' Billy had no idea what he was talking about. Thimbles had been simple. What remained was not.

Who sent the texts? Was Alain really sleeping with Mariah? Did Taylor know about Cheyenne and her husband? How do two separate affairs overlap into the same string of murders? These were the questions Heather was asking herself, and even though she had yet to answer any of them, she knew that the tandem affairs held the key.

The affairs had also added two new players to the arena: Hunter and Taylor Sherman. That made four, and in some ways, all four were credible suspects, but none of them, as of yet, were perfect fits.

If Taylor knew of her best friend's betrayal, that was a strong motive for enacting her revenge. Yet there were plenty of holes there. Was she strong enough? Was she hateful enough? And why Mariah? Why her own sister? If anything, Heather was less worried about Taylor striking again than she was about her being next in line.

As a suspect, Leah Durand suffered from the same conundrum. Kill the mistress, sure, but why the others? She might have made Heather's gut twist and tighten and was almost certainly hiding something, but she lacked the motive for serial killing.

Alain was more confusing still and bordered on joining Thimbles in verifiable innocence. The hotel had sent over the CCTV, confirming that he had not left the night of Mariah's death. Like his wife, he also had no link to the other women, especially considering neither were Glenville residents. However, due to his possible extramarital involvement, Heather was not ready to bench him just yet.

Hunter was the most suspicious. He was large, strong, cocky, and not only had a big secret but had been Mason's best friend. Maybe they killed Jenny together, and he was just carrying on the legacy. However, despite having encountered plenty of domestic homicides, Heather couldn't quite marry the passionate affair with the state of Cheyenne's body. Usually, these situations culminated in strangulation or a gunshot. Such extremities and something that seemed so premeditated and meticulous were unusual. How could anyone do that to someone they'd loved? Or perhaps, she reasoned, love had never been part of the equation, only lust. Much easier to take a pipe to a piece of meat than a soulmate.

Heather needed to start answering questions, so she'd offered to deliver the bad news about Cheyenne to Taylor herself, hoping to dot some *i*'s in the process. Thus, she had spent the past half hour driving past the Sherman residence, waiting for Hunter to leave. For a long list of reasons, she thought it best to speak to Taylor privately.

On her third loop around town, she stopped at the red light and looked over to the community center. There was a martial arts class occurring on the other side of the big window, and Heather recognized two faces in the crowd. Briana Taylor—Gabriel's overenthusiastic ex-girlfriend—and fry cook extraordinaire Victor Wu. Just as the young man was called up to the mat to face off with the instructor, a car honked from behind, and Heather took off, turning back toward Suburbia.

Hunter was gone this time, saving Heather from having to ask Joe, Ollie, or Martin to fake an emergency at the mill. She pulled up, took a deep breath, and approached the house. She rang the bell, and Taylor answered with a smile. She was glowing, her skin dewy and smooth and her happiness reaching her eyes. Yesterday, Heather would have been happy to witness this transformation, but today it only exacerbated her guilt for bearing bad news.

"Good afternoon, Mrs. Sherman," Heather said.

Taylor rolled her eyes and scoffed. "If I can call you Heather, please, for the love of God, don't call me Mrs. Sherman. Makes me feel old."

"Fair enough. Can I come in?"

"Sure," Taylor said hesitantly, her expression falling. "Is this about Mariah?"

"Sort of," Heather replied. "It'd be better if I came in."

They both looked around; nosy neighbors were dotted around, pretending to idle as they openly stared.

"HOA?" she asked.

"Yeah," Taylor said, scowling at the onlookers. "In retrospect, we should've moved into my place instead."

"No kidding."

Taylor stepped back, ushered Heather in, and slammed the door shut. "Ugh. Those people are vultures." She examined Heather's face and shifted uncomfortably. "Do I need a drink for this?"

"You might," Heather admitted, even though it was only two in the afternoon.

"Do you want one?"

Heather wanted to say yes but shook her head. "I'll take a glass of water."

"Suit yourself," Taylor said, her voice already shaky.

She turned, the skirt of her rust-colored peasant dress spinning out, and strode down the narrow hallway to the door at the end. She yanked it open, and as Heather struggled to remove her shoes with cold hands, she could hear Taylor clinking glass against glass from afar. By the time Heather joined in the large sage green kitchen, Taylor had poured their drinks and situated herself at the table.

There was a beautiful bouquet in the middle of the table, and Heather gestured toward the peonies and wildflowers.

"From Hunter?"

"Mariah, actually," Taylor said.

"Mariah?" Heather asked, lowering herself into the seat opposite Taylor.

"Yeah. It's our friendaversary, and apparently, she was more of a planner than I realized. Scheduled email nearly gave me a heart attack."

"I bet."

"It's actually been nice. Now that the shock's over. Hunter's been on his best behavior, and it feels like my best friend is still alive. All in all a great day until you showed up."

Heather sighed. "Sorry."

"Don't be. Just tell me why you're here."

"I won't beat around the bush," Heather began.

"Wait," Taylor interrupted, a hand raised.

Heather waited patiently as Taylor brought the rim to her lips and sipped. Her eyes were already wet with tears when she gave the okay in the form of a shaky thumbs-up.

"I'm so sorry to have to tell you this, but we found Cheyenne's body this morning by the lake."

A squeak escaped Taylor's tightly drawn lips, and she clasped a hand over her mouth to silence the mournful scream that begged to be let out. She kept it there for almost a minute, rocking and turning red before fading back to tan. Slowly, she dropped her hand, opened her mouth, and let out a loud guffaw. It was a honking sound that was unexpected when coming from such a demure woman.

"Oh, I see. This is a joke!" Taylor exclaimed, throwing her hands around and splashing her drink across the table. "Ha ha, how funny, all four of my friends are dead. You know, you're lucky I have a sense of humor, Heather. Most people wouldn't find that funny at all."

"Taylor," Heather said softly.

"No, I get it. It's funny. Really," she insisted, wiping a hysterical tear from her cheek.

"Taylor. Look at me."

Taylor fell silent and made eye contact as she swayed back and forth. "What?" she asked, another giggle escaping her forced grin.

"Taylor, I'm not joking. You know I'm not."

Taylor watched Heather carefully before crumpling. She swallowed and retched, letting out a raucous belch before covering her mouth. "Sorry, that's… You're serious… You're serious… You can't be serious," she pleaded.

"I'm so sorry," Heather said, pulling tissues from her bag and simultaneously striking Taylor from the list. No one was this good of an actor.

Taylor didn't grab them and let the tears stream freely as she shifted one hand to her stomach and the other to her glass. "Did her parents…"

"Yeah. Her dad did. About an hour ago. It was a tough identification, but it's her."

"Tough identification?" Taylor questioned. Heather wished she hadn't said anything, but fortunately, Taylor didn't push. "So it wasn't Thimbles?"

"No, it wasn't. Thimbles is…" Heather hesitated. "Also dead. We found his body two days ago, and he'd been gone for a few days by that point."

"Wow. You must be loving your job right now," Taylor said sarcastically. "So whoever did this is still out there?"

"Correct."

"You think I'm next, don't you?"

"Yes," Heather answered, sticking to her promise of not beating around the bush. "Which is why I need you to pack a bag and go stay with your parents. We'll have two officers monitor the house 24-7 for your protection."

Taylor furrowed her brow. "My parents' house? Why can't I stay here?"

Heather looked at the bottle of wine, wishing she'd accepted that drink, and said, "This might be hard to believe. Especially coming from me. But I think you could be in danger if you stay here."

Taylor said nothing, so Heather continued, "We found photos of Cheyenne and Hunter on her phone together. Sexual photos. Videos too. Selfies of them kissing. We believe from the time stamps that the affair had been going for the past year."

Taylor did not react as Heather expected. There was no laughter, tears, screaming, or throwing Heather out of her home. Instead, she lowered her glass carefully and spoke steadily, "I knew it… I mean, I thought I was crazy, but I knew it. He was gone all the time, and she had a crush on him in high school and… This is crazy." She shook her head as if Heather had just relayed some scandalous celebrity gossip.

Eye of the storm, Heather thought.

"You know, on the night she died, Mariah had something she wanted to tell me," Taylor said. "I guess I've just found out what." She laughed again, bitterly this time. "And I've spent all this time convincing myself that he'd never… In fact, yesterday, I *was* convinced. He was so sweet I just told myself I was being crazy. Glad to know I'm not crazy, less thrilled about being an idiot."

"You're not an idiot."

"Sure."

"Where was Hunter last night?" Heather asked.

"I know what you're thinking, Detective," Taylor said sternly. "You think he killed Mariah for wanting to blab and Cheyenne because he had me back in his arms or whatever, but

I know my husband, as ridiculous as that sounds. He might be a cheating pig, but he didn't do this."

"Where was he?" Heather pushed.

"He was here!" Taylor half yelled, the hysteria returning.

Heather raised an eyebrow.

"Okay. I'm pretty sure he was here," Taylor admitted. "I fell asleep on the couch, but I don't think he went anywhere."

"You think, or you know?"

"I *think*, all right? I was really deeply asleep, which is weird because..."

"Because?"

"I'm usually such a light sleeper." She looked down at her wine glass, and though Heather didn't know why, the gesture chilled her.

Sensing that Taylor was running on low battery, Heather kept pushing, hoping to squeeze a little more out of her.

"Did you know Mariah was also having an affair? With a married man."

"Wait, what?" Taylor asked blearily.

"Yeah. Cheyenne told me that Mariah was sleeping with a man named Alain Durand over in Hallington. She received a text about it apparently, as did his wife, Leah."

"No, Mariah wouldn't do that. She had a rule about... Doesn't matter. Cheyenne told you that? Why wouldn't she... Why were they... Wait, did you say Leah?"

"I did."

"Not Leah Reed, by any chance?"

"Yes," Heather answered, the pendulum of confusion swinging to her side of the table. "I'm assuming you know her."

"Oh yeah. We were best of friends back in school actually. Had a major falling out just before senior year. She hated our guts so much she actually moved towns, if you can believe that."

Mentally noting down that Leah would also need to be under police protection if she too was in the group, Heather paused before asking, "Why did you—"

Perhaps the most crucial question of all was cut short by the sound of a car pulling up outside. The pair fell silent—Taylor's black-rimmed eyes wide and frightened—as footsteps approached the front door and keys jingled.

Hunter was back, and it was too late to leave.

CHAPTER TWENTY-FOUR

THE DETECTIVE

The door opened, and Hunter hollered down the hallway, his voice breaking. "Is it true? Is she dead?" Keys in a bowl, boots thumping to the ground. "Taylor? Where the hell are you?"

Taylor pursed her lips and topped up her drink as she stared expectantly at the doorway, not bothering to answer. His emotion confirmed everything Heather had said. If she hadn't believed it then, she certainly did now.

"Taylor!" Hunter roared, storming ahead.

It was then—with her head turned, the light shining just right, and the layer of foundation dripping from her jaw—that

Heather noticed a mark on Taylor's cheek. A bruise left by the monster that barreled toward them. Hunter let out another roar of pain, and Taylor's flinch was enough to guide Heather's hand to her gun holster.

"If you're wearing those goddamn headpho—" Hunter burst into the room, his mouth open to continue the onslaught until he saw Heather. He gaped silently, stiffening, and cleared the phlegm from his sinuses. "Oh. You're here."

"I am. I was just confirming Cheyenne Welch's death," Heather said, turning her chair toward him.

Hunter looked as if she had slapped him. "So it's true."

"It is."

"Why are you crying?" Taylor asked coldly as Hunter wiped a trickle of snot on his sleeve. "I mean, you hated Cheyenne, right?"

"Because it's messed up!"

"Was it not messed up when Jenny and Mariah died?"

"Of course it was," he insisted, his pained expression switching to neutrality in a split second.

"You're a shitty actor," Taylor laughed.

Or an amazing one, Heather thought, staying silent and letting Taylor run the show.

He stuttered. "I… I'm upset *for* you, babe."

"You've never been upset for me before."

"That's because I never wanted to make it about me. This just caught me by surprise." Then he said to Heather, "Why haven't you"—pointing an accusatory finger—"caught this asshole?"

Taylor sighed, calm and collected, as she scraped her chair back and stood. "I'm going to pack a bag and go to my parents' house."

"What? Why?" Hunter demanded, his sniffling ceased for good as indignation and rage took hold.

"Well, Heather here says she found your penis all over Cheyenne's phone."

Despite the situation, it took everything in Heather's power to prevent the laugh threatening to burst out of her.

"Wha-what?" Hunter stuttered, looking as if the carpet had been pulled out from under him, but in a way that seemed like he was expecting it enough to keep his balance.

"Wha-wha-wha?" Taylor mocked. "Be a man and own up to it."

"I don't know what you're talking about."

"Your penis is all over Cheyenne's phone," Taylor repeated loudly.

"Well, admittedly, those photos were harder to attribute to you," Heather admitted. "But the videos cleared it up for us."

"They're photoshopped!" Hunter yelled over his wife's laughter. "Do you know what they can do with AI now? Someone is setting me up. I'd never cheat on you."

"Mr. Sherman, have you ever heard of digital forensics?" Heather waited, watching the veins bulge in his wide neck. "I guess not. Well, digital forensics is where very smart people receive digitally stored evidence and analyze it. They're able to tell if a photo is faked."

The red rose to Hunter's face. "It was just a fling. It didn't mean anything."

"A year, Hunter. You were sleeping with her for a year. One of my best friends."

"Taylor... I can explain. I love you," he moaned, and Heather started to wonder if the apology had more to do with his secret than Cheyenne's death.

"You're so full of shit it's coming out of your eyes," Taylor jabbed as Hunter began to cry again. "How do I know you're not behind all of this? Trying to bury your dirty laundry and keep me locked up with fear."

Hunter stepped forward, his pointing finger aimed like a gun at Taylor's face. "Stop saying that," he warned. "I am not a killer."

Taylor laughed. "Yeah, because you look so sane right now."

Hunter ignored her, turned toward Heather, and lowered his hand. "I heard you found blood at Thimbles's tent. Do you have him in custody?"

"Thimbles is dead," Taylor said. "But I bet you already knew that. Probably why you're so upset. No one else to take the blame."

Hunter froze, stunned. That hit him where it hurt, and though she didn't sound remotely convinced by her own accusation, she seemed satisfied with the outcome.

"I didn't do this," Hunter said, looking at Heather desperately.

"I'm not here to arrest you," Heather clarified. "Just providing an update and moving Taylor to a safer location while we proceed with the investigation."

"So, I'm a suspect?"

"Everyone's a suspect, Mr. Sherman. Especially men whose genitalia appears on the belongings of the deceased."

"That doesn't mean I did anything!"

"No, but I'm sure you can agree that maybe you and your wife need some time apart," Heather said. "You'll be able to contact her, and I will provide updates to both of you."

"You can't just—" he protested, a hand reaching out for Taylor.

"She can't what?" Heather asked calmly. "Leave? Your wife is not your property, correct?"

"Yes."

"So she can leave whenever she pleases?"

"Yes."

"Excellent. Now take a seat. Taylor, please head upstairs and pack. Take your time, and when you're done, I'll escort you out."

"You don't have to do that," Hunter growled. "I'm not going to hurt her."

"Mr. Sherman, as I've stated, I cannot know if that's true. You certainly could be innocent, but considering the affair, the bruise on your wife's cheek, and the fact two women have been bludgeoned to death within the last week, you can understand my desire to be safe rather than sorry."

"Sure," Hunter said, sitting down hard, struggling to keep his temper tamped.

Contented by his settling, Taylor exited the room.

They waited in silence, hearing Taylor rummage and slam drawers upstairs—all the while, the threat of Heather's holstered weapon kept Hunter firmly in his seat. Only when Taylor emerged in the doorway did he move to stand. Taylor strode toward him, and he looked momentarily relieved as if she might kiss him goodbye or change her mind altogether. Instead, she snatched up the bouquet, turned sharply, and headed toward the door.

Heather looked at Hunter, who looked as if he'd had his soul ripped out of his nostrils, and said, "I'll be in touch, Mr. Sherman."

Outside, Heather helped Taylor pack her belongings into her car when Taylor stopped abruptly.

"This is going to sound weird, but do you want to get dinner at Luigi's?"

Heather, taken aback by the answer, didn't answer. Instead, she asked, "Why?"

Taylor flushed. "Oh, it's just... Remember the friendaversary I mentioned earlier? Mariah booked us a table at Luigi's for two. I called, and it's still booked into their system, and I just feel like I have to go. I was going to take Hunter, but..."

"Why me?"

"Because I don't have anyone else."

Heather nodded, a knot forming in her throat. "Sure, why not. We'll say I'm a police escort. Official business."

"Thanks, Heather."

"Just doing my job, ma'am."

Taylor smiled for the first time since Heather had arrived at her home, loaded the last of the suitcases into the trunk, and handed Heather the keys.

CHAPTER TWENTY-FIVE

THE DETECTIVE

Although Hunter's lack of a solid alibi, relationship with the deceased, and life-ruining secret made him a near-perfect suspect, Heather wasn't ready to pull the trigger on an arrest. The evidence that he was more than an adulterer was flimsy, and there were still questions to answer, namely regarding the Durands. Not only were the texts and Leah's gut-churning behavior still a mystery, but Leah had also failed to mention that she had once been friends with the deceased. Surely, your husband sleeping with your ex-best friend would be an aspect worth mentioning? Unless there was a reason to hide it.

Heather intended to uncover exactly what that reason was. So she walked over to the Sherman residence at first light, retrieved her car, and ventured to Hallington. Despite Tina and Gabriel's protests, she made the journey alone. The last person Leah would open up to right now was a man, and Tina, happily married and stinking of roses, was a worse sidekick still. What Leah needed was commiseration, and Heather—divorced and lacking in love—was going to give it to her.

Baby Theo was screaming as she pulled up, and as Heather opened her door and turned toward the sound's direction, she stifled a yelp. Leah Durand was staring at her through the front window, the dark circles around her eyes emphasizing the effect of her glare. She was dressed in a white nightie, her arms limp and at her sides, her exhaustion having reached a familiar summit. Leah might have looked like a ghost, but Heather knew she was the only one doing the haunting here.

She offered an apologetic wave, regretting her decision to surprise the woman, and made her way down the path despite Leah's blatant displeasure. She knocked, and to no one's surprise, Leah did not answer. Heather, however, was not giving up that easily. As it turned out, judges gave little credence to gut instincts, so a search or arrest warrant would be near impossible to obtain. So knowing it was now or never, she opted to sit on the stoop and wait her out. It took about four minutes for her to consider resignation, and just as she was about to leave for fear of being arrested by Hallington PD, who by all accounts was much more organized than Glenville could ever hope for, Leah opened the door and looked down, her lip curled with disdain.

"What do you want?" Leah asked.
"I just want to talk to you."
"I think we've talked enough."
"I disagree."

Leah huffed. "Okay, make it quick."

Heather got to her feet and looked into the dark house. "Can I come in?"

"No."

"We found Cheyenne Welch."

"I heard. I also heard she was having an affair with Hunter Sherman." Leah tutted. "Seems to be a lot of that going around. Interesting that it all stems from that group of harpies."

"So, you do know them."

Leah threw her hands up. "Yeah. Okay? I know them."

"Why didn't you tell me?"

"Because I knew how it would sound. One of my best friends turned bullies screws my husband and shows up dead? Yeah, that doesn't look great for me."

"Neither does lying," Heather said.

"You cops love to twist the truth, don't you?"

"Really? I hadn't noticed."

Leah rolled her eyes. "Facetious too, huh? Well, I didn't lie. I just kept my mouth shut."

"Well, you're talking now. Would you like to continue?" Heather asked wryly, trying to match Leah's personality.

"If it will make you leave."

"It will."

"Great." She waited, arms folded. "Go on, ask your questions."

"So, you said Mariah bullied you."

"She bullied everyone. They all did. Cheyenne, Taylor, Jenny, Hazel. I knew Hazel from Girl Scouts, so I joined her friendship group when I transferred schools. A few months later, I had a wake-up call and cut them out of my life. Apparently, that wasn't an option, and they turned on me, and I became their newest punching bag."

"Do you mind if I write this down?" Heather asked, retrieving her notebook and clicking her pen.

"Go ahead."

"Thanks. So, what caused this turning point?"

"Nothing in particular," Leah said. "I guess just a bunch of little things turned into a big one."

There it was again. That funny feeling that Heather couldn't quite place. A tightening in her gut and her chest. It was akin to anxiety, and she wondered if Leah's body felt the same way as she lied to a detective's face.

"Your husband's infidelity must be even more painful considering Mariah's role in your life. It must have felt like your bully had returned."

Leah laughed. "Oh, she never stopped. There have been numerous 'pranks' over the years. I guess they just decided to up the ante."

"What kind of pranks?"

"Oh, getting me fired from my barista job by leaving fake reviews, glitter bomb cards congratulating me on my marriage, a size zero dress delivered while I was eight months pregnant with a note that said 'For motivation.' That sort of thing. Fun stuff, you know?"

"Jesus," Heather said, pausing her scribbling to look at Leah. "That's…"

"Shitty? Yeah. But I never took it very seriously until they involved my husband. Honestly, it just made me feel sorry for them. Imagine being twenty-eight and still stuck in high school."

"No thanks," Heather replied with visible disgust. "So, what's going on with you and Alain?" When Leah didn't answer, Heather continued, "I'm sorry to ask. I know marriage is hard at the best of times. I myself just went through a divorce and—"

"Save it, Detective. I don't need your friendship. What I need is to sit down."

"Oh, of course."

Leah began to walk away into her house, leaving her door wide open. She paused and looked back. "Are you coming?"

Heather perched awkwardly on a chair in the corner of a living room that had clearly once been a classy place for adults but had since been wrecked by Hurricane Theo. Everywhere Heather looked, she noticed disarray. The laundry was unfolded and mounting high, the white table was covered in coffee cup rings and mysterious stains, the pillar candles on the china cabinet sat in wax pools, and the many half-drunk mugs were filled with fungus. It also stank faintly of dirty diapers and strongly of baby powder—the combination of which did little to quell the bile that had been slowly rising since Monday morning.

Leah returned, having thrown a chunky-knit sweater over the top of her nightgown and slipped on some thick winter socks. Theo was no longer crying, and the relief Leah felt was palpable, aiding the tightness that Heather had been feeling in her chest.

Despite her relaxed body language, Leah looked decidedly gray in the dim, curtain-filtered light. She collapsed onto an armchair and slid down, her legs stuck out far in front of her and her rear positioned at the seat's edge.

"Do you have kids?" she asked.

"No, I don't."

"Then you have no idea how hard it is doing this alone, but let me tell you, it's hard, and I'm exhausted. I haven't left the house in days."

"No chance of Alain moving back in then?"

Leah let out a whimper, her stoic expression crumbling. "Jesus," she muttered, rubbing her already-sore eyes and wiping away tears before they had the chance to fall. "Look at what motherhood has done to me. You know, before I got pregnant, I hadn't cried in about seven years. Now I cry every single day."

"Hormones are a bitch."

"That they are."

"So, what's going on with you and Alain?"

Leah glared. "You're not going to drop it, are you?"

"It's my job, Mrs. Durand."

"Yeah, and what a job it is. How did you get into it?"

"I wanted to help people."

Leah laughed coldly. "It's funny, you all say the same thing as if the rest of us don't want to help people too. How many people do you think you actually help, and how many more do you hurt?"

"You're deflecting," Heather said.

Leah pushed herself upright with her palms. "Alain is in the hospital. He tried to kill himself last night at around two in the morning. Fortunately, the old beam snapped. Owes a lot of money to the hotel, I imagine."

Heather flinched. "I'm sorry to hear that. Is he all right?"

"He'll live. You know, he left a note. Says he's innocent but knows that no one will ever believe him and he can't live without his family." She swallowed, and her voice grew thick. "He'll be back home tomorrow. I have no idea if he cheated or not, but I refuse to let those evil bitches ruin our lives. For all I know, Mariah hit him with her car all those years ago on purpose."

"You really think she would do something like that?" Heather asked.

"Come on, you're a detective. You should know that anyone is capable of doing anything."

"I know. I'm just surprised. It doesn't match up with the women I've met. Especially Taylor and Jenny."

Leah tilted her head, greasy blonde hair falling into her eyes, and bore a look of pity. "Then you're more naive than I took you for. You should really work on that."

"Are you happy they're dead?"

"Come on," Leah protested with a laugh.

"It's just a question. Feelings and opinions aren't crimes," Heather said.

"But they can be evidence," Leah countered.

"Only if you're guilty."

Leah surveyed Heather. "I'm not happy. I'm relieved. And I'm sure I'm not the only one. They were nasty pieces of work, and I think they got what was coming to them."

"You think they deserved this?" Heather asked, keeping her voice psychiatrist-neutral.

"I think the best way to deal with a viper is to bash its brains in. Maybe that makes me sound guilty. Honestly, I'm too tired to care."

"I don't believe anyone deserves death."

"Really?" Leah asked, her eyes wide in fascination. "Not even the Paper Doll Killer?"

"I think prison is a more fitting punishment," Heather answered coolly. Had anyone else asked a question so pointed, it might have been harder to deflect, but Leah was running on fumes.

"I'm inclined to agree, but these girls were never going to go to prison. So, in the absence of, it's not a bad second option."

"What have they done that's so terrible that you believe that?" Heather questioned, leaning forward. "There has to be something because otherwise you would not sit in front of a police officer and tell them the victims of a serial killer deserved to die."

Right on cue, Theo began to scream from upstairs, and Leah stood. "That's enough for today."

"Of course," Heather said, getting to her feet, her backside completely numb.

She followed Leah out into the foyer, and although Leah yanked the door open impatiently, Heather paused momentarily, noticing something she hadn't on the way in—a metal softball bat in a glass case perched on the shelf above the coat hooks.

"Do you play?" Heather asked.

"I did," Leah retorted, her grip on the doorknob tightening as Theo continued to wail. "Another thing ruined by the den of snakes."

"Maybe you should get back into it."

"I think that ship has sailed. Now, if you don't mind."

Heather snapped out of her haze and hastily stepped through the doorway. "Thanks for your time, Mrs. Durand."

"Yeah, yeah. Contact our lawyer if you want to talk again, or better yet, leave us the hell alone."

"Of course," Heather said, walking away. "Have a good afternoon. My regards to Alain."

"Oh, and, Heather," Leah called after her.

Heather turned. "Yeah?"

"Don't let them ruin your life too."

Slam.

CHAPTER TWENTY-SIX

THE DETECTIVE

Jeff and Diane Brooks's house looked exactly the same inside and out as it had done that fateful day in 2018 when Heather had questioned them about the death of their daughter, Jenny. The plinth-mounted couches were still cobalt blue, and the same hardback books about travel, food, and interior design were piled in the center of the glass coffee table. The only new addition was one of those televisions that could be disguised as artwork. It hung on a distant wall in a gold frame, and though Jeff delighted in showing Heather this miraculous piece of technology, he seemingly had no idea how to use it.

"We don't use this room much," he admitted, confirming what Heather had always assumed. "I prefer the 'man cave' downstairs while the ladies tend to use the rec room, which is toward the back of the house. The rec's okay, though what it lacks in craft beer, it certainly makes up for in surround sound." He looked at Heather. "Would you like a beer? I just cleaned the lines, and I owe you one for getting my daughter away from that asshole." He shook his head. "We've always liked Hunter, so this whole thing has been quite the shock."

"I bet."

"So, how's about that beer?"

While Heather had always wanted to see a man cave in the flesh, she kindly denied the offer. "Honestly, I need to get going pretty soon."

Jeff smacked his forehead. "Forgive me, Detective. Here I am talking your ear off about a TV when you need to talk to Taylor."

"It's fine," Heather said. "It is really cool."

Jeff chuckled. "Thanks for humoring me. Taylor is upstairs in her bedroom." He paused, a familiar, solemn expression washing over his round face. "Don't push her too hard. That girl's been through far too much. You make her cry, and I won't be as welcoming next time. Understood?"

"Yes, sir."

"Great. First door on the left."

"Thanks."

Halfway up the stairs, the distinctive voice of Britney Spears beckoned Heather like sirensong to Taylor's childhood bedroom. The door was half open, and Heather knocked as she peered in. Taylor startled and turned with a hand on her chest before laughing. Heather, too, felt a cardiac pang from the reaction and waved sheepishly as both of them turned red.

"Sorry," Heather said.

"No, it's fine, just couldn't hear you over—" Taylor picked up a CD "—*Now That's What I Call Music* number 57."

"Having a nostalgia trip?"

"Hard not to in this room," Taylor laughed, gesturing around. "I moved out when I was eighteen."

Heather stepped inside and looked around at a room fit for a teenage princess. The queen-sized bed and the accompanying ruffled white sheets were covered in stuffed animals, the carpet was pastel pink, the posters were of pop stars, the shelves were full of DVDs and diaries, the vanity table was covered in an impressive collection of body sprays, and a faux-marble plinth bore a prom queen scepter and crown.

"Wow," was all Heather could say.

"Ugh, I know. It's so cliche. Cheerleader dates football player and is crowned prom queen."

"Yeah, I think I've seen that movie before."

"It's called *Prom Night*," Taylor joked wryly. "Starring Jamie Lee Curtis. It's pretty good, you should check it out. Might help you solve the case."

"I'll do that," Heather said, taking a seat at the fluffy pouf next to the vanity table.

"So, how can I help you, Heather?" Taylor asked, pressing Pause on the pink CD player just as Kelis's "Milkshake" began to play.

"So, I went to Hallington today to speak with Leah Durand, née Reed."

"Please tell me she did it. That would make my day."

"Guessing you hate her as much as she hates you, huh?"

Taylor frowned. "I don't hate anyone. I just want the case solved. Did she say she hated me?"

"Does that surprise you?"

Taylor barked a laugh. "Yeah! Considering I haven't seen her in a decade."

"That's not how she tells it."

"And how does she tell it?" Taylor asked, arms crossed, suddenly looking and sounding as teenaged as her room.

"That you and your friends have been 'pranking' her over the years," Heather replied, sounding like a mother segueing into a lecture.

"What kind of pranks?"

"The mean kind. Sending her a size zero dress as 'motivation' when she was heavily pregnant, for example."

Taylor held up her hands. "I don't know anything about that, I swear. I'm way too old for pranks."

"And the others?"

"I guess it does sound like something Cheyenne would do," she admitted, grimacing. "She had a bit of a mean streak."

"Apparently, you all did."

Taylor stiffened. "Isn't everyone an asshole in high school?"

"Maybe, but I'm not asking about everyone else. I'm asking about you."

Taylor clucked her tongue. "Leah's the suspect here. Why the third degree?"

"Because suspects need motives, and making her life hell is a good one," Heather explained.

"Okay, maybe I was an asshole in high school, but Leah was no saint either, and I don't know anything about these so-called pranks, I swear." Taylor unfolded her arms to cross her heart. "What else did she say?"

"That she thinks Mariah's 'affair' with her husband was orchestrated by your friends. That Cheyenne took that photo and sent the text."

"No way. They wouldn't do something like that," Taylor insisted.

Heather raised an eyebrow.

"Fine, maybe they would've back in high school, but not now. Seriously, that's too far even for them. I mean, who would do something like that? That could ruin someone's life."

"See, that's what I'm trying to figure out. Maybe she had dirt on them. Maybe they envied her marriage. I have no idea. And where does Jenny fit into all of this? It's like I've got an outline of a story, but I need somebody to color it in. This all has to stem from something. Nobody kills three people, maybe four, for no reason."

"I wish I could help you, but beyond schoolyard bullying and girls being bitchy, I really don't know anything about any of this."

"So, you have no idea what she was talking about?"

Taylor shrugged. "Sorry."

"So why did you fall out with Leah?"

"We just stopped liking her!" Taylor said, raising her voice. "I feel like I'm taking crazy pills. We have a nice time at Luigi's, and then Leah goddamn Reed puts all this crap in your head, and you come over acting like my friends deserved to be killed."

"Of course, I don't think…" Heather exhaled. "I can't help get your friends justice or arrest the person who did this if you keep secrets from me."

"I'm not." Taylor pinched the bridge of her nose. "I'm suddenly tired, Detective. And hungry. I think we should save this conversation for another day."

"Sure," Heather said, getting to her feet. "Feel free to call me if anything else comes to mind."

"Yeah, sure."

"I really hope we can be allies, Taylor. I'm close, but I'm running in circles around something. I'd like to know what that something is."

Taylor watched Heather move to the door, her mouth ajar. She stood, her folded arms morphed into a self-embrace.

"I don't know what else to say about Leah, and despite what I said yesterday, I still don't think it's him…"

"But?" Heather pushed.

"But I have a prenup."

Heather paused, hand on the doorway. "What kind of prenup?"

"The kind where if he cheats on me and I file for divorce, I get everything. The money and the house."

"Thank you," Heather said, a splash of color landing on her rough sketches, adding depth and texture to Hunter's part of the page.

CHAPTER TWENTY-SEVEN

THE DETECTIVE

Heather sighed and fell sideways on her couch, her head landing on a sleeping Beam and her phone pressed to her ear.

"I don't know. Both Leah and Hunter fit the bill. She has the bat, the hatred, the lust for revenge, and her baby is her only alibi. He has the peavey, the secret, the prenup, and a pretty hazy alibi. But there's still so much I don't know and can't figure out. Sure, she might kill Mariah and Cheyenne for faking the affair, but why Jenny? Why the gap between kills? What happened in high school?"

"And then we have Hunter," Gabriel said. "A guy who loses everything if his wife discovers his affair. But then again, why Jenny? He wasn't even married yet, and Cheyenne's cloud data goes back to 2015, and though there are plenty of guys on there, Hunter doesn't make an appearance until 2022."

"Maybe Mason really did kill Jenny," Heather theorized, looking at her corkboard. "Or Hunter helped him do it."

"I can get with that theory. They get high, head to the diner, and then she runs off, and they follow her."

Heather sat up. "Things get out of hand, they hurt her and have to kill her to save their own skins."

"Mason takes the fall, but Hunter's caught the killing bug. He suppresses it, but then years later, he feels his future and life slipping through his fingers again, and he falls back into old habits."

"Thimbles becomes the scapegoat," Heather continues. "But throws a spanner into the works by dying."

"Case solved," Gabriel said.

Heather chuckled. "It's a solid theory. You know, you're a pretty smart kid. Ever considered becoming a cop?"

"Nah. Sounds like a headache."

"Smart."

"I think he's our guy. Sure, Leah's a strong suspect, but didn't she just have a baby?"

"She did," Heather confirmed, her head bobbing up and down in sync with Beam's unconscious breathing.

"And how would you describe her physically?"

"About five feet four, petite, slender."

"And Hunter is a brick shithouse," Gabriel stated.

"He is," Heather agreed.

"And a cocky one. The kind of guy who considers himself a jack of all trades."

"But is a master of none," Heather said. "I know. It would explain the poor knot-tying. Plus, Leah was a Girl Scout."

"So, we've got him?" Gabriel asked, the slight crackle of his cigarette audible through the receiver.

"Maybe. I just need something more to hold on to. Hunter is rich, well connected, and there's no way he's speaking to us without a lawyer. Without DNA or an eyewitness, they'll have him out of the station in a few hours, and we will lose in court."

Gabriel groaned. "This is so frustrating. What did Julius say?"

"Well, once again, there was no DNA present. No signs of sexual assault, no fingerprints, nothing. However, despite the bludgeoning's increased severity, the knife wounds and bruising were identical."

"Bruising?" Gabriel questioned.

"Yeah, on the upper arms. I assume from being pulled along and pinned."

Gabriel took another noisy puff. "Jesus. Was there anything in the report about the weapon?"

"Likely a hunting knife. There's a curvature there. And as far as the bludgeoning goes, he says it's curved and metal. He also said I don't want to know how he can tell the difference between wood and metal."

"Jesus. Have you considered exhuming Jenny and getting him to examine her too?"

"Her parents would never agree to that," Heather said.

"But they're lawyers!" Gabriel protested.

"And she's their daughter."

Whatever Gabriel said next, Heather didn't hear it. She'd pulled the phone away from her ear as soon as the first crunch sounded. Someone was walking around outside of her house, making their way up the alley between her and next door, trampling the frozen leaves.

"Got to go," she whispered to Gabriel.

"Wait, wha—"

She hung up and leaned forward, the couch springs creaking as she plucked her belt from the coffee table and unsheathed her gun from its holster. She listened to the person walk back and forth on the other side of the closed blinds above her TV, and her dogs joined her, their ears pricked. Heather looked at the two on the far couch and shushed them as she stroked Beam's back and held his collar. By some miracle, they all stayed silent as whoever was outside made their way to the front door and scraped their feet on the concrete.

Heather pictured a myriad of ghosts standing on the other side of the barrier, eager to seek revenge for their arrest or execution. There were the truly dead, like Dennis Burke, and the egregiously alive, such as the Paper Doll Killer or Gustavo Molina. All of them wanted a piece of her, and though none could logically be at her front door, they haunted her still as the mysterious stranger failed to knock.

Then the sound came. A tepid rapping. Heather didn't want to answer, her body almost refused, but she forced herself to the door, gun in hand. Telling herself she could take on whoever it was, she turned the lock and pulled the door ajar. The chain held it in place as she peered through the gap, and the light of the living room shone on Taylor Sherman's face.

"Can I come in?" she asked, teeth chattering, wearing nothing but thin pajamas and rubber boots.

Heather closed the door, unhooked the chain, and reopened to find Taylor walking away.

"Come on!" she called, entrance wide open.

Taylor turned, and her eyes locked on to the tip of Heather's gesturing gun. Whether Taylor was too cold to care about the weapon or a closet gun nut, Heather wasn't sure, but the woman ran inside and into the warmth. She stood by the console, frost melting from her boots as she rubbed her hands together. The dogs wagged and made happy grunts before quickly going back to sleep. Usually, their increased age was a point of sadness for Heather, but today she was grateful for their elderly laziness.

"Not allergic, are you?" Heather asked. "Because this might as well be a hair factory."

"No, I love dogs."

"But you don't have one?"

Taylor shook her head. "No. After Jenny, I just... I can't put my heart on my sleeve like that. Not voluntarily."

"I understand."

"No husband?"

"No husband," Heather confirmed. "No kids."

"It must be lonely."

"Sometimes. Do you want tea or something?"

"Whiskey," Taylor stated. "And don't pretend you don't have any."

"All right," Heather relented, despite smelling alcohol on Taylor's breath. She grabbed two glasses from the liquor cabinet and poured doubles into each. It had been a while since she'd foraged for bourbon since she rarely drank alone, but the situation called for it, if only to convince Taylor they were on an even keel.

"Your house is weird," Taylor said.

"Thanks," Heather replied dryly.

"Sorry, it's just not what I expected."

Heather handed Taylor her drink as the woman sat between Turkey and Fireball and then moved back beside Beam and turned on the heating. The furnace roared to life, but Taylor was still shaking even as the room warmed. Looking blue, she pulled a hairy blanket over herself, not seeming to care that her flannel navy pajamas would be coated in short prickly hairs.

"Did you walk here?" Heather asked.

"Yeah," Taylor said, raising her slush-covered boots.

"Does anyone know you're here?"

Taylor shook her head.

"How did you get past the officers?"

"Went out the back and jumped the fence," Taylor admitted.

"Jesus," Heather groaned. "You know they're there for your safety. The curfew too. You know how much crap they're going to give me for stationing them in your backyard?"

"I know. I'm sorry, I just needed to talk to you."

"Okay. What about?"

"Terrible things," Taylor whimpered, her grasp tightening on the glass as she took a sip. She pulled a face as it burned, but as the warmth settled, Heather saw her expression soften slightly.

"Terrible things?" Heather prompted.

Taylor stared at her for a long time, and Heather half expected her to pull a knife from her pants and admit to the murders. She made a noise, a choke catching in her throat as her eyes watered. When she began to sway, Heather wished she hadn't left her gun so far out of reach, and when she started to shake, Heather realized she was no longer cold but affected by the terrible chill that came with unearthing something terrible.

"You were right," Taylor whispered. "We all did something unforgivable, and now somebody is after us."

CHAPTER TWENTY-EIGHT

THE BRIDE

2012

"What do you think?" Cheyenne asked, revolving on the fluffy vanity stool and unveiling what she'd been working on for the better part of an hour. Her dark eyes were ringed with black, a perfect cat-eye lining the upper lid, and her new contour kit enhanced her already-angular bone structure. Her eyebrows were sharp, her false lashes looked heavy, and her lips were covered in a pale iridescent gloss. Frankly, Taylor—who had yet to master the complexities of liquid eyeliner—thought it was a little much, but she undeniably looked like a superstar.

"It looks good," she said. "I wish I could get my eyebrows to look symmetrical."

"Well, mine are naturally symmetrical, which makes it easier," Cheyenne replied sympathetically, jutting her lower lip. "What do you think about the hair?"

Cheyenne's glossy black hair was parted down the middle, and the twists at her temples were held in place with sparkly, pale-blue butterfly clips the same color as her racerback crop top. She stood and spun, taking the phrase "If you've got it, flaunt it" to new heights. She tottered in her high-heeled sandals to scattered applause, her whale tail making an appearance from the top of her white miniskirt while a shimmery pear drop gem swung fiercely from her navel.

"You're basically in your underwear," Hazel said, exchanging disapproving looks with her symbiotic parasite, Leah. "You look like *Dirrty*-era Christina."

Cheyenne halted and put a hand on her bony hip. "Don't be such a prude, Hazel. And Christina wishes."

"Yeah, Hazel," Mariah chimed in, forever loyal. "Maybe if you showed some skin, you'd finally get laid."

"All I'm saying is that it's a bit… Y2K," Hazel said, not backing down.

"Whatever, Hazel. As if you know anything about fashion. You're as bad as Jenny half the time."

"Hey!" Jenny exclaimed indignantly. "I think you look nice."

"What do you think, Tay?" Cheyenne asked, staring her only standing friend in the eye.

Taylor, halfway through pouring another round of sour apple shots, paused. "You look hot," she said, stating what Cheyenne was fishing for.

Cheyenne faced the mirror. "I do, don't I?"

Taylor scoffed and finished pouring the drinks. Cheyenne had changed a lot since turning eighteen three months ago. Suddenly she was allowed to wear what she wanted, and her mom even took her to get her nose and belly button pierced while the rest begged their parents for a second lot of lobe studs. It was hard to watch your best friend's liberation from curfews and open-door policies and not feel like a total baby. She even managed to buy alcohol without needing an ID from the dodgy liquor store by the gas station. Still, Taylor tried not to be too jealous. There weren't many other perks that came with being held back a year.

Cheyenne smiled at all of them as Taylor handed out the drinks. "Of course, all of you look hot too. I love you bitches. Cheers!"

Taylor caught sight of herself in the mirror, dressed up in Cheyenne's clothing for the first time, having lost some puppy fat toward the end of junior year. She felt far from comfortable in the halter-neck, leopard-print, shirred body-con dress and black ankle-strap heels, but she couldn't deny that she looked good in the getup.

"Why are we so dressed up anyway?" Leah asked.

"Well, we want to look nice for our guests, right?" Cheyenne asked.

"I thought it was just us," Taylor said, rushing to open a window as Mariah lit a cigarette without asking.

Cheyenne grinned at her silently while everyone else looked around cluelessly. Everyone except for Jenny, who stared down at the carpet, her ears turning pink and her nails in her palms.

"Jenny, who's coming?"

"I don't know, just Mason and Hunter," Jenny lied, not breaking eye contact with the floor.

Taylor tutted, stormed toward her little sister, pinched an ear between her thumb and forefinger, and lifted Jenny from the bed.

"Ow! Get off of me, you lunatic!"

"Who else?"

"Nobody."

"Tell. Me. Who's. Coming."

"All right!" Jenny squealed. "Just let me go." Taylor relinquished her grip, and Jenny sat back down, rubbing at her now-crimson ear. "I invited Penelope."

"Penelope?" Taylor repeated in disbelief. "Penelope we hate? That Penelope?"

"Yes. Jesus. Why are you being a freak about this?" Jenny asked.

Cheyenne laughed. "Yeah, Tay, why are you being a freak about this?"

Taylor looked around at the others, her arms held out wide. "Am I the only one who thinks this is insane?"

The other three shook their heads.

"Great. At least I'm not crazy."

"You're definitely not crazy," Hazel replied, obviously baffled. "Why would you do that?"

"Seriously, why?" Leah interjected. "Actually, scratch that—why would she agree to come? I mean, no offense, I love you guys, but you can be a real pack of 'See You Next Tuesdays' when it comes to that girl."

"Jenny here has been patching things up with Penelope at some adorable little pottery class," Cheyenne said. "So, I asked her to invite Penelope to our little soiree so we can all apologize and start over with a clean slate for senior year."

"Ugh, Cheyenne," Hazel moaned. "This is going to be so weird."

"Come on, guys. It'll only be weird if we make it weird, and we're way too old for all of this mean girls crap. Personally, it's giving me acid reflux. Plus, Jenny said she was excited to come over, so don't be a bitch. I'm talking to you, Mariah."

"She did seem pretty excited," Jenny admitted, looking up at Taylor.

"I don't want to apologize to that slut," Mariah added, wiping the sting of cigarette smoke from a smudged eye.

"What did I just say about being a bitch?" Cheyenne snapped. "It's not a good look on you. Neither is being a child. It's bad enough that you dress like one. Black dungarees and a striped T-shirt? Seriously?"

For a split second, Mariah looked as if she might cry, but instead, she stuck out her tongue and raised her middle finger before returning to her pack of noxious cigarettes.

"Besides," Cheyenne said, "we don't want this kind of unpleasantry hanging over our future success. Imagine if one of us becomes a celebrity and she hits the tabloids with stories about insults and catfights. I've seen plenty of promising careers take a nosedive over that sort of thing."

"So, you acknowledge you're a bully then?" Leah asked, eyebrow raised.

"God no," Cheyenne said. "Well, maybe a bit. But my granddad says weak kids need bullying. If he didn't get thrown in the trash as a kid, no way he'd have been tough enough to make it in New York as a chef. Penelope will thank us one day when she's a CEO who takes no shit. You have to break a horse for it to become a champion."

"You're a psycho," Taylor laughed, shaking her head.

"Is it so hard to believe I have good intentions?"

"Yes!" everyone said in sync.

"Well, you'll see when you're older. A big part of being an adult is—"

"Oh, please spare us," Hazel interrupted. "You're a year older, we get it."

"All I'm saying is that I used to hate spicy food, but after forcing myself to eat it a hundred times over, I love it. Maybe Penelope is just an acquired taste and worth pursuing."

"Whatever," Taylor said. "Pass me the bottle, I want to be drunk for this."

In their too-high heels, they made the perilous journey from bedroom to rec room and got the party started while Hunter and Mason drank beers and shot the resulting cans with BB guns in the backyard. Taylor checked in on her boyfriend now and again, glancing through the glass sliding doors and watching proudly as he kicked Mason's ass repeatedly. She smiled smugly at her sister, who rolled her eyes as she turned on the rotating party lights and turned up Cheyenne's playlist on the speakers.

Through the doorway—and the banister of the staircase in the adjoining hallway—Taylor could see the others in the kitchen setting up snacks, opening pizza boxes, and pouring drinks into plastic cups. When the doorbell rang, they—all considerably inebriated by this point—dropped what they were doing and cheered.

"Better let your friend in," Taylor said coolly to Jenny.

"Please don't be an asshole," Jenny scolded, getting to her feet.

"It's not me you have to worry about," Taylor replied, glancing between Hunter in the backyard and Mariah in the kitchen.

The rest of the group, excluding the boys, filtered into the room and waited expectantly for their guest. They reminded Taylor of a pack of wolves waiting for a deer to stumble into their territory, poised to ambush. Taylor did not join them in hovering and instead planted herself firmly on one of the many beanbags and sipped her cherry-flavored drink with a scowl.

Jenny and Penelope entered the room to more cheering, and Penelope awkwardly waved before being bombarded with hugs. Taylor didn't move to embrace but offered a tight-lipped smile and reluctantly got to her feet.

"There's pizza and booze in the kitchen," Taylor said over the chatter. "Help yourself."

"Thanks," Penelope said shyly, tucking the front strands of her elegant bun nervously behind her ears. Her lips were painted plum, her smoky eye shadow extended her slender eyes, and she wore a black velvet A-line dress paired with a pair of flat ballet-style shoes. Begrudgingly, Taylor admitted that Penelope looked nice, even if she kept these thoughts to herself.

"Hawaiian and pepperoni," Cheyenne added. "The best two, wouldn't you agree?"

"Oh, I'm a vegetarian," Penelope replied. "But I'll take a drink."

Taylor held her breath, waiting for a catty comment, but instead, Cheyenne snatched Penelope's wrist and said, "Let me show you to the bar," before dragging the helpless fawn into the kitchen.

"Maybe this won't be so bad," Jenny said hopefully, sidling up to her sister.

Taylor frowned, not yet convinced. "Yeah. Maybe. Go make her some toast, would you? I don't want her drinking on an empty stomach."

"Seriously?"

"*Seriously.* Remember Leah's first party with us?"

Jenny shuddered. "Vividly. Mariah still calls her pea soup." She sighed dramatically. "Fine, I'll make her some stupid toast, though it's not like you don't have hands."

"She's not my guest."

Every bit the typical sixteen-year-old, Jenny stomped into the kitchen but pulled out the niceties as she made Penelope one pathetic slice of buttery toast. Taylor gave her sister a disapproving look as Penelope thankfully ate it, but she supposed it was better than nothing as Cheyenne lined up seven oversized tequila shots.

Grumbling to herself, Taylor joined the others and plucked a shot from the row as Cheyenne nudged one toward a wide-eyed Penelope. She looked like a puker, and Taylor waited for the fallout as the girl gulped down her shot on the count of three. Surprisingly, perhaps to everyone, she held it down without blanching, and when Cheyenne topped her up to the brim, she eagerly went again.

"I love a girl that can drink," Cheyenne cooed as she lined the glasses back up and filled them all of them halfway, except for one, which she filled to the brim and slid back toward Penelope.

Taylor stared at Cheyenne, who eventually noticed and mouthed, "What?"

Taylor shook her head and drank her shot. It was fine, she convinced herself. Penelope had a lot of catching up to do and seemed more than capable of handling her liquor.

Fortunately, after that, it was back to plastic cups full of unpleasant soda-vodka mixtures, and one by one, they returned to the rec room, where they threw themselves down on comfy furniture and cast furtive glances at a still-mute Penelope.

It took about an hour of forced conversation and heavy drinking for her to finally open up, and when she did, she bloomed splendidly, and even Taylor found herself enamored with the girl, her anecdotes, and her biting sense of humor.

"I'm sorry for how we've all behaved," Hazel started after a side-splitting story about a holiday abroad that had come to a disastrous end.

"Yeah, seriously," Leah added.

Cheyenne kept the ball rolling. "Yeah, we've been a bunch of cows. And I'm not too big to admit it."

Jenny nodded. "We've talked already, and you know how I feel. But I'm sorry too."

Taylor hesitated. She hadn't warmed up as much as she'd liked but more than she'd hoped, so she swallowed her pride and said, "I hope you can forgive us."

Penelope's giggle was punctuated by a hiccup. "I mean, you guys only made my life hell for the past year." Everyone held their breath, waiting for salvation. "But what's a year, you know? In the grand scheme of things."

It was a well-earned dig, but when she laughed, they followed and raised their newest round of shots—a concoction of rum and Kahlua that Taylor feared would end up in the sink or toilet at some point—high above their heads.

"To clean slates!" Cheyenne exclaimed, and down the hatch it went.

"What's all the cheering about?" Hunter asked, stepping through the back door with Mason in tow.

The pair of them did a double take as they caught sight of Penelope kneeling on the rug at the center of the room.

"Penelope?" Hunter asked, laughing loudly. "What the hell are you doing here?"

"Forgiveness," Penelope slurred, her face flushed and shiny.

Taylor watched with a frown as the boys looked the fresh meat up and down. They were a pair of hungry dogs staring at a steak they knew they weren't allowed, and Taylor saw red. Despite her glammed-up look—a makeover he'd frequently encouraged—Hunter hadn't even glanced in her direction since earlier that day. All because she'd rejected his advances after he'd tackled her to the bed. She'd claimed it was because of her lipstick and the curlers in her hair, but really, it was because he was pathetic when he begged, something he frequently did and something she often gave in to out of sheer frustration. He'd never overstepped the line and always accepted the no, but he did so bitterly, leaving them both out of sorts until she said yes days later.

"This is girl time," Taylor said loudly. "Get your beer and go back to your guns."

"Yeah," Penelope began, giggling and hiccupping. "Go back to your—"

Vomit everywhere. The girls ran to Penelope's side, scraping her hair back as the boys mocked and jeered before moving toward the kitchen. Furious with them—not Penelope, but furious all the same—Taylor and Jenny looked at each other and lamented telepathically as a multicolored pool ran into the gaps between the floorboards.

"Jenny, Hazel, take her upstairs to the guest room to sleep this off and give her some pajamas," Taylor instructed. "I'll try to clean this up."

"Aw, but I don't want to go," Penelope said, her eyes unfocused, as she reached pleadingly for Taylor's hand.

"Too bad, drunky," Cheyenne jeered. "Next time, eat some damn pizza."

Penelope frowned, clearly wounded, as she was lifted to her feet by the pits and escorted up the stairs. Taylor shot Cheyenne a nasty look, who batted her lashes innocently as she moved to the kitchen to gather cleaning supplies.

Thanking her lucky stars that the floor wasn't carpeted, Taylor succeeded in her task as Hazel and Jenny descended the stairs. Taylor looked up at them, throwing her latex gloves in the bucket.

"Is she okay?"

"She'll be fine," Jenny said. "She didn't look as pale after going for round two. We left her some water and put her in the recovery position."

"Great," Taylor exhaled, sobered somewhat as she gathered her supplies. "I think that calls for another drink."

Drunken *woo*'s agreed, and the party was back on. Having heard each other's stories a million times, they opted for dancing and karaoke instead while Leah—who was not as hardened as the rest—slept on the couch underneath a blanket.

After about an hour of getting drunker than Taylor thought possible, the boys returned. They were in a similar state, having nabbed the rum to take outside, and looked around with sloppy grins, their gazes low and nowhere near anyone's eyes. Despite feeling silly for doing so, Taylor puffed her chest out, hoping to bear the brunt of their lechery. It didn't do the trick, and their eyes continued to wander, landing frequently on Jenny in her low-cut top.

"What do you want?" Taylor asked, failing to keep the disgust out of her voice.

"Just grabbing more beers," Hunter said, not seeming to notice the discomfort among the group.

"Where's Penelope?" Mason asked.

"Upstairs, sleeping," Jenny answered, seemingly ignorant of her boyfriend's x-ray vision.

"Aw, that's too bad," he pouted. "It seemed like she was having fun."

"Get out of here," Cheyenne scolded. "You heard Taylor. This is girl time."

"All right, all right, don't get your period everywhere," Mason mocked.

Hunter, clearly sensing the rising apathy, grabbed his friend by the jacket and guided him toward the kitchen. "Sorry to bother you, ladies," he sneered before departing.

They stayed in the kitchen for a long time, for which Taylor was grateful. She didn't want them in the rec room, but firearms under the influence seemed like a bad idea. So she left them to it as gossip and deep discussions replaced the dancing and singing. Then, at around two in the morning, she noticed the boys slide their stools back from the kitchen island and head up the stairs. The conversation grew quiet as they all watched them make the trudging ascent, but soon enough, the chatter started up again, and Cheyenne turned the music up.

Taylor's instincts were on fire, but she fought them fiercely with a hose. It was late; they were drunk and had gone to sleep in their girlfriend's beds. That's all there was to it. Nothing sinister. Just two guys going to bed.

"Hey, what's wrong?" Jenny asked, realizing her sister had long since tuned out their conversation.

Taylor turned to her and smiled. "Nothing. I'm just being stupid. What were you saying?"

Then she heard it. The creak of the second step. Slowly, she craned her neck and watched the doorway, hoping it would be Penelope coming to rejoin the party. Instead, Hunter and Mason appeared on the landing, a little sweaty and muttering conspiratorially between hearty laughs. They moved into the rec room, making foul gestures and sounds as they slid the back door open and returned to their rum. The pit in Taylor's stomach was hard and heavy, but she tried to ignore its weight, hoping the alcohol would dissolve the lump. It was fine. It was nothing.

It was nothing. It was nothing. It was nothing.

CHAPTER TWENTY-NINE

THE DETECTIVE

Now

"**B**UT IT WASN'T NOTHING, WAS IT?" Heather asked, harrowed by the imagery that Taylor had provided in abundance.

Taylor shook her head tearfully, wiping away the saline, one of her fake nails missing and her fake tan patchy.

"No, it wasn't nothing. It was something. We didn't even notice her leave, but in the morning, she was gone. A few of us—bar Leah, who was asleep, and Cheyenne and Mariah, who thought we were crazy—put two and two together and tried to call her. Not that we voiced our fears out loud, but something was wrong."

"Where were Mason and Hunter at this point?"

"Asleep in our rooms," Taylor answered, combing her soggy hair with her fingertips, grazing her scalp until it was raw. "God, I saw him when I woke up. You know how even the toughest guy looks sweet when he's asleep? He looked perfect, and I just couldn't… I felt awful for thinking badly of him."

"But you still did."

"Yeah," Taylor said. "I just prayed Penelope would pick up and tell us she was just hungover and wanted to be in her own room. But…," she continued, her voice cracking, "she didn't. All of our attempts at contacting her bounced back. She'd blocked all of us on everything. Then we knew something was really wrong. Cheyenne made excuses, saying she only forgave us because she was drunk and then sobered up and changed her mind, but I knew it wasn't us. I knew it was them."

"Then what happened?" Heather asked, writing in her notebook without apology or permission.

"The guys came downstairs, hankering for pancakes, but then they saw our faces, and… they got angry. That was the second confirmation. The third came when I outright asked them if they'd…"—Taylor paused to breathe—"raped that poor girl. They denied it, of course, but Mason was a shitty liar, and soon even Cheyenne woke up to what had happened. They still never directly admitted it, but they stopped protesting and let us figure out what to do."

"What did you *want* to do?"

Taylor hesitated. "Only Leah wanted to go to the cops. The rest of us were scared, I guess, or selfish. I lean toward the latter nowadays. We didn't want to be implicated. Didn't want to get busted for underage drinking either."

"So, what *did* you do?" Heather asked.

"Well, Jenny and I broke up with Mason and Hunter on the spot. Though I'm ashamed to admit that only lasted six weeks for me and two for her."

"Wow," Heather said, passing judgment aloud for the first time. "Why? Why would you go back to someone like that?"

Taylor drained her drink. "I want to say it's because we loved them, but if I'm being honest with myself, it's that we didn't care as much about Penelope as we'd tried to."

Heather stared at Taylor in disbelief. Here was a woman she'd liked, that she'd gone to dinner with, that she'd gone above and beyond to protect. She hated that it lent credence to her "trust no one" ideology—something she had been trying to unpick from her tightly woven psyche.

"Don't look at me like that," Taylor sobbed. "You think I don't feel guilty? That I don't wish I'd made a different decision? I was a kid!"

"Yeah, so was she," Heather said coldly. "So, Penelope didn't go to the police."

"Nope. We were waiting for it, the day the sirens came, but it never happened. Nearly died from lack of sleep in the meantime."

"Poor you." Heather tapped at the page, dotting it with ink. "So, does anyone else know about this?"

"Just you."

Heather sighed. "Well, I guess I have a new suspect. What's Penelope's last name?"

Taylor shook her head. "It's not Penelope."

"She has plenty of motive."

"It's not her," Taylor said firmly.

"Did she move country or something?" Heather asked.

"Her mom did. After the divorce."

A cold chill ran through Heather. "Taylor, what happened to Penelope?"

Taylor looked up at Heather, tears running in torrents down her blotchy face.

"Taylor," Heather insisted, "what happened to her?"

"She killed herself," Taylor moaned. "Slit her wrists in the bathtub two weeks later."

Heather put her head in her hands, her drink perched between her knees. "Jesus," she muttered. "That's…"

"I know," Taylor wailed. "I know. And I know it's all my fault. I've spent years convincing myself that it wasn't. That it was Jenny for not giving her enough toast, Cheyenne for the shots, or the guys for what they did to her, but it was me too. I saw them go upstairs, and I did nothing."

Taylor stood up suddenly, crying too hard to speak, and held out her hands, her wrists pressed together, begging to be cuffed.

Heather at her hands and took a swig. "Sit down. I'm not going to arrest you. You committed a gross misdemeanor by not reporting them, but the statute of limitations ran out on that a long time ago now. However, there's no time limit on rape in the first degree, so if you want to come with me to the station, then you can finally do the right thing."

"No," Taylor said, retracting. "I can't. He's my husband. It was a mistake."

"You know that's not true, and I know you know he's done more than that," Heather implored.

Taylor fell back to the ground, knees pressed to her chest.

"Taylor, we can't let him get away with this. He raped that girl and killed your friends. He killed your sister. Taylor. Taylor. Taylor, wake up!" Heather yelled.

"It's not him. It's not him."

"It *is* him," Heather insisted. "Your friends, Jenny, they wanted to come clean, and he killed them for it."

"No, no, no," Taylor croaked, sounding on the verge of vomit. Then her nose erupted, and crimson flowed with pressurized intensity from her nostril.

As it started to dribble all over Heather's belongings, she stood suddenly, handing a pack of tissues over and hovering over Taylor with concern.

"Taylor," Heather said sternly. "I need you to listen to me. What I'm saying makes sense. Your husband is a violent man. He hurts women, he hates women, and he will do anything to keep his reputation. I mean, who's to say he and Mason didn't kill Penelope too?"

"No, they wouldn't. He wouldn't. It was ruled a suicide."

Heather leaned back. "Yeah, I've heard that one before."

"What about Leah?" Taylor asked, painfully hopeful. "Maybe she's seeking revenge. Sure, she kept the secret, but she hated us. I mean, really hated us. She hated us so much she dropped out and moved town. Got married right away. Changed her last name. Tried to leave us all behind."

"And you guys just couldn't let her go," Heather snarled, her upper lip curled in disgust.

"I...," Taylor began, "I wasn't involved in any of the pranks."

"But you knew about them."

"Some. But I had no idea about the affair."

"Well, whether it's her or not, the police are parked outside her house, keeping her safe and contained. Just like you should be."

"It's her," Taylor insisted.

Though Leah was undoubtedly still on the board, Heather only had eyes for one suspect after the story she'd heard. Hunter Sherman. Leah had certainly been hiding something, and though Heather was unsure if this awful act was the entirety of it, her being the killer seemed less and less likely.

"You think I'm a monster, don't you?" Taylor sniveled, a pathetic writhing worm on the carpet.

"I don't know. Is a person a monster if they knowingly marry one?"

"I think so," Taylor murmured, the blood making her hard to understand. "And I think I deserve whatever's coming for me."

Heather sat, sighed, and swilled the ice around in her empty glass. "I have my opinions on what you've done, but I'm not going to let you die. So, tonight you'll sleep here, and tomorrow morning I'll drop you off at your parents' house and double the security. No more sneaking out."

"Thank you," Taylor whimpered.

"Think about what I said about coming clean. Without your testimony, there's nothing I can do to get Penelope justice. Or your sister. Or your friends."

"It's not him," she said again. "It's just not."

"We'll see about that. Let's get you into bed."

CHAPTER THIRTY

THE DETECTIVE

After the confession, the night took a frustrating turn. The problems started with Taylor asking for dry clothes. Considering the state of her soggy, hairy pajamas, this seemed a reasonable request, so Heather happily handed over some spares. Then Taylor asked for a toothbrush. Once again, Heather acquiesced her request, providing a toothbrush and a cupful of mouthwash. Taylor thanked her, but she wasn't done yet. Next came a glass of water, socks, a spare blanket, a snack, and a shower. Heather wavered at the final request. It was already after midnight, and she was lagging, but Taylor seemed desperate, so Heather—a more reluctant host than usual—agreed.

Taylor's shower took over forty minutes, and Heather spent the entire time outside the door, coffee in hand, knocking intermittently, though she knew Taylor was alive and breathing from the consistent sobbing. Though Taylor's guilt was a good sign for her life going forward, Heather was losing patience with her behavior. Mainly because she was struggling to drum up any sympathy for any character in that terrible story besides Penelope. Yes, Leah had been asleep, but she still chose not to go to the police.

Taylor emerged from the shower wearing a smile, the spare pajamas, and Heather's most expensive perfume. It was as if nothing was wrong. Despite Heather's unhappy body language, she even attempted to hug the detective who'd saved her from the bleak weather. Taylor, unfortunately, was not as cute as a stray animal, and it took most of Heather's self-control not to shove her away. Still, she kept her at arm's length and put her foot down. It was time for bed.

Alone in her room, Heather debated whether or not taking a sleeping pill was a good idea. Ultimately, she decided against it. It was too late, and she didn't want to oversleep. Irrationally, she was also afraid that Taylor would realize what she'd done by confessing and crush Heather's skull with the cast-iron Dutch oven that was soaking in the sink. Less irrationally, she was concerned that Taylor might tell Hunter everything, and he might show up and attempt to murder them both. Neither situation allowed for unconsciousness, so Heather attempted to sleep the good old-fashioned way and failed miserably, leaving her tired and irritable.

In the morning, she knocked on the spare room door, woke Taylor up, loaded her into the car, still dressed in borrowed clothes, and drove her to her parents' house. It was awfully reminiscent of her time as a patrol officer, which had been chiefly spent returning drunk teens to their worried parents.

Jeff and Diane were even standing outside, dressed in nightgowns. Who could blame them, after what happened to Jenny? Heather felt another pang of irritation as she turned to look at Taylor, half asleep in the back seat.

"You see your parents?" Heather asked.

"Yeah," Taylor groaned, her hangover beating her into submission.

"Don't scare them like that again. If you want to see me, call me, and I'll pick you up."

Taylor nodded sheepishly.

Heather sighed. "And I hope you do. I really hope you do."

"I'll sleep on it."

Heather twisted back and pressed a button to unlock the back doors. "Yeah, you do that. Stay safe, Taylor."

"You too, Heather."

Heather kept an eye on Taylor as she trudged toward her parents with a trash bag filled with her own clothes. They looked worried, furious, and confused all at once. Heather could relate, and as she drove toward the rising sun on the horizon, she pulled over, called Tina, and told her everything.

Her reaction was much the same as Heather's had been. If the affair with Cheyenne hadn't been motive enough, rape in the first degree and a subsequent suicide certainly were. So it was decided Hunter and Mason killed Jenny to keep her quiet, and Hunter killed the rest later on once they too considered coming clean. What they needed now was Taylor's testimony and any other evidence they could get their hands on. Unfortunately, upon looking up Penelope's name in the local system, Tina came up blank.

"She's seriously not in there?" Heather asked, grabbing the pack of newly purchased gum from the cup holder. "Nothing about a suicide investigation in 2012?"

"Nope. There's a domestic homicide from 1966 involving a woman named Penelope Armstrong, but that's it. I guess I can ask Ellsworth for his burial records. I imagine he runs a tighter ship than Gene ever did."

"While I'm sure you're right—considering what Gene has told me about his file-keeping habits—I don't think Foster can help us with this."

"Why?" Tina asked through gritted teeth, mumbling about Gene under her breath.

"Well, according to what I squeezed out of Taylor this morning, Penelope was buried out of state. Something about a family plot. She had no idea where though."

"Somebody has to know something," Tina insisted, her voice distant as she slammed metal drawers and flicked through what sounded like manila folders.

"What about the state death records?"

"I can't search them without a last name. Taylor really couldn't remember it?"

"She 'thinks it began with a *Y*,'" Heather mocked, using air quotes that Tina couldn't see.

Tina shook her head and tsked. "That's really something, isn't it? Drive a girl to suicide, and you can't even remember her last name. What about a yearbook?"

"It's with Hunter. If she provides testimony against him, we can grab it when we search the place."

"Do you think she will?" Tina asked skeptically.

"I hope so. I don't think she can live with this hanging over her head, especially now that I know. I think she wants this to be over even more than we do."

"Well, you better do more than hope and think because you're running out of time," Tina said, her pointed tone suddenly directed at Heather.

Heather sat up, her weary heart palpitating two times before regaining a steady beat. "Wait, what?"

"Hunter did this. We know this. And in knowing, it's our job to arrest him so he can't hurt anyone else. So, I'm going to be generous and give you forty-eight hours to convince Taylor or find whatever it is that you're looking for, or I'm bringing him in."

"Tina, come on. We both know that a guy with a rich daddy who raped someone ten years ago probably won't see more than a year behind bars. I want him locked up for life. Not to mention his lawyers aren't exactly going to let us grill him without evidence."

"I'm sorry, Detective. Forty-eight hours and it's out of your hands. I'll catch Gabriel up and get him to tail Hunter in the meantime. Clock's ticking."

THE BRIDESMAIDS

Tina hung up before the inevitable protest could begin. In the silence, Heather collapsed. She knew her boss was right. It had been too long, and they knew too much to twiddle their thumbs. Yet Heather also knew that they didn't have nearly enough evidence for the conviction they sought. She even considered calling Tina back to wave a white flag, to tell her to just pull the trigger and get the warrants signed, but she knew she owed it to everyone involved to keep trying.

She turned on the engine and headed toward Greenman Grocery. Having eaten out excessively all week, what remained in her fridge could not be considered edible, much less brain food. Worse still, her coffee supply—instant or otherwise—was running dangerously low, and she'd need caffeine and plenty of it to get through the file-combing, evidence-compiling day that lay ahead of her.

In the frozen aisle of the always-overlit Greenman Grocery, she ummed and ahhed over unseasoned frozen curries and microwaveable lasagnas until a familiar cologne filled her sensitive nostrils. It wasn't Julius's, Gabriel's, or even Beau's. It was hazier than that. Distant. At first she considered Paul Warren—a CK One kind of man—but this was sharper, peppery. Old Spice but stronger, the type of thing a high schooler might wear because the ads were filled with adoring bikini babes.

Despite its insistent acquaintance, she stiffened and didn't turn with a smile. Instead, she twisted her neck and spotted Hunter Sherman standing a few feet away, grabbing a bag of frozen french fries. The only other thing in his basket was an $8.99 bouquet of mostly wilted flowers.

Despite her attempted subtlety, Hunter caught her staring and bared his teeth. Jaw clenched, she looked back at the shelves, but his heavy footsteps, supporting a large frame, made their way toward her anyway. Heather kept her eyes focused on the side of an Aloo Gobi box but greeted him regardless.

"Mr. Sherman."

"Miss Bishop," he retorted. "Not much of a cook?"

"Not while investigating a homicide, no."

"It must be tough work, especially without a husband to keep house. I certainly missed my wife's cooking last night."

Heather hummed, pretending to scan the offerings indecisively.

"Are you getting close? To the killer, I mean?"

"Very close," Heather replied, her eyes straining to the sides.

Hunter smiled and leaned on the rim of the freezer bins. "That's great news. Can you tell me who it is?"

Heather straightened to her full height and pivoted to look him full in the face but soon wished she hadn't. Usually, a killer's countenance and proximity set her instincts on fire in one way or another. Her "gut"—seemingly a nasty form of empathy—reflected their fear, hatred, and innate violence. It was never precisely the same, person to person, but it was often similar. This was something she'd never experienced before. Nothingness. She felt devoid of anything, and a chill whistled through the hollows where her guts had once been.

"What's with the flowers?" she asked, turning away, the emptiness growing, cloying at the skin that held it in.

"They're for Cheyenne," he said, and she heard his jacket shift as he shrugged. "Thought I'd lay them where she died."

"That's nice of you."

"Well, she always loved flowers. Roses especially. Apparently, they're out of season, so she's getting whatever these are instead. Honestly, I'm a little scared she'll haunt me over them. She always was picky as God himself."

"Is God picky?" Heather questioned, opening the cupboard door and grabbing things from the shelves that she didn't even want.

Hunter chuckled. "Have you read the Bible? No adulterers, no homosexuals, no drunks, no rich men, no lobster eaters." He paused. "No fornicators."

"Well, consider me screwed on the lobster front. Sounds like a lame party anyway," Heather said dryly. With her basket full of what could only be described as overpriced crap, she tilted. "Well, let me know if you see anything down there. Killers often return to the scene of the crime."

"Ah, of course. Sick bastards," Hunter said, almost jovially. "You're a smart woman, Heather."

"Detective," she corrected sharply.

"Detective," Hunter laughed. "My mistake. You know I like smart women. Not enough of them around."

"Oh yeah? I hadn't noticed," Heather replied coldly.

"Yeah. It's a real epidemic. Lots of empty-headed girls around, causing drama and telling lies. You, though, you seem like you have your head screwed on, maybe even a little too tightly."

"I'll see if I can find any WD-40."

Hunter barked a laugh. "I hope after all of this is over, we can become friends. When Taylor and I start having kids, it would be great for them to have a powerful female role model."

"Is Taylor not powerful enough?" Heather inquired, her face the epitome of neutrality.

"Well, there's no harm in having too many role models, wouldn't you agree?"

"I suppose I would."

Hunter reached past her and grabbed some samosas from the open cupboard. "I can't cook either, truth be told. I suppose some people are the gatherers and others are the hunters." He paused. "Which one are you?"

"I have no idea."

"Oh, you know. I think we're more similar than you realize."

Heather flashed a fake smile. "Maybe you're right. I've certainly taken down my fair share of wild animals."

"That you have, Detective. That you have."

"Well, I guess that's me," she said, closing the door. "I'll be seeing you, Mr. Sherman."

"I hope so, Detective. Enjoy your slop. And, um, see you in hell," he joked, a finger gun pointed at her chest.

Heather nodded curtly, turned, and strolled to the end of the row without looking back. In the shelter of the end display, she veered into the next aisle over and pressed her back against the pantry goods. She breathed heavily as feeling returned to her body, and she fumbled for her phone. With numb fingertips, she alerted Gabriel—thankful for her phone's autocorrect function—of Hunter's location and pried herself away from the shelves once he replied with a thumbs-up.

On unsteady feet, she wandered in a fugue toward checkout, the tinny loudspeaker music sounding warped and full of negative notes. Hunter was still etched into her vision, the smell of cologne still remained in the pore of her nostrils, and the emptiness—though it grew smaller with distance—still clawed at her insides. She was desperate for a shower but knew it would do little to remove the stench or melt the permeating interior frost. In her experience, evil tended to linger.

CHAPTER THIRTY-ONE

THE BRIDE

"Are you sure you're going to be okay?" Diane asked kindly, sitting behind her daughter on the couch and brushing her silky blonde locks.

Taylor turned and pulled a face, her crackling cucumber mask conjuring a ghoul in place of her usual pleasant visage. Diane giggled and pressed both sets of fingers to her lips.

"What? Is there something on my face?" Taylor asked, the mask crumbling at the center of her knitted brows.

"No. You look lovely," Diane insisted, squeezing her daughter's hands. She continued to giggle as she forcibly turned

Taylor's head and brushed her hair into a shiny, low ponytail before securing it with a satin scrunchy. "So… you're sure?"

"Mom!" Taylor whined. "I've told you fifty times already that I'll be fine." She paused, embarrassed. She hated that staying with her parents turned her into a child and a bratty one at that. "I have plenty of ice cream and a lot of TV to catch up. Not to mention four police officers watching my runaway ass."

"Okay, honey," Diane said, hugging her daughter from behind.

"I'm sure. Plus, you cannot miss this date night. Luigi just added calzones to the menu."

"Calzones!" Jeff exclaimed from a distant alcove.

"Now you have to go," Taylor said, rotating toward Diane, the action made easier by the slickness of her silk pajamas.

"When did you go to Luigi's?"

"I went with Heather the night before last. Mariah booked us a table in advance for our friendaversary."

"Oh, that's…" Diane trailed off. "That was nice of her. Of both of them. Did you have a good time?"

"Yeah. I mean, she was on her best cop behavior, but she had some crazy stories to tell."

Diane rubbed Taylor's arm sympathetically. "Making new friends already. Not that the others can be replaced," Diane insisted. "God, that was a stupid thing to say."

"It's okay, Mom. Really."

It really was, and before last night Taylor had thought so too—that Heather could be a friend. However, after the events of last night and the unpleasantness between them this morning, she feared that they were doomed to be nothing more than cop vs. criminal.

Diane sighed. "Everything's going to be okay. You know that, right, baby?"

"I know."

"You really scared us last night."

"I know. I'm sorry. I just really had to talk to her."

"Well, newsflash, kiddo," Jeff said jovially. "They already invented something for that. It's called a phone."

Taylor rolled her eyes. "I know, Dad."

Diane stood, wearing her favorite figure-hugging red dress, and toyed with her diamond tennis bracelet. "I won't push, but you know we're here if you need us. No judgment. No questions. The police don't need to be your only ally."

"Thanks, Mom. You look beautiful."

"Not half as much as you do, my love," Diane said, swooping in for a cheek kiss despite the cucumber mask. "Have a nice evening. We'll be back around ten. Oh, and don't forget—"

"To feed George, I know."

"That's my smart girl."

Jeff opened the front door for his wife and winked at his daughter. "Enjoy yourself, kiddo. Don't watch anything too scary. I don't want a repeat of last time."

"Oh my god, you guys. I was thirteen. How was I supposed to know *Rosemary's Baby* was a horror movie?"

Jeff chuckled. "I'm only kidding. Call us if you need us." He made a phone gesture and gave a thumbs-up.

Phone equals good, got it, Dad, Taylor thought, amused.

She gave a thumbs-up in return. "I won't," she replied in singsong.

"We just want you to know we love you."

Taylor groaned and tossed a cushion at him. "Get out of here!"

He raised his hands in defeat. "All right, all right. See you later."

"Bye. Don't get too drunk," she chided and watched through the window as her parents, arm in arm, made their way to the car under the surveillance of several police officers.

Taylor envied their freedom, but as she waved to the friendly officers and closed the curtains, she was glad for their presence as she hunkered down for the night. She still wasn't—having known the man since she was thirteen—convinced of Heather's Hunter theory, but it was an undeniable fact that someone was out there killing and that she was likely next in line. Having an armed security detail, as claustrophobic as it was and was going to be, would at least allow her a good night's sleep. Not that she was tired after her four-hour-long nap.

She was surprised that she'd been able to sleep so easily, but strangely, despite a tumultuous prior night, her day had been one of alleviation—at least during the periods between the bouts of anxious puking. She supposed unearthing your darkest secret inevitably resulted in some sweet dreams and anxiety attacks. On the one hand, it was off her chest, and on the other, it was out in the open, acknowledged, admitted to.

Yet it seemed the positives outweighed the negatives. The denial had been soaking up her energy like a parasite since she was seventeen. She'd never been a great liar before Penelope; even white lies sounded unnatural coming from her, and what they'd done—what they'd *all* done—was a black lie. The kind of black that swallowed light. The kind of black that the holes in space were made of. It was astronomical, suffocating, all-encompassing, and now it was gone. The guilt the self-deception had left in its wake was relieving compared to the suckling void. She was a monster, but she knew the antidote, and come morning light, she would make things right.

Her phone buzzed as she washed off her mask, and she flipped it over absentmindedly, only to see Hunter's name on her screen. She wanted to ignore it, she did, but something—deep-seated love or morbid curiosity—compelled her to read on.

Hunter: *I know you don't want to see me right now. In fact, I know you're not allowed to see me right now. But I owe you an apology, and I need to do it in person.*

She frowned and didn't reply. Heather had warned her about sneaking out again, and it wasn't like the cops would let him come over. No, his apology could wait until all this was over. She just hoped their talk wouldn't be through prison glass.

Her phone buzzed again, and she sighed impatiently as she stared at the screen. Hunter again. As expected.

Hunter: *Please. I love you, Taylor. You know I would never hurt you. I just want to talk.*

The idea of talking through prison glass stuck with her. There was a lack of closure there, something she desperately needed. It would be hard to get past the cops but not impossible. There was a crawl space under the house, a loose lattice panel, and a broken fence plank that she knew she could fit through. She knew this because George—her parents' excessively overweight and elderly beagle—used this particular trajectory to make his miraculous escapes. Everyone else thought he was Houdini reincarnated, but Taylor had caught him in the act in her teenage years and used his secret for her own devices. After all, he never wandered far—just a few doors down to sniff his best friend, Buck, the German shepherd—and she, in turn, had always been back by midnight.

Taylor: *Fine. Meet me in an hour at the park.*

She could practically see his big goofy smile as the three dots popped up in reply.

Hunter: *Just like old times. See you then.*

Taylor smiled and, when she realized what her face was doing, forced it into a frown. She cursed under her breath. It was hard to love someone who'd done terrible things, but it was even harder not to. They'd been together for twelve years, and she wanted to hear him out, if only to suffocate the persistent butterflies once and for all. Then she would offer him a choice: he'd turn himself in or she would.

Hunter was sitting at Alice Warren's pondside memorial when Taylor arrived, her flashlight pointing forward, shining a spotlight upon his perfection. He turned, smiled, and stood, holding a bouquet of wilting flowers. He strode ahead, the bunch of daisies and carnations losing petals with each step, but before he reached her, he began to sob and fell to his knees.

Despite herself, she ran toward him, pulled his face to her middle, and massaged his short crop of hair.

"Jesus, Hunter," she murmured.

"I'm so sorry, babe," he cried into her belly. "I don't know what I was thinking. We were so distant, and one day I bumped into Cheyenne at Sherwood's after work. She bought me a drink, and we got to talking, and one thing led to another."

Taylor loosened her grasp. "She was one of my best friends."

"I know, I know," he sniffled.

Taylor frowned, his patheticness nauseating her. It felt insincere and manipulative, and slowly but surely, the butterflies stopped flapping their wings and fell to the pit of her stomach, waiting to be consumed by the acid that was broiling inside of her.

"It was a stupid mistake. I'll never do it again. I'm so sorry about everything."

"Including Penelope?" she asked, her tone colder than their surroundings.

Hunter froze and unfurled, getting to his feet but not stretching to his full height. If he thought a hunchback or puppy eyes would save him from his wife's wrath, he was sorely mistaken.

"Huh?" he asked, wiping his nose with the back of his hand.

"Are you sorry about what you did to Penelope?" she asked again.

"Yes, of course, I'm sorry! I promise I'll never touch another woman as long as I live." He moved forward, wrapping his arms around her despite her lack of reciprocation.

Taylor frowned with disgust. "So you're sorry for… cheating?"

"Yeah, babe," Hunter said, clearly confused.

"Not for raping a drunk girl and driving her to suicide?"

She felt him stiffen, and with his hot breath on her scalp, he said, "I never said I raped her. That was what all of you said. You weren't in that room. You don't know how she begged for it. It's not my fault she regretted it in the morning."

"People don't kill themselves over sex they regret," Taylor snapped. "If they did, I'd be long dead."

Hunter pulled back, his shadowy face stony. "She didn't say no."

"Because she was wasted!" Taylor yelled.

Hunter lunged and clasped his hand over her mouth. She toppled, but he stayed latched, and as they moved into the streetlamp's light, Taylor could see that his eyes were bone-dry. Taylor bit down. Hard. Hunter retracted and raised a hand before stopping. He inhaled shakily and used the same hand to slick his hair back.

"It was a long time ago, Taylor," he said firmly.

Taylor spat, the taste of his palm in her mouth. "Not according to the statute of limitations."

Hunter straightened, growing several inches, turning from a tall man into a giant, his muscles bulging and chest inflated. "What are you saying?"

"I'm saying I can't live with this anymore, and we need to tell the police what happened to Penelope. For her family's sake. For our sake."

Hunter didn't reply.

"You'll be out in no time. And won't it feel better to come clean?" Taylor pleaded.

"Taylor, I'm not going to tell the cops. And neither are you," Hunter warned.

"You know," Taylor said, taking several steps back as Hunter did the same, his enormous form turning back into a silhouette. "Jenny wanted to tell the cops. Back in 2018. Talked about it constantly. She was going to dump Mason, turn you both in, and hit the road. She brought it up that night, actually. The night she died. Funny that."

"You better not be implying what I think you're implying."

"Oh, I am. I'm saying that maybe Mason caught wind of that fact, and you two shook on it with spit and went rat-hunting."

"Taylor," Hunter said emotionlessly, "you know I'm not a killer."

"I know you lied to the cops about that night. The night my sister died."

Hunter clenched his fists so tightly that they cracked. "Okay, fine. I admit it. I was in the car with Mason that night, and I made up the alibi to save our skins. Not to mention, he was innocent. We saw Jenny, they argued, and she ran off into the woods."

"You always told me he was guilty," Taylor said. "I think *that* was the truth. You just left out the part about you playing second fiddle."

"Taylor, I was lying. I was just telling everyone what they wanted to hear," he hissed from the shadows. "Mason was already dead. So I let people believe what they wanted to believe. I would've gone to prison if I'd said I was in the car with him, even though we didn't do anything."

"How do I know that's true?"

"Because I'm telling you it is," he growled, frustrated.

"All you do is lie!" Taylor laughed hysterically. "You just admitted to lying this entire time!"

Hunter stepped forward again, and despite Taylor's doubts, Heather's theory weighed heavily at the back of her head and pulled her back, stumbling toward the road. Here was a man she'd loved for twelve years, but this wasn't a shape she recognized. Here was a monster, not a man, and regret seeped in as she glanced around the dark, isolated park.

"I admit it. I've lied to you. So now here's the truth," the dark monster said. "I raped Penelope. I don't feel bad about it, and I wasn't upset when she died. I had an affair with Cheyenne for a year. I liked her but didn't love her. It was all about sex. I have slept with two other women since we've been together. One of them once, one of them four times. I have never killed anyone directly. Call me a rapist, a cheater, a sex pest, a pervert. Whatever. But you can't call me a killer because it's not true."

Taylor stood, staring at him in silence, reaching for her phone and finding it absent. It was still in the bathroom back at home. She thought of running but wasn't sure if she could outpace him.

"Use your head," Hunter snarled. "Why would Jenny have told us she wanted to turn us in? Why would any of them?"

"I'm telling you," she whispered, "that I want to turn you in."

"You are, and I'm not going to kill you either, Taylor." He reached out but didn't move forward. "But I'm not going to confess anything."

"Then I'll report you myself," Taylor said, standing as tall as she could. "And serve you up divorce paperwork while you're behind bars."

For a second, she expected Hunter to lunge, run, hit her, grab her by her throat, and pin her to the ground.

Instead, he remained still and looked up at the stars. "You're making a mistake."

"No, I'm owning up to them."

"So, this is it? The end?" he asked.

"The end," Taylor confirmed.

Hunter began walking, and Taylor moved backward. She tripped on a rock and fell to the ground, waiting for a fist to strike. Instead, Hunter kept on going back toward the road without a word. She flipped herself onto her hands and knees, mud coating her palms, and watched as he left her alone in the dark.

CHAPTER THIRTY-TWO

THE DETECTIVE

Hand on the railing, one toe touching the surface of the bubble bath, Heather's phone began to ring. She glared at it as if it was the technology's fault and not whoever was on the other end. She retracted and wiped on the bath mat before pulling on the oversized, hot-sauce-stained T-shirt she'd been wearing since the moment she got home.

The phone stopped ringing as she picked it up from the aquarium-themed resin toilet lid, and though she hoped it was just a spam call or someone she could call back later, her hopes were quashed by an immediate second attempt.

Heather looked at the steaming bathtub longingly. The pink salts—gifted to her by Karen Wells, who was in the process of starting some sort of organic soaps and bath salts business—smelled amazing, and her muscles ached from clenching. It had not been a fruitful day, and knowing that time was rapidly running out had only worsened her tetanus-level tension.

Whoever was calling didn't give up so easily the second time, and Heather sat on the porcelain rim, turned the phone over, and answered Tina's call. She knew it was bad news, but she prayed it was the kind of bad news that didn't involve getting dressed.

"Ghostbusters, whaddya want?" Heather croaked, rubbing her eye with the back of her hand.

"Taylor Sherman is missing," Tina replied.

Heather's joints locked, the phrase sending a bolt of electricity through her nervous system. Her jaw locked, and she struggled to speak but managed to strangle out, "What do you mean she's missing?"

"Jeff and Diane just got home from dinner, and Taylor isn't there."

Heather reached into the tub and pulled the plug. "And nobody saw anything?"

"Nope. Four officers on watch, and nobody saw a thing. She must've snuck out somehow. Again."

"Goddammit, Taylor," Heather muttered. "What time did Jeff and Diane leave?"

"Around seven."

"So in those three hours, no one thought to, I don't know, look in a window, knock on the door, check in on her?"

"She'd drawn the curtains and clearly wanted to be alone. They heard the TV going the entire time and assumed everything was fine."

Heather's blood pressure was rising, and an invisible band was tightening around her head as a tension headache took hold. "Where's Hunter?"

Tina hesitated. "We don't know."

"You don't know?" Heather asked in disbelief.

"Gabriel stopped tailing him a couple of hours ago. A drunk driver smashing into a tree distracted him. I sent Reeves out, but he couldn't find him."

"Anything else?"

"We have her phone, but her parents don't know the code."

"Try 0909."

"Zero nine, zero nine," Tina repeated back to herself. "I'm in."

"Check her texts."

"Already on it." Tina fell silent as she read. "She went to meet Hunter at the park. I'm assuming Whitetail. She said 'in an hour,' meaning she arrived there at eight."

Heather checked the time. It was ten fifteen.

"I'll be there in five," Heather said before hanging up.

Carefully, blankly, Heather padded to the bedroom to get changed, her towel dragging along the floor behind her. In her room, she got changed, unblinking, and once she was ready to go—belt and all—she took a second to press the towel to her face and unleash a mighty, lung-shredding scream that triggered a chorus of howls from her dogs. She kept going, their mournful wailing hiding her own.

Tina was right. They should've locked him up. In Heather's pursuit of perfection, she'd failed the victims, and now there was nothing left to save.

Heather didn't win the race to the park but came second by moments, pulling up behind the infamous Sheriffmobile just as Tina and Reeves stepped out of the vehicle. Then came the EMTs, Lisa Simmons, and finally, Gabriel. As the others chattered, called out, and turned on flashlights, he appeared in the distance, speeding along the main road in his beat-up Suzuki Swift. He parked haphazardly up on the sidewalk to disapproving looks and exited the vehicle apologetically.

"Sorry. That crash was a real mess. Is she here?"

Tina and Reeves had already ventured deeper into the park, and Heather tilted her head toward them. "Come on," she said.

"Hey, I'm sorry about Hunter," Gabriel panted.

"Don't beat yourself up," Heather said, not sounding as sympathetic as she was aiming for. "She wasn't supposed to be out here."

"I know, but still."

"Seriously," Heather warned, her heart pounding. "Let's just get this over with."

"Okay," Gabriel said quietly, pointing his flashlight at Reeves's back and following the pair into the darkness that lay beyond the halo of the single street lamp.

Heather trailed behind them, not wanting to be the first one to find the body of Taylor Sherman. Somehow it felt like someone else seeing her first would dilute the pain or, at the very least, the shock. She knew she'd gotten her wish when Gabriel gasped up ahead before stumbling, leaping, and rolling to save himself from falling. Heather shone her light in his face, his terror cast in white, and knowing that the burden was hers to bear, slowly lowered the bright light to the frozen ground.

Taylor Sherman was lying on her back, unmoving, her arms sprawled snow-angel style, just as Cheyenne's had been. Heather waved Tina and Reeves over, and they jogged toward her before beckoning Lisa and her floodlights onto the scene. Without the need for communication, everyone got to work, and soon the generator was humming and the lights were on.

Despite knowing it was important to look at, Heather resented the influx of detail. The blood was still fresh, pouring from the massive headwound at the top of Taylor's head. Her cheekbone was smashed, her lips split and blue. There was blood-imbued down spilling out of the stab wounds in her puffer jacket, and one of her earrings had been torn through the lobe and was discarded a little way away. She'd put up a fight, Heather thought, his eyes drifting to Taylor's mitten-covered hands.

Carefully, Heather removed the knitwear and noted that her knuckles were a little red. She gestured for Gabriel to do the same on the left side. He crouched, removed the powder-blue mitten, and furrowed his brow.

"What?" Heather asked.

He raised her limp hand. "Her wedding ring has been torn off."

Heather shook her head angrily, knowing exactly who took it, and looked at Taylor's seemingly restful face, her eyes having been forcibly closed by whoever killed her.

Then Heather saw something. A cloud of condensation. Heather held her breath and looked at Gabriel, who slid his thumb to Taylor's wrist and opened his eyes wide.

"Holy shit," he said. "I think I can feel something."

"Oh my god," Heather exhaled, getting down to her knees and laying her head on Taylor's chest. It was faint but distinct.

Ba-bum. Ba-bum. Ba-bum.

"Tina!" Heather yelled, looking over her shoulder. "Get the EMT over here now!" Heather scooched to Taylor's head, and while the EMTs got the stretcher, she pressed a warm hand to Taylor's neck and addressed her in a low, soothing voice.

"I don't know if you can hear me, but it's all going to be okay."

"Coming through," one of the EMTs hollered, and Gabriel hastily moved to Heather, helped her to her feet, and moved her out of the way.

In shock, they watched as the pair lifted Taylor, placed her on the stretcher, secured her, and raced her toward the ambulance. Heather heard mentions of unconsciousness, low heart rate, and possible hypothermia as they became distant and prayed that her injuries were not too severe. If she survived this, not only would she get to live her life, but she would also be able to tell them who the killer was once and for all. Stuck inside an unmoving mouth was all the evidence they needed.

They took off quickly, alarm blaring, and once she was gone, Heather and Gabriel scoured the scene, helping Lisa to find a couple of aspects worth marking.

Eventually, Tina—who had been talking to Reeves by her car and making phone calls—trudged over and asked, "What have you found?"

Heather looked at her, almost twitchy from her mania. "Prints. Size 12 men's hiking boots and two indents, which I'd hazard belong to a set of kneeling knees. Both are fresh, left after the rain shower at"—she paused and checked the Weather app—"quarter past nine."

"So he took an hour to work up to killing her?"

"Or he came back." Heather shrugged. "There was also a knife in her bag, which means…"

"That Hunter scared her enough to bring protection. You ready to bring him in?"

"Oh yeah. Let's get him. But keep Taylor's status under wraps. I want doctors and nurses sworn to secrecy," Heather ordered. "Hunter thought she was dead when he left. I want to keep it that way."

"Why?" Tina asked.

"He'll stay put if he thinks he's gotten away with it, but if he knows one of his victims could wake up and provide eyewitness testimony…" Heather trailed off and huffed, frustrated by explaining her frantic thoughts. "I don't want him to disappear or, worse, pull a Mason. I'm not letting that happen."

"Understood. We'll keep this quiet, and I'll get people looking for him tonight. As long as he's in town, we'll have him in a cell by sunrise."

"Great," Heather said, taking a step and stumbling.

"You okay?" Tina asked, catching Heather's arm.

"Yeah, think the lack of sleep is catching up to me. I'm fine though. I'll grab some coffee from Dottie's and—"

"Go home, Detective," Tina said. "We've got it from here. I'll call you when he's in custody."

"Tina, come on. Don't bench me. Not now."

"I'm not benching you. I have six squad cars covering every inch of the town. We have Taylor on her way to the hospital. I have Leah Durand under Hallington PD's protection. And we have our killer."

"But—"

"Go home," Tina insisted. "I need your interrogation abilities sharp."

"All right, fine. See you at sunrise."

Back at home, the relief Heather had felt from Taylor being alive began to fade. The stab wounds, the head wound, her lack of response. What if she died anyway? The difference between a case failed and a case solved hinged on Taylor's ability to speak. What if she couldn't? What if they couldn't save her?

An anxious mess of tight tendons and sore muscles, Heather reattempted her bubble bath. Unfortunately, it didn't soothe her half as much as she'd liked, and with no updates from anyone on the force as of yet and Gabriel having gone to bed early, Heather opted to call her favorite night owl, Julius. She reasoned that he'd worked on the case just as much as she had and deserved to know how it was shaping up, but really, she selfishly needed to talk to someone to retain some sanity.

"Heather?" he asked, clearly half asleep.

Crap, Heather thought, realizing it was later than she thought.

"Sorry, I just got back from a crime scene, and… I don't know, I wanted to talk about it. You're asleep, my bad. I'll call you tomorrow."

"Hold on," he groaned. "Just let me grab my glasses."

"You don't need glasses for a phone call."

"You non-glasses wearers don't understand anything."

Heather smiled weakly. "I guess not."

"So, what's going on?" he asked, his voice progressively clearer.

"We found Taylor Sherman. Alive, but she's in rough shape, and I have no idea if she's going to pull through. I really need her to pull through. I can't lose another one." She sounded more broken and pathetic than intended. It was the lack of sleep and adrenaline depletion mixed with one of the most frequently disappointing cases she'd ever worked on. It was Alice Warren times four. So many women let down.

"Are you all right?"

"Yeah, I'm fine," she croaked.

"I'm coming down."

Heather shifted, a wave making its way from her torso to her feet. "No, you don't have to do that, I'm going to be busy and—"

"Are you in the bath?"

"...Yes."

Julius tutted. "Do you know how many autopsies I perform on people who've drowned in the bath per year?"

"No."

"A lot. Don't take baths when you're tired," Julius scolded.

Heather had been half expecting an inappropriate, flirtatious comment and couldn't help but laugh at the lecture. "All right, hold on until I get out then."

"Don't let it happen again," he half-joked. "And if you're busy, that's fine. But I'm coming down. Should she die, I'll be there for the autopsy. Should she live, I'll be there to help build the case. Either way, we'll grab a drink and go over everything. I'll bring the reports with me if you like."

"You really don't have to," Heather half-heartedly objected, though it didn't sound like he was asking.

"I do. It's my job, remember?"

"Yeah, I think I remember something about that."

Heather didn't protest further. She needed to speak to someone who wasn't a coworker, a murder suspect, or a grieving family member. Someone who knew her past but wouldn't coddle her like a parent. Julius could tell it like it was but was far enough removed from the pressures of being on the force to provide comfort and rationality instead of frustration and panic.

"Thanks," she said after a beat of silence.

"As I said, it's my job. Now get out of the bath and go to bed," he replied warmly.

Heather did as she was told.

"Put the phone up to the drain; I want to make sure you're not tricking me. It would affect me greatly to have to perform your autopsy."

Heather pulled the plug and watched the pink water swirl down the drain. "Did you get that?"

"I did. It sounded crunchy."

"Bath salts."

Julius chuckled. "I hope the legal kind. Now, get some rest. I'll text you when I'm in town."

Heather yawned. "Night."

"Good night, Heather."

CHAPTER THIRTY-THREE

THE DETECTIVE

They did not find Hunter by sunrise, and now, at 5:00 p.m., it didn't seem likely that they would find him by tomorrow's dawn either. He was not in his house, he did not show up to work, and his truck was missing. He was no longer in Glenville, likely having left while they scoured the park for Taylor. This, of course, could mean only one thing: he was on the run.

Heather wanted to hurl accusations, despite Tina's assurances that Taylor's status—which remained unstable—had been kept a secret. Still, the entire department—including Heather to a degree—was confident that he would soon be found, his attempt to flee only furthering his guilt, and subsequent sentence, in court. It was messy, but they had him. It was just a waiting game, leaving Heather—still barred from the hunt—with plenty of time to meet up with Julius.

She waited quietly in the booth, a martini and a glass of merlot in the middle of the table, trying to ignore the numerous sets of eyes burning holes into her skin. She knew some were staring for the sake of gossip—wondering if she'd been stood up on a date—but most were trying to gain insight from her expression. Did a furrowed brow mean they'd found another body? Did a chewed lip mean the killer was still at large? Did her lifeless eyes mean they were all in danger?

There was the hum of a frenzy beginning, not helped by the influx of journalists around town and the enforced 11:00 p.m. curfew. The former had been camped outside of the deceased's families' homes for the past twenty-four hours, and though they were frequently ushered away, like herpes, they always came back.

Heather herself had pushed away three microphones on her front lawn as she'd gotten into her car and was grateful that Bobby had enacted a "No Media Allowed" rule within his establishment. Though legally discriminatory and technically unenforceable, the chalkboard sign had worked thus far. Not that it stopped them from waiting on the sidewalk, eager for her to emerge and hopeful she'd be loose-lipped when she did.

With the exception of Hunter's parents—who expressed their outrage loudly and litigiously—everyone else had kept quiet. For this, Heather was grateful, though she knew their rage burned just as hot as the killer's outspoken parents.

Taylor's parents, in particular, were furious, partly at themselves, the department, and their daughter for sneaking out; but mainly with Hunter, a man they'd once trusted. Heather felt their unawareness regarding their son-in-law's capabilities was the only reason they hadn't demanded Tina's—or Heather's—head on a spike. Sure, the police were supposed to know more than civilians, but no one had ever thought Hunter could commit such crimes. In fact, Jeff and Hunter frequently went golfing together, and Diane had always found him to be polite and charming, especially at Christmas when he'd volunteer to do all the washing up. They were also begrudgingly thankful that the police had, as of yet, saved Taylor's life, even if it was too little and maybe too late.

Tina had relayed all this to Heather over the phone after the sheriff met Jeff and Diane at the Glenville Memorial Hospital. They didn't cry, didn't scream, didn't yell. Instead, they were zombies, wandering aimlessly, reciting irrelevant anecdotes about their daughters and their murderous partners. Tina ended up having them treated for shock, and with Taylor's health worsening, they were at home under suicide watch. Heather thought that was a good idea, especially in the event that Taylor didn't pull through. No parent should outlive their child, let alone two. It was the cruelest thing she could imagine enduring, and she wasn't even a mother.

That, too, reminded her of the Paper Doll Killer. So many parents left without daughters, so many killed before Heather could catch up, and so many broken homes as a result. The similarity was unsettling, and as she sipped her wine and waited for Julius, déjà vu took hold. Here she was again, apparently stuck in a time loop—a sick six-year-long *Groundhog Day* that gave no sign of ending. Each time it started the same: serial killer on the loose, hunt serial killer, catch serial killer. And each time it would inevitably end with a nervous breakdown she'd struggle to emerge from. Unable or unwilling, she wasn't quite sure, to change careers, she was doomed to repeat the pattern over and over until the day came that she'd lose her mind completely.

She was tallying how much more of this she could take before her nervous system failed when the front door to Sherwood's opened. Suddenly all eyes were on the entrance, everyone wondering if a journalist or podcaster dared to enter. Heather understood why as Julius—sticking out like a sore thumb among all the flannel and boots—stepped inside and wiped the mud from his brogues. Bobby eyed him suspiciously, unsure if he was an interloper or a city tourist. Julius—who was nearly as empathetic as she was and far more astute—offered a friendly wave to the barkeep.

"Not a vulture," he said. "Just here to see a friend. Is Detective Bishop here?"

Bobby's severe facade melted away as he pointed to Heather with a smile, causing all the curious patrons to turn their gawping fascination back to her.

"Thank you," Julius said, squinting behind his small oval spectacles and lighting up when he spotted her.

He wore a crisp white shirt, unbuttoned at the top, tucked into gray slacks and a fine leather belt. Jacquard socks poked out the bottom of his cuffs, his leather satchel swung to and fro, and his thigh-length wool coat flared as he strode through the bar. He offered a slight wave at the halfway point, unaware that every woman in the room was watching him with the voracity of a fox scouting a chicken coop.

"Hi," he said, hand on the top of the booth bench. "Do you mind if I sit here? I don't have many friends in town."

Heather rolled her eyes dramatically. "If you must."

"Much obliged," he replied with a wink before sitting and facing Heather, his elbows on the table.

Heather pushed his martini toward him, trying to ignore the whispers of locals and trying harder not to glare at their brazen gawping. She supposed it was just one of the many "perks" of being a local celebrity: people cared about who you associated with. More than that, they cared about the exact nature of the said association.

Julius plucked his drink from the table. "You are truly a lady and a scholar." He sipped. "Mm. They've upped their game since last time. How's your merlot?"

"It certainly is merlot," Heather replied, tilting the glass back and forth and watching it reconvene in the base of the bowl.

"It's got good legs," Julius said, pointing to the slow-moving droplets.

"That's probably why it's already gone to my head."

"Have you had anything to eat?"

Heather attempted to penetrate the fog surrounding her day, conjuring a headache and little else. So she turned to her body for answers, and a growl ripped through her that she knew even Julius must've heard. "Nope," she said. "Completely forgot."

Julius pulled his wallet from his pocket before shucking his jacket. "What would you like? My treat."

Heather glanced at the colorful illustrated menu on the table and let her hunger guide her. "A cheeseburger with extra bacon."

"You know what? I'll have the same," he said, standing, cash in hand.

He moved to the bar, where even Amber bore the same look of fascination as she took their order. Julius didn't look or behave like the men did in Glenville. He was too foreign with his Mediterranean looks and mixed-bag accent. He was also too well-spoken, well-dressed, and well-groomed. The few locals that did sport a beard did so in a lumberjack way, not a university professor way. Even the rich tourists looked different. Those people were gaudy, all fast cars and indoor fountains. There was nothing quiet about their luxury. Not to mention they wouldn't be caught dead in Sherwood's despite its face-lift. Once again, Julius seemed oblivious.

No wonder you're single, Heather thought, highly amused.

Julius returned to the booth and examined her face with narrowed eyes, his mouth lifted at the corner. "What are you smiling about?"

Heather dropped her grin. "Nothing."

"Whatever you say. So, shall we get the medical talk out of the way before food?"

"Good idea." Heather took a deep breath. "If we compare the doctor's reports to yours, it's clear that Taylor Sherman was attacked by the same person who killed Mariah King and Cheyenne Jackson. And from what little we know of Jenny Brooks's autopsy, I'd say she also fits the pattern, stab marks or otherwise. Intracranial hematoma, blunt-force trauma to the head, and identical stab wounds to Cheyenne's and Mariah's. Aside from the fact that she suffered two more punctures in each palm, the only other difference is that she was found nowhere near the lake and in a public park."

"He's taunting you," Julius said thoughtfully. "Trying to display his skill. Odd that he'd leave footprints behind, considering he'd tried so hard to hide them previously."

"I have a theory about that."

"Hmm?"

"The prints were fresh, according to CSI at least. I think he 'killed' her and returned to be with the body."

"You think he regretted killing his wife?"

"Maybe. Yeah. And I think his grief, or realization, made him sloppy. Then his demons, or whatever, drove him out of town."

"Makes sense. And what about Jenny? Did he kill her too?"

"I think they both killed her. Hunter and Mason. Mason killed himself out of guilt, and Hunter let him take the fall. Then when Hunter found out Mariah, Cheyenne, and Taylor were going to reveal his big secret, he murdered them too. Or tried to."

Julius combed his fingers through his salt and pepper curls. "You know I don't make a habit of weighing in on theories, but I must admit, I think this is a good one."

"Nothing else makes sense, right?" Heather asked, her question tinged with desperation.

"As I said, the theory is a good one, and all the evidence is there. So why do you sound like you're trying to convince yourself?"

Heather sighed and threw herself back against her seat. "Leah Durand. I don't know what it is, but I know there's something there."

"She was withholding information about Penelope. You felt her guilt about doing so. Maybe that's all it is."

"Yeah, maybe." She paused. "Yeah, you're right. I'm overthinking it."

"Case closed," Julius said.

"Let's hope so."

Julius wavered, sipping his drink before speaking. "On the subject of cases—and please tell me to go fuck myself should you see fit—but why did you drop the Lilly Arnold case?"

"I told you," Heather said, feigning confusion.

"No, you told me you didn't want to do it anymore, but you didn't tell me why that was."

"Is that not a reason?" Heather snapped.

Julius lowered his drink. "I suppose this is the part where I go fuck myself. Apologies."

THE BRIDESMAIDS

"No, I'm sorry. It's just a touchy subject for me right now. And I know that just adds to the mystery, but I can't. I really can't right now. Okay?"

"I don't mind a bit of mystery," Julius said kindly, though his brain whirred behind his dark eyes. He'd put two and two together. He'd been there, on the phone, when she'd found out about her ex-husband and the murder of his fiancée, Katy Graham. And he knew the Lilly Arnold case—which she'd dropped less than twenty-four hours later—like the back of his hand. It was an obvious equation, but whatever Julius had figured out, he kept to himself.

"Changing subject," he said, shifting in his seat. "How involved are you in the documentary?"

"What documentary?" Heather asked, a million possibilities running through her mind.

Julius frowned. "The one about Peter Anderson. Considering you were the lead investigator—" Julius stopped after seeing Heather's mortified expression and apologized hastily again, "Sorry, I've misspoken again. I thought you knew."

"It's fine. I just hadn't heard… I didn't know they were doing that," Heather said quietly, her stomach churning. She hadn't heard the Paper Doll Killer's name in years, and each syllable felt like a bullet in her chest.

"Yes, well, apparently, he's joined the ranks of Bundy and Dahmer in notoriety."

"Are they going to be interviewing him?" Heather asked. "Anderson?"

"Don't say his name." She took a breath. "Please."

Julius nodded, withholding another apology with great difficulty. "I suppose they will. He sure is a chatty fella. It won't be hard to get him going."

"Jesus, why do they keep making these sickos famous?" Heather lamented. "Are you going to be involved?"

"No. It sounds a bit tawdry to me." He examined his already empty glass. "Would you like another drink?"

"Yeah, why not. I've basically been kicked off the case while Tina handles the rest, so I guess I might as well."

Just as Julius moved to stand, Amber strode over, red plastic tray in hand, and delivered their delicious burgers and fries, complete with American flag sandwich picks and red gingham napkins.

She set them down, beaming ear to ear, and slid their respective plates toward them. "Here y'all go. Enjoy!" she enthused before turning.

"Oh, before you go, could we get another round?" Julius asked, pulling three ten-dollar notes from his wallet. "Keep the change."

"Of course," Amber chirped, pocketing the cash and hurrying away to the bar.

Heather laughed once she was out of earshot. "You're not in Seattle anymore. You just gave her like a fifteen-dollar tip."

"I'm sure she's earned it."

Heather smiled momentarily until her face couldn't take the strain anymore. She slumped and propped her head up in one hand and drummed on the table with the other.

"Are you okay?" Julius asked.

"Not especially."

"I suppose that's a pretty stupid question, isn't it?"

"Little bit," Heather said, the corners of her mouth quirking before collapsing.

"Is it everything or something specific?"

"It's everything. It's Daniel. It's the job. It's this town. It's the case. It's letting down the Brooks family again. It's letting four innocent women down. I just..." Her voice cracked, and she swallowed. "Sorry. I think I really messed this one up. Maybe I should just move to another town and start again. Somewhere far away. Canada maybe."

"Oh, please don't move to Canada."

She laughed. "What's wrong with Canada?"

"They serve milk in bags. Dreadful stuff."

Heather laughed again but choked up at the end. Embarrassed by the display of vulnerability, she looked away until she felt the warmth of his hand on hers. She flinched, and he retracted hastily. There was an awkward silence until she reached, straining across the table, and returned the gesture. He examined her hand—tan wrapped around brown—and explored the lines in her palm before flipping it over and rubbing the soft dorsal side with a rough thumb. Despite this, his grasp was gentle, and she looked up at the same time as he did, a single tear escaping her eyes.

"I don't get to be sad about this," she insisted.

He didn't let go, didn't tell her she didn't mess up or that everything was going to be okay. He didn't say anything. What he did communicate, however, was that he was going to stick around regardless.

They stayed like that until Amber's clomping heels approached, and they severed contact. Amber sheepishly dropped off their drinks and hurried away, but they didn't reunite. Whatever the moment was or whatever it had meant was over. Heather wanted it back so badly she could scream, but she kept her hands to herself as she picked at her food and sipped at her drink.

She only looked up when she heard a creak from Julius's side and watched as he stood and took two steps to her side of the booth.

He gestured to her bench and asked, "May I? My side is a bit lumpy."

Heather silently scooched and allowed him to join her, and when he wrapped an arm around her shoulder, she exhaled and tapped her head against his before straightening. He unraveled shortly after, needing both of his hands for food and drink, but his proximity remained, their shoulders pressed against each other, warmth transferring through layers of fabric.

It was nice, Heather thought, to be touched by another person. It had been a long time since she'd received any intimacy beyond a hug or a handshake. It had been so long, in fact, that she'd grown to fear the concept. However, like most phobias, she found the confrontation wasn't so scary after all.

CHAPTER THIRTY-FOUR

THE DETECTIVE

Not wanting to impose, Julius spent the night at the Black Bear Motel, and Heather spent most of the night wishing he hadn't. It was nice to have company, and she felt—if given the time to work up to it—she had plenty more guts left to spill. In fact, the list was seemingly endless, but it seemed the emotional disemboweling would have to wait for another visit because when they reconvened at Dottie's in the morning, all Heather wanted to say was, "Thank you."

"For what?" Julius asked, unlocking his car as they neared it.

"I don't know. I feel better today, I guess. Calmer."

"I don't think I can take all the credit. That cheeseburger was quite the remedy."

"Well, either way, consider my wounds licked."

Julius opened the door to his brand-new Jaguar F-Type in British Racing Green but lingered before dropping into the driver's seat.

"Should you need them licked again..." He flushed. "I mean, should you need to talk—"

"Yeah, I know," Heather interrupted. "I'll talk to you soon. Drive safe."

Julius nodded and sat in the beige leather seat. "Heather?"

"Yeah?"

"I'm sure Tina is a fine boss, but don't let her cut you out before the ending. You deserve to see this through."

Heather glanced at her car, parked at the edge of the diner lot, and felt elation fill her chest. Every ending needed a beginning, and Heather had a feeling that Hunter was a full-circle kind of guy.

"Yeah," she said, lighting up, "yeah, I do."

Julius looked as nonplussed as he did amused. "Well, I'm glad that resonated with you, but you know the chief would have never benched you, especially at a time like this."

"Uh-huh," Heather said, barely listening as she texted Gabriel to meet her at Dottie's.

"Heather," Julius said more insistently.

"Yeah?" Heather asked, looking up from her phone.

Julius chuckled. "Doesn't matter. Go get him, Detective."

Heather beamed and bounced from foot to foot, impatiently awaiting further goodbyes when Julius shooed her.

"Go on," he said, his eyes crinkled at the corners. "Go do your job."

"Thanks, Julius," Heather said breathlessly before darting to her car, hopping in and starting the engine. "Come on, come on, come on," she said, reading Gabriel's replies.

Three minutes later, once Julius was already long gone, Gabriel sprinted into the lot, looked around wildly, spotted Heather's car, and ran at her full tilt. He yanked the passenger door open, tossed himself into the seat, and looked at Heather.

"So, what's going on? What's the emergency?"

"I know where he is," Heather said, glancing over her shoulder as she reversed with a screech.

Gabriel immediately gripped the grab handle and looked at Heather with wide eyes. "Where is he?"

Heather didn't give him an answer, revving her engine before taking off. Just as they reached the other end of the lot, a wall dangerously near, Heather pushed the clutch while pulling the hand brake and twisted her wheel into the turn. She pressed the hand brake back down, hit the clutch again, and counter-steered, whipping the car ninety degrees to the right and leaving a cloud of smoke behind them as she careened onto the main road.

"You're a lunatic."

"Sane people don't catch killers."

"They also don't die in preventable car crashes."

"You'll be fine. Put your seat belt on."

Gabriel turned white as he realized he'd been unbuckled through the entire stunt and hastily clipped himself in as Heather put her pedal to the metal and headed toward the place that had started it all. The crime scene of Jenny Brooks. It wasn't far from Dottie's, considering that was where she'd disappeared from, but the actual location itself had been a couple of miles out, accessible only by a dirt road that only the most local of locals knew about.

Lo and behold, as Heather slowed her vehicle to avoid any deer-related accidents, Hunter Sherman's work truck was parked by the side of the road, only partly obscured by the trees. Heather pulled up behind the pickup, keeping a distance of about ten feet, and parked.

"Holy shit. You were right," Gabriel said.

"Yup," Heather replied, unsheathing her gun. "You ready to do this?"

"Oh, I've been ready."

They exited the vehicle—guns by their side and their body language neutral—and split into two paths, Heather taking the driver seat left and Gabriel taking the passenger seat right.

"Hunter Sherman," she called. "You are under arrest for the murders of Jenny Brooks, Mariah King, Cheyenne Welch, and your wife, Taylor Sherman. Please exit the vehicle with your hands behind your head."

They paused on either side of the tray—Heather on the road and Gabriel in the woods—and waited for him to do this the easy way. Though Heather could see his hair above the headrest, he didn't move.

So, she spoke again."Mr. Sherman, I am asking you to get out of the car. I will arrest you either way. So you can make this harder than it needs to be, or you can get out, kneel, and let us take you in."

Heather's anxiety mounted as Hunter neither exited the car nor moved at all, but as she gave the nod to move in, they soon found out why Hunter Sherman was motionless: he was as drunk as a lord after a Christmas banquet. He was so drunk he couldn't speak, couldn't move beyond hazy blinking, and hardly seemed to notice Heather's presence at all as he attempted to lift the mostly empty whiskey bottle to his lips.

"Good morning, Mr. Sherman. Do you mind if I take a look around your car?" she asked.

Hunter made an unintelligible noise, and Heather looked at Gabriel through the opposite window.

He shrugged. "Sounded like a go-ahead to me."

"Thank you, sir," Heather said scathingly as she opened the back door of the oversized GMC cab.

There were empty beer bottles, a six-pack of undrunk plastic water bottles, a sleeping bag still in its toggled pouch, a yellowing pillow, a phone and its charger, a box of energy bars, and a still-unopened bottle of Jack Daniels. Clearly, he hadn't intended to evade the law for long—not even he was that cocky—but he had provided the right supplies for about seventy-two hours of abject misery.

"Heather," Gabriel said, his voice low, "you better come look at this."

She rounded the front of the cab, ran her fingertips along the spotless grill, and made her way to the passenger side. Following Gabriel's subtle gesture, she looked past the tip of his discreet finger and saw a yellow peavey on the ground. It looked heavy, not to mention metal and rounded, and just small enough to swing without throwing yourself off balance. More than that, it was absolutely covered in blood.

"Call it in," Heather said quietly. "We need Gretchen if we're going to get this asshole out of the car." She raised her voice back up to a normal level. "Okay, Mr. Sherman. We'll just wait here until you're ready. Let us know if you need your rights, some water, a hospital. Anything."

Once again, Hunter didn't reply, so Heather and Gabriel closed the pickup doors and sat on Heather's car's hood, waiting for the heavy lifters to arrive. It was anticlimactic, but Heather felt on top of the world.

CHAPTER THIRTY-FIVE

THE DETECTIVE

Hunter sat beneath the fluorescent beams of the interrogation room, his wrists shackled to the bolted-down metal table. He looked haggard and downright Kubrickian as he glared, chin tilted down, at his captors. His eyes were bloodshot; his five-o'clock shadow was rapidly turning into stubble; and his usually quaffed, prematurely graying hair was unkempt and frizzy from the dampness of the lake.

"Did you go for a swim, Mr. Sherman?" Heather asked as Tina quietly set up the recorder, pressed Play, and dictated the time and circumstance.

Hunter didn't answer, though Heather knew it was a yes. When they'd finally removed him from the car, his clothes had been soaked through. He hadn't been permitted a shower as he still needed to be swabbed and scraped, but he'd been given clean clothes: an unzipped gray hoodie, matching sweatpants, and a white T-shirt that matched his sickly hue.

"It must be cold this time of year," Heather continued, still smiling despite Tina's repeated scoldings.

She couldn't help it. The blood on the peavey matched Taylor's, and the tip looked identical to the cast they'd made of the hole found next to Cheyenne's body. It was over. They had him. How could anybody not smile at that?

Tina sat, the tape rolling, and acknowledged Hunter with professional sternness. "Good afternoon, Mr. Sherman. How are you feeling today?"

"Hungover," he replied, his eyes fixed on Heather's happy expression.

Heather hummed sympathetically. "I'll bet. There was barely anything left in that bottle by the time we found you. Have you had some water? Some aspirin?"

"Yes," he snarled.

"Good. That's good," Heather replied cheerily, opening her notebook and clicking her pen. "So, I'm sure you know why you're here."

"Yeah. Somebody killed my wife."

"Somebody killed a lot of people," Heather said, avoiding derailing the interview by mentioning Taylor's living, but still comatose, status. "And we have good reason to believe that somebody is you."

"Yeah? Well, I hope you've got some evidence," Hunter growled, leaning forward, all his charisma washed away to reveal the monster below. "Or else my lawyers are going to rip you limb from limb."

There you are, Heather thought, examining his body language with the fascination of a nature documentarian.

Where there was once a straight spine and a winning smile, there was now a hunched back, a lowered neck, and a slight underbite as he swilled his churning jaw around. His enormous hands gripped the table's edge, and his sneakered feet were poised to pounce. He was every bit the rabid animal she'd suspected lurking just beneath the fraudulent flesh.

"Actually, we do," Tina said, spinning some paperwork and sliding it toward him. "The boots you were wearing earlier match those found at Taylor's crime scene, the peavey in your truck matches what was discovered at Cheyenne's crime scene, and the blood on this potential murder weapon was covered in Taylor's blood."

"Type O negative," Heather said. "Universal blood type."

"Yeah, she donated a lot," Hunter said, ignoring the pile of proof that lay between them. "Even though she barely had enough to give."

Dark implications abundant, Heather's expression faltered. "What do you mean by that?"

"She suffered from chronic nosebleeds," Hunter clarified with disdain. "In fact," he added wryly. "she had a nosebleed last time she was in my car. I was driving her to Sherwood's for work, and we got into an argument about what time she should come home. As usual, she started bleeding all over everything. Including the peavey."

"Can you prove that?" Heather asked.

"The car? No. The nosebleeds? Yes. Just talk to her doctor." Hunter looked confident, and Heather believed him and hoped such a minor possibility wouldn't win over the jury. "I'm sure you've seen her have one."

Heather had witnessed said nosebleeds in the flesh but avoided the question. "So, you're saying you didn't use the peavey to kill Taylor or anyone else?"

"No, because I didn't kill my wife."

"Okay, maybe what you're saying is true. The peavey is unrelated. I'll humor you. But that doesn't explain why we found your boot prints at the scene."

A flicker of pain ran across Hunter's face, and he straightened as if the question had zapped him with a cattle prod. He cleared his throat and looked away.

"I went out there to meet her. We talked, and then I left."

"What time did you leave?"

"I don't know."

"What time, Mr. Sherman?" Heather pushed.

"Twenty past eight," he snapped.

"It didn't rain until 9:15, Mr. Sherman. According to our team, the boot prints in question were only visible because of the brief but heavy rain. Before that, the ground would have been too solid to be impacted. There were knee prints too, by her head. Riddle me this, if she'd been alive and standing, why would you have been kneeling?"

"I was begging her on my knees," Hunter protested. "I was trying to win her back. She must have landed there when this freak hit her."

Heather slapped the table with a bang. "Remember the rain, Mr. Sherman. These prints are from after the rain."

"Fine!" Hunter yelled, standing as much as he could.

"Please take a seat, Mr. Sherman," Tina instructed.

"Okay," he said, fingertips raised in surrender as he lowered himself and his voice. "I was there, we talked, and I left. Then a little while later, I realized I'd dropped my wallet, so I went back to the park to look for it. That's when I found her."

"What time did you leave, and when did you go back?" Heather asked.

"I guess 8:20 and 9:40."

"So, you're saying that somebody else came along in that time and killed your wife, leaving no trace."

"They must've gotten her before the rain," Hunter replied snidely.

"And what happened when you found her?"

"I knelt by her body and said my goodbyes. Then I drove back to our house and took off. I knew you'd arrest me eventually, but I needed time to grieve. I wasn't on the run… just taking a breather."

"A breather?" Heather sighed. "Let's say your story—despite all the evidence and motive—is true, who do you propose killed your wife and the others?"

"I don't know, Detective. It's not my job to solve the case for you."

Heather flipped through her notes. "Did you regularly beat your wife, Mr. Sherman?" she asked, feeling Tina's disapproving eyes on the side of her face. Push too hard and they'd lose him; she knew that, but she had to try.

"What the hell are you talking about?"

"That was one hell of a bruise on her cheek. And please save me the walking-into-a-door excuse. I've heard it enough to know when it's true. And let me tell you, it rarely is."

"I…," Hunter began, losing confidence, stumbling over his words. His fists clenched, and he took a deep breath. "Okay, I slapped her. But that was the only time anything like that has ever happened."

"So, you don't make it a habit of hurting women?"

"Of course not." Hunter shifted, sweat appearing at his temples despite the frigidity of the concrete room. "Can somebody take this goddamn jacket off of me?"

"That would require removing your cuffs," Tina said. "And I'm afraid we can't do that."

"Fine," Hunter grumbled, rolling his shoulders and shucking his hoodie until it fell to his elbows.

Heather's brow raised, her focus drawn to his right bicep. On his strawberry skin was a singular sun-faded tattoo of what she assumed was his wedding date written on a ribbon and coiled around a poorly drawn dove. It didn't take long for her to place where she knew it from—the blurry photo of Mariah and her beau attached to the text sent to Leah. The man in the photo was Hunter. This begged the question, why would he sleep with both of his wife's best friends?

Fortunately, this was easily answered. Mariah and Cheyenne wouldn't go to the cops about Penelope if they were being threatened with losing Taylor and their reputations, right? So he'd seduced them, taken photos and had photos taken, and blackmailed them into keeping their mouths shut. It worked for a while, but when Mariah's guilt became too much to bear and her lips became loose, he escalated to murder. So he sent the text to Leah, blaming his blurry look-alike Alain (knowledge he'd gained from likely joining in their post-high school pranks), and casting guilt in a different direction before he moved in for the kill.

Heather couldn't prove any of it yet, but with the help of the Durands and the digital forensic analysts, she would be able to soon enough.

"Hurting women," Tina whispered, prompting Heather to continue.

"Right. Yes. You say you've never hurt a woman, but I have a feeling the deceased would disagree with that. In fact, Taylor told me something very interesting the night she came to my house. Do you know what that was?"

"No, I don't," Hunter said, jaw clenched.

"Okay, let me give you a hint. It was about you, Mason, and a girl named Penelope. Does that ring a bell?"

The remaining color drained from Hunter's face, and he stood again but was forced to stoop from his chains. "Get me my goddamn lawyer. This is over."

"Of course, Mr. Sherman," Tina said, moving to turn off the tape.

Heather, furious, had already stood, knocking her chair over in the process. She looked down at the hunched figure in disgust before making her way to the door. There she stopped, her hand on the knob, and said, "I look forward to seeing you in court *and* hell, Mr. Sherman."

Tina followed her out, and two burly officers replaced them to move Hunter back to his cell. Not wanting to brush past him in the hall, Tina ushered Heather into the staff room.

"We could have gotten more out of him," she said quietly.

Heather shook her head. "No, we couldn't have. He had an egg timer on in his head and was about to ask for his lawyer regardless. I've seen it before. And at least this way, we know Taylor was telling the truth. He really did rape Penelope, and I believe he'd stop at nothing to stop that from getting out. I mean, did you see the look on her face when I mentioned her?"

"What about the nosebleed?" Tina fretted. "A good lawyer could do a lot with that."

"Screw the nosebleed. We've got so much more than that."

Tina didn't look convinced.

"It'll be fine," Heather assured her boss. "We've got him."

CHAPTER THIRTY-SIX

THE DETECTIVE

As it turned out, Heather was wrong. It was neither fine, nor did they have him. She realized this a few hours post-arrest when a strange man appeared in the window. Dressed in a bespoke suit and wing-tip shoes, he shook the slush from his umbrella and offered a long-fingered wave through the glass. Before anyone could meet him at the door, he let himself in, repurposing his parasol into a walking stick with a flip, a twist, and a strike. The tip dented the hardwood, and his hand coiled around the golden duck head handle as he stepped toward Heather, who was, unfortunately, the closest.

"Raymond Duck," he said, hand outstretched. "I'm here to see my client."

Heather moved to shake but, at the last second, realized that was not his intention. In between his index and middle finger was a business card. Heather begrudgingly plucked it and pocketed it without further inspection, much to Raymond's apparent displeasure.

He slicked his undercut silver tresses back over—an unusually modern haircut for a man in his sixties—and leered at Heather, his teeth crooked but blindingly bleached.

"You must be Detective Bishop," he said. "Hunter's parents told me to look out for a little Indian. Though I'll admit, I thought teepee rather than curry."

"Excuse me?" Heather asked, loudly enough that the department fell silent.

"I meant no offense," Raymond said, feigning horror.

Tina's tiny, tottering footsteps approached rapidly, and Heather turned to see a warning gaze that told her to stand down. She did so happily and drifted toward Gabriel's desk while Tina ushered Raymond toward her office in an apparent panic.

Heather tried to remain optimistic, but her feeble sanguinity dwindled as the meeting reached and surpassed an hour in length. Then when Raymond and Tina reemerged—the former still picture-perfect and the latter's hair looking like she'd gone ten rounds with some gorse bush—her hope was dashed into microscopic pieces.

As Raymond took a seat by the front desk, Tina approached and explained the situation in hushed tones. The lawyer had done it. Hunter had been transferred to a cushier house arrest less than four hours after his arrest. He had to wear an ankle monitor, and while the lawyer didn't fight this aspect, he did propose a compromise. If Hunter wore an ankle monitor, there was no need for a police detail stationed outside of his home. Tina had agreed but made one final counter. Hunter would receive an 11:00 a.m. checkup from an officer every day until a court date was arranged. They'd shaken on this and gotten it in writing. So that was that. He wasn't in a cell, he wasn't being guarded, but Tina assured Heather that it was impossible to remove an ankle monitor.

"So, he's just going to wait there?" Heather asked, gesturing toward Raymond.

"Yeah. There's some paperwork to do and an ankle monitor to arrive."

"Right," Heather said, standing up. "I'm going home."

"You are?" Tina asked.

"Yeah, I can't watch Hunter walk out of here," Heather said, her eyes on the door that led to the cells. "Plus, it seems like you have everything handled here. I'll make myself useful by putting everything together for the prosecutor."

Tina exhaled. "Good idea. Though maybe—"

"Don't worry. You'll get to polish it," Heather laughed. "I have zero desire to speak to the attorney myself. That's all you, Sheriff." Heather looked at Raymond, his long legs crossed, his eyes staring into nothing. "Have fun. I'm out of here."

"Can I trust you two to check in on Hunter tomorrow morning?" Tina asked as Heather pulled on her coat, her gaze still fixed on the unsettling lawyer.

"Oh yeah. I'm not subjecting anyone else to that asshole. Plus, who knows, he might spill some more beans if I play my cards right."

"Don't do anything stupid," Tina chided.

Heather looked at Tina and grinned. "When have I ever done anything stupid?" She paused. "Don't answer that. Sheriff. Buster. See you tomorrow."

With one hand on the icy front door, the bell half jingling, Raymond spoke softly, his voice snakelike. "You seem in a good mood."

Heather slowly turned to look at him, incredulous. "Yeah, I just caught one of the most prolific killers of my career."

"Or so you think."

"I don't think. I know."

"Do you now?" Raymond inquired. "Well, here's something that I know. Hunter Sherman will have that ankle monitor off soon enough."

"Yeah, no need for an ankle monitor in prison," Heather retorted.

"Oh, he won't be going to prison. None of my clients do."

"Even with all that evidence?"

Raymond shrugged. "Plausible deniability. I believe his story about the nosebleed and his wallet. So will the jury once they've been reasoned with."

"And the first-degree rape charge?"

The lawyer cocked his head, his neck clicking. "As an officer of the law, I'm sure you're aware of the incarceration statistics regarding that particular crime."

He paused, and Heather wondered whether he already knew about this.

"Who was the victim?"

"She's dead."

"Shame," the lawyer pouted. "You'll struggle without a testimony. Rape kit?"

"No."

"Did she report the crime?"

"No."

"Hmm."

"We have his wife's testimony," Heather said.

"Well, you better hope she wakes up then," Raymond replied.

Heather must've looked taken aback because he laughed.

"Yes, I know about that. Though I wonder why you haven't told my client." He tutted as he checked his watch. "Would your boss mind if I popped out for an hour or two? I'm expected at the country club in Hallington. A thank-you from one of my most recent clients. Ran his wife over with his Land Rover. I suppose he should've gone to Lenscrafters," Raymond said coolly.

A chill began to creep into Heather's bones, and she opened the door wide.

"Have a wonderful day, Detective Bishop," Raymond said, and when Heather didn't reply, he tutted again. "Bad manners won't get you far in the courtroom. Not that it matters. I doubt this case will ever get its day in court."

Heather stepped through the front door and stood frozen on the street before storming toward her car, her fingernails digging into her palms and her molars aching under the pneumatic pressure.

CHAPTER THIRTY-SEVEN

THE DETECTIVE

"I CAN'T BELIEVE THAT LAWYER BROKE HIM OUT OF JAIL so quickly," Gabriel said.

He checked the time on his phone and turned it to Heather—10:55 a.m., right on schedule if the people carrier in front would get a move on.

"Yeah. That's rich people for you," Heather grumbled.

"It's just … You can't just *do* that. He's been accused of three counts of first-degree murder and rape in the first degree."

"I know. It's not fair," Heather sympathized.

"Have you seen this happen before?"

"To a degree. This is particularly egregious," she said through gritted teeth. "But it happens more than you think. The closer you look at the judicial system, the more you realize most people are locked up because they're too poor to get out."

"Do you think Dennis Burke would've if I hadn't…"

"Yeah. He looked guilty. The jury would've torn him limb from limb."

"Like Thimbles."

Heather sighed. "Yeah, like Thimbles."

"Was the…" Gabriel stopped and started again, "Was the Paper Doll Killer rich?"

"He was, but not in money so much as community. Don't get me wrong, he was upper middle class, but it was his neighbors' determination to turn a blind eye and not look at what was right in front of him that kept him out of a cell for so long. Plenty of them testified in his defense too."

"Seriously?" Gabriel asked, brows raised.

"Seriously. He ran the local post office, went to church every Sunday, ran the soup kitchen, rescued stray cats, was a hit at the Thursday potluck, and donated all of his disposable income to children's charities."

"Jesus. Do you think he did all of that to hide the truth?"

"I don't know. For a while, I thought—because of his faith—that he was just assuaging his guilt. Then, worse, I thought that maybe he really was a kind man, just not all the time. I thought that, somewhere mixed in with the evil, there was good in there too. And I'll tell you, after following a trail of dead little girls, that was a tough pill to swallow."

"What do you think now?" Gabriel asked.

"I don't. Or at least I try not to."

"Understandable."

"You know, he was so polite when I interviewed him. This doddering old man in a reindeer knit vest and oversized glasses. He stuttered, sniffled constantly, and chewed on his thumbnail as if he wanted to suck on it. It was bizarre. And what's weirder still is that all of that was gone when Julius—who'd never met him before—went to see him in prison. He didn't pick up on any of that. He had no idea how the freak in front of him had ever existed in society. It's like once it was over, he let the facade go."

"Leaving only evil."

"Yep. And whatever that is—that bug, that virus, that lack of humanity, that ability to disguise yourself among the sheep—Hunter has it too. I just talk to him, and I feel this darkness." She held up a hand. "I know that sounds woo-woo. But I don't mean it in a 'magical powers' way. I just think I've… I don't know, tapped into some sort of empathetic frequency after years of doing this. It used to just be a lurching or a twisting, but now I get palpitations, cold sweats, specific stuff. And in Hunter's case, I get nothing. Just this awful emptiness."

Gabriel looked at her, torn between concern and fascination. "All my gut tells me is when it's time to eat."

Heather laughed. "Swapsies?"

Gabriel grimaced. "I'm good." He paused. "Can you tell what I'm feeling right now?"

Heather looked at him—his stiff stance, his hand wrapped tightly around his phone, the condensation around the edge of his palm from sweat—and she took a second to feel his energy. The creaking tension in his bones, the pounding of his pulse.

"You're anxious," she said.

"Yeah," he admitted. "You're good."

Heather laughed again. "Just a little hot and cold reading mixed with intuition."

"Does it make people less unpredictable?" he asked. "More trustworthy?"

"No. Mostly it just makes them more frustrating. I know that they're lying, I know that the questions I've asked are stressing them out, but I don't know about what or why."

"Well, if it makes you feel any better, I'm not secretly a serial killer. I am way too poor and Mexican to get away with that."

"You make it sound like you want to," Heather joked.

Gabriel shrugged. "I could go for a *Dexter*-type situation. A serial killer who kills serial killers and is also a cop."

"God, the ending to that show sucked," Heather groaned.

"I thought you didn't watch crime shows."

Heather smirked. "I don't. That one was the final straw."

"Makes sense. It definitely put me off of being a serial killer."

Heather rolled her eyes as they pulled into Hunter Sherman's driveway. "I wish it had that effect on more people."

"Hey, maybe it did. Maybe we'd be up to our eyeballs in killers without it."

"Are we not already?"

"It could always be worse," Gabriel said with a grin. He seemed considerably less anxious now, and knowing that they were both ready to face the evil within, they exited the car and once again slammed their doors in sync.

"We're getting good at that," he enthused, waving at the old lady across the road who was pretending to water her roses despite the hose being turned off. She didn't wave back and hurried back inside, much to the delight of her snarling chihuahuas in the window.

"I wonder what the HOA's policy on murder is?" Heather queried.

"It's probably okay as long as you mow your lawn and only kill the people that dare to have lawn gnomes."

Heather chuckled and rang the doorbell, noticing a small camera above through which Hunter almost certainly was watching them on his phone. Heather neutralized her expression and stared into the lens expectantly. She only waited a minute before trying again.

"He's making us work for it," Gabriel said, amused, his arms crossed.

"Yeah," Heather murmured and tried a third time.

It was not the charm, and she resorted to knocking loudly.

"Mr. Sherman," she called through an open upstairs window.

Still nothing. Her gut tightened to the size of a peach pit, and she banged again. Nothing, nothing, nothing.

"Check under the flower pot," she instructed.

A clunk of terracotta on the stone step and the jingling of keys followed before Gabriel straightened. He hesitated in handing them over.

"Are we allowed to do this without a search warrant?"

"That depends. Did you hear that sound that indicated Mr. Sherman might be having some sort of emergency?" she asked.

"What sou… Oh yeah, I heard it. Sort of like a banging noise?"

Heather nodded. "Yeah, followed by a crashing."

"That's the one."

"He could be hurt."

"He could," Gabriel agreed.

Heather put the key in the lock and turned. The door swung backward—the cheaply made suburban home apparently on an imperceptible lean—and hit the coat rack before Heather could stop it. The wooden stand, which only sported a singular jacket, hit the floor with a clatter, and Heather stepped hastily into the dark, curtain-drawn interior. Despite the noise, Hunter didn't stir, and Heather looked around, half expecting to find him choking on his vomit on the living room floor.

Cautiously, Gabriel shut the door behind them, and using the flashlights on their belts, they moved left through the vacant living room and then forward into the similarly unoccupied kitchen. There was an empty bottle of bourbon on the table and a watered-down whiskey glass by the sink.

"Drunk again," Gabriel whispered.

Hoping that was all it was, Heather kept moving, peaking into the sunroom and office before reentering the hallway through the kitchen's secondary but narrow door.

"Only way is up," she said, moving to the base of the stairs and unsheathing her weapon. "Mr. Sherman," she called out, giving him a final opportunity to respond. "It's Detective Bishop."

As expected, he did not reply, and they made their way up the stairs in a single file. At the top were four doors, three on the left and one at the end. All there was to their right was another closed curtain and a vintage console topped with an initialized doily—*JB*. Jenny Brooks, Heather figured, wondering whether Taylor would ever live in this house again.

In order, they checked the rooms: a bathroom, a bedroom, and a dusty nursery. The only living thing in any of them was a curious little mouse who had made a home among the dusty toys of the latter room. She closed the door after a brief scan. There was something unnerving about an empty cradle and unused toys, though she thanked the universe—and the invention of birth control—that no child had been brought into this situation.

There was only one door left, and if Hunter was there, he was behind that door. She faltered—her outstretched arm bent slightly and falling short of the knob—until Gabriel clapped her on the back and moved them both forward. She twisted, pushed, and looked toward the occupied king-sized bed.

"No, no, no," she moaned, striding forward and holstering her gun.

"Fuck!" Gabriel yelled, turning around in anger.

Hunter was propped up in bed, fully dressed and lying atop the tucked covers, the interior of his skull splattered against the headboard and white walls. In his right hand was a gun, and on the nightstand to his left was a note. Just like his best friend, Mason, he'd eaten a bullet instead of seeing the inside of a cell, and everything they'd worked toward had ended in a bang.

"Why would he...," Gabriel began, pawing at his mouth and pacing at the foot of the bed. "That skeezy lawyer was going to get him off."

"I don't know," Heather replied. "Maybe he couldn't live without Taylor after all." She cursed loudly and repeatedly. "Or the goddamn lawyer told him she's still alive and could testify if she woke up."

"Planting him in high security for life," he added. "What an idiot." He stopped moving. "What does the note say?"

Heather pulled a pair of gloves from her pocket, put them on, and gingerly grabbed the sealed letter. She tore along the top as neatly as possible, attempting to keep the seal intact for forensics, but made a mess anyway. She unfolded the card stock and noted that the letter had been written with a fountain pen, the letters duplicated on the blank upper half. The handwriting was loopy but legible—the benefits of private tutorage—and she read aloud to Gabriel.

Detective Bishop. You win.

Heather took a beat, her heart pounding.

You were right about everything. Mason hurt Jenny badly, and I helped him finish her off. He couldn't take it, but I could. I lived with myself for a long time, not guilty but resentful of her actions. Mariah was easy too. A death for my life. Cheyenne was harder. I didn't love her, but I cared for her. Taylor was the straw that broke the camel's back. Alive or not, I can't live with what I did to her, and a court case—lost or won—won't change my fate. I believe in God and the Devil, and I think the latter has ahold of me. So I'm going downstairs to meet him early. I've never been a patient man, and I can't live my life tortured by what is coming to me, so I might as well get it over with. I'm sorry to those I've hurt. I'm sorry to Penelope. I'm sorry to Mason. I'm sorry to you. Until we meet again, Heather. Hunter Sherman.

"Poetic," Gabriel said sourly.

Heather folded the letter back up, put it back in its place atop the envelope, and looked at Hunter, his eyes glassy and jaw slack.

"So that's that," she said. "Full confession."

"Full confession," Gabriel confirmed before putting his hand on her shoulder. "You were right all along."

It was of little consolation, but Heather tried to see the upsides. No more deaths, an unhappy ending for Hunter, and no court case, aside from the possibility of his parents suing the department.

"He didn't mention Hazel," she said.

Gabriel dropped his hand and furrowed his brow. "Maybe that one really is a coincidence. Some frat boy killed her at a Halloween party. I guess that's Pullman PD's problem now."

"Yeah, I guess so."

"Hey," he said, moving in front of her, breaking her line of sight, "it's over."

"Yeah."

"Do you want me to call it in?" he asked, his voice much steadier than hers, though she could practically hear his heartbeat drumming in every word spoken.

"Yeah," she answered quietly, despite being his superior.

Gabriel pulled his phone from his pocket. "I'll be outside. You coming?"

Heather leaned and grabbed the letter. "I'll follow you down. I just need to check something."

"Okay," Gabriel said, brow quirked. "Come on, let's get out of here."

They shuffled out of the room, leaving the door open, and headed down the stairs. At the bottom, Heather turned up the hall as Gabriel opened the front door. He didn't ask questions as he pressed dial on Tina's contact, and Heather watched him greet their boss before moving forward.

She opened the narrow door to the kitchen, moved through to the office, and approached Hunter's organized desk. There were a few pieces of paper stacked beside his desktop computer. There wasn't much to each of them—ticked to-do lists, notes about employee bonuses, and a grocery list—but as she laid the letter down beside them, even she could tell the handwriting was a perfect match.

CHAPTER THIRTY-EIGHT

THE DETECTIVE

Hunter Sherman was a killer, and his status hit the papers by the following day. An expert confirmed what Heather already knew—that the handwriting was a match—and forensics verified the saliva on the envelope was his, and he had residue all over his hand. Mason's guilt was also confirmed by the legitimacy of the suicide note, and soon Heather was shaking hands with the mayor—Kenneth Ward—before camera flashes. Like Dennis Burke, another serial killer had been halted with a bullet to the brain, and her credibility was restored.

Yet the rest seemed a distant fantasy. There was paperwork to fill out, an unconscious Taylor to visit, and innumerable funerals and memorials to attend. Not that she minded. The closure and invites felt positive, and first on the docket was a memorial for Thimbles at the end of the week. Then the victims would follow, their funerals taking more time to plan than a slapdash gathering at Sherwood's.

As it turned out, Thimbles, or rather Michael Ford, had been telling the truth about his tragic backstory. Heather had done a little digging, and using his real name, it didn't take long to find out his daughter had been murdered by her husband, and his wife had passed shortly after. He had lived in Hallington before she died, working as a butcher, explaining his ability to survive on wild-caught meat without getting sick. Additionally, it seemed some people still remembered him fondly at his old place of work, so Heather passed their details along to Bobby and Amber, who organized the whole thing. It was unlikely to be busy—the jury was still out considering his more recent behavior—but it seemed the least she could do for tarring and feathering his posthumous reputation.

Despite all this, technically, Heather's job was done. However, there was still something bugging her—the Durands. Yes, Alain was innocent, and Leah's involvement had been explained, but when trying to tie up the case in a bow, Leah jutted awkwardly from the package, piercing the smooth wrapping paper. There was still something there, and Heather—unwilling to let anyone else down—intended to find out what.

So she waited for the news of Hunter's demise and guilt to reach Hallington so that Leah was no longer under lock and key and headed to the Durand household, hoping that Leah's lockdown would leave her itching to leave the confines of her home. Not that the tail was likely to lead them anywhere interesting, but Heather thought it was a good place to start in the absence of other options.

She told no one about this, not Gabriel, not Tina. No one. This was for her satisfaction alone. Leah Durand had a secret, and she was going to lose her mind if she didn't unearth it. Then, maybe, she could relax—that was, until Hunter Sherman's relatives drove her out of town with pitchforks.

Maybe it would be for the best, she thought, the window down and the wind in her hair. Then Glenville would be free of their curse and she could change her name, get bangs, and start over somewhere new as a dog groomer or an antique store owner. She smiled at the thought. It was nice to dream, even if said dream was packed into the bowl of a pipe.

Julius had countered about the curse when she'd accidentally mentioned it. Ever the professor and scientist, he said it was all about statistics. It would be like saying he was cursed because he saw dead bodies every day. People didn't start dying around her until she became a cop. Not to mention, most of this was in motion before she even stepped foot in Glenville. Hikers had already gone missing, and Penelope was already dead. Sure, the crime statistics were worse than your average small town, but Glenville didn't even break the top five hundred.

"So, you're not cursed," he'd said. "You just don't have the reprieve everyone else has. You don't get to turn a blind eye to this. You're the only detective in a town of over two thousand people. There's no ignorance in our world."

It was nice and most certainly reassuring, but as she drove around Hallington, waiting for Leah to hopefully make a move, she couldn't help but feel like a plague, a blight, spreading sickness into another beautiful town. Yet she was compelled. She supposed it was how bacteria felt—compelled to infect.

After three hours, Heather nearly abandoned ship. Leah wasn't coming out, and her plan to tail her started to feel downright insane. However, when a car pulled up and a sweet-looking lady with gray hair wearing a lot of knitwear emerged, Heather's motivation returned. She stayed put in the distance, her car hidden behind a horse-shaped topiary, and watched as the storybook grandma knocked on the door. Leah opened quickly and embraced the woman, his face scrunched and reddened, before ushering the older woman inside. With the woman in the doorway, Leah began to dither until her assumed mother shooed her and blew her a kiss. Then Leah finally got into her car.

It was go time, and Heather carefully followed Leah, always remaining three cars back to avoid suspicion. After six minutes, they approached the hospital, and with great disappointment, Heather realized that this entire plan was ridiculous. Leah was visiting Alain, her husband, in the hospital and then would likely run some errands while Grandma enjoyed some quality time with baby Theo. It was boring, normal people stuff because Leah was a boring, normal person.

Except… she didn't stop at the hospital, the shops, or the cafés; instead, she continued toward the back of the "Welcome" sign with only one car between herself and Heather and headed out into the wilderness and onto a road that led straight to Seattle.

"Where are you going, Leah?" Heather muttered, catching sight of the Hallington sign in the rearview mirror and feeling decidedly grateful that the car in between them was one of those huge Dodge RAMs with the animal demolishing grills. That gave Heather a decent amount of hiding space as she continued to pursue Leah toward Seattle.

Forty minutes later, just outside of the city limits, Leah veered off the road, and Heather continued to drive for half a mile before making a U-turn and returning to the spot that Leah had turned off into. Leah's car was parked on a dirt patch: off, empty, and surrounded by undergrowth. It was clearly somewhere only she knew about.

Heather pulled up beside her, exited the car, and looked around at the endless forest. On the one hand, Leah was now apparently on foot and thus much easier to stalk, but on the other, tracking a person through an unknown wilderness was much more difficult than following a car on the road.

Fortunately, this wasn't Heather's first rodeo, and after inspecting the perimeter of Leah's vehicle, she spotted her footprints—Converse, if she wasn't mistaken—and followed them toward trampled bracken. With a vague destination in mind, Heather followed the snapped branches and crumpled leaves into the expansive state forest.

Though it took twenty minutes to catch up, Heather eventually found her. Ultimately, it was not her instincts or even her tracking abilities that led her to her mark but the other woman's incessant muttering and stomping. Heather, on the other hand, remained completely silent as she followed from a distance, hiding behind trees, darting from trunk to trunk as Leah gesticulated wildly.

If Heather didn't know any better and hadn't seen the woman's careful driving, she would assume that she was looking at someone suffering from schizophrenia or some other type of delusion-inducing psychotic illness. Sure, it was possible for her to be having a manic episode, but Heather knew that this was something else. This was seeing a person who thought they were utterly alone, allowing their emotions to run rampant.

Leah paused suddenly and turned, and for a terrifying second, Heather thought she had been caught until the woman stooped to pluck a purple flower from the ground and then continued on her way, still talking incoherently to herself.

Heather caught her breath, her heart still pounding. She had no idea why she was so terrified. She had the gun and power, yet she was fearful of being caught in the act. What if Leah reported her or tried to sue the station? What if she also had a gun in that fanny pack of hers? What if they never made it to the mysterious destination? Somehow the last option was by far the worst one.

They walked for another five minutes at least and were a good mile from the road and at least a dozen from anything else when Leah suddenly disappeared. Heather moved forward quickly, worried she'd accidentally fallen from a cliff ledge, only to see Leah skillfully scramble down a ridge using rocks and vines to slow her descent. Finally, she reached the base of an overgrown clearing, and Heather watched with intrigue from higher ground as Leah knelt beside something obscured by a tree.

Heather moved carefully, cautiously, trying to improve her scope, and yet as Leah stooped to lay the flower on the ground, a branch snapped from beneath her boots. Heather froze, and Leah looked up sharply and stared directly at Heather. At the same moment, Heather caught sight of what Leah had come all this way for. A little wooden cross hammered at an angle into the earth.

They looked at each other, and Leah, a deer caught in the headlights, unzipped her fanny pack. Heather unholstered her gun and pointed it at the woman, and Leah let out a terrible moan, dropping her pepper spray to the ground.

"Seriously?" Heather asked from afar. "You were going to pepper-spray a cop?"

"Don't shoot!" Leah begged hands on her head.

Heather sighed and put her gun away. "I'm not going to shoot you, Leah. Keep your hands on your head. I'm coming down, and then we're going to talk."

Heather's descent was far from graceful, but Leah still stared at her as if a mountain lion was coming her way instead of a bumbling detective covered in mud. At the bottom, Heather straightened and brushed herself off. She took two steps forward, keeping her own hands raised.

"Okay, on the count of three, we'll both put our hands down, but no funny business. You pepper-spray me, and we're going to have a problem, okay?"

Leah nodded.

"Okay. One, two, three."

They lowered their arms, and Heather looked between Leah and the grave marker.

"So, Leah, who's in the dirt?"

CHAPTER THIRTY-NINE

THE DETECTIVE

"Y OU'RE NOT GOING TO BELIEVE ME," LEAH WHIMpered, her palms in the dirt and her body wracked with sobs.

Heather reached out and grabbed Leah's upper arm in an attempt to haul her to her feet. Leah scurried backward, wrenching her arm from Heather's grasp and holding it to her chest. Heather raised her hands and took a step forward.

"I'm not going to hurt you, Leah."

"No," Leah moaned, curling into herself.

Heather sighed impatiently and held out a hand. "Come on, stand up. You look ridiculous."

Leah glared at Heather, and though the expression packed a punch, Heather preferred contempt to melodrama.

"Leah, I'm not going to leave you alone, so that leaves you with two choices: tell me who's in the grave or put these cuffs on."

"All right! I'll tell you. But you're going to end up arresting me anyway."

"We'll see. Come on, let's go sit on that log," Heather said, stepping forward again, her hand still outstretched.

Leah hastily got to her feet with a sneer. "I can do it," she snapped. "I'm not a child."

"No kidding?" Heather asked dryly, following Leah to the mossy log and sitting at the opposite end. "Here I was thinking I'd finally caught the baby bandit."

"Ha ha."

"It's no laughing matter. Toddler crimes are on the rise."

Leah cast another filthy look in Heather's direction. "You're not funny," she said informatively.

"And you're a crappy liar, so we both have our flaws."

Leah bobbed her leg. "I've never told anyone about this. Not even Alain."

"Please don't tell me you're actually the 'Glenville Ripper' or whatever they're calling him. I don't think I'll survive the headache."

"The Glenville Ripper, huh? That sucks."

"Yeah, it does," Heather said, staring at Leah's profile.

"I'm not a serial killer."

"But you've killed somebody?"

"Not exactly."

Heather nodded toward the grave. "Then who's that?"

"That," she replied, "is Hazel Brock."

"Ah," Heather replied, staring at the cross.

"Yeah."

Heather looked around at the woodland. "We're a long way from Pullman."

"About five hours if you take the WA-26."

"So, are you going to tell me how she ended up out here?"

"As I said, you won't believe me."

"Try me."

Leah started at the beginning.

October 2022. She'd just gotten home from an anniversary dinner with Alain when she received an email. It was from Hazel, who was pursuing her doctorate in English at the Washington State Graduate School. Maybe it was the wine, but Leah read it eagerly. They'd been best friends in high school but severed connection after the Penelope incident. Leah had wanted to go to the police and had tried to reach out to Penelope to persuade her to do so. In doing so, she was ostracized, even by a reluctant Hazel, and then the torture really began. Though Leah hadn't cared about being bullied half as much as she'd missed Hazel. It was the worst breakup she had ever experienced, and sometimes it still hurt to think about it, even a decade later.

The email read:

Hi. I know this is weird, but not only do you deserve an apology, I need to give one to you. It's been a long time since high school, and with distance comes realization. I was a bad friend and a terrible person. I should've never said what I said to you, I should've never taken their side, and I should've gone with you to the police. I know it's too late to undo any of that, but I'm hoping that maybe, for us, it doesn't have to end in misery. We can't change the past, but we can change the future by healing, growing, and making things right. I miss you a lot. I've never entirely managed to replace what we had. If you're interested, there's a Halloween party on my campus next Saturday, and you could stay in my apartment if you want to catch up. No pressure.

Hazel.

Leah, tipsy at the time, was over the moon about Hazel's olive branch extension and quickly accepted the invitation with a typo-riddled reply. Like Hazel, she too had struggled to replicate their perfect friendship, especially since she'd moved town and married young. In fact, all of her "friends" were actually Alain's friends, and though they were nice, they were much older and far more interested in academia and dinner parties than they were in celebrity gossip and baseball games.

For whatever reason, Leah didn't tell Alain whom she was going to meet. Instead, she kept it simple, saying she was going to the WSU campus to go to a party with an old friend. Alain, neither a jealous nor suspicious man, encouraged her to have a good time, stay safe, and text him when she got there.

So when Saturday rolled around, she excitedly got into her costume and headed toward Pullman, Washington, with nothing but pajamas, makeup wipes, a toothbrush, and a bottle of strawberry vodka—just like old times.

When she arrived, she parked in a small shady lot, wanting to avoid drunken damage to her expensive sports car, and tentatively wandered onto the campus. She had worn the only Halloween costume she owned—a haunted doll that looked more akin to Pippi Longstocking—but from the stares she received, she knew she looked good. The grounds were packed full of costumed students, and she felt young again for the first time in years. Not that she was unhappy to be a married homeowner at twenty-seven with a baby next on the agenda, but she was far from carefree. So with a negative pregnancy test taken that morning, she took the opportunity for one last hurrah before the inevitability of that second line changed her life forever.

A group of strangers beckoned her over for shots, which she gladly accepted and topped up with her bottle. Just as she was about to introduce herself, somebody grabbed her shoulders. She turned and saw a bloody sheet ghost watching her with sparkling eyes. She could tell it was Hazel immediately from the warmth of her expression and her signature coconut body spray.

Hazel smiled, the corners obscured by the ragged edge of the third face hole, and pulled Leah in for a hug.

"It's so good to see you!" she gushed before pulling away, hands on Leah's shoulders. "Raggedy Ann?"

"Haunted doll," Leah corrected. "Sheet ghost?"

"Charlotte Brontë. I know it's hard to tell. As it turns out, all ghosts look the same."

Leah laughed and offered Hazel the shot she was holding. As Hazel downed it appreciatively, Leah swigged from the bottle, and suddenly they were teens again. After another squealing hug, Hazel took Leah by the hand, and off they ran, weaving through the crowd, looking for a place to sit, drink, and catch up before the dancing began.

They talked as if nothing had ever happened, and though they both could've stayed on that bench, passing a bottle back and forth all night, eventually, the time came to party. Soon the night was in full swing. They did karaoke at the campus bar, tore up the dancefloor among flashing lights, and were chased out of a corn maze by a guy wielding a chainsaw. Leah was having the time of her life and was keen to keep the party going. So when Hazel received a text about an apple-bobbing contest in one of the apartments, Leah encouraged her to say yes. All they needed to do was stop by Hazel's place to freshen up and change into sneakers.

Hazel's apartment was cute and just as organized as expected, and as Hazel excused herself for a lengthy bathroom excursion, Leah looked around. Then an idea struck her. As teens, they'd delighted in scaring each other, and Halloween seemed to perfect opportunity to continue the tradition. So she grabbed one of the many awful Halloween masks from the coffee table, headed into the tiny kitchen, and using a stool, climbed on top of the fridge and turned off the lights with a broom handle.

Hazel returned to the living area and called out for her friend.

"Come on, bitch, we've got to go. There's this really hot girl there that I'm trying to hook up with. She's a poetry major with a buzzcut, and I think I'm in love." She paused, opening a cupboard door. "Leaaahhhhh. Come on. Please don't scare me."

Leah considered getting down then, but as Hazel paced toward the kitchen, she decided to follow through with her plan. Hazel turned on the lights, looking all around, but not up, until Leah unleashed a terrible scream from atop the fridge, her hands raised like claws.

Hazel shrieked and fell back, tripping on the bottom of her costume as she went and hitting her head on the kitchen counter. It didn't seem like a particularly hard blow—her thick hair and the costume itself cushioning the impact—but she sank to the floor and lay flat on her back as Leah clambered down from the top of the fridge.

"Hazel, are you okay?" she asked.

Hazel didn't move—a common revenge tactic.

Leah laughed. "I'm sorry, okay? I couldn't resist."

She knelt by Hazel's side. Her friend's eyes were open but unblinking.

"Okay, very funny. Way to get me back. The problem is, I know your weakness."

Leah positioned her hands and zapped Hazel's side, a trick that had always put an end to playing dead in the past. She assumed, at first, Hazel had simply become less ticklish in the past decade, but then she felt it. The wet. Blood was pooling around Hazel's head, and when Leah lifted the sheet, her friend was unmistakably dead, her head dented by the sharp edge of the marble counter.

"Does... does that count as manslaughter?" Leah asked, turning to Heather.

Heather rubbed her forehead. "Honestly, I have no idea. Maybe, maybe not. If you'd called an ambulance..."

"But I didn't."

"No," Heather said, her fingers tingling from holding her breath. "So, what did you do next?"

"I wrapped her head up in bandages and duct tape to stop the bleeding, put the costume back on, and propped her up in the living room. Then I cleaned. Luckily, there wasn't too much blood, and Hazel was a clean freak, so she had every cleaning supply known to man. I ended up doing the whole house, just so the kitchen wouldn't look so suspicious. She had a UV light for her fish tank, and I used that to double-check. When I was sure there wasn't a drop left behind, I picked her up, put her arm over me, and pretended that she was really drunk if anyone looked in our direction, which almost nobody did. Then I went to the parking lot, which didn't have cameras; put her in the back seat; and took off. I figured, the further away, the better, so after five hours, when there were no cars around, I pulled over here. Then I took her out of the car, dragged her down here, and buried her."

"With what?"

"I had a shovel in the trunk I bought the day before. I was planning to redo the garden. Not that I ever got around to it. Didn't have much interest in digging after that."

"That's convenient."

"You don't believe me."

"Actually, I do," Heather said, all the tension she'd felt around Leah in the past vanishing. "But I don't know if anyone else will. Did anyone see you together? I know there was an investigation."

"Yeah, they did. There was CCTV too, but no one knew my name, where I'd come from, or even what car I drove. I was wearing *a lot* of makeup too."

"Thank God for Halloween," Heather said flatly, harrowed by the tale and genuinely sorrowful for what Leah, and Hazel, had been through. "Alain's a true crime fan, right?"

"He is."

"And he didn't question anything when you came home covered in blood?"

"I changed into my pajamas and used the makeup wipes. Slept in my car too and came home in the morning."

"And he never saw you and your costume on the news?"

"If he did, he never said anything. He was a little reserved that week, but then a month later, I was pregnant, and whatever he knew, he chose to forget."

"That's lucky," Heather said.

"All of it was. Until you came along."

"Sorry," Heather replied, unapologetic but not unkind.

Leah breathed deeply. "Honestly, it's a relief. This has been tearing me apart for the past year. I haven't been a great wife or a good mother because all I can think about is her. I visit when I can, but I know it's not enough."

"No, it's not."

"I guess I'm under arrest?" Leah asked.

Heather frowned. "Leah, as much as I'd like to keep your secret, you know I can't. I wouldn't be good at my job if I did. But I'm not going to arrest you, not yet. I'm going to let you go home, cuddle your son, talk to your mom, visit your husband, and then, in the morning, you're going to turn yourself in at the Hallington precinct. I'll call them around midday if you haven't, and know that if you run, I will find you."

"I understand. Thank you, Heather."

Heather smiled sadly, stood, and held out a hand, helping Leah to her feet.

"I told her that you caught the killer," Leah said, addressing the grave.

"Does she seem happy about it?" Heather asked.

Leah looked sadly at the lonely little cross. "I wish I had an answer for that, but I guess it'll be a long time before I know for sure."

Birdsong interrupted them, a beautiful, haunting melody that reverberated through the lush forest. The corner of Leah's mouth curled upward, and she looked at Heather with a shrug.

"Maybe?"

"Yeah. Maybe," Heather agreed.

CHAPTER FORTY

THE DETECTIVE

As Heather watched Leah drive away from the side of the road, she attempted to relish in tying up her most frustrating loose end, yet reprieve did not come willingly. Aside from Leah, Alain, and hopefully Taylor, everyone involved in the case was dead. It was strange and perhaps naive, but Heather—like Taylor identifying Mariah—had been holding out some degree of hope that Hazel would be out there somewhere, having fled the pressures of academia or a messy breakup. The confirmation was gutting, and all of it weighed heavily on her as she trudged to her Granada.

She sat behind the wheel, exhausted in the dark, and as her lids joined her body in being weighed down, she decided to continue toward Seattle instead of turning back toward Glenville.

She considered heading to her parents' apartment but knew she'd only worry them to death and would be forced to tell a story that her mouth was too sore to recite. So instead she scrolled back through her texts, found Julius's address, put it into her phone, stuck it in the cup holder on full volume, and hoped he wouldn't mind an unexpected visit.

She parked in the complex below the modern high-rise, balked at the ticket expense, and took the elevator to the lobby. She explained to the friendly desk clerk, who was watching TikTok videos on her phone, that she was there to see Julius Tocci.

The woman caught sight of the detective badge on her belt and asked, "He's not in any trouble, is he?"

"No, he's a friend."

"Oh, good. He's one of my favorites. Good tipper and easy on the eyes. Would hate to see that face behind bars."

Heather smirked. "Which floor is he on?"

"Oh, he's in the penthouse. So, just press the *P*. Don't worry about the code, I'll okay it."

Heather's raised her eyebrows. "Will do."

The girl went back to her videos, which echoed around the gilded room, and Heather made her way to the elevator and did what she was told. She pressed *P*, waited for the keypad to beep, and up she went. Eleven stories passed in a blink, and the double doors opened to reveal a smaller secondary lobby with a tiled floor, gold brocade wallpaper, and two enormous monsteras. Straight ahead was a wooden door with a doorbell and another keypad.

She approached and pressed the button with a buzz, but when she heard a woman's tinkling laughter in the distance, she flushed furiously and hastily backed toward the elevator. He had a guest over—of course, he did—and she was being unforgivably rude by showing up announced.

"What were you thinking?" she hissed at herself, pressing the elevator button repeatedly, praying she could disappear without being caught.

The penthouse door opened as the elevator arrived, and Julius called out, "Heather?"

She twisted to look at him, her foot stopping the door from closing. He was dressed in pajama pants and an oversized T-shirt, and his feet were clad in socks and slides. She'd never seen him look so informal. He pulled his glasses from his curly hair and positioned them in the proper place before staring at her as if there was a full-body apparition on his doorstep.

"Sorry," she said, waving goodbye as the elevator arrived. "You have company, and I'm being so rude. I just was in the area, and—"

He pulled a remote from his pocket, pointed it into the room behind him, and the laughter stopped. "Surround sound," he explained. "Sounds real, doesn't it?"

"It does. What are you watching?"

"*Real Housewives*," he admitted with an embarrassed laugh. "I know it's stupid, but it's a good—"

"Distraction," she finished. "I know. I like it too. Well, maybe *like* is the wrong word. Sometimes it stresses me out too much to enjoy. I'm mostly a home-shopping type of gal."

"Ah, the good old HSN. I know it well." Julius smiled briefly but grew stony-faced as he looked her up and down. "Heather, you're filthy."

Heather looked down at her mud-caked clothes and brushed some debris from her slacks to the ground. "Sorry," she said sheepishly.

Julius waved her apology away. "I own a vacuum. So, where have you been?"

"It's a long story."

"Would you like to come in and tell it?" he asked.

"Actually, I'd rather not."

"Okay," Julius replied, clearly confused.

"Tell the story, that is," she clarified. "But I'd like to come in."

"*Casa mia è casa tua*," he said, stepping back from the door.

"Don't people usually say that in Spanish?"

"Well, I'm not Spanish."

Heather plodded forward, wiping her shoes on the mat before abandoning the cause and removing them altogether. She looked at Julius apologetically.

"Do you have a chair you don't care about that I can sit on?"

"I have something even better. A shower and some clean clothes."

Heather put her hands together in prayer. "My savior."

"It's at the end of the hall, I'll put some options outside the door."

"Thank you," she said softly, moving in for a rare hug.

He hugged back, and when she released, he darted forward, his hand moving toward her face. She froze, but what she expected—and perhaps feared—didn't occur. Instead, he tugged at her temple and removed a thin twig, the dead leaves still attached. He waved it around questioningly.

She laughed. "Today has been interesting."

"I can tell. I'll have some food and wine waiting for you when you get out."

"Thanks," she said sleepily before shuffling along the long hallway to the enormous bathroom.

Though she barely acknowledged it in her exhausted state, the beauty of the penthouse was still apparent. The floorboards were dark, the walls were charcoal, and though the combination might have been gloomy in a smaller building, the high ceilings, downlights, abundance of stylish decor, and plentiful lamps made it not only chic but cozy despite the enormity.

In the marble-walled bathroom, she took one of the best showers of her life so far beneath the overhead rain spout. Afterward, dressed in a towel, she opened the door a crack and grabbed the flannel pants, oversized T-shirt, tube socks, and baggy boxers from the pile. All of them were clean, the labels still intact, and once she'd pulled them on, she noticed a dozen pairs of white fluffy slippers on a rack. The sign above said, "For Guests," so she retrieved a pair and slipped them on before emerging. She felt like a brand-new woman and planned to get a quote for a rain shower as soon as she got home.

As she made her way up the hallway, Julius turned and looked at her as he sat on the enormous couch, two full glasses of wine in hand.

"Sorry, I didn't have anything in your size."

"No, this is great. I always used to wear Dan's clothes when I wasn't working. Women's clothes lack comfort. And pockets."

She rounded and collapsed onto the chaise section of the ash-gray couch and looked around at the enormous room.

"This place is insane," she said, noting that the ceiling was two stories high and the second story of the apartment's balcony overhung the TV unit. Then she twisted and gasped, her sore back cracking in the process. The huge windows and balcony were impressive enough, but it was the glittering city view that really took her breath away.

Julius chuckled. "You know, I take it for granted, but whenever someone comes over and makes the face you're making, I feel like the luckiest man alive."

"You should. This is crazy. Like really crazy. I thought it would be nice, but wow."

Heather scooched and sat, accepting the glass of wine and bringing it to her lips. It was made of thin glass and had a flat base to the bowl. It looked like something stolen from a film set for a movie about rich people from the future, and as she watched Julius take a sip, she readjusted her hand to mimic his form. It smelled expensive, and a singular sip confirmed this fact.

"Jesus," she moaned.

"Good?"

"Mm-hmm."

"So," Julius began, clearly not knowing where to go from there.

"So, you want to know why I was in the forest."

"I'll admit my curiosity is piqued, but please don't tell me if you don't want to."

"No, we can talk about it," she said, leaning forward to pick at the charcuterie board. "I think if I don't, I'll go insane. But then"—she pointed the cracker in his direction—"I need you to distract me because God knows I need it."

Julius chuckled. "Deal."

Heather swallowed painfully, a fraught day and exhaustion wearing at her emotional resolve and bodily functions.

"I found out what happened to Hazel Brock."

"The one who went missing from campus?" Julius asked, dutifully recalling what Heather had told him about the case, even though she knew it was not the only one on his plate.

"Yeah, I followed Leah Durand out into the woods, and she led me to Hazel's grave. Turns out she went to a party at Washington State and accidentally scared Hazel to death in her apartment."

"Like a heart attack?"

"No, she made her jump, and she fell and hit her head."

Julius shook his head, removing his glasses to polish them on his shirt. "That's dreadful. Poor woman. Poor both of them. Did you arrest her?"

"No, I let her go under the agreement that she turns herself in in the morning."

"So, that's everything? No holes?"

"No holes," Heather answered.

"You must be pleased."

"Yep," Heather replied, choking up, but not because of the sourdough that filled her cheeks.

"Heather, what's wrong?" Julius asked, scooching closer, his face fraught with concern.

"I screwed up. I didn't catch him quick enough, and he killed three people that I could have saved. It just feels like a repeat of the goddamn Paper Doll nightmare all over again. Except I didn't even catch Hunter. He caught himself."

Julius frowned. "I'm sorry, this must be uniquely painful for you, and with everything else going on with Dan…" He caught himself. "Sorry, I know you don't want to talk about that."

Heather smiled weakly. "Not just yet. But I know you know what's going on."

"I do, and you know I will never push you—and this is the last thing that I'll say on the matter—but if you believe that there is a connection between your ex-husband and the Lilly Arnold case, you know what you have to do."

Heather exhaled and washed her mouthful down with wine. "Yeah, I know. This case especially has taught me how deadly secrets can be." She paused and looked him in the eye. "Not today, but soon. I promise."

Julius nodded fervently. "Of course. No rush."

"A little rush," Heather replied, her voice creaky.

"Well, as you said. Not today. But regarding today, do you feel any sort of relief? Now that it's all over?"

Heather closed her eyes, feeling the tension in her body. "Not yet."

"I hope it comes soon."

"Me too."

"Well," he said, "I suppose it's my turn to distract you. So pick your topic: food or autopsies."

Heather pretended to think deeply. "I think I'll go with food."

"Excellent choice. Let me tell you about these cheeses. Now this one comes all the way from—"

"Can I crash on the couch?" Heather asked abruptly.

"Can you crash on the couch?" Julius repeated, his brows knitted together in disapproval.

She hung her head in her hands. "Sorry, I—"

"When I have a perfectly good guest room? No way."

Heather looked up to see an amused smirk on his face. She exhaled in something like relief and popped a chili-stuffed olive in her mouth. "Thanks, Julius."

"Heather, I'm sure you know by now that you never need to thank me."

Heather shrugged. "And yet, I'm still going to."

"Well, if you must," Julius said, "Anyway…"

Heather watched intently as he enthused about each cheese on the board. Though her eyes grew heavier, she caught every word and swallowed every sample offered. Époisses de Bourgogne, Comté, Parmigiano Reggiano, Fromager d'Affinois, Gorgonzola Piccante were music to her ears and a miracle in her mouth. She realized as she chewed another sliver pasted to a cracker that there was so much man-made beauty in the world. Humans could be evil, but they could also be wonderful, and though relief over this case might never come, she could perhaps find it in other facets of her life. Maybe that was good enough.

CHAPTER FORTY-ONE

THE DETECTIVE

"There she is!" Heather heard Beau exclaim as she squeezed past Sludge's oblivious juggernaut of a bouncer.

She looked around, able to hear but not see her friends through sardine-packed patrons.

"Heather, over here!" he called, and finally, she spotted him, lifted up on tip-toes, extending his lanky build.

Heather pushed through the crowd with difficulty, her new wide-legged, black boiler suit—courtesy of Julius's ex-wife and her unworn belongings—causing her to blend in with the hip crowd for the first time. She emerged by the table where Gabriel and Beau looked her up and down with fascination.

"You look different," Gabriel noted. "Are you wearing makeup?"

"Yeah," Heather admitted, suddenly self-conscious. "I still had the eyeshadow palette Jason Fleming gave me."

"Why did Jason give you makeup?" Gabriel asked, a brow raised.

"For when I went undercover in Texas. Have I not told you about that?" Both men shook their heads. "It's a long story. I had to wear a wig, which sucked way more than I imagined."

"Sick," Beau said. "Like in *Alias*."

Heather chuckled. "I guess."

A passerby bumped into Heather, pushing her into the table, and she gestured around at the crowd.

"What's going on? Is someone famous performing?"

Gabriel shook his head. "Everyone's out celebrating. The Glenville Ripper is dead, the curfew is canceled, and the streets are safe again."

Heather surveyed the room again and noticed that for the first time since Mariah's death, the female population of Sludge outweighed the male one. She also noted that short skirts and low-cut dresses had replaced the conservatism that had taken hold and that even the men seemed metaphorically unbuttoned.

"Huh," she said, unable to suppress a grin. If nothing else, that felt like a win.

"Speaking of celebrating," Gabriel said, gesturing toward the bottle of champagne on ice at the center of the table.

"Don't worry, I won't be having any," Beau added, cracking a nonalcoholic beer. "Just pour me a glass to clink, and then you can double-fist."

Heather chuckled. "I didn't even know they sold champagne here."

"Oh, they don't," Gabriel said. "Beau bribed the owner into letting him bring his own."

Heather looked at Beau fondly, and he gesticulated bashfully. "Least I could do."

"Would you like to do the honors?" Gabriel asked.

Heather chewed her lip. Considering the case's many failures, such a luxurious reward felt unearned and would undoubtedly result in a nasty headache. However, her friends had gone through a lot of trouble to supply it, and even if she didn't deserve any form of congratulations more frivolous than a handshake, Gabriel—who still felt guilty for his failure in tailing Hunter—was in desperate need of a good time.

So she plucked the bottle from the bucket and popped the cork unceremoniously, attracting the attention of the meaty bouncer. She lifted the bottle high in the air, explaining the sound, and poured each of them a glass. They clinked, Beau handed his glass over, and much to the delight of the two men, Heather sipped from both glasses.

"So, what's with the getup?" Gabriel asked. "And where the hell have you been? I stopped by your place, but the lights were off. Your neighbor told me she'd fed the dogs but had no idea where you were."

"I fancied a change."

"And?"

"And I was in Seattle," Heather admitted.

"Seattle," Gabriel muttered. He clicked his fingers and pointed wildly. "It was you!"

"What was me?"

"Leah Durand. She confessed to accidentally killing Hazel Brock this morning. They found her body in the woods just outside of the city."

"I don't know what you're talking about," Heather replied slyly.

"That was nice of you. Letting her confess on her own terms." Gabriel shook his head. "You knew there was something there, and you were right."

"As I said—"

"Yeah, yeah," Gabriel waved her off. "Miss Modesty over here. So, did you stay with your folks?"

Heather hesitated. "Julius, actually."

Gabriel's eyebrows raised up to his hairline, and Heather scowled.

"What?"

Gabriel smirked as he took a sip. "Nothing."

"Who the hell is Julius?" Beau asked, looking back and forth between the pair.

Neither answered him, and he folded his arms.

"Oh, I get it. Heather's bagged herself a bigshot city guy. Gabriel, tell me, is he handsome? Big muscles? I know, he's a bodybuilder. A real *himbo* type. That's why you don't like me. I'm too smart."

Gabriel was nearly on his knees laughing as Beau flexed his pale, wiry arms, taking them all on a trip to a particularly underwhelming gun show. In between tear-inducing hysterics, Gabriel managed to choke out, "*Doctor* Julius Tocci is the best forensic pathologist in the state. And yes, he's handsome. Kind of in a 'distinguished snooty professor' sort of way."

"A snooty professor?" Beau whined. "Heather, are you serious?"

She could only shrug in response.

"I see," Beau whispered, clutching his breaking heart. "I'm the dumb one."

"Of course you are, you idiot," Gabriel wheezed.

"Is he rich?" Beau inquired, ignoring Gabriel with a raised palm.

"Richer than you. Which isn't saying much," Heather retorted.

"Ohhhh, Heather with the zinger," Gabriel laughed.

Beau pretended to wipe away a tear before composing himself. "That's fine, I don't mess around with gold diggers," he replied indignantly.

"Yeah, no shit," Heather teased.

Gabriel exploded again and high-fived Heather with great gusto. Soon all three of them were laughing, and though Heather felt compelled to explain the situation, she stowed it for the sake of comedy. In all honesty, she wasn't sure she could explain what was going on without sounding like an insecure teenager who'd never been kissed. She was clueless as to whether she was misinterpreting Julius's kindness. Her feelings were a mystery even to herself, and having only been in two relationships—both of which had ended in varying degrees of terrible—she was terrified of repeating the past.

Gabriel looked at her as her laughter faded, his expression suddenly serious, and she braced herself for a quizzing when a shy voice interrupted his attempt.

"Gabriel?" the person asked, and all three turned to see Victor Wu standing sheepishly by their table. He was dressed in a white dress shirt and obviously ironed blue jeans, which revealed a lithe muscularity his usual hoodies hid.

"Victor," Gabriel said, surprised. "How's it going, man?"

"Can't complain," Victor replied, running a hand through his '90s-style, middle-parted curtain-bang hairdo. "My parents lifted curfew for the night."

"Curfew, huh?" Beau asked. "That sucks."

"They're worriers," Victor explained. "If I'm not working late, it's home by ten." He paused, clearly embarrassed by the juvenility of the statement in the face of his peers. "How's everything going for you? I mean, you just caught the Glenville Ripper."

"That name," Gabriel said, shaking his head.

"I think the Glenville Hunter has a better ring to it," Beau added to silence. "What? Too soon?"

Gabriel punched him in the arm and continued to talk to Victor. "So, what have you been up to? It's been a while."

He shrugged. "Oh, just working at the diner."

"Don't forget the beetles," Heather added with a grin, much to the confusion of the others.

Victor blushed. "I could never forget them. I actually just pinned a few that passed if you're interested."

"Hell yeah," Heather enthused. "My dad's got loads of stuff like that. Bat skeletons and wet specimens. Might make me less homesick."

Victor smiled. "I'll bring a rhinoceros beetle to work and put it in my locker for when you next stop by. Gold, black, or silver for the frame?"

Heather gestured to her jumpsuit. "Black, always."

"Got it."

"We'll probably be there bright and early," Gabriel said. "I may lack Heather's instincts, but I'm predicting a hangover in our futures."

"I start at eight," Victor replied keenly.

"When do you finish?" she asked. "So I don't miss you."

"Just before lunch," he answered. "How's Taylor Sherman doing?"

"Touch and go," Heather answered.

Victor looked glum. "Well, I hope she recovers."

"Yeah, us too."

Victor shifted awkwardly, clearly unsure how to keep the conversation going. "Anyway, I won't keep you guys. Nice to see you, Gabe."

Victor launched forward for a hug, which Gabriel reciprocated at the last second, and patted Victor on the back as he tossed a confused look in Heather's direction. Victor let go, shifted awkwardly, and gave a small wave goodbye before making his way to the bar.

Gabriel tutted. "I should've invited him to hang out with us."

"I didn't realize you two were still close," Heather said.

"We're not. Haven't talked in years. We were best friends until he dropped out. After that, he just kind of disappeared."

Heather frowned, watching Victor sit at the bar and quietly wait to order. "That's a shame. He seems like a nice kid."

"Yeah, he is. I should've tried harder to stay in touch, but you know how it is."

"Yeah," Heather said quietly. "I'll be right back. He's looking at the menu like it's written in a foreign language."

"You and your big heart," Beau taunted. "Always helping out the underdog."

"You would know," Heather responded, walking toward the bar as Gabriel kept the banter going.

Once close enough, she put a hand on Victor's shoulder, who turned, startled, before smiling.

"Oh, hi," he said.

"So, what's your poison?"

"I honestly have no idea," he said, looking up at the specials board. "What do you recommend for someone who hasn't had a drink since the Fourth of July?"

"A beer," she said. "A light one."

Victor retrieved his Velcro wallet from his pocket and pulled out a debit card. "All right, Bud Light it is."

Heather stopped him, fingertips on his wrist. "Don't worry. I've got it."

"You don't have to do that."

"Consider it payment for the beetle," Heather said.

Victor wavered before reluctantly placing his wallet on the counter.

"Also, I want to thank you."

"For what?" he asked.

"For reminding me that not everyone in this town sucks. Some people are just beetle collectors trying to get by."

Victor beamed. "Well, I'm glad I could be of assistance."

The bartender approached, and Heather ordered for Victor, paid, and looked at the younger man from her standing position.

"And if you want my opinion, I think you should get that GED and see where it takes you. You know, forensic entomologists are pretty sought after. I could put a good word in for you if that's a direction you're ever interested in."

Victor lit up. "Really?"

"Really."

"That would be awesome."

"You know what, I'll check in with you in six months, and if you're on your way to graduating, I'll introduce you to our CSO, Lisa. With everything that's been going on, I think Glenville's police department is in need of a serious upgrade."

"No kidding," Victor said, hesitantly cracking the frosty beer can as if it might explode. "I promise I'll get my GED."

"You better. Have a nice night, Victor."

"You too, Heather."

Back at the table, Heather picked up her glass of champagne, and Gabriel looked at her inquisitively.

"He looks happy. What did you say to him?"

"I said we could do with a forensic entomologist on the team. I know he's into bugs, so I suggested that if he gets his GED and goes to college, we'll have a place waiting for him."

Gabriel smiled. "I'm sure you've made his year. Poor guy deserves better than being a fry cook. He was probably the smartest kid in our year. I always thought he'd go on to great things."

"What happened?" Beau asked. "Like, why did he drop out? He doesn't seem like the druggie type."

Gabriel leaned forward and lowered his voice. "His sister killed herself."

Heather's ears started ringing, and the world around her fell silent as her knees weakened. She put the empty glass on the table at an angle, and it toppled before straightening.

Gripping the edge of the table, she asked, "When?"

"When what?"

"When did she kill herself?"

"Um, 2012, I think. Summer break."

"What was her name?" Heather asked, her heart pounding painfully hard.

"Penny Wu," Gabriel said, looking at Heather with wide-eyed concern. "Why, what's wrong?"

"Penny isn't short for Penelope, is it?" Heather asked through gritted teeth.

"I... Holy shit," Gabriel breathed, glancing over his shoulder at Victor. "I never... I only knew her as Penny. Honest to God, I thought that was her real name. And you never said what year, and... I'm such a goddamn idiot. I'm so sorry, I..." He stopped and poured himself another glass that seemed anything but celebratory.

"What the hell is going on?" Beau asked, bewildered.

"Have you been reading the news?" Heather asked.

"Here and there."

"So, I'm sure you're aware that Hunter Sherman and Mason Fowler raped a girl named Penelope."

"Yeah," Beau said, nodding. "That's why they killed Jenny, Mariah, and Cheyenne, right? They were trying to hide what they'd done."

"Right. As it turns out, Penelope—apparently better known as Penny Wu to those who actually cared about her—was Victor's older sister."

Gabriel repeatedly swore under his breath. "I can't believe this."

"Why wouldn't he say anything?" Heather asked, looking over at the shy man sipping his beer with a look of disgust.

"Maybe he didn't know before now," Gabriel reasoned. "That's probably why he's out celebrating."

"Hey, maybe he can start healing now. I know what it's like to have a dead relative looming over you," Beau said sympathetically.

Heather chewed her lip and said nothing, her eyes still locked on Victor.

"What are you thinking?" Gabriel inquired.

"It's a strong motive," Heather said. "They kill his sister, and he kills them. Not to mention both of his testimonies were wrong. Why is that?"

"Heather, come on," Gabriel protested. "I'm sorry, but that's insane. It's done. It's over. He's just another victim."

"Gabriel."

"Seriously, leave him alone," Gabriel begged.

"You know I can't. I have to talk to him."

Gabriel sighed. "Fine, but you're not going to find anything."

"I really hope I won't," Heather replied, unable to pull her eyes away from her sixth and final suspect.

CHAPTER FORTY-TWO

THE DETECTIVE

Plastic bag in hand, Heather stood in the middle of the dead-end road already piling up with early snow and pressed the End Route button on the digital map. Before her lay 143 Carpenter Street—a vision of bright yellow paint and premature Halloween decorations—and though her feet were literally and metaphorically cold, she had no choice but to follow through with her plan. Sweaty from the long walk and sweatier still from mounting guilt, she sidled up to the modest house, weaving between plastic graves and animatronic zombies as she went.

Cute, she thought as she wiped the slush from her boots on the pumpkin-print "Welcome" mat. It was nice to see that, despite everything, the Wu household had not lost their sense of whimsy.

A gush of water caught her attention, and she turned to watch as the white plastic drainpipe parted in the middle, causing the lower segment to fall sideways and the upper segment—clogged by its bottom counterpart—to explode with dirty water. Heather watched the deluge blankly as the water pooled around the basement window and flinched when the door flew open.

A woman—barefoot aside from the thick woolen tights and wearing a fluffy white cardigan over a cream floral dress—stuck her head outside, and together they witnessed the ebbing disaster.

"I promise it wasn't me," Heather said.

"No, *that* would be my husband and his supposed DIY abilities. I knew we should've just hired a plumber. Serves us right for being so cheap." She turned to Heather, her round face full of sunshine despite the intensifying scent of rot and stagnation. "How can I help you?"

"Hi, sorry, are you Mrs. Wu?"

"I am. And you're Detective Heather Bishop. I've seen you in the local paper." Mrs. Wu looked her up and down. "I must admit, you're much prettier in person."

Heather reddened. "Thanks. It doesn't seem to matter how much time I spend in front of a camera. I never get any better at it. My poor mom only has one halfway decent photo of me, and she uses it for everything. I'm even blinking in my baby pictures."

Mrs. Wu nodded sincerely. "I know her pain. Victor hates having his picture taken. So does his father. Our Christmas cards always look like I'm holding them at gunpoint." She chuckled, though Heather considered it to be more of a tinkle. "So, how can I help you, Detective?"

"Just Heather is fine. And I'm looking for Victor. Is he here?"

"He is," Mrs. Wu replied, scrutinizing Heather's off-duty outfit. "He's not in any trouble, is he? He came back a little tipsy last night. Normally, we have a curfew, but he seemed in such a good mood..." She trailed off, fiddling with the pearl choker that dug into her plump neck.

Not wanting to lie, Heather raised the plastic bag containing two large hardback books and said, "I'm here to deliver a present. I bumped into him last night at the bar, and we got to talking about taking the GED and pursuing forensic entomology. And believe it or not, I was walking around town this morning and saw *An Entomologist's Guide to Crime* in the window. So, I went inside, and one thing led to another, and now I'm here."

Despite not wanting to lie, Heather was doing an awful lot of it. She wasn't even sure if Glenville had a non-used-books bookstore, and if they did, they certainly would not be selling specialized nonfiction such as these. No, these two tomes had come from Lisa's personal collection per her agreeing to their immediate replacement.

Mrs. Wu slid her hand to her chest, her amiable expression becoming tearful. "The GED? Studying? My gosh. That's just..." She paused for breath. "That's wonderful. Please come in."

"Thank you, ma'am."

"Oh, honey, you can call me Janet. And my husband—who is around here somewhere—is Kevin."

"My ears are burning," blurted a jolly voice from somewhere down the hall.

Seconds later, Kevin Wu peered around a doorway with a grin. Like his wife, his face was moon-shaped and his figure hearty. He stepped into full view wearing a "Kiss the Cook" apron and brandished a cake-batter-covered spatula in Heather's direction.

"Hello," Heather said, offering a small wave.

"Oh, Detective Bishop!" Kevin exclaimed. "To what do we owe the pleasure?"

"She's here to give Victor some books," Janet said gleefully. "Apparently, she's convinced him to go back to school."

Kevin's eyes widened, and his grin widened to cartoonish proportions. He looked between Heather and his wife and asked, "Are you serious?"

Heather's deception was backfiring, even if only she could smell the fumes. Here she was, lifting these people up under false pretenses while trying to determine if their son was a serial killer. More than ever, she wished for a suspect's innocence and hoped that Gabriel's instincts were sharper than her own. If he wasn't and they weren't, what was to follow would be the most unpleasant arrest of her career.

"I'm serious," Heather replied, a little nauseous. "I think your son is very bright and could be a great asset to our team."

"Your team?" Kevin questioned. "Wow. Well, isn't that something? We were going to have a little barbecue on Sunday anyway to celebrate the demise of Hunter Sherman, but now we have a much happier reason to celebrate."

"You'll come, won't you?' Janet asked. "If you have the time."

"We'll see how everything pans out," Heather said kindly.

Kevin smiled appreciatively. "Of course. You must be a very busy woman. Though if I can just have a moment of your time."

"Of course."

Kevin Wu began to break down, his face turning red, and Janet ran to his side and rubbed his arm.

"I'm okay, honey," he said sweetly, his voice thick. "I'm sorry, Detective. I just wanted to thank you for solving this case. I had no idea… She never… Penny never said a word, and then I blinked, and she was dead. I had no idea what had happened, but I knew it was something to do with that damn house party. She was different after that. We failed her by not pushing her, and I…" Kevin began to sob. "I'll never forgive myself for that. But you found out, and you took those monsters down. I can never thank you enough for getting my baby justice. And now you're giving my other baby a future."

Heather didn't feel deserving of the praise, but now was no time for self-deprecation. "I'm so sorry for your loss, Mr. Wu. I hope with Hunter gone, your family can begin to heal."

"Thank you," Janet mouthed as Kevin continued to cry. "Victor's upstairs. The second door on the right."

Janet and Kevin merged into one, arms wrapped around each other as Heather made her way up the stairs, crinkling all the way. Glad to be out of eyeline at the top, she took a second to compose herself before rapping on Victor's door.

"Come in," a voice answered.

Slowly, Heather opened the door and peeked inside the cramped and crowded room.

"Hi," she said quietly.

Victor shut his laptop lid and hastily twisted toward her, clearly too shocked to speak.

"Sorry to barge in like this," she added, retreating slightly.

"No, I… I thought you were my stepmom. Please come in. Sorry about the mess."

"Don't worry about it," Heather replied, venturing further into the confined space.

"I missed you at the diner this morning. Sorry to say your beetle is still in my locker if that's why you're here."

Heather shook her head. "I'll grab it next time. My hangover was worse than I predicted. I'm actually here to give *you* something."

She extended her arm and handed over the bag, and he took it, his head cocked in confusion. Though polite, he didn't thank her as he unwrapped the books—which were sheathed in brown paper and string bows—allowing her an unobserved opportunity to snoop.

She addressed the photos first, but they offered little insight. Most were of Victor, his dad, his stepmom, and some older ones of his biological mom. Several were of a very beautiful girl with long dark hair that was blatantly Penelope, and strangely, there were a couple of Victor and Gabriel when they were younger, their arms wrapped around each other. If he had other friends, they were not on display, and Heather felt the loneliness pang in her chest. His only friend was Gabriel, and Gabriel barely remembered that he existed.

Next, her eyes traveled to the most prevalent feature of the room—insects. Some crawled around in jars and plastic terrariums while others were framed on the wall or in the process of being displayed, their limbs and wings pinned symmetrically to varying boards.

"I don't know what to say," Victor said, attracting Heather's attention back to his boyish face. "These are amazing. Thank you so much."

"No problem. I just saw them in town today and thought you might get a kick out of them."

"I will. Can you pass me that pen?"

"Sure." Heather grabbed a ballpoint pen from a pot on his work table and handed it over.

With his left hand, he proceeded to write "Property of Victor" on the first pages.

"Lefty, huh?" Heather inquired.

"Ambidextrous," he clarified, looking down at the chicken scratch. "And yeah, I know it's lame. It's a holdover from being a kid and my sister stealing all of my stuff."

"I actually wanted to talk to you about your sister," Heather said quietly, pushing the door closed. "I want you to know that I know what happened to her. Taylor Sherman told me everything. I know it's of little consolation, but I hope you feel better now that he's gone, and I'm so sorry for your loss."

Victor's glossy eyes cracked her heart, and the way he shut the book and pulled it to his chest threatened to shatter it. "Thank you, and I do. A little."

"Good."

"Not just for her sake either. I think everyone's better off without guys like Hunter around. He was a real monster. I mean, what did he do to the bodies? The stabbing? That was sick. You should search his place for like Satan worship books or something."

"We did," Heather said, her blood freezing over. "CSI found some works by Aleister Crowley and Anton Lavey."

"Huh," Victor replied mildly. "I didn't take him as academic enough for Crowley."

"Yeah. Neither did I."

"Well, I guess he was full of secrets."

"Most sickos are," Heather responded, her intuition unusually numb, preventing her from getting a read. So instead she used logic, the stronger of her abilities.

In order to avoid copycats, the nature of the stab wounds—or that there were any at all—was still not public information. Even the parents of the deceased didn't know about them, not yet. The only people who were privy to these aspects of the crimes were the investigators, Julius, and the killer. Victor was neither an investigator nor was he Julius. So how did he know about the stabbings?

Despite how badly her body begged to crumple, she tried to keep her composure as Victor smiled up at her, his body still wrapped around his gift.

"You should come by on Sunday and celebrate with us," Victor said. "Dad nearly didn't make it after Penny died, and though he got better, I could still see the pain there. But after everything came out, I could see this fog lift. He's happier today than he's been a long time. Between all the crying anyway. And it's all thanks to you. So, if anyone deserves a plate from Chef Wu, it's you."

"Yeah," Heather said quietly, "I'll see how my week goes."

"Awesome," Victor said as he opened his second book to sign.

Heather looked back to the work table. There was a praying mantis pinned to a large rectangle of foam. She looked at the needles one by one, left to right: forearm, bicep, chest, bicep, forearm. The connection almost felt ridiculous, but the manner in which the deceased creature was arranged and punctured reminded her awfully of the wounds on Mariah, Cheyenne, and Taylor's bodies.

"You know, I've been thinking a lot about your offer," Victor said, interrupting her train of thought.

Heather turned back and saw that his eyes, too, were trained on the praying mantis.

"I think that's something I really want to pursue. I mean, I can't stay in the diner forever."

"No, you cannot," Heather agreed.

Victor's eyes flicked up to meet hers, and for the first time, she saw something dark there, beyond the black. "You're a good person, Heather. Just in case nobody's told you that recently."

Heather's lip quivered as she tried to hide her horror behind faux friendliness. "Thanks," she said. "So, I've got to ask, what is it with insects?"

"Honestly, after Penny died and Gabriel abandoned me—no judgment—I needed something alive to fill the void. Something nonhuman. Something that wouldn't rape or betray. Something that wouldn't lie to my face. I guess that's why you like your dogs—"

"How did you know I have dogs?" asked defensively.

Victor blushed and nodded toward her shoulder. "The hair."

"Ah, right."

"Anyway. After all you've seen, you need to come home to something with a heartbeat, something that doesn't know what malice is, something to love and love you in return." He laughed. "Not that these guys love me, not really, but it's nice to pretend."

"Yeah, it is." Heather swallowed. "Well, I'll leave you to your books. I've got to put on the monkey suit and do some media crap."

Victor looked taken aback, clearly wanting to continue their conversation, but he nodded and wished her luck. "I hope I'll see you Sunday."

"Should I bring anything?" Heather asked, keeping the facade going.

"How's your potato salad?"

"Not bad."

"Great, because truth be told, Janet's is terrible." He grimaced. "Raisins. Lots of raisins."

"No raisins in mine," Heather said, crossing her heart. "See you around, Victor."

"I'm sure you will, Detective," Victor said.

Heather paused, her hand on the knob, before opening the door and stepping out into the hallway.

After closing it, she put a hand over her mouth and stared at the unflattering high school portrait of Victor hanging on the opposite wall. She dug her nails into her cheeks and clenched her jaw to stop an angered yell from escaping. She didn't have much evidence—far less than she'd had for Hunter—but there was something wrong with Victor Wu, and this time there would be no hesitation in finding out what.

Next stop, the station, where she'd request a warrant, and tomorrow she'd arrest him herself.

She made her way quietly down the stairs, but even still, Janet and Kevin emerged from the woodwork. She thought to feign something—joy, benevolence, goodwill toward men—but couldn't conjure up anything aside from profound disappointment. So even though she heard them call out, she turned the handle, stepped through the entrance, and walked away, leaving the door banging in the breeze.

CHAPTER FORTY-THREE

THE DETECTIVE

"Okay, so he's ambidextrous," Gabriel said. "Lots of people are."

"His left hand's writing looked a lot like Mason's."

"Which you haven't seen in five years," Gabriel protested.

"I remember."

Gabriel sighed. "What about the other handwriting samples? The ones you found in Hunter's office?"

Heather didn't answer, her eyes on the road and her hands tightly wrapped around the freezing-cold steering wheel.

"Okay, forget the handwriting. What about his curfew?"

"There was a broken drainpipe," Heather said. "I think he was using it to sneak out."

Gabriel pinched the bridge of his nose. "Heather, you're a genius, there's no denying that. But you're seeing evil where there isn't any. This case has gotten to you and—"

Heather shot him a nasty look.

Gabriel raised his hands in surrender. "I'm just saying. Being ambidextrous and pinning insects does not a murderer make."

"Gabriel, he knew about the stab wounds."

"So? Everyone at the precinct, you, Julius, and Lisa know about the stab wounds. That's sixteen people. Somebody probably had a few too many over at Molly Malone's and got blabby."

"Molly?" Heather questioned.

"Malone's. It's where all our coworkers go to drink. See how little you know about them? Maybe Gretchen can't hold her liquor, maybe Reeves is a gossip. Not to mention all of these people have husbands, wives, and friends. Of course, the information was going to leak."

"Gabriel," Heather said wearily.

"Seriously, Heather. What do you have on Victor other than him having a dead sister and a creepy hobby? Mason and Hunter actually raped the girl, not to mention their history of violence against women, the prenup, and the affair. Victor's just some guy who's had a shitty life."

"Well, we're here, Tina agrees with me, and I've got an arrest warrant. If I'm wrong, I'm wrong, but I can't just let him go without knowing for sure."

Gabriel looked crestfallen as Heather turned off the engine. "He was my best friend as a kid."

Heather exhaled. "I know. But you have to trust me."

"I do. Usually. I just…" He trailed off. "Hunter makes so much more sense, and you said yourself you couldn't get a read on Victor. None of your usual gut-grinding or whatever."

"I know," Heather repeated. "But I won't be able to live with myself if I don't do this."

"You're going to have a lot of peace-making to do with his family. And he clearly idolizes you. You told him he could work for you."

"Gabriel, please stop," Heather begged quietly.

"Okay," Gabriel said softly.

"Okay. Come on. Let's not drag this out. I see Janet in the window."

"All right," Gabriel said, bracing himself and taking a little longer than Heather to exit the car.

Victor opened the door and stood on the porch step with a grin. He waved at both of them, his oldest and newest friends, as they approached. If Gabriel hadn't maxed out her guilt levels, the young man's happy expression certainly would have.

"Hi, guys," Victor chirped. "What are you doing here? The cookout isn't until Sunday."

Heather looked him right in the eye with a steely expression. "Victor Wu, you are under arrest on suspicion of murder. You have the right to remain silent. Anything you say can and will be used against you in a court of law. You have the right to an attorney. If you cannot afford an attorney, one will be provided for you. Do you understand the rights I have just read to you? With these rights in mind, do you wish to speak to me?"

To her surprise, Victor calmly held out his wrists. "I'll speak once we're out of earshot," he said without wavering.

Heather saw all the confidence drain out of Gabriel's face as he cuffed Victor and gently led him toward the car. Kevin and Janet appeared in the doorway, once again wrapped around each other, looking at Heather in shock.

"What's going on?" Kevin asked. "What has he done?"

"We have reason to believe your son is the Glenville Ripper," Heather replied calmly. "We're taking him in for questioning. Should our fears be substantiated, he will be allowed one phone call, and I'm afraid to say if he does confess, he will be denied bail."

"But... but... but...," Kevin stuttered. "That's not possible. He was here. He has a curfew. I... He's my son."

"He won't confess. He hasn't done anything wrong," Janet insisted, much angrier than her husband. "He's a good boy." She yanked at her pearls, nearly snapping the string. "We invited you into our home."

"I know, I'm so sorry." Heather glanced over her shoulder as Gabriel opened the back door and Victor ducked to take his seat. "I'll try to keep you updated."

"Don't bother. I'm calling the sheriff," Janet snapped.

More protests followed as Heather silently approached the squad car, and she watched as Victor calmly waved at his father and stepmother from the back seat before facing dead ahead, unblinking and meditative. Gabriel must've noticed because he strained his eyes to look sideways at Heather from the passenger seat, determined not to turn his head toward his childhood friend. He looked devastated, and Heather clapped his shoulder as she sat beside him and began their slow journey toward the police station.

"So this is it," Victor said once Janet and Kevin were out of sight. His voice was oddly childlike in its airy breathiness, and there was a lisp there that Heather hadn't perceived before. The latter was often a sign of exhaustion. He'd been up late, and Heather figured it was because he was waiting for this.

"What do you mean?" Gabriel questioned, pain throttling his vocal cords. He might have been a smoker, but he was never this raspy.

"You've figured it out," Victor explained. "Honestly, I thought it would happen sooner. Not that you're not a good detective," he hastily clarified. "I still think you're one of the best. I suppose I'm just surprised I did such a good job. I've never been much good at anything."

Gabriel shut his eyes, and Heather looked at Victor in the rearview mirror.

"Well, you're hardly an amateur."

Victor chuckled meekly. "I guess not. Not anymore."

"So, you really did it?" Gabriel asked. "You killed all those women?"

"I'm sorry, Gabe," Victor began. "But yes. I couldn't... I couldn't let them live. Not after what they'd done. Especially not Mason and Hunter."

Victor was as calm and mild as one might be when discussing the weather or dinner plans, the expected melodrama nowhere to be found. He was polite, too, easygoing and open. All this only made it more painful and bone-chilling.

"So you killed them too? Hunter and Mason?" Heather asked.

"Everyone except Hazel." He shook his head. "I didn't think Leah had that in her. I figured that one out long before you did by the way. I knew that ugly doll costume anywhere. She wore it religiously in high school. There she was at every party in October, demented Raggedy Ann. I'm surprised she didn't go straight to jail, considering the CCTV was all over the news, but I suppose no one around here much cared about Hazel Brock or Leah Reed."

"You could have turned her in," Heather said.

"I'm not a monster, Heather. I wasn't going to send a pregnant woman to prison, especially one who did my dirty work for me and at least tried to stand up for Penny. Not that I was going to let her get off scot-free, considering she was too much of a coward to go to the cops. I suppose you could call that my falling-off-the-wagon moment, my ruining her marriage."

"So you sent the texts," Gabriel groaned.

"I did."

"Who was the man in the photo?" Heather asked.

Victor shrugged. "Just some random guy. She was with random guys most days of the week, and one of them just happened to look exactly like both Leah's husband and Hunter Sherman, so I took my opportunity."

"I know you're angry that none of them confessed, but why didn't you go to the police?" Heather inquired.

"Heather, come on," Victor laughed, though he sounded closer to crying. There it was, some humanity. "You know they wouldn't have gone to prison. The girls especially. Maybe Mason would've gotten a few years, Hunter a few less, but after half a decade, they'd be back to their lives. Sure, if the world was different, and they'd stare at the inside of a cell till their dying day, I would have gone straight to Gene. But come on, it was Gene, and I know how this works. Penelope did too. I had to make this stick. I had to make it permanent. For her and all the other women they planned to hurt. Rapists don't just do it once. They do it over and over again. Who knows how many other women are out there celebrating right now? There's probably at least five just in this town."

"Why start with Jenny?" Heather asked, noting that Gabriel was entirely checked out, his eyes still closed and his shoulders hunched. "Why not just kill Mason and Hunter? You could've cut their brake lines, made it look like an accident."

Victor looked contemplative as Heather glanced back at him. "Honestly, I don't know. I never meant to kill anyone. It's not like I fantasize about that shit. I didn't torture animals as a kid or hate my mom or anything like that. I was a totally normal guy my whole life, but then they paraded into my place of work, their lives completely untainted by what they'd done. I watched you and Jenny talk. I saw how happy she was, and then when Mason and Hunter showed up and scared her off into the woods, I took off after her like a rescued greyhound with a rabbit. It was complete animal instinct. I was a family pet, but I was also, as it turned out, a killer. No one noticed. Grady was on meth, and Missy was pill-popping, so the fact that I was gone for an hour did not register at all. She was terrified. So was I. It was awful, but once I started, I couldn't stop." Victor stopped to look at his trembling hands. "I was shaking worse than this. That's probably why I failed to finish the job."

"Do you think she deserved it?" Heather questioned, her tone neutral. She planned to squeeze every drop from Victor, and it seemed he had far more blood than a stone.

"Maybe. I mean, she pretended to be Penny's friend to lure her to that party in the first place. Then they all got her drunk, abandoned her, and let those cavemen have their way with her. Sure, they didn't touch her, but everyone at that party was guilty."

"What did you use to kill Jenny?"

"An old piece of pipe from the junk pile out back. Dottie's has been good to me, but it's kind of a crap hole."

"Did you stab her too?"

"No. That inspiration came later."

"Where's the knife?"

"In the duck pond. It was a hunting knife, just as you suspected," he elaborated. Heather raised an eyebrow, and he explained, "Some of your coworkers are pretty chatty."

Gabriel peeled his eyes open, and he and Heather exchanged withering looks. However, the department was a problem for another day, so Heather pressed on.

"Where'd you get it?"

"Don't you remember, Gabe?" Victor asked, addressing his friend. "I'm one of the lucky seven. I actually succeeded in going down to Thimbles's tent when I was like fourteen. We were supposed to go camping together, but your parents wouldn't let you come along, but I went anyway, and I guess I wanted to impress you. I even showed you the knife, but you didn't believe me about where I'd gotten it." He paused. "Honestly, I feel pretty guilty about that part. I never wanted you to blame Thimbles, but my parents are precious about their kitchen knives."

Gabriel was balking, leaning forward as if he might vomit, but Heather couldn't stop now.

"So, what about the rest? Did you use the peavey?"

"You were wrong about that one. I did steal a peavey and stick it in the ground to implicate Hunter, but I found it unwieldy, so I used a steel club. Dad was on a fitness kick last year, so we have all kinds of workout junk in the garage."

"Huh, I never thought of that one," Heather said, still maintaining impartiality, though she was compiling the fury for later.

"I'm sure it seems obvious now," Victor noted politely. "As I said, you're a very good detective. I mean, hey, you got me in the end."

"Maybe I'm not as good as you think. Or maybe you should start writing murder mysteries because I'll hand it to you, I never saw this coming."

"I'll bear that in mind. I need something to do in my cell," Victor said weakly, his resolve weakening.

Nearly at the station, Heather noticed the tape recorder in Gabriel's hand and pulled over by the side of the road.

"I'm sorry, I still have a few more questions."

"Sure," Victor replied, seemingly relieved by the stillness.

"When you gave your eyewitness account back in 2018, why didn't you say Hunter was with Mason? Why did you say that Jenny got into the car with him?"

"Because without Hunter lying—which I knew he'd do—I knew you'd have them thrown in jail, and then I'd never be able to get to them. At that point, I didn't know *what* I wanted to do to them, but I knew inaccessibility wasn't an option."

"What about your curfew? I figured you were escaping using the drain, but…"

Victor laughed. "Nope, the broken drain is all Dad. Yeah, my curfew is 10 unless I'm working the night shift, which I do three nights a week. So, once again, I seized my opportunities when I had them."

"And when you come home bloody and filthy?"

"Dad and Janet are retired. Sleep in until 9 on the dot every day, and nothing wakes them. Dad uses a CPAP, and Janet wears earplugs because of it."

"And how'd you kill Mason and Hunter?" Heather asked, almost enjoying the most easily obtained confession of her career. "That must've been hard, faking their suicides. They were a lot bigger than you are."

"I got into martial arts and MMA after Penny died. I needed to do something with my anger, so I'm stronger than I look. But it helped that they were both blackout drunk and had conveniently forgotten to lock their doors. All I did was wander in, find their guns, threaten them into position, and together we'd blow their brains out. Then I wrote the notes—Mason with my weaker left and Hunter with my stronger right."

"What about the matching samples?" Gabriel asked.

"Oh, I wrote those too and put them in the office. Then I made him lick the envelope by grabbing his tongue with forceps. I guess you're right. By the end, I was no amateur."

"Jesus," Gabriel moaned.

"I just have one more question," Heather said, ignoring her partner's meltdown. "How did you get to Cheyenne and Taylor? The other two, I get, but how did you know where they'd be?"

"I followed Hunter and waited for him to stop arguing with them and leave. Nothing complicated—aside from their relationships."

"Nothing complicated? I can't believe this," Gabriel said, shaking his head. "You should've talked to me, man."

Victor whimpered, Gabriel's disappointment affecting him more than anything else. "Do you know what it's like to come home to your older sister floating in her own blood, a razor blade by her side? Do you know what it's like to try to revive her, to hug her cold body?"

"No."

"No," Victor confirmed. "You don't. So you'll never understand why I needed to do this."

"Why are you telling us this?" Heather asked. "If you'd kept your mouth shut, you probably could've gotten away with this."

"Haven't you heard? Taylor Sherman is going to wake up. And when she does, she'll tell everyone that I was the one who attacked her. Sure, I wanted to get away with it. No one wants to go to prison, but if I'm going to go, I'd rather do it on my own terms."

"You've left your parents without any children," Heather said. "You've ruined your life."

"I don't care," Victor said quietly. "I just don't."

"Okay," Heather said, not believing him. "Gabe, you got all that?" she asked.

Gabriel nodded. "Yep. Unless you've got any more to say?" he asked Victor, twisting slightly in his seat and facing his friend for the first time.

Victor shook his head. "No, that's everything, Gabe. Now I'd just like to enjoy the snow in silence."

Gabriel pressed the Stop button.

CHAPTER FORTY-FOUR

THE DETECTIVE

Addled by a long day, Heather blearily tipped Carl of Whitetail Taxis, muttered her thanks, and forced herself out of the warmth of the vehicle. Gabriel wasn't far behind her, groaning like a man three times his age as he unfurled, a bag of Chinese food clutched to his chest as if it was in danger of being stolen.

"Hey, Detective. Your change," Carl rasped, sticking five two-dollar notes out of the cracked window. Heather only took one, and Carl saluted her. "Oh, and congratulations," he added. "Four consecutive life sentences. Doesn't get much better than that."

"Thanks," Heather said weakly.

Carl looked at her expectantly, but after three days of sitting in a courtroom, she had no desire—nor legal ability—to discuss the trial.

"Have a nice night," Carl said, rolling the window up, clearly disappointed to get so close to the case and come away empty-handed. His wife—whom he constantly mentioned throughout the journey from the precinct to Heather's home—was sure to be disappointed, but Heather couldn't force herself to care about the desires of yet another true crime junkie.

She couldn't help but wonder, what with Leah's upcoming court case—which would hopefully only culminate in a couple of years, if that—whether Alain had lost his love for the genre. Regardless, Heather was happy to hear that they were back together, despite everything. At least there were two lives that Victor didn't completely destroy.

Gabriel was standing by the front door, hopping from foot to foot, dinner in one hand and a mysterious parcel in the other.

"What's this?" he asked.

"No idea. My x-ray specs are in the shop."

"Pity."

Heather jogged to the door, exhausting herself in the process, and grabbed the parcel in exchange for the house keys. She examined it as Gabriel struggled with the stiff lock and realized it was wrapped and tied with the same paper and string as Victor's entomology books had been. Heather shouldered past Gabriel as he opened the door, and as he switched on the light and greeted the dogs, she tore into the thick brown paper, ignoring questions and barks alike.

Inside was another wrapped item, a sealed letter, and a folded note. She started with the note and quickly realized it was from Kevin Wu. She'd received a lot of letters over the past few days from the parents of the deceased—some good, some bad—but the parent of the killer was something else entirely.

Dear Heather Bishop,

Victor asked me to give you these. I have no idea what's inside of them, and I hesitated in giving them to you, but after much discussion with my wife, it seemed the right thing to do.

Apologies for the wrapping paper; we didn't have anything non-festive in the house.

Regards, Kevin Wu.

PS. Should you find it in your heart to do so, I'm sure Victor would love to hear from you as he begins his new life at Washington State Penitentiary.

"What does it say?" Gabriel asked as Heather laid the parcel on the liquor cabinet, unwrapped the gift bottle of bourbon from Julius, and retrieved two glasses from the cabinet.

"It's from Kevin Wu. Apparently, Victor had something he wanted to give me," she replied, holding up the letter and wrapped rectangle.

"Are you going to open it?"

"It'll kill me not to."

Gabriel sighed with relief. "Yeah, me too."

She poured herself a double and turned to Gabriel, who nodded, and poured one for him too. She drummed her fingers on the wood, picked up the items, and traversed to the couch. Turkey and Fireball snuggled up to her, and she gave them each a scratch before tearing the top of the envelope.

Written in loopy, legible handwriting, it read:

Dear Heather,

It's been a difficult few weeks for myself and my family, and though I'm sure some of your colleagues are celebrating my upcoming sentencing, I imagine you have not joined them in the festivities. I'm sorry for the pain I have caused you and for turning out to be such a disappointment. However, I have discovered that the prison offers a GED program, and should you wish to check in on me in six months as originally planned, it would mean the world to me. Who knows, maybe with the wonders of technology, I can work for you on the inside. Thank you for everything, Victor Wu.

Heather handed the letter over, her mouth turned down at the corners. She hated that she was happy that he might still get his GED because, in the end, it didn't matter. He was going to die in prison.

Gabriel shook his head as he skim-read. "Jesus," he said. "Do you think you'll write to him?"

"I don't know," she said.

She really didn't. Contacting him went against all her carefully compiled convictions. He was a sadistic killer, and Taylor Sherman—who woke up two days ago and told all to any journalist that asked—would be traumatized and in chronic pain for the rest of her life.

Yet as Heather watched him shrivel before the court in his ill-fitting suit and cry as he talked about his sister, she couldn't help but pity him and his family. Even the judge looked uncomfortable as Victor relayed his crimes with a sorrowful expression and lilting, lisping voice. His face didn't match his offenses, and all Heather could think was how right Cheyenne had been about the halo effect.

"Probably not," she said after a beat. "I don't write letters to any other killers."

Gabriel nodded. "What's the present?"

Heather braced herself, tore into the Christmas paper, and revealed the rhinoceros beetle he'd promised her. She clutched the black frame and examined it. It was beautiful, it was art, and it pained her more than she could have ever imagined.

"Can you go put this in the drawer?" she asked, peeling her gaze away.

"Yeah," Gabriel said quietly, gathering up the package's contents and burying them away in one of Heather's many junk drawers. He sat back down in an armchair and took a moment to speak. "I think I will. Write him, that is. He was my best friend once upon a time."

Heather looked up at him. In all the chaos, she'd almost forgotten about that aspect. "Are you okay?" she asked.

Gabriel shrugged and began rummaging through the bag of Chinese food. "Not really. Sure, we've taken down a couple of killers now, but none of them have been my friends. It's different when it's someone you care about. I can only imagine how his parents feel."

Heather fell silent, realizing that, to some degree, Gabriel was in the same situation she was with her ex-husband, Daniel. It was the golden opportunity to come clean, no need to bring it up out of the blue. It was still going to be painful, but Julius was right. Secrets were dangerous, secrets hurt innocent people, and worst of all, secrets could kill.

"Are *you* okay?" Gabriel asked.

"I need to tell you something," she said, standing. "And you can't interrupt, or else I'll never say it, and it'll just continue to burn a hole inside of me forever, okay?"

"Okay. Go ahead."

Heather began to pace.

"So I was married to a guy named Daniel Palmer for four years. We met in late 2011, and at the tail end of 2017, he left me. I wasn't doing well. The Paper Doll Case messed me up, and I was not only drinking, but I was a mean drunk. Argumentative, combative, you name it. I also suspected that he was sleeping around, and things got messy. Honestly, his leaving in the middle of the night wasn't exactly unexpected, but it hurt. It really hurt. So I blocked him on everything after I signed the papers and moved to Glenville. I hadn't heard his name until I met up with Julius earlier this year, but despite my curiosity, I still had every intention of leaving him in the past."

Heather was nearly out of breath and saw that Gabriel was watching her manic breakdown with the wariness one applies to a bear entering a campground. She slowed her roll and lowered herself onto the couch, her voice back to normal.

"And then you told me to stop running away from my past. So I looked him up. Not that I blame you," she clarified. "Do you have a cigarette?"

"I do," Gabriel said, startled by the question. "But I'm not giving you one."

Heather nodded. "Okay. Okay. For the best," she convinced herself. "So I looked him up. He had a new fiancée. Katy. Katy Graham. Don't worry, that's not the bit I'm upset about. Under different circumstances, I'd be happy for him. No, the bit I'm upset about is that he killed her."

Gabriel inhaled sharply. "Wait, what?"

"Well, they think he killed her. Seattle PD. Lead suspect, as far as I'm aware. I don't know exactly. I stopped looking after that. I couldn't wrap my head around it. I mean, Julius said they had problems, but so did we, and he never killed me. Anyway..." She paused to take a big gulp of air. "I get all mushy and nostalgic, trying to convince myself he's innocent, so I got back through the photo albums. I find our trip to London. There's a picture of us standing out the front of a pub called the Thistle & Pig right next to Hyde Park in 2016. Okay, fine. But there's something nagging me. I know that pub, I know that park. Then it hits me. Lilly Arnold, the Hyde Park cold case I was working on for Julius. She died while we were staying in London. Not only that, but she's actually in the background of our photo." Having run out of air, Heather stopped abruptly and waved at Gabriel to speak while reaching for her glass.

"So, you think he killed Lilly Arnold and Katy Graham? Jesus, Heather, that's…"

"I don't know what I think," Heather clarified, not convincing either of them. "I don't know. I just know he disappeared that night, but if he was a killer, how come I never figured it out?"

"Maybe it's just like how Victor's parents never figured it out. We see what we want to see."

"But they're not detectives," Heather protested.

"You said yourself you were drinking a lot and overwhelmed by the case. Maybe you just looked the other way."

Heather groaned and rubbed at her face, her heartbeat finally slowing down. "All I know for sure is, I don't want to be like Taylor Sherman and protect my evil husband. I don't want my affections to get in the way, and I don't want to be an unwitting accomplice. I want to find justice for Lilly and Katy. I want to know the truth."

"Okay," Gabriel said.

"Okay?"

"I'll help you," Gabriel replied, unboxing his noodles, seemingly unfazed. "We'll figure it out. I'm sure Julius will help too. You said that was his friend's case?"

"Yeah."

"Well, there you go. We've got everyone we need."

"And the autopsy reports," Heather admitted.

Gabriel nodded. "It's going to be hard, but you've been through harder. And no one is going to let you do this alone."

"Yeah," Heather said, floored by his maturity. As she watched him eat, she felt herself descending from untethered heights, grounded by his gravity.

"Yeah?" he asked.

"I don't think I have a choice, but I think I can do this."

"But not today," he insisted. "Today we watch crap TV and eat MSG. Then tomorrow we begin our investigation into Daniel Palmer."

"Sounds good to me," Heather replied, the magnitude of her secret shrinking, allowing her body enough room to eat. She took a bite and felt relief.

AUTHOR'S NOTE

Thank you for joining Heather on her journey and delving into the mysteries of Glenville in *The Bridesmaids*, the fourth book in this mystery series. Your decision to continue on this adventure means the world to me.

If you haven't already, I invite you to explore the gripping prequel novel to the series, *The Bachelorette*. And the best part? You get to download your copy and read it for FREE! (I wish I could make it free on all the Amazon stores worldwide but Amazon only chose the US/.com store to have the book be free).

As a new indie author, I am incredibly appreciative of your support. Your reviews and word of mouth recommendations fuel my passion for writing and for bringing these stories to life. If you could spare a few moments to leave a review for The Bridesmaids and The Bachelorette, it would make an immense difference. Your thoughts and feedback play a crucial role in shaping my creative process, enabling me to craft an even more captivating reading experience for you in the future!

Are you feeling up to another mysterious and thrilling adventure right now? Don't miss out on my other series, the *Mia Storm FBI Mystery Thriller* series. In the latest addition to the series, Missing in Paradise, Mia is facing a challenging case in beautiful Honolulu. A local businessman went missing without a trace, leaving behind a trail of enemies and cryptic clues. With a number of suspects turning up at every corner, it's a real puzzle trying to narrow down who might be responsible for his disappearance.

Thank you again for your support, and I hope you continue to enjoy my books in the future!

Warm regards,
Cara Kent

P.S. I will be the first one to tell you that I am not perfect, no matter how hard I try to be. And there is plenty that I am still learning about self-publishing. If you come across any typos or have any other issues with this book please don't hesitate to reach out to me at cara@carakent.com, I monitor and read every email personally, and I will do my very best to rectify any issues that I am made aware of.

Get the inside scoop on new releases and get a **FREE BOOK** by me! Visit *https://dl.bookfunnel.com/513mluk159* to claim your **FREE** copy!

Follow me on **Facebook** - *https://www.facebook.com/people/Cara-Kent/100088665803376/*
Follow me on **Instagram** - *https://www.instagram.com/cara.kent_books/*

ALSO BY CARA KENT

Glenville Mystery Thriller

Prequel - The Bachelorette
Book One - The Lady in the Woods
Book Two - The Crash
Book Three - The House on the Lake
Book Four - The Bridesmaids

Mia Storm FBI Mystery Thriller

Book One - Murder in Paradise
Book Two - Washed Ashore
Book Three - Missing in Paradise

An Addictive Psychological Thriller with Shocking Twists

Book One - The Woman in the Cottage
Book Two - Mine

Made in United States
Troutdale, OR
03/02/2024